Nia

About the Author

Penny Parkes survived a Convent education largely thanks to a ready supply of inappropriate novels and her passion for writing and languages.

She studied International Management in Bath and Germany, before gaining experience with the BBC. She then set up an independent Film Location Agency and spent many happy years organising shoots for film, television and advertising – thereby ensuring that she was never short of travel opportunities, freelance writing projects or entertaining anecdotes.

Penny now lives in the Cotswolds with her husband, two children and a geriatric spaniel. She will often be found plotting epic train journeys through the Alps, baking gluten-free goodies or attempting to prove that you can, in fact, teach an old dog new tricks.

Follow Penny on Twitter: @CotswoldPenny

Penny Parkes

Out of Practice

**SIMON &
SCHUSTER**

London · New York · Sydney · Toronto · New Delhi

A CBS COMPANY

First published in Great Britain by Simon & Schuster UK Ltd, 2016
A CBS COMPANY

3 5 7 9 10 8 6 4 2

Simon & Schuster UK Ltd
1st Floor
222 Gray's Inn Road
London WC1X 8HB

www.simonandschuster.co.uk

Simon & Schuster Australia, Sydney
Simon & Schuster India, New Delhi

A CIP catalogue record for this book
is available from the British Library

Paperback ISBN: 978-1-4711-6866-6
eBook ISBN: 978-1-4711-5305-1

Typeset in the UK by M Rules
Printed and bound by CPI Group (UK) Ltd, Croydon, CR0 4YY

MIX
Paper from
responsible sources
FSC® C020471

Simon & Schuster UK Ltd are committed to sourcing paper that is
made from wood grown in sustainable forests and support the Forest Stewardship
Council, the leading international forest certification organisation. Our books
displaying the FSC logo are printed on FSC certified paper.

For Rosie and Bertie
With all my love, always

Out *of* Practice

Chapter 1

Holly blew her fringe from her eyes and the familiar hot prickle of embarrassment began to crawl across her chest. 'Please don't let anyone be watching,' she murmured under her breath, as she turned the steering wheel even harder to the right, until the ancient suspension on her beloved Golf groaned in complaint. Tentatively, she lifted her foot off the clutch, gingerly checking that, this time, she actually was in reverse.

It made no sense to anyone who knew her. As a doctor, a mother, a bright, articulate woman, she had always been the capable one – the one you'd go to in a crisis – but somehow the part of Holly's brain that was required for parallel parking simply refused to engage.

The sound of metal on metal always made Holly shudder. This morning, her first day at her new job, the sound of Golf on Mercedes nearly made her sick.

It was hardly the first impression she'd been hoping for and Holly swallowed hard to regain her composure. She slipped out of her car to survey the damage. She was just reassuring herself that her own car had taken the worst of the impact when a tiny powder-blue Fiat whipped into the car park. The driver was barely visible above the steering wheel, but

nevertheless executed a faultless one-two-slide into the minuscule space that Holly had previously given up on.

'Perfect,' muttered Holly, awkwardly rubbing at the ding
in the Mercedes' paintwork with her sleeve, 'out-parked by
a pensioner.'

'Well, good morning to you!' called the Fiat's driver, as
she attempted to exit her car and untangle herself from the
seatbelt at the same time. Holly turned in surprise, recognising the voice and struggling to place it. As she watched,
a glamorous old lady, probably as vintage as her vehicle,
emerged from the Fiat and it only took a few seconds for
Holly to realise who it was.

Elsie Townsend, star of stage and screen and Larkford's
resident celebrity, stepped out as if she were on the red carpet.
She was sporting a glamorous confection of scarves and drap-
ing cardigans that were clearly eye-wateringly expensive and
belied the fact that they were standing in a rather muddy,
country doctors' car park at 8:30 on a Thursday morning.

'Hi,' managed Holly, quietly in awe.

'Chatty little soul, aren't you?' said Elsie drily. 'Don't be
shy now. Do please tell me that you're the new GP. We've all
been simply *longing* for a lovely lady doctor.'

Holly felt her fingers being taken in a surprisingly strong
clasp by a delicate hand that looked and felt like paper, but
somehow supported a sapphire the size of a gull's egg. Before
she could reply, she'd been pulled into a half embrace and
powdery air kisses were whistling past both cheeks.

'You'll be like a breath of fresh air around here, young
lady,' Elsie said.

Holly felt her cheeks growing pink and she couldn't help
smiling. All the nerves this morning, not to mention the
hideous sweatiness of the parking debacle, slipped from her

mind in the warmth of Elsie's appraisal. 'First day today, in fact. I'm Holly Graham by the way. It's a pleasure to meet you Ms Townsend.'

Elsie's eyes danced with delight at being instantly recognised, 'Elsie, please. Well then, Dr Graham, may I be the first to welcome you to Larkford. We've all been looking forward to your arrival. I'm afraid some of our residents may even have been speculating about your reasons for joining our little community. They can't help it – not a lot to do but gossip, some of these old biddies.' She gave Holly a conspiratorial look.

Holly laughed, loving the fact that even though Elsie herself was clearly in her eighties, she certainly didn't regard herself as one of the 'old biddies'. 'Ah, well, then I'm sure I shall provide plenty of fodder for the gossip machine, especially if I make a habit of reversing into expensive Mercedes.'

Elsie shrugged and waved a hand. 'That's just Dr Bruce's car. He's actually a bit of a shit,' she pronounced incongruously, 'so I rather think you'll win Brownie points from the locals for that one. Might even bring him down a peg or two. If there's one thing people round here don't like, it's uppity people looking down on them, and Henry Bruce is just so full of himself, he can't see how offensive he can be.'

'Brilliant,' said Holly quietly, having met the indomitable Henry Bruce at her interview and already suffered his condescension for having the nerve to be a woman, a mother and a doctor all at the same time. She knew full well that he was the only partner not to have supported her application and now she'd reversed into his car!

'Worry not, my petal. We, your loyal patients, will support you,' Elsie announced, holding out an arm as if she were on the stage at Stratford and reeling off a bit of Will

Shakespeare. 'Come on, or I'll be late for my slot with the delicious Dr Dan. I've been summoned in for bad behaviour,' Elsie confided disgustedly. 'Again! It's unseemly, apparently, for a woman my age to be caught having fun. Gets all the neighbours in a pickle, you see. Quite why I can't dance around my garden in a nice evening frock doing a bit of gardening, I do not know. But here we are and the dementia drums are beating . . .'

Holly felt Elsie tuck her arm through hers. 'Well then,' Holly said, 'we can't miss your slot now, can we? Not if it's with Delicious Dan Carter. He always was rather easy on the eye, even when we were teenagers. He's my best friend Lizzie's cousin actually.'

'Excellent,' replied Elsie, 'I do love a bit of healthy nepotism. I hope that's why you're here in Larkford?'

'Partly,' replied Holly diplomatically. The car park was hardly the place to divulge the intimate tangles of her life, but it did remind Holly that she needed to work out a public version of events sooner rather than later.

Elsie's intent gaze missed nothing, as she appeared to clock Holly's discomfort and nervous anticipation all with one assessing look. 'My darling girl, I'm sure you'll be an asset to our little community whatever your reasons. And here you are on your first day . . . Such bliss to have a new project – all those new people to meet, new adventures to have, the possibility of an *affaire du coeur*. Oh, I envy you a little, I really do.' Elsie's hand fluttered to the diamond pendant at her throat, highlighting the sharp contrast between the perfectly smooth skin of Elsie's cheek and the crêpe de chine of her neck.

Holly flushed a little, discomfited by the picture Elsie was painting. Searching for a change of subject, she eyed up Elsie's perfectly parked vintage Fiat, the early sun glinting off the powder-blue bonnet. 'I must get you to show me how to do that snazzy parking manoeuvre one day, Elsie. My husband, Milo, has given up trying to teach me. It was going to end in divorce if he didn't!' She just about managed a gentle laugh.

Elsie followed her lead, albeit watching her expression closely. 'Well, I'll teach you my little trick, if you like. Steve McQueen taught it to me in 1965 and it's never let me down yet. Now, what was the name of that movie we did together? Oh, that's going to annoy me all day now . . .'

Holly guided Elsie around a puddle in the gravel, trying not to be a little jealous of the old lady's stylish leather boots, and they walked over towards the main entrance. The Practice building itself was newly renovated and nestled comfortably on the edge of the market town. The older part of the building was warm local stone and the windows were capped by arches of red brick, giving the building the appearance of having eyebrows. A sweeping wisteria climbed the walls and the tiny pendulums of buds promised a stunning display to come.

The newer section was clearly bolder by design, featuring huge picture windows with frosted glass. Having already been inside for her interview, Holly knew that the light now flooded into the building, relieving the dark, oppressive feeling that haunted so many doctors' practices. All in all, the building had a pleasant airy feel that was welcoming and spacious.

She pushed open the doors and breathed in the ubiquitous smells of Deep Heat and antiseptic. It felt like coming home. Whatever her reasons for leaving the hospital behind, Holly knew that the move to The Practice was the right thing for her professionally. All she had to do now was to make sure it worked for her disastrous personal life too. She couldn't help smiling as she saw her name newly painted on to the list of doctors at The Practice.

Elsie gave her arm a squeeze, '*Bonne chance*, Dr Graham. It's been a pleasure.'

'Holly? Holly Graham?' A petite woman with a harassed expression managed a welcoming smile as she bustled across the office, 'I'm Grace Allen, the Practice Manager.'

'Grace, hello. So lovely to see you again,' said Holly sincerely, recognising her from the interview day, and comforted to be met by a familiar and friendly face.

Grace flushed a little and Holly remembered how thoughtful Grace had been to all the candidates, briefing them beforehand on areas of special interest, making sure they knew about schools and housing in the town.

'I can't thank you enough for all the information you sent through to me, Grace. It made the move so much smoother and the boys are settling into Pinetrees Nursery already. I won't say it's been a painless transition,' said Holly, with classic understatement, 'but your tips made all the difference, truly.'

'Well . . .' parried Grace, obviously delighted by the compliments but embarrassed nevertheless, 'it's stressful enough moving house, let alone starting a new job. But I do remember what it's like juggling work and the little ones, so if you ever need someone to talk to, I'll be right here.' Her cheeks flushed a little more, setting off the auburn highlights in her bob, as she leaned in a little. 'Although, I also seem to remember that some days it was nice to come to work for a rest! Now let's see what we can do about getting you some coffee and we'll sort out that bit of porridge on your skirt at the same time.' Grace gave her a sympathetic smile which made Holly want to hug her, despite having known her for all of five minutes.

She looked down at the small white handprint on her skirt and shook her head in dismay, frustrated with herself for fulfilling the ditsy working-mother-stereotype right off the bat. She really needed to get her act together. She always aimed to be professional, calm and compassionate at work. This morning, it was fair to say, she was falling well wide of her target. She scooped a wet wipe from her handbag and rubbed at the stain ineffectually. 'I don't know how they manage it. I walked all round Tesco with yoghurt down my back when the twins were tiny and nobody said a word.'

Grace laughed and patted Holly's shoulder. 'We'll watch your back for you now you're here.' Her expression darkened as a tall, blonde woman swept through the office without even acknowledging their presence, merely dropping a stack of paperwork on Grace's desk and leaving. 'Well, most of us will, anyway. But we can save that one for later.'

Holly craned her neck, wondering who this woman was, to provoke such a reaction in seemingly mild-mannered Grace. Other than being slightly in awe of the endless legs, the perfect make-up and the expensively tailored dress, Holly struggled to form an opinion on the basis of one fleeting moment. The stethoscope looped around her neck marked her out as one of the doctors and the jigsaw pieces clicked into place: Julia Channing. No wonder everyone seemed so delighted to have a new female GP starting, if this über-perfect ice maiden had been their previous option. Holly could easily believe that such perfection would hardly be conducive to baring one's intimate issues.

*

A few minutes later, coffee in hand, Holly was taking notes as Grace whistled through the daily schedule at The Practice with a ruthless efficiency directly at odds with her genteel appearance.

'I've popped you in for your own afternoon surgery later, but I thought we'd spend the morning just showing you the ropes, the systems and making sure you feel at home,' said Grace. 'Dan has requested that you sit in with him for one or two patients and you can meet the rest of the team for elevenses. Now, how does that sound?'

'Sounds perfect, Grace,' Holly smiled, all her worries about finding her feet unfounded, and relieved to have such a welcoming and well-organised Practice Manager. She knew that, in reality, it was probably Grace that held the whole show together. 'I can't wait to meet everyone.'

A little white lie on that front couldn't hurt, justified Holly to herself. After all, Grace didn't need to know that she was quietly terrified at the prospect of meeting the rest of the team. Not Dan, obviously, but she'd have to meet Julia Channing properly at some point and there was still Henry Bruce to win over. Holly couldn't see any hope of a lasting friendship with the terrifyingly young and overly confident nurse they had passed in the corridor either.

She was suddenly pathetically, ridiculously glad to have Dan here. There were some days, Holly decided, when it took more than a medical degree and a pair of lucky pants to keep one's confidence up.

Grace took her cup and ushered her down the hall towards a door marked Dr D. Carter. 'Well, you've already met Larkford's most glamorous resident, so I'm afraid it'll all be downhill from here.'

Holly crinkled her brow. 'Do you mean Elsie Townsend?

Isn't she wonderful?' she said with genuine warmth, quietly thinking that if she were able to choose her own old age, eccentricity was looking pretty appealing.

'Oh she's a card alright. Fabulous fun, but a terrible influence. Whatever you do, never let her mix you a Martini – you'll be dancing on tables before you know it. Trust me. But if you're ever bored, buy her a drink and she'll tell you about her cat fight with Marilyn Monroe and her steamy affair with Steve McQueen.'

Holly laughed, before coming back down to earth with a jolt as she remembered their earlier conversation about Steve McQueen. 'Actually,' Holly dropped her voice to a whisper, 'I do need to find Dr Bruce at some point. I ... well, I ... I kind of need to speak to him about his car.' Holly's throat flushed red and Grace didn't miss a trick.

She looked left and right and pulled Holly sharply into the ladies' loos. 'You know, Holly, after you've been here a little while, you'll find that all the doctors have their weaknesses,' she said, with a studied intensity. 'George Kingsley for example, is a sucker for a decent steak and kidney pie. Dan Carter gets his shorts in a twist about discovering a new running trail. And what you need to know about Dr Bruce, is that when it comes to his car, he can sometimes be a little, well, obsessive. So all I'm really saying here is that, unless his bumper is half way across the car park or you're a secret petrol-head, I would aim for a nice positive introduction. Yes?'

'Um,' said Holly, still desperate to make that first positive impression on all her colleagues, but also knowing that Dr Bruce would doubtless notice the two-inch dent on his beloved motor sooner rather than later. 'But I really need to tell him it was me that ...'

'That noticed nothing at all in the car park as you walked in?' said Grace carefully and deliberately.

Holly shook her head. 'No, that it was me that . . .'

Grace was the one shaking her head now, her voice surprisingly forceful as she continued, 'Holly, you're a very sweet girl and clearly a very good doctor or you wouldn't be here. But tell Dr Bruce that you scratched his car and your first day could well be your last. Okay? So, as I was saying, you noticed nothing at all . . .'

Holly was struggling to remove the stricken expression from her face, when Grace leaned in and whispered kindly, 'He's off to do rounds later and the lanes are really muddy. Trust me on this one. Just let it go.' She squeezed Holly's arm and bundled her out of the ladies, leaving Holly with the distinct impression that Grace was turning out to be a bit of a dark horse.

Chapter 2

Moments later, Holly settled herself quietly in the corner of Dan's consultation room and tried not to be obvious about the fact that she was staring. She always felt that you could tell a lot about someone by the state of their desk and, if that maxim held true, then Dan appeared to be suffering from some sort of split personality.

One side of his imposingly solid desk was arranged with almost military precision and, whilst there were serried ranks of various gadgets and gizmos, there was definite order in the chaos. By contrast, the other side was a teetering mass of paperwork, unopened post and empty coffee cups.

Holly looked up. Caught in the act, there wasn't much she could do but smile. 'Sorry. Just being nosey,' she managed. 'Trying to get a feel for the place . . .'

'And trying to work out how it's possible to have so much paperwork in a paperless office?' said Dan wryly. 'Just don't tell Grace. It's my guilty little secret.' He sat down and swivelled his chair until he was facing her. 'It's great you're here, Holls. You're going to love it. Quick question though? Dr Graham? Was it just too much paperwork to change when you got married or should I read something into that?'

Holly shrugged. To Milo, she'd blamed the paperwork,

but in reality? 'Nothing sinister afoot. Just that I didn't really want to be known as Dr Payne. It's nearly as bad as Dr de'Ath at med school.'

Dan laughed, 'God, yes, I remember him. But Milo Payne – ooph – that's a tough one to carry off. When you put it like that, Dr Graham is probably the way to go. But, I will warn you, it's a little bit old-fashioned round here some-times – you may find yourself constantly explaining that you haven't upped and left him.'

Holly laughed nervously, earning herself a quizzical look from Dan, so she quickly filled the conversational black-hole. 'It seems like a really friendly town, though. The boys are settling in well and I'm obviously over the moon to be nearer Lizzie. How often, as grown-ups, do you get to see your best friend every day?'

'It's great,' Dan agreed, thankfully letting any awkward-ness about Milo pass. 'Although half the people in this town are completely eccentric and there's rarely a dull moment. In fact, to be honest, even the staff at The Practice can take a little getting used to. There are one or two characters here that you'll either love or hate, but I'll let you form your own opinions on that.'

Dan looked at his watch and made an obvious gear change to professional mode. 'In fact, the first thing you'll notice today is that General Practice is a rather different beast to being at the hospital and we all have our own individual style. The important thing for you, Holly, is to hold your own. Don't be swayed into any decision that makes you feel uncomfortable, but try and stay open to other possibilities. Granted, it's a bit of a balancing act, but give it a go.'

'Okay,' nodded Holly, suddenly unable to formulate any-thing more eloquent. She watched as Dan pushed back his tousled mop of chestnut hair that appeared to be resilient to any cut, style or product.

'Okay then,' echoed Dan. 'And I gather you've already met Elsie Townsend? Who, by the way, is simply fabulous, but she does rather keep us all on our toes here.' He grinned. 'Bit of a handful really, but we do love her. Watch out though, she has a sort of mesmerising voice, and before you know it, you've agreed to anything ... So, up you hop and get her from the waiting room then.

'Dr Carter's first rule of medicine, never miss an opportunity to get a little insight into what's really going on. Most of our patients will lie through their teeth at some point, but you can tell so much about someone's health from the way they stand up and the way they walk. Why would anyone want to miss that, if it might help with a diagnosis? But still, you'll find some people here just love their intercom.'

Holly left the room, secretly over the moon that she was getting to see Elsie again and that Dan seemed to be exactly the kind of doctor she'd hoped. Even if all the local tales about the other doctors were true, at least she'd have one friendly soul to chat to.

Pushing open the door, she cast her gaze around the spacious new waiting room in the atrium. Light and airy, it was certainly relaxing and welcoming: windows that actually opened, along with heating that actually worked and cosy chairs in clusters, all combined to make the inevitable wait a little more restful. Sure, there were the predictable and pervasive wafts of Olbas Oil in here, together with the Deep Heat and antiseptic she'd noticed earlier, but it was easily the most inviting doctors' surgery Holly had ever visited. She sighed happily, still unable to believe her luck in landing the position here.

'Elsie? Elsie Townsend?' she said, trying to catch the old lady's attention from where she seemed to giving an impromptu poetry recital to a huddle of toddlers in the play corner. She certainly had their rapt attention and as Holly got nearer she could understand why. Elsie's poem seemed to be almost exclusively about poo. Well, technically, farts *and* poo, but she had her miniature audience in the palm of her hand.

Having finally prised Elsie away and got her settled in Dan's consulting room, Holly had to acknowledge that he had a point. In fetching Elsie from the waiting room herself, in guiding her down through to the consulting rooms, waiting for her to catch her breath after only a few short paces, Holly had learned more about her patient than she would have done in a five-minute conversation. She had also learned a very funny limerick about potty training a koala that she knew would delight her twins no end.

'Am I in trouble again, Dr Carter?' asked Elsie with a winsome smile. 'I was only having a bit of fun, you know. I haven't completely lost my marbles.'

'Indeed,' said Dan, 'but I did get an awful lot of phone calls, Elsie, and we did agree . . .'

'Phooey,' dismissed Elsie instantly, with an edge to her voice. 'Just because my neighbours are a bunch of boring busybodies, it doesn't mean they can boss me around. I've been waiting a very long time to be old and eccentric, Dr Carter, and I'm not prepared to start being all straitlaced now because Cassie Holland has got a bee in her bonnet about appropriate behaviour.'

Holly noticed Dan glance sideways at her to see if she

was taking all of this in. Taking it all in was the least of her challenges, though. She was actually hooked, wanting to know more – frankly, if she was honest – wanting to join in with whatever inappropriate behaviour Elsie had been up to, because no matter how much it had obviously shocked her neighbours, Elsie seemed to have mastered a skill that Holly had been struggling with lately – she knew how to have fun.

Holly watched Dan as he listened intently, rolling his fountain pen between his palms, his soft brown eyes filled with concern. Elsie's latest misdemeanour was obviously the latest in a long line and Dan had clearly had a number of calls about her, judging by the scattering of Post-its on his desk.

Holly had to smother a smile, as Elsie began to justify why she'd been found at midnight in the Market Place. Dressed for the Oscars and gaily planting daffodil bulbs in erratic clumps amongst the grass verges, she'd clearly been having a wonderful time. Although, if her celebrity status was to be believed, it was probably a small mercy that none of the nosey neighbours had thought to alert the press.

Sensing in Holly a kindred spirit and not missing a trick, Elsie clasped Holly's hand emphatically. 'My darling girl, you've no idea how stultifying tedious it *is* being old. There really is only so much *Antiques Roadshow* I can sit through without being bored senseless and needing a little pick me up.'

Elsie was on a roll now, playing to her audience of two and clearly loving the attention. Her husky voice made the simplest of statements sound like an invitation and her accent was crisp and redolent of a bygone era. The light danced for a second in her deep grey eyes, every inch the star of stage and screen. 'Every time I have a bit of fun, everyone says I'm going dotty. By my reckoning, I've been going dotty for the last six decades then . . .' She laid a weightless hand on Holly's arm, paper-thin skin and fragile fingers still somehow supporting the enormous sapphire Holly had noticed earlier, not to mention several eternity rings, each no doubt presented with love by a succession of eligible husbands. 'We girls are allowed to let our hair down occasionally, aren't we?'

Holly tried to remember Dan's cautionary words, but felt unable to resist the captivating pull of Elsie's fabulous personality, wavering further as Elsie fixed her with a determined and persuasive smile.

'Back me up here, Dr Graham. I really don't want to take any more of those pills that Dr Bruce gave me. They make me feel so muzzy-headed and slow. And I can feel old and stupid and clumsy without the help of pharmaceuticals, thank you *very* much.'

Holly breathed in and caught a stern hold of her medical objectivity. Every personal instinct was suggesting that she and Elsie nip to the pub later, for lunch and a couple of G&Ts, but her professional voice was nudging insistently at her conscience. Even putting aside the question of medication, Holly could see that, beneath the veneer of glamour and sophistication, all was not running smoothly for Elsie. Holly's gaze took in the mis-buttoned silk blouse, the tell-tale food stain on the sleeve of her cashmere cardigan and the eyeliner that had been carefully and immaculately applied to only one eyelid.

If Elsie was in fact starting to deteriorate, then they were hardly going to get to the bottom of things in a ten-minute appointment. In fact, at that moment, the light on the desk phone flashed repeatedly to remind them that there was indeed a waiting room full of patients demanding attention.

Holly was about to speak up when Dan leaned forward in

his chair. 'Elsie, no one is begrudging you your right to have a bit of fun, but there are a lot of people in this town who care about you and are worried about how you're doing. So, I'm going to get Lucy on reception to book you in for a triple appointment with me and we can review all your medication and if,' he held up a hand to stop her interrupting, 'if you still feel that we need to tweak things a little bit, we can take our time. In the meantime,' he continued in an affectionately commanding voice, 'I am going to send one of the team over every day to check in with you. It's all very well you putting on a bravura performance every time you come in, but I want you to accept that we're all here to help. You might even have to come clean and tell us if there are things that you're struggling with. Now how does that sound?'

Holly nodded along as he spoke, delighted to find that this was a practice where it clearly wasn't frowned upon to get involved in their patients' lives, rather than simply reaching for the green prescription pad.

Elsie tilted her head to one side to consider his offer, finding comfort in the pretence that she actually had a choice in the matter. 'Fine,' she said with some authority. 'You can send young Jason round. It would be such a treat to have a male nurse to corrupt.'

Dan and Holly both laughed: Dan, because he knew that 'young Jason' was finding his first year with The Practice an eye-opening experience and a visit to Elsie's beautiful Georgian townhouse would doubtless be an entertaining one; and Holly, because she was a little bit shocked, a little bit in awe and a little bit smitten with the feisty Elsie Townsend.

'We'll see,' said Dan, gently guiding Elsie towards the door, and holding it open to usher her through, his height and broad shoulders only serving to emphasise her petite fragility. 'If you're really good, I might even let Dr Graham here pop round. It is her first week though, Elsie, so you'd have to be gentle with her.'

Holly had to satisfy herself with a simple goodbye, appreciating how unprofessional it would look to be excited at the prospect of a house call. Elsie gave her wrist a squeeze as she left, flashing another conspiratorial grin, leaving Holly with a mixed-up excitable feeling that she couldn't begin to place.

Dan sat down at his desk and began typing his notes into the system. 'Don't worry if you feel a bit all over the place, by the way. She seems to have that effect on everyone – a sort of star-struck, post hurricane sort of thing. To the best of my knowledge, she has half the town wrapped around her little finger.'

Holly took a calming breath. 'I would actually love to look in on her though, Dan. Yes, I mean, I know she's fabulous and all that, but it's fascinating, isn't it? So together and eloquent in here, but I'd put a fiver on the table that there's more to these funny episodes than boredom.'

'I'm not sure I should take that bet. We'll let Jason go tomorrow and you can pop round on Saturday morning and see what you think. I'd be delighted to have another of the GPs on my wavelength. Between you and me, and you'll find all this for yourself soon enough, Dr Bruce can be a bit quick on the draw when it comes to prescribing. He doesn't feel it's our job to look too deeply. But actually, one of the reasons I supported your application is that you clearly look at your patients' ailments as a part of the big picture too. So, now you're here, don't let me down and start handing out the hard stuff as if it were Smarties, okay?'

'You won't have any worries on that score, I can promise you. It never ceases to amaze me that people are so quick to risk all the horrible side effects of some of these drugs. I mean – well! – some of them are worse than the original problem aren't they?' Holly said fervently. It was something she felt passionately about and had been the cause of many heated debates with her last boss at the hospital. He'd been more of a 'Treat-'em-and-Street-'em' kind of doctor.

But not Dan, whose face broke into a grin, 'Well said.' He swivelled his chair from side to side, watching her carefully. 'How crazy is this then, Graham? Who'd have thought we'd end up working together? I might even have to be nice to my mad cousin for pulling this off.' The lines crinkled at the side of his eyes and Holly was reminded of how extremely attractive Dan Carter always had been.

She shrugged, her cheeks a little pink. 'I can't tell you how pleased I am to be here. Hospital life was wearing a little thin and, now there's the twins to consider ... Well, this is exactly what I needed. So, thank you.'

'Well, to be honest, we should probably be thanking you. The other candidates were awful. You know that mentality some people have where they think they're absolutely bloody wonderful, with nothing at all to back it up? It was like the X Factor or The Apprentice in here for a week. Lots of bullshit and very little skill. And then you walked in. Sensible, experienced, eloquent ... we'd have been idiots *not* to hire you.'

Holly sat back in her chair, feeling any residual awkwardness evaporate. She hadn't realised it, but Elsie's comment about nepotism had hit a nerve. She had wanted the job so badly, that she'd been prepared to overcome her principles and hope that Dan could pull a few strings. If there had been no need for string-pulling, she could finally breathe a little easier. All she had to do now, was live up to their expectations.

Chapter 3

In the doctors' lounge, Holly cradled a cup of coffee in her hands and tried to remember everyone's name, as Grace introduced her to the support staff.

So far, she'd had a lovely conversation about hand-sanitisers and antibiotics with Maggie, the germ-phobic pharmacist, who had surreptitiously wiped her hand only moments after shaking Holly's. Holly had tried not to react or to take offence, but had watched in amazement as Maggie had wiped down the handle of both her mug and her teaspoon before even attempting to make a drink. Nevertheless, it was easy to warm to Maggie – her curly hair and dancing eyes making it look as though she was always on the verge of laughter. It also seemed that Maggie was self-aware enough to make jokes about the irony of choosing a career in medicine that called for industrial strength wet wipes on an hourly basis.

Holly had tried to ignore the blatant head-toe-head appraisal and subsequent snub she'd received from Jade, the junior nurse she'd seen earlier. Jade, who appeared to have got her uniform off the internet simply by googling 'slutty nurse' and then doing her utmost to live up to the label. Clearly a Lad's Lass, Jade couldn't even bring herself to pass the time of day with Holly, before fluttering over to Dan Carter with a flirtatious smile and shoulders well back.

Holly had also gained a deeper understanding of why Elsie Townsend might think 'young Jason' would be fun to have around. To be fair to the male nurse, he seemed like a nice enough lad, but his passion for his fitness regime was bordering on the evangelical. Holly had certainly struggled to muster the requisite enthusiasm when discussing interval training techniques, although the results of said training schedule were clear to see. It remained to be seen whether there was anything of substance lurking beneath his chiselled exterior.

It was hardly the most auspicious of beginnings and Holly began to wonder what she'd taken on, or indeed whether she would ever fit in here. At least at the hospital, the medical staff had all been thrown together into a kind of siege mentality, where bonds of friendship quickly formed and were not so easily broken. Shared adversity had indeed increased intimacy among her colleagues – often beyond the bounds of 'civilian' acceptability.

At least by consciously stepping out of the intensity, Holly knew that her statistical likelihood of death, divorce and depression had halved. Whether spending more time with Milo would counteract those statistical improvements, remained to be seen.

Grace gave her shoulder a nudge and interrupted her train of thought, as the door to the doctors' lounge swung open. 'Now then, Holly, plaster on a smile and come with me. It's time to play nice with Dr Bruce. But remember, he's a suave old bugger, so don't take any nonsense, and whatever you do, don't mention the car!'

*

'Dr Graham. How wonderful to see you again. I trust you're settling in well.' Henry Bruce stroked his pink silk tie and Holly could feel his eyes travelling appraisingly down her body. He seemed to have conveniently forgotten that he was the only partner to oppose Holly's appointment and was now laying on the charm. 'I am sorry we haven't had chance to catch up. Busy-busy, you know.'

'No problem,' Holly replied, cradling her cup of coffee in front of her, subconsciously blocking Henry's assessment of her physical attributes and creating a natural barrier between them. 'Grace has been wonderful in showing me the ropes.'

'Good, good. Obviously we're a team here, but you may find that some of us are a little more on the ball than others, so my door is always open if you need to discuss anything. Not literally, of course!' He leaned in closer as he laughed at his own feeble little joke and Holly could smell the coffee on his breath mingling with his potent aftershave.

Holly suppressed a slight shudder as Henry's little pink tongue darted out and moistened his lips. He certainly was Mr Smooth, standing there in his Savile Row suit and highly polished brogues. He looked as though he'd come straight from his Harley Street practice and he'd certainly look at home behind the wheel of his obscenely expensive Mercedes.

Holly flushed at the thought of her deception and was about to confess all, when Dr Bruce clearly misinterpreted her blushes. 'Any questions, Holly, I mean it, do come to me. Bright young thing like you though, won't take you long to work out the lay of the land, will it?' He placed a soft, mani-cured hand on her arm and gave a gentle squeeze.

Holly awkwardly took a step back as he leaned yet further into her personal space. 'That's very kind, Dr Bruce. But I'm finding my feet already and as you rightly say, you have such a wonderful team here,' she hesitated for a moment, slightly caught off guard, quietly longing to 'accidentally' spill her coffee down his front and tell him to Back Off. Politely, of course. 'In fact,' she said, finally managing to locate her resolve and looking him straight in the eye, 'they have all gone out of their way to get me fully up to speed with everybody's little foibles.'

Dr Bruce looked at her sharply, but Holly just smiled innocently. She'd met his type before amongst Senior Doctors – give this one an inch and he'd certainly take a mile. She'd already heard rumours of his extra-marital activities and she had no desire to become his new pet. She was actually rather inclined to agree with Elsie Townsend's earlier assessment.

His face tightened, his advances clearly rebuffed, but then he just shrugged, ever the professional, 'There's a lot to be said for a small community, of course. What you sacrifice in privacy, you gain in intimacy.' He gave her a long appraising look. 'I happen to believe though, that this Practice could be more efficient if we stopped resting on our laurels and looked to the future. Simply delivering half the town's population into this world and still dealing with their snivelling offspring twenty years later, doesn't automatically make anyone the best doctor here. It's not James Herriot, you know.'

Holly followed his gaze towards the door where George Kingsley, the genial Senior Partner had ambled in with a smile and a kind word for everyone he passed. He'd been so lovely to her at the interview that Holly felt as though she already knew him, and his benevolent approach to The Practice made her like him even more.

She jumped as Henry clasped her upper arm firmly and dropped his voice, coffee fumes still wafting warmly across

Holly's cheeks and the warmth of her cup now sandwiched between them. 'Don't make the mistake of confusing compassion and medical care, Holly. It's all very well knowing the entire family history, but I think you'll agree that this touchy feely approach to medicine can cloud the judgement. We'll have a drink one evening and have a chat about it, shall we? I think we'll be of a like mind, you and I, both being from a hospital background.'

Holly took another step back, but Henry just leaned in closer. 'It's not a popularity contest, being a GP, Holly. It's the curse of living in a small town, you see – your patients are also your neighbours, blah, blah, blah ...' He made a small winding motion with his hand, clearly dismissive of anyone who might have the temerity to disagree with him. 'Take my word for it, you'll find that keeping a bit of distance is more illuminating – helps you keep your perspective professionally.'

Holly's relief was palpable as Dan's gravelly laugh interrupted them, 'Do put her down, Henry. And how about you follow your advice about keeping a bit of distance?' Dan fished the end of Henry's expensive silk tie out of Holly's cup of coffee and grinned. 'Not quite dipping your pen in the company ink there, Henry, but ten out of ten for effort. Holly, all this time and you never said you took your coffee with a spoonful of smarmy lechery.' Dan grinned cheerfully and patted Henry on the back. 'Cheer up, Henry, surely even you can see that the delectable Dr Graham is off limits.'

Henry drew himself up to his full height, which would have been more impressive if Dan didn't still tower over him, even casually slouched against the doorframe. Muttering something about childish behaviour, Henry left the room, head held high and perfectly tailored shoulders firmly back.

Without the handful of limp, stained pink silk in his hand and the seething expression on his face, he would have looked almost impressive.

'Thank you,' Holly said simply and with feeling.

Dan just shrugged. 'I'd like to tell you he's harmless, but he just does seem to think he's God's gift to women sometimes, smarmy git, and he really does need to learn a bit of discretion.' He grinned broadly. 'Besides, anyone can see, you're way out of his league.'

Dan plucked Holly's cup from her fingers and plonked it down beside them. 'Now, come and say hello to a few friendlier faces. Oh, and Julia. You'll need to meet her too ...'

Dan steered her across to the battered old sofas that formed a U-shape at one end of the room. 'Now this reprobate is Taffy Jones, our ever-present locum and my best mate.'

Dr Taffy Jones unfurled himself from his slumped position at the end of the sofa and stood up, holding out his hand for Holly to shake. He was tall and strapping and his hand enveloped Holly's in a firm grip. 'So you're the infamous Holly Graham? It's a pleasure to meet you at last.'

His face, already welcoming and friendly, broke into an enormous grin. His soft Welsh lilt was strangely hypnotic and Holly was sure it must have melted the inhibitions of many a local girl. She was disgusted to find herself blushing yet again, not quite sure how to respond and feeling completely wrong-footed.

'Don't worry, Dr Graham, it's all been good so far. Mostly, anyway. But your reputation does precede you, I'm afraid. Dan and the lovely Lizzie have been spilling the beans on all your youthful exploits. I do hope you'll return the favour, I could use some dirt on our golden boy here.' Although he was standing still and, Holly couldn't help but notice, still holding her hand, the energy simply radiated from him. He was basically a spaniel, Holly decided, with his eager expression, slightly chaotic hair and chocolate brown eyes. She felt her cheeks burning and panicked slightly as she realised that there were simply no words forthcoming from her addled brain.

Luckily Dan stepped in to rescue her yet again. 'Back in your box, Jones, and be nice to her, okay. She's just had Henry Bruce leering all over her and I haven't even introduced her to Julia yet.'

'Understood,' replied Taffy seriously, finally releasing Holly's hand from his. 'I shall be the soul of discretion and I *certainly* won't take this opportunity to dish the dirt about Henry shagging young nurse Jade behind his wife's back. And I certainly shall *not* let on, that until a few months ago, Dan and the terrifyingly ambitious Julia Channing were quite the hot item around here.' His face was a picture of amused innocence and he gave Holly a conspiratorial smile that knocked the breath from her chest. 'Now, was there anything else I'm supposed to be keeping quiet about?'

Dan shook his head. 'I give up, I really do.' He sat down on one of the sofas and started rummaging around in the biscuit tin. He snaffled a couple and passed it over to Holly, who perched on the arm beside him. All the good ones were gone, she noted, casting aside half a Jammie Dodger and the broken corner of a chocolate Bourbon. Settling resignedly for a rich tea finger with the consistency of cardboard, she was frankly just glad of the distraction. Anything that meant she didn't need to add to the speedy back and forth banter around her. They clearly were the best of friends, she decided, as the two men mocked each other mercilessly for her benefit.

By the time she'd finished off her biscuit, she knew more about their personal lives than was probably healthy.

Dan had clearly had a hideous break-up with Julia Channing. Holly was actually really looking forward to meeting her properly now, because the mental picture building from their descriptions was somewhere in the region of Cruella de Vil. She also got the impression that Dan wasn't quite as together as he'd have her believe. There was the occasional sharp glance in Taffy's direction that seemed to be warning him not to overstep. But, if Julia was even half as awful as Taffy maintained, it was hard to imagine Dan being too upset about the split.

Holly didn't miss the warning look from Taffy either, as Dan teased him for being the local Romeo. 'Quite the heart-throb of the Larkford Rugby Club, aren't you, Taffs?' It seemed his commitment issues extended into his work life too – preferring to have the freedom and flexibility of a locum contract, despite working here almost every day. And it certainly seemed as though Taffy was not short of female company, if everything Dan was saying happened to be true, much though Taffy protested.

An inexplicable wave of disappointment washed over Holly. She managed to smile and laugh along with the joke of course, but every time she looked over at him, Taffy's gaze was resting on her. She felt a little stupid and embarrassed now, for imagining that it meant anything more than a friendly welcome.

Holly was actually getting quite exasperated with herself. She really didn't feel that she was putting her best foot forward today. She'd been nervous, of course, but she hadn't expected to feel quite so drowningly overwhelmed. Obviously, it would take a little while to settle in – she was walking into a tight-knit practice, where the team's personal and professional lives clearly overlapped. Grace, Dan and Taffy were going out of their way to put her at ease and to bring her into their circle, but Holly was getting frustrated. Here she was, tongue-tied and blushing like an imbecile. She wanted them to meet bright, witty, attractive Holly. So far today, she had less charisma and drive than a Victoria Sponge.

With no warning, Dan suddenly stood up and strode across the lounge to where Julia Channing, the tall slender blonde, had made an entrance. She clearly wasn't running short in the self-confidence department, thought Holly tetchily. Words were being exchanged and Julia was waving a day-glo Post-it in Dan's face. Holly strained to hear what was being said, but Taffy reclaimed her attention.

'It's like watching a train wreck in slow-motion with those two. Personally, I can't help thinking that to dislike each other quite so very much, there must still be something there . . .'

Holly watched as Julia flicked a silken curtain of hair over her shoulder and, giving Dan one last disparaging look, she sashayed across the lounge towards them.

'Incoming,' muttered Taffy under his breath. 'Brace, brace, brace.'

Holly took a deep breath and willed herself to make a better showing. She didn't wait for Dan to introduce her, but stood up and took a pace forward. 'Dr Channing? Hi, I'm Holly Graham. We didn't get chance to meet earlier.' Remembering Julia's earlier performance, Holly tried very hard not to let an edge creep into her voice.

Julia herself was also clearly having issues with tone. She

shot Dan another filthy look and forced a smile on to her face. 'Yes, yes, lovely to have you here . . .' Julia rattled off insincerely. 'Hope you settle in okay . . . do feel free to ask if you've any questions . . . etcetera, etcetera . . .' She turned pointedly to Dan, ignored Holly, and waved the Post-it at him. 'Happy now?'

From where Holly was standing, she could just make out Dan's handwriting:

Please welcome Holly to the team and FOR FUCK'S SAKE - <u>BE NICE</u>!

Holly couldn't help it; the pressure of the morning had clearly got to her. Rather than getting her hackles up, as was obviously the intention, she burst out laughing. 'Oh, Dr Channing, thank you for that. Here I was, feeling all nervous about meeting everyone, and you manage to make me laugh. Brilliant. Just brilliant!'

Julia turned slowly, her mouth puckering until it closely resembled a duck's arse. She clearly had no idea how to react to Holly's mirth, especially since Taffy and Dan also seemed to find the whole situation so amusing.

Holly felt a moment's guilt as she watched Julia's internal struggle. After all, she didn't personally know this woman from Adam, but she was damned if she was going to be bullied from the start. Holly knew instinctively that if she didn't lay down her marker now, there would be no way to earn Julia's respect later. Humour had been the only way to go. Well, conceded Holly, it was that or a spot of mud-wrestling . . .

It briefly crossed Holly's mind, looking at Julia's expression, that Julia may be one of those people who actually had no discernible sense of humour, in which case, she might have been better served to opt for the mud. Holly felt the first bite of panic that she'd completely misjudged the situation, before deciding that she was already in for a penny.

There was an awkward pause and then Holly reached out and took the Post-it from Julia, smoothing it between her fingers. 'This just has to go on my noticeboard, Julia, I hope you don't mind. It's just so funny. And you're so kind, putting me at ease. Now, I gather from Lizzie that your *Larkford Life* column's going really well. You must be over the moon.'

Dan and Taffy swivelled their heads back and forth, as though they were watching Wimbledon.

'Yes,' said Julia tightly. 'I had forgotten that Lizzie's your friend. You must be pleased to be living nearer to each other? Where were you before – Reading, wasn't it?' she said, unclenching a little and struggling to make an effort. Clearly Julia was not familiar with the concept of small talk.

'Yes, at the hospital. It's a big change, coming here. I'm actually quite looking forward to meeting all the locals. Maybe you can give me a heads-up on the ones to watch out for? The bonkers ones? The hypochondriacs?'

Julia smoothed her dress over her enviably taut stomach and, if Holly hadn't known better, she would have thought that Julia was the one to be nervous. Her own heart was still thudding ominously against her ribcage and she felt as though she were in a scene from a David Attenborough wildlife programme, where the pecking order was being established: *'See the doctors of the Serengeti posturing for position . . .'*

Holly just needed Julia to understand that she was posing no threat to her role as Alpha female at all, but she refused to be dismissed or discounted. A little healthy respect was all Holly was aiming to achieve at this point.

Julia softened still further, 'Okay then,' she said, as she made to walk away.

'Great. Lovely to meet you, Julia,' Holly said brightly, slowly breathing out and willing her pulse to return to normal. She took another calming breath and turned to the two men who were gaping at her. 'Well, I thought that went rather well, don't you?' Holly could feel her confidence flowing back and she couldn't help but smile. Sod Victoria Sponge – that had surely been a Chocolate Roulade performance.

'Bloody hell,' said Taffy in amazement, once Julia had left the room. 'Who *are* you, Holly Graham?'

'Told you she was a keeper,' said Dan with pride, giving Holly a wink.

'Rites of Passage have been negotiated,' said Taffy seriously and in wonderment, sounding so very Welsh it was almost musical. 'I never thought I'd see the day!' He turned to Holly and laid his hands on both her shoulders. 'You're a bloody marvel, you are.' His eyes danced with mischief. 'You have tamed the notorious Channing and without bloodshed. I could kiss you, I really could.'

Holly's heart rate rocketed again, as her moment of eloquence dissolved, a mental picture of that very scenario already taking precedence in her mind.

Chapter 4

'Come on. You sit down and rearrange your face, try and look like you're happy to be here, and I'll go and order us some lunch. What do you fancy?' said Lizzie, taking control of the situation as Holly had known that she would.

Holly felt her shoulders instantly relax, free from the responsibility of making decisions. 'Whatever contains the most calories – it's been that kind of morning,' she said gratefully. She couldn't really let on in the genteel surroundings of Larkford's organic deli-slash-café-slash-fair-trade-emporium, that what she was really craving was a big juicy burger – the kind where you could actually feel your arteries clogging with every delicious bite. She spent her days advising patients to have their five-a-day, to stay away from saturated fat and processed sugar, and then felt honour-bound to live by those same strictures herself. And most of the time she did.

'Right then, Holly, lunch will be here in a sec. Now spill,' ordered Lizzie in full executive boss mode.

Holly didn't really know where to start. All she'd known was that there was a forty-minute window in her day and her best friend worked around the corner. The opportunity for moral support had seemed too good to pass up.

'How great is this – having lunch together on a work day?' she dodged. 'It's like being back at uni.'

Lizzie's glamorous façade wobbled for a second and Holly saw a flash of the girl she used to be: the girl who had dodgy braces and flat brown hair. This Lizzie sitting in front of her now was altogether more glamorous, as her job as Editor of local glossy magazine *Larkford Life* dictated. But the twinkle in her eye was sheer retro and Holly felt instantly more comforted and less intimidated.

The downside to having a best friend whose life revolved around material gratification was that Holly genuinely struggled to give a stuff and it sometimes put a strain on their friendship. She'd rather look nice than ghastly, of course, but she'd also rather read her boys a bedtime story than blow-dry her hair to perfection. In a way – a way that she would never confess to – she felt a bit sorry for Lizzie. The pressure to be perfect, to live the dream, must be exhausting, but she'd tentatively mentioned it once and been instantly shot down. She wouldn't be mentioning it again.

'I have to confess, your call came at the perfect time,' Lizzie confided. She looked around the room as if checking for eavesdroppers. 'Work's hellish at the moment.' She talked about print deadlines, fluctuating ad revenues and temperamental columnists until she ground to a halt. 'But that's old news. Tell me then – how's the first day going?'

'In a sec, but I'm starving. What did you order? Pasta? Panini? Pie? I'm in need of comfort food.'

Lizzie wrinkled her nose apologetically. 'Oh. I didn't think you meant it! I've ordered you a goat's cheese salad. It's organic and the goat is called Betsy and lives down the road, if that helps.'

Holly shook her head and smiled. 'Good old Betsy. Where

would we be without her? I don't suppose there's an Aberdeen Angus around here who's planning to give his life for the enjoyment of others, is there? I could literally kill for a burger.'

'Nope, not in here anyway ... Strictly veggie. But I am reliably informed that there's an organic grapevine in Herefordshire whose self-sacrificing actions have made this possible ...' Lizzie proudly produced a bottle of cloudy liquid that claimed to be Organic Sauvignon Blanc. She unscrewed the lid and waved the bottle vaguely in Holly's direction before pouring herself a large glassful.

Well, glassful wasn't really the word, thought Holly, as she put a hand over the top of her own vintage jam jar and sighed. 'Not for me. I've got my first solo clinic after this and I'm not sure that turning up sozzled is the right note to start on. Although, frankly a bit of Dutch courage might just be what the doctor ordered.'

Their meals arrived and Holly sighed deeply, poking at her salad without enthusiasm. 'I am not my best self today, Lizzie. You know how you only get one chance to make a first impression? Well, if that's actually true, then I'm a little bit screwed.'

Holly recounted her morning, starting with denting the Mercedes and ending up with her *Life on Earth* stand-off with Julia Channing.

She grimaced slightly as she ran out of steam. 'Be honest. How bad is it?'

Lizzie clapped a hand over her mouth and tried to stifle the laughter. 'Oh Holls, what are we going to do with you? It's not that bad, honestly. I mean, given, when you string it all together like that, it's not really ideal ... Did you really stand up to Julia?'

'Yup,' said Holly despondently. 'I just didn't want her to

think she could walk all over me, like she does every other female at The Practice.'

'Well then, hats off to you – she's horrifically ambitious, that woman. Her bedside manner may leave a little to be desired, but she's a cracking doctor. Her column's getting loads of really positive feedback and, strictly between you and me, I had a call from a TV production company last week, asking for a reference. You never know, she may not be around for too much longer.'

'Cool,' said Holly. 'I get the impression that everyone's a little bit scared of her. Apart from Dan, obviously, since they went out.'

'Oh he told you that, did he? I wondered if he would,' Lizzie said with studied casualness.

Holly frowned. 'No, Taffy Jones let it slip. Is there a story there I should know about?'

Lizzie shook her head. 'Let's just say that seeing those two together was World War 3 just waiting to happen. The only irony being, that they were actually really smitten with each other to begin with; we even got a glimpse of the softer side of La Channing. Then it all sort of imploded and nobody really knows why.'

'Another reason not to get involved with a colleague,' said Holly vehemently.

Lizzie gave her a strange look. 'Quite.'

There was a lull in the conversation, then Lizzie picked up where she left off, reviewing Holly's opening act. 'Did you really go all tongue-tied with Taffy then? I wouldn't worry. He's such a sweetheart, he won't hold it against you and he's been a good mate to Dan too. Actually, your job is starting to sound much more fun than mine. Assuming you can avoid interacting with the patients, of course!'

'They're quite the comedy duo,' said Holly, ignoring Lizzie's theatrical shudder. 'They seem to have a really good bantering thing going on – it was almost like being back at med school. They even eat like teenagers. And obviously, I still have the emotional maturity of a nineteen-year-old – all it takes for me to go all pathetic is some dishy rugby player to hold my hand and smile, and I forget how to speak!'

Lizzie raised a deprecatory eyebrow but said nothing.

'What?' demanded Holly.

'Nothing. Nothing at all. I just suddenly can't help feeling that this thing with Taffy has thrown you more than all the other stuff put together. Am I right?'

'Maybe,' replied Holly slowly. 'I'm really not nineteen any more. It is a bit feeble, you have to admit.'

Lizzie tilted her head to one side and took in her friend's obvious discomfort. 'I'd just let it go, Holls. I'm pretty sure that nobody noticed but you and you've got a lot on your plate at the moment. Stressing about this is just easier than focusing on all the changes you've got going on.'

Holly half-heartedly chewed on a spinach leaf. Lizzie certainly had a point. It was a lot nicer to think about Taffy Jones holding her hand than it was to think about the reality of her situation at home.

'I don't know if I can do this, Lizzie,' she said quietly. 'The pressure in my head is crazy. I just can't get past the responsibility, you know? Of knowing that it's my call.'

Holly looked up to see her friend watching her appraisingly, jam jar full of cloudy moonshine pressed against her bottom lip. Lizzie cleared her throat, took another slug of wine and sat forward in her seat. 'Are you honestly saying that checking a bunch of old biddies for high blood pressure and the odd nit-check is more stressful than being at the hospital? You were in A&E for years – I don't get it.'

Holly shrugged, frowning slightly as she realised her ramblings had given Lizzie the wrong idea. 'I didn't mean the patients. That bit's easy. Shit – that sounds arrogant. What I mean is . . .'

Holly pushed her uneaten salad away and slumped in her chair. 'Please don't make me burn my bra – for one thing it's actually my only nice bra that fits and for another, I'm not letting down the sisterhood by saying this. It's just a fact of life. If we'd relocated for Milo's job, it would be fine, yes? If we'd sold the house and moved the boys to a new nursery and uprooted everyone, it would just be . . . well, something we all had to do.

'But, Lizzie, I've kicked up such a fuss about this. I've essentially forced the move and now, I'm here: the buck stops with me. And if this doesn't work out, if the boys aren't happy . . .'

'It will all be your fault,' suggested Lizzie calmly.

'Well, yes,' said Holly quietly. 'I never really felt responsible for everyone else's happiness before. And now, because *I* insisted on moving as part of our whole "Fresh Start" . . .' She mashed Betsy's special cheese into a paste with the back of her fork and swallowed hard.

Lizzie refilled her jam jar and looked Holly straight in the eye. 'Do you want me to say "there, there" or can I give you some home truths?'

'Why do you think I needed an emergency lunch summit? You may be drinking for one, but I need you thinking for two. Give it to me straight.'

Lizzie grinned. 'Ooh Carte Blanche – where to begin. Shall we start with the new fringe or those hideous shoes?'

She flapped a hand at Holly's open-mouthed protest. 'Only joking, Holls. But let's just put a few things in perspective, shall we?

'One, you've hated working at the hospital since the boys were born and you've been a trouper and just got on with it. But then, you were offered a choice. Something a bit different: a way to see the boys more, to see me more and to be happy in your work.'

Lizzie paused for breath and another drink and then began ticking her points off on her beautifully manicured fingers. 'Two, Milo isn't on a voluntary research sabbatical from the University and I don't care what he goes around telling everyone. You and I both know the truth. Frankly I think the University Board were pretty amazing for not firing him and you're made of sterner stuff than me for not punching him, leaving him or let's face it, castrating him. If I thought Will was mucking around with a student, he'd be out on his ear . . .'

'Hey, that's not entirely fair,' interrupted Holly. 'There was no *actual* misconduct, the Board said so . . . Milo said so . . . And, for what it's worth, I do believe him, Lizzie. The Board just thought it would be better all round if he took some time out to work on his manuscript.'

Lizzie's eyebrows rose under her fringe and she took a deep breath, clearly restraining herself. 'Putting aside for another day, whether you do or don't believe he'll ever *really* change, I will say this and I'm going to be harsh, okay? His book is niche publishing: he might sell twelve copies if he's lucky. He's not on paid sabbatical. He has, to all intents and purposes, been banished. You, my darling, are now the primary and sole breadwinner in the family. And forgive me, if I think that gives *you* the right to choose what job *you* do – endless nightshifts full of car crashes and drunks in Reading A&E, or a nice set up as a country GP, seeing the boys, supported by your oldest friend and earning more money than you were before!'

There was an awkward moment when the café fell silent just as Lizzie was building to a crescendo and Holly's face flushed to a painful hue. 'Don't mince your words there, will you, Lizzie?'

The pregnant pause went on so long it was in danger of having triplets, before Holly sighed, the breath seeming to come from the much loved but much maligned ballet slippers on her feet. Perhaps Lizzie had a point – maybe Holly's value system was as dated as her footwear? 'Look,' she managed, 'in my head, I agree with everything you're saying, Lizzie, you know that. But, in my heart, I still feel that the pressure is on me to make a go of this. I've got Milo brooding at home and spending hours bemoaning the lack of a decent research library for his manuscript. I've got his mother breathing down my neck and questioning my priorities at every turn. And I just know that I have to make this job work.'

She reached over and took a slug of Lizzie's wine. 'Which is presumably why I'm behaving like an absolute imbecile on my very first day.'

'Well, jack it all in then. I'll give you Julia's column and you can stay home all day in your ghastly yoga trousers being my roving reporter.' Lizzie was playing devil's advocate and Holly knew it. They were the best of friends, but their approach to work came from opposite ends of the spectrum. Working together was not a good idea.

'I can see the headlines now,' said Lizzie, giving her a nudge as she made a rainbow headline with her hands. 'Local Doc Discovers Chemical Weapon in Laundry Hamper!

'Or,' she said enthusiastically, getting into her stride, 'Local Doc Slays Cheating Husband with Cyanide!'

'That's it – I'm cutting you off – no more Agatha Christie for you!' Holly grinned, glad to be back on lighter, more bantering terms with her oldest friend, but slightly alarmed at the way Lizzie's hand had tightened possessively on her jam jar when Holly had proclaimed she was cutting her off.

'Go on – I dare you,' said Lizzie, with a glint in her eye. 'I cannot stand that bitch Channing anyway. I'd much rather work with you. She thinks she's oh-so-bloody-perfect. I keep hoping that pride comes before a fall with that one,' Lizzie confided gleefully, 'but no ... It's just not normal to be that accomplished at everything.

'Still, you never know, maybe she'll burn out and have a complete nervous breakdown by the time she's forty?' Lizzie suggested hopefully, a spiteful undertone to her voice that indicated she wasn't really joking, which took Holly by surprise.

No matter how many years they were friends, Holly still found it hard to get her head around how competitive Lizzie could be. Woe betide anyone who got on the wrong side of her. Holly was even ashamed to admit that, on occasion, she'd been known to edit her own stories and news, if she felt there was even a chance of provoking Lizzie's ire.

Truth be told though, it had been so long since they'd seen each other every day, that Holly had simply assumed it was a trait her friend had grown out of – like leg warmers, dodgy haircuts and retro music.

Holly watched her friend drain her jam jar and decided to continue as though Lizzie's outburst had never happened.

'If we were men, we wouldn't be worrying about any of this,' said Holly bluntly. 'And we wouldn't have worried about appearances either. We'd be in the pub now, with a big juicy steak.'

'And you might be forgiven for wearing tragic shoes and we'd be talking about the new motor, the latest rugby results and our friendship would be about as deep as a puddle,' countered Lizzie with a grin, following her lead. 'But alas alack, no. We are instead Mothers-with-Jobs, which roughly translates, as you very well know, as the brave (or possibly futile) attempt to Have It All, by the simple application of Doing It All.'

'Speaking of which,' said Holly, looking at her watch and ignoring the scene of devastation on her plate, 'I'm on in five.'

Lizzie pushed her chair back, batted Holly's wallet away and threw a twenty-pound note on the table. She leaned in and kissed Holly firmly on both cheeks, gripping her shoulders hard. 'Don't let the bastards get you down, okay. And don't let them walk all over you either. You're a bloody good doctor and they're lucky to have you. As am I. Kitchen supper at mine tomorrow?

'Oh and Holly?' called Lizzie as they parted. 'No funny business with anyone at work today, okay?' She grinned like a loon, waggling her fingers in parting, as her mobile phone began to ring, her Barry O'Connor ringtone blaring cheesy 70s schmaltz across the Market Place. For a stylish, savvy woman, it had to be said that Lizzie had appalling taste in music.

Holly looked around her new consulting room and breathed a sigh of relief. She'd run the gauntlet of the outer office, remembering everyone's name and at no point had she crashed into anything, blushed like a teenager or engaged anyone senior in a battle of wills. Cool. Calm. Confident. How hard could that be?

'Come on then, Graham. You can do this,' she murmured. She made sure all her bits and pieces were unpacked, lingering over a photograph of the twins swinging like monkeys from the climbing frame, Ben's little face wrinkled with the sheer effort of keeping up with his brother. It was all the incentive Holly needed; if her boys could make the most of their fresh start, then so could she.

She pushed back her chair and walked through to the waiting room. 'Prue Hartley?' she called. This may not be A&E, there may not be much call for her excellent wound cleaning and stitching skills, but she knew her stuff. It wouldn't be such a bad thing for her to remember that occasionally.

'I need to talk to you about my poo.' Prue settled herself into the seat opposite Holly and shuffled a little to get her generous bulk comfortable as she cradled a capacious tangerine leather bag on her lap. 'I've been meaning to come in for ages actually and when my Alan told me that the new lady doctor had started, well, I thought it was about time.'

Holly nodded. 'Okay. What in particular is worrying you?' She liked to start out with a few open-ended enquiries, get a more accurate picture of the problem, without any leading questions.

'It's tricky to describe really. It's just *not quite right*, you know?'

'I see. In what way do you mean, *not quite right*?' Holly asked delicately, wondering how to get Prue to open up a little, but her patient seemed more interested in ferreting around in the enormous handbag.

'Now before I forget, this is for you, Dr Graham.'

Prue proudly handed Holly a small brown paper bag and nodded encouragingly. Holly tentatively unrolled the top of the bag and looked inside, trying and failing not to look shocked.

'That's ... well, that's just ...' Holly struggled to find the right words. 'It's wonderful that you've planned ahead for your appointment obviously, but to be honest, we normally prefer you to use the special plastic pots provided. It's just a little more, um, sanitary.'

Prue Hartley looked blank for a moment and then a delighted grin rippled across all five of her chins. 'Oh, Dr Graham, you are such a hoot! You had me going there, you really did. Ooh wait 'til I tell my Alan ... It's a brownie, Dr Graham! A brownie!' She chortled merrily, not in the least offended. 'Prue Hartley? The clue's in the name – Hartley Bakery? My chocolate brownies are the best in Larkford and I thought you could have it for your afternoon tea, by way of a little welcome.'

Holly found herself lost for words. Of course it was a bloody brownie! She was beginning to think that living with two small boys was beginning to warp her view of the world. 'I'm so sorry, Mrs Hartley. Do forgive me. I have two-year-old twin boys at home and you'd be surprised how much of my day is spent discussing poo.'

Prue was still tittering away to herself, but at least she now looked relaxed and at ease, even if it hadn't been achieved by conventional means. 'That's the best laugh I've had in days. I knew I was right to wait and see you. That Dr Channing's a right cold fish.' Prue shifted her not inconsiderable bulk in the chair and leaned forward confidingly. 'When I gave myself an injury trimming my bikini line, she was right sniffy about it. Kept making comments about me in a bikini that I did not appreciate. I didn't dare tell her about my purple poo.'

'And when you say purple,' replied Holly, without missing a beat, 'are we talking Professor Plum or Miss Scarlet?'

Prue nodded approvingly, clearly getting Holly's Cluedo reference straight away. 'I'd say Professor Plum, in the downstairs cloakroom, for a good half hour, with a rather pointy candlestick . . .'

Holly started jotting down notes before losing her nerve. 'So just to clarify – it takes you half an hour to have a bowel movement and when you do, it's a bit sharp and uncomfortable – and of course – purple?'

'That's about the size of it,' said Prue, tapping the round crystal paperweight on Holly's desk for emphasis.

'Okay, so nothing else unusual?'

'No, I mean that paperweight there – that's about the size of my poo!'

'Crikey,' said Holly a little taken aback. 'Then we need to talk about stool softeners and samples. All very routine. Probably nothing to worry about, but better safe than sorry.'

Holly began to run through the usual chat about keeping regular and the benefits of lots of water and fruit and veg. Prue took it all in and seemed to be happy with the plan that Holly outlined for her, even shaking her hand when it was time to go.

'Do stop by the bakery, Dr Graham. We've some lovely unusual bakes – I bet your little lads would love my meringues and if it's vegetables you're after, my Alan does some lovely carrot cakes and his little beetroot cupcakes are to die for. I can't get enough of them, with a nice cup of tea.'

Holly's expression lit up with amusement. 'Erm, Prue? Obviously we'll stick to the plan we've outlined, but to be honest, you might just want to stay away from the beetroot cakes for a couple of weeks. Just to see if it helps.'

Prue's face flushed a decidedly beetroot-y colour and she let rip the most echoing chuckle. 'Oh for God's sake, Prudence Hartley, you dolt. Beetroot cake!' She shook her head. 'I'm so sorry, Dr Graham. I just didn't think . . .'

Holly opened the door to usher her out, making Prue promise to drop in a sample anyway and up her water intake, and the two of them were laughing like old friends by the time they got back to the waiting room.

'You seem to be finding your feet there. Nice to see a happy customer,' said Dan Carter, as he came through to call his next patient. It threw Holly for a moment, to think of her patients as customers, but of course he was right. It was all about customer service these days, wasn't it?

It was probably a timely reminder, as her next patient appeared to have more piercings than Holly had thought physically possible. But, in a society where the customer was always right, did it mean that Holly's job now was to patch up the one through his nose that was clearly infected, or could she give him a stern lecture on the risks of self-mutilation and refer him for psychiatric evaluation?

She made do with a brisk talk about hygiene and sent him off with lots of antibiotics and sterile cleansing solution, since it turned out that his Prince Albert was also causing him a bit of grief in the bedroom since he'd had a few issues with 'snagging.' Holly had gamely managed to keep a straight face, showing neither the bubbling humour nor burgeoning disgust, that was threatening her resolve to remain Cool, Calm and Confident.

It was fair to say though, that she was never going to look at a willie in the same way again. And to be absolutely fair, she didn't feel terribly keen to eat that brownie either.

Chapter 5

Holly pressed rewind on the Bob the Builder DVD, to the twins' incredulous delight. There was a time to be strict about these things and a time to be practical. At this anti-socially early hour of the morning, practical beat principles every time.

Although it was only her second day at The Practice, Holly was still determined to get their morning routine running smoothly, even if that meant a few compromises on the television front. Somehow, tiptoeing round their tiny terraced house while Milo slept on made everything so much harder. Not that he would have been helpful if he'd been awake. It was just that quietly rushing seemed to be an oxymoron in Holly's experience, especially when you added a pair of two-year-old boys into the mix. So, as far as Holly was concerned, as long as she could hear Neil Morrissey's dulcet tones coming from next door, it meant she had a chance at some breakfast.

Milo's unprecedented appearance in the kitchen made Holly do a double-take. He lounged back against the kitchen worktop, hair artfully tousled and yawning widely. He stretched his arms above his head, giving the yawn a deeper resonance and lifting his t-shirt to reveal perfectly honed (and time-consuming) abs. He yawned again, stretching still further and adding in a little satisfied sigh.

Holly tried to think gracious thoughts as he picked up *her* toast and chomped on it contentedly – she probably wouldn't have time to make another piece, but it seemed petty to complain. Milo didn't like it when she was petty and, to be honest, neither did she.

Pinching the last of her coffee, he dropped a sleepy kiss on her forehead. 'Morning, Holls. Aren't you going to be late?'

'Probably,' sighed Holly, flicking a glance towards the station clock that took pride of place on her kitchen wall and which dictated her schedule in a more benevolent manner than her husband or children.

She looked wistfully at the empty coffee machine, forgoing the time to make a fresh cup in favour of shovelling a pile of crockery into the dishwasher, before rushing through to the sitting room to give the boys their ten-minute warning of imminent departure, as advised by Baby Whisperers everywhere. She wondered if it ever actually made any difference to the mad scramble out of the door, but nevertheless it had become part of her routine.

Captivated by the sight of the pair of them snuggled up together, Holly simply watched for a moment, pausing in her frantic rush, to focus on committing this picture to memory. She leaned against the door frame, enchanted as always by her boys, cross-legged in front of the TV, their soft cord trousers riding up their plump little legs. She adored the way their actions unconsciously mirrored one another, as they always had done, leaning inwards like a pair of book-ends. All the stresses, all the compromises – all totally worth it in moments like these.

The phone pealed suddenly throughout the house,

prompting a volley of grumbles from the kitchen about who could be calling at this ungodly hour. Milo had settled down to read the newspaper and showed no sign of movement so, with a harried glance at her watch, Holly grabbed the receiver before it disturbed Bob the Builder's big announcement or set Milo off on another one of his spiels about telephone etiquette.

'Hello,' she managed, her voice sounding unusually gruff and strangled.

'Jesus Christ, Holly, if that's your best doctoring voice, it certainly needs some work,' said Lizzie with a snigger.

'Morning, Elizabeth,' managed Holly. 'Only you could sound this chipper at stupid o'clock in the morning.'

'Only because I've been up for bloody hours! Anyway, I know you're dashing but I just wanted to check you survived yesterday afternoon and that you're still up for supper tonight? I want all the gory details.'

'Sounds perfect,' said Holly, secretly longing to dissect the rest of her first day at work. Milo's enquiries last night had been brief to the point of disinterest, but then, she had been fast asleep in front of the television by nine o'clock: hardly scintillating company herself. 'The boys are looking forward to it already.'

'Then I shall have something entirely pointless and non-educational lined up for them to do. Speaking of pointless, will your darling husband be joining us?'

'Lizzie!' Holly protested, feeling disloyal for the laughter that automatically bubbled up. It was just that Lizzie had this unerring knack of putting into words exactly the feelings that Holly would never admit to. Lizzie firmly maintained that Milo's primary role in family life was purely decorative and Holly tried to remind herself daily that he was doing his best and that not everyone could multi-task or prioritise on the hoof.

True, there were times, like last night, like this morning, when it grew increasingly difficult to ignore the deteriorating state of her marriage, but Holly knew that if she stopped to dwell on it, even for a second, she would lose the momentum she relied upon to carry her through each and every day. It was all about keeping focus. Much better to focus on the things that made her happy – her boys, her work, her friends . . .

'Can I bring anything?' Holly asked simply.

'Wine. We'll definitely be needing wine. Quite a lot of wine probably.' Lizzie's laugh was a little strained and Holly wished she had more time to talk, but Lizzie, like Holly, was banking on momentum and pushed on with her plans. 'We'll give the kids a treat and pop on a DVD or something – you never know, we might even finish a sentence.'

And Lizzie had a point: with everyone's various offspring around, there wasn't much scope for adult conversation in Holly's home life. The snatched exchanges with the other mothers in the Nursery corridor, or at the various children's parties that seemed to monopolise many a weekend, often felt unsatisfying and left Holly feeling out of sync with the people around her.

Lizzie had it right as always. What Holly fancied was a proper gossip with her friend, without the need to censor her words and cram every concept into three sentences or less. Holly had recently decided that motherhood was a lot like Twitter – you had 140 characters to get your point across, before the next distraction came bowling along and you'd missed your window.

'Have you got time for this?' Milo called through from

the kitchen, feet up on the table and sports pages spread open.

'Is that His Lordship I hear summoning you?' asked Lizzie drily. 'He's doing well to be out of bed this early.'

Whilst absolutely true, Holly once again felt torn: her honour dictated that she should defend her husband, mention that he'd been up writing until the wee small hours, but the exhausted mother in her welcomed the acknowledgement that help and support from Milo were in short supply. Some days she wondered whether it might actually be easier to be a single parent, before promptly and repeatedly quashing the notion. She simply couldn't do that to her boys. So, she did what she always did these days, and dodged the issue. 'I'd love to chat but I really must dash, Lizzie, I can't be late on my second day.'

'Quite right too – go forth and heal the sick, placate the whiney and be virtuous for the both of us. Just promise me you're not wearing one of those tired old jersey dresses again or I shall be forced to intervene.'

'Good Lord, is that the time?' deflected Holly as Lizzie hit a sensitive nerve. Holly was actually still mourning the fact that, as a GP, she would no longer get to fall out of bed and pull on a set of scrubs every day. Okay, so she had secretly rather enjoyed going into Jigsaw with Lizzie at the end of her maternity leave last year, and picking out three stylish outfits, but a year down the line she was still wearing those self-same outfits day in, day out – and now for work as well as play.

Biting at yet another loose thread, she conceded that a little more effort probably was required on the clothing front, but at 6 a.m. every last moment spent in bed was precious. And if she did sometimes worry that she might arrive at work looking as though she'd got dressed in the dark, it just didn't seem terribly professional to let on, that some days she actually had.

Lizzie's laugh echoed down the phone as Holly hung up and started gathering yet more kit together for the day ahead. She could hear Bob the Builder heading for its exciting denouement and knew she didn't have long.

She grabbed the twins' kit bags from the kitchen table and dashed into the utility room, turning her back on the sorry heap of laundry that lay neglected in the basket. 'You'll still be here when I get back,' she told it, as she filled the bags with drinks for the twins and shook her head in disbelief. 'I can't believe I'm talking to the bloody laundry now,' she said to the contents of the fridge, as she rummaged around for a few snack-time treats.

She filled a separate plastic tub with Ben's special homemade biscuits and unearthed some non-dairy chocolate buttons. It had been a long road to uncover the source of Ben's allergy, but the endless exclusion plans had been worth the effort. Of course it meant that most of his food had to be prepared from scratch, just to be sure that no dairy products were creeping into his diet, but Holly figured that a little extra cooking was a small price to pay. Watching her miserable, screaming, snotty baby transform before her very eyes had been almost miraculous.

If only they could get to the bottom of his other issues so easily. Although it was fair to say that Ben suffered by comparison with his gregarious, over-confident twin, it was equally obvious that Ben shied away from other people. Given the choice, Ben liked habit, routine and his twin. He was happy enough with Holly, but he only really sparkled for Tom. Anyone else, anything else, was simply perceived by Ben as an unwelcome interruption.

*

Holly emerged from the utility, bags fully laden and running through her day's To Do list in her head. The twins were now running noisy loops around the kitchen table, Ben lagging behind as always. She'd been meaning to book him in for another development assessment, but somehow, with the move, it had slipped down the list and guilt needled at her over-burdened conscience.

Holly looked up, distracted, to find Milo still blissfully unperturbed by the chaos now surrounding him. He sensed her gaze, looked up at her and smiled. 'If you're up, Holls, I'd love another cup of coffee.'

'Yes, yes, very funny,' Holly replied. 'Kettle's on. You'll have to make your own. I'm late.'

'I did warn you that you didn't have time to be nattering on the phone,' he said, turning the page. 'I'm not sure that this morning routine of yours is really working.'

Holly took a deep breath, refusing to rise to the bait. Sometimes she wondered whether Milo just wanted to provoke a reaction, to prove that he could.

To say that Milo was not a morning person would be an understatement of Jurassic proportions, but since she was utterly wiped by supper-time, their window for civil communication was rapidly shrinking. She constantly reminded herself that his writing was important and that his hours were long and erratic – she wasn't making excuses for him, whatever Lizzie might say – she was just stating a fact.

But it didn't excuse the elephant in the room: Holly's new policy of keeping her head down and ducking the debate was hardly a long-term strategy for marital bliss.

She checked the clock and pulled her battered make-up bag out of her handbag and quickly smudged some eyeliner into place.

'You want some help?'

Holly distractedly covered up the stress spot on her chin and didn't think before answering. 'You could get the boys into their boots and coats?' she suggested, ever hopeful.

Milo leaned forward and plucked the make-up from her hands. 'I meant with that muck on your face – there's probably a trowel kicking around here somewhere!' He laughed at his own joke and tossed Holly's make-up bag to one side. 'I think you might have to admit defeat there, Holly. Only so much you can do with a bit of slap, my love.'

She stared at him, stunned. He may have been laughing, but these recent jokes at her expense simply weren't that funny. 'Give it a rest,' she said, properly needled by his comments, hitting her on the soft underbelly of her own insecurities as they always did. For Milo, words weren't just his profession, they were also his weapon of choice and these days his aim was unerringly accurate.

Later on, when she thought about this conversation, she knew she'd be second-guessing herself. There was a chance, of course, that she was simply over-reacting to Milo's odd sense of humour. But then there was also the possibility that Lizzie was right and that he was actually doing his level best to put her down and gradually shred her self-esteem. The problem was that Holly could no longer tell the difference.

Fresh starts were all well and good, but surely they had to be built on a level foundation? And right now, living with Milo was like walking across a ploughed field in high heels. It was all about balance.

As ever, it took an age to wrestle Tom and Ben into their gloves, hats and coats, muddling up their identical pairs of shoes, and by the time they were ready to leave the house, Holly felt as though she'd run a mile.

She manhandled their enormous double-pram, dubbed the Beast, out of the hallway and into their quiet little road. Holly had actually been looking forward to walking to work whenever the weather allowed. If nothing else, the opportunities for denting expensive Mercedes when she was merely wielding the Beast were marginally lower.

This morning, though, her thoughts refused to be quieted by the beautiful scenery around her. The boys were gabbling away in the pram; their own little language indecipherable even to Holly.

She leaned in to the pram as the road sloped upwards and wondered where it had all gone wrong.

Milo's comments about her appearance used to build her up, not pull her down. Lizzie had been extremely vocal on the subject whenever his jibes had been overheard, leaping to her defence unreservedly, so at least she knew she wasn't imagining it.

Holly sighed. It wasn't just the comments about how she looked; it was everything she did these days. Milo somehow managed to know exactly how to play her, yet always pulling back just before he crossed that line, leaving her uncertain and confused.

The travel mug of coffee that he had lovingly pressed into her hand with a gentle kiss as she'd left just now was a case in point.

He was an expert at sowing just enough seeds of doubt, just enough to unsettle her, before abruptly changing tack – sometimes she honestly thought she might be going mad.

If it weren't for the boys ... Holly shook the disloyal thought away. She'd made the decision to try again and she was damned if she was going to give up without giving this her very best shot. She wasn't going to let her own insecurities ruin her family. So she might need to make a few compromises; it had to be worth it for her boys to grow up in a secure family unit. Didn't it?

'Hello there, Dr Graham!' called out Marion Gains from across the narrow street, bustling towards them with unstoppable purpose and jerking Holly from her reflections. 'How are you settling in?'

Holly smiled despite herself. She couldn't help liking Marion and her kindly interest in every living soul in the town, which spoke more for her maternal nurturing side than for any malicious gossip. As the manager of the little supermarket in town, Marion was basically Larkford's all-seeing-eye. She knew about pregnancies, diets, minor ailments and visiting relatives before anyone else, simply based on her skilled evaluation of your shopping basket. Who needed market research when you had a Marion?

Marion gave the twins an adoring smile and couldn't resist ruffling Tom's hair – she already knew better than to try that with Ben. A few moments of small talk and Marion was off again, heading down the road with the energy and intensity of a woman on a mission.

Larkford was a funny little town in many ways, but Holly had no regrets in moving here, even taking into account the proximity of her formidable mother-in-law. And if ever Jean's ever-looming presence became too much, Holly had only to walk through the streets of the town to know she'd made the right decision.

Every time she came out of her narrow residential road, whether on foot or by car, Holly would pause for a moment. From this mini vantage point, the hills outlined her view in every direction and the woodland seemed to creep down into the edges of the meadows that surrounded the town like a moat.

Holly took a deep breath, slowly drawing in the crisp morning air, and allowed herself just a moment to indulge. Here, Holly had always felt that her little family would be safe, cocooned from the realities of the outside world. Her own childhood had been rather different and she certainly tried to be selective with her memories, for the most part.

The happier years, before her father, a policeman, had been promoted to the Public Protection Unit, she allowed through. Everything after his death in the line of duty was sharply, brutally, edited, leaving her only with the disturbing echoes, whenever she was confronted with a decision of her own.

It had been an easy choice in the end, between the practice in central Bristol, or moving to a nice quiet backwater like Larkford.

She turned into the Market Place just as the sun burst through the heavy blanket of cloud, unwittingly mirroring Holly's state of mind. Just as she never allowed herself to think about her father's passing, Holly mentally filed all thoughts of Milo's thoughtless comments, and how rubbish he'd managed to make her feel, into the Pandora's Box in her mind. In Holly's world, it seemed, nobody had the capacity to hurt her more than the ones she loved the most. She rubbed at her face, her skin taut and irritable, and gave herself permission to draw comfort from her new hometown laid out before her.

There really was something for everyone in Larkford – the statuesque Georgian townhouses at the far end of the Market Place lent a certain elegance to the town and the soaring simplicity of the Norman church provided the perfect relief for the otherwise fussier pastel-coloured terraces that lined each side of the square and led off down the rabbit warrens of residential side-streets that could still get Holly in a muddle.

The acres of wooded parkland, criss-crossed by paths and running trails brought the countryside right into the town. Even the car parks had wrought-iron lamp posts and benches, and a town ordinance from decades before prevented any local businesses using gaudy signs to promote their location. To the tourists' eyes it was a picture-postcard scene.

But walking the length of the town on a day like today made it all too obvious which end of Larkford belonged to the Haves and which to the Have-Nots. Even though the Pound Shop had a suitably tasteful sign, its very presence was an indicator that not everyone in town could afford the decadently fresh sea bass from Larkford's renowned fishmonger, Waves.

As always, as she made her way through town, it was the bit in the middle that fascinated Holly, not the obvious issues in the outlying council estate or the genteel wealth of those Georgian town houses. In between lay the residential streets, small shops and offices that spoke of families trying to get by – juggling time and money whilst dealing with the realities of whatever life may throw at them.

The bit in the middle was where Holly lived and she didn't really think that the tourists swarming through Larkford every summer would have any interest in that at all. But, as far as she was concerned, this was where her patients lived and where her children would grow up and, for her, it didn't get more interesting than that.

Chapter 6

Holly made it to work on time with moments to spare. Tom had predictably leapt from the pram with boundless enthusiasm, whilst Ben, unsettled by the tension at home, had thrown the mother of all tantrums as she dropped them off at nursery. By mid-morning, Holly's stomach was growling as if it were lunchtime and she was already feeling drained and exhausted. Being a working mum was all about stamina and the ability to multi-task – Holly was unconvinced she qualified on either front this morning.

She'd already seen a decidedly spritely and well-rested looking chap, who'd come to her desperate for help with his insomnia. Apparently the poor fellow was barely getting seven hours sleep a night! Seven hours! It had taken a super-human amount of restraint for Holly not to give him a piece of her mind. Instead she'd given him a list of suggestions that might help – hot milk, more fresh air during the day, stay away from cheese in the evenings, oh and get a freaking clue!

Okay, so that last one hadn't been said out loud, but the sleep-deprived portion of Holly's brain had stepped in and she was aware that she was now muttering 'seven hours!' incredulously under her breath at random and inopportune moments.

On the plus side, she felt she'd been sensitive, supportive and skilled in handling several patients with depression, one with horrific acne and had passed no judgement at all on the 70-year-old resident with a raging case of gonorrhoea! She had given him a little pep talk about safe sex, but she feared he'd already nodded off by then.

All in all, it was a slightly different pace to hospital doctoring and Holly was looking forward to finding her feet and getting to know her patients.

She even quite liked the idea of having 'regulars' – feeling that she really might be able to make a significant difference to their long-term care. At the hospital, the notion of 'regulars' was restricted to Mad Derek (who turned up drunk and bruised at 1 a.m. every Saturday morning, having consumed his pay-packet over the course of the evening and picked a fight) and Pervy Brian (who managed to insert something inappropriate into one or other of his orifices on a weekly basis). Holly was therefore understandably excited by the idea of a gentler pace of medicine.

She also knew that, on some level, her new job wasn't just about healing her patients. She was secretly rather hoping that Larkford might also be able to heal her spirit, to give her a much-needed confidence boost that she was a valuable and worthwhile person, whatever her husband may think.

Gradually, the early morning rush had subsided. Grace had forewarned her that there was always a full-on start to the day, as overnight reports of admissions came in to be read, urgent requests for repeat prescriptions were called in, not to mention the ever-looming spectre of triage.

'All the doctors are on a triage roster,' said Grace, 'so it's completely fair. But to be honest, the triage shift is rather the short straw, even compared to the Tuesday morning Boil Clinic. So it's best to just crack on and get it done. And do try not to swap shifts around.'

Lucy the receptionist had chipped in then, keen to get Holly on side, 'It really does work better if we work as a team. I'll warn you, I'm constantly surprised how rude people can get when they're asking for help. I know, I know, they're ill or frightened, but seriously!'

As she spoke, Lucy's little blonde ponytail bounced up and down. Their petite blonde receptionist may look like the angel that fell off the Christmas tree, but she managed to combine her sweetness with a core of steel. Holly had quickly realised that nobody got by Lucy's front desk without her express permission, or possibly a severed limb.

Breaking off from their conversation to tactfully deal with whoever was having a nervous breakdown on the other end of the phone, Lucy gave Holly a grin and Holly couldn't help but respond. There was something intrinsically likeable about Lucy. Even as she then turned to deal with the blustering gentleman at reception, Lucy managed to remain respectful and polite, whilst calmly maintaining the upper hand. Holly was impressed to see this young girl using a firm no-nonsense voice to explain to the patient that turning up at the right time but on the wrong day did not necessarily mean that the doctor could squeeze him in, no matter how much he paid in income tax!

Holly quietly wondered if Lucy might be up for a spot of babysitting – she clearly had the necessary skills.

A few moments later Grace continued the briefing, every now and then earning a supportive nod from Lucy. 'Every morning on the dot of eight o'clock the phone will start ringing with patients requesting an urgent appointment.

Now, more or less every single one of them believe their need to be the greatest, their illness to be the most severe and will be utterly convinced of their right to *instant* medical attention. The poor soul on triage duty needs to evaluate these calls. Obviously, deal with matters on the phone where you can and then fit the others, the ones that do in fact need urgent attention, into the handful of slots that we hold available. Okay?' Grace queried before barrelling on, 'Now, on occasion, you'll need to make a judgement call to send someone straight to hospital and Lucy or I will help you with whatever calls and admin that entails to smooth the way.'

Lucy swivelled around on her chair and re-joined their conversation, 'Yeah and whatever you do, don't swap shifts with Dr Bruce or Dr Channing. Triage duty is the only thing that stops those two being unbearably smug. I'd give them extra shifts if I could, but Grace won't let me.' She nodded her head across the office and Holly followed her gaze.

This morning, the triage shift had clearly fallen to Dr Henry Bruce and his mood was none the better for it. Striding purposefully into the doctors' lounge, he was ruffled to the point that his usually immaculate hair looked dishevelled and the knot in his tie was askew. He looked almost human. 'Please tell me there's a decent cup of coffee in this hell-hole this morning?' he bellowed as the door to the doctors' lounge swung shut behind him.

'See!' said Lucy with a scowl.

'I see our Dr Bruce has been working on his interpersonal skills again,' said Taffy, as he wandered through to the front office with his cup of coffee. 'Morning Luce, morning Dr Graham.'

'It's Holly, remember.'

'I know,' said Taffy with a slow smile. 'You look like you've been up all night, if you don't mind me saying. Bad night with the kids?' he said sympathetically. Whilst he had no desire to populate the world with his own offspring, his sisters' tribes were cute enough that he could at least claim to understand the basics of child-rearing. He surrendered his own cup of hot, sweet coffee to her without a thought, clearly delighted to cause the flash of gratitude that lit up Holly's tired eyes and caused the faintest of blushes to colour her pale cheeks.

'Stinker,' Holly sighed, too tired to be proud, wincing as she attempted to down the steaming coffee in three large gulps. 'When one of the twins is asleep, the other one's awake. I swear the little sod-pots have a rota.'

Holly rummaged in her enormous handbag for something to eat, pushing aside Lego cars, baby wipes and a miniature Buzz Lightyear. Initially discarding the notion of a half-chewed rusk, Holly hesitated as she realised there was nothing else on offer, bar a slightly mangled pouch of mango puree. She hovered in indecision by the bin, the crumbled rusk in hand and stomach rumbling. It was only when Taffy quietly plucked the rusk from her fingers and tossed it into the bin that she realised he'd been watching her and a wave of mortification washed over her.

'I wasn't going to eat it,' she said, defensively.

He just laughed. Not a mean, teasing laugh that made her feel useless and pathetic, but a warm, compassionate laugh that made her feel as though she was a part of the joke and that she was actually funny.

He hopped off the corner of the desk and made the decision for her. 'Here. Sit down and play with your Lego for a bit,' he said kindly, pulling out a chair. 'I'll bring you a fresh cuppa and a Mars bar in a minute. But I should warn you that I'll be expecting a turn with your Buzz Lightyear in return.'

Holly's look of total bafflement only went to show how very rarely she was on the receiving end of such a thoughtful gesture. This time it was Taffy who blushed and he waved away her thanks. 'It's my random act of kindness for the day. Look, all done before elevenses. Some days it takes me 'til bedtime.

'Now while you're here, let's talk about getting you up to speed on the office acronyms,' said Taffy with a devilish grin.

Grace just sighed and pushed back her hair. 'Holly, you listen to this one at your own risk, okay?'

'Aw Gracie, you love my notes really don't you? It's just so convenient. Here's a few of my favourites to get you started, okay . . .'

Holly grinned. 'You may have a bit of competition on that front, Dr Jones. We weren't short of the odd acronym at the hospital either.'

'It's Taffy.'

'I know,' said Holly.

'Challenge accepted then – FFFF?'

Holly thought for a moment, unwilling to show her hand too soon. 'Female, Fat, Fifty and Flatulent?'

'Well, I would have said forty, but I guess fifty's the new forty these days.'

'Erm, isn't that completely sexist?' interjected Lucy indignantly.

'It is a bit,' admitted Holly reluctantly, 'the problem is though, that it's quite often true . . . What about FTW?'

'Easy. Fucking Train Wreck! CTD?'

Holly was stumped. 'I don't know that one.'

'There's a clue here for Lucy if she's still playing and it doesn't offend her delicate sensitivities ... Mr Carlisle ...'

'Ooh, ooh I do know that one – it's Circling The Drain isn't it? I mean, that guy's been at death's door since I started here and that's three years ago!'

'And the lady with the fetching ponytail has it! Bad luck there, Dr Graham!'

'It's Holly,' she said automatically.

'I know,' he replied, before sliding off the desk and heading back to work, leaving Holly feeling as though something important had just happened.

The tension was palpable in the doctors' lounge that Friday lunchtime. Not only was everyone forgoing a much-needed break, but there were mutterings and speculations as to why the meeting had even been called at such short notice. There was a spate of impatient texting, as anyone with a social life scrambled to rearrange their lunch plans.

Holly looked around the room and realised that she still had so much to learn.

She was very much the outsider when it came to understanding the undercurrents and the dynamics in the room. It didn't take a genius to see that there was tension between Julia and Dan; indeed there was an almost elegant rhythm to the way they managed never to physically cross paths. They seemed to be instinctively aware of one another's location at all times and when their eyes did occasionally meet, Holly felt as though she was intruding simply by noticing.

The rest of the staff seemed to naturally fall into small cliques and huddles that crossed all the traditional, departmental boundaries and so left Holly feeling very unsure of where she should be.

For example, Lucy the receptionist was perched on the back of the sofa with Dan, Taffy and Maggie the germ-phobic pharmacist. Holly noticed that Maggie had now brought in bottled water to drink, rather than risk the tap water, and that she was deeply engrossed in conversation with both the male doctors in hushed, urgent tones. They were shooting glances around the room that suggested to Holly that it was their own colleagues that were falling under scrutiny.

Henry Bruce seemed to have gained a small female entourage, led by the sartorially challenged young nurse that Holly had met yesterday. The snotty, rude one who'd looked down her nose at Holly – Jade, was it? Holly didn't recognise the other two girls, although Grace had mentioned something about a senior nurse and a midwife, hadn't she? The Henry Bruce Appreciation Society seemed to be in full swing and he was clearly delighted to have three such attractive young ladies hanging on his every word.

Smarmy bugger, thought Holly with an involuntary shudder, as she watched him smoothing down his tie and leaning in close to hear Jade's breathy comments.

Stupid girl, thought Holly, as she watched Jade flick back her hair and laugh, making a great show of checking the time on the little watch pinned to the chest of her nurse's uniform. Either she really was a bit slow and was struggling with that tricky little analogue watch, or she was loving the fact that Henry was leaning in even closer to help her out.

Holly felt a small growl rise in the back of her throat but took a calming breath, as she made her way across the lounge, swallowing opinions left and right. It was an appalling habit of hers to make snap judgements, but it was one that she was trying hard to break. Ours is not to reason why, she chastised herself. There were clearly years of back-story and history in this room. It was going to take a lot longer than a few days to form a considered opinion.

In the meantime, she had to rely on her gut and her gut was telling her that she needed to be over by the sofas with Dan Carter and the others.

She walked past Julia Channing, who was sitting at the table, tapping away at her iPhone. The speed with which her fingers pecked at the screen was at odds with the casually relaxed air she was cultivating. Well, that and the nervously tapping foot under the table. She glanced up and gave Holly a very intense look, as she noted Holly's planned trajectory towards Dan. Julia leaned across to Jason the nurse who was sitting beside her and seemed smugly satisfied with whatever snide little titbit she whispered in his ear. Jason looked over at Holly then, a long appraising glance, before huddling back down to their tête-à-tête.

For a moment, Holly was back in the Sixth Form Common room and it did not feel like a happy memory. She glanced back in their direction, unnerved to be their topic of conversation. She was relieved to find that they were now discussing their health shakes, which looked for all the world like silage slurpies, but were obviously doing the pair of them a power of good. Bitter greens, thought Holly – shelving all her good intentions not to judge – figures.

Indeed, whereas everyone who congregated around the sofas with Dan looked pretty normal – for that, read tired, peaky and several seasons out of date on the fashion front – Julia and Jason were positively shining with conceited health. To be fair, Henry Bruce was shining too, but in a slightly more over-polished, oleaginous way.

Holly had only just settled beside Maggie, when Grace

came into the lounge and made her way over. 'Someone really should teach that poor girl to tell the time better,' said Grace wryly. 'How's Jade working out with the patients anyway, Dan? Probably not the best idea to put her on blood pressure duty until we've found her a bigger uniform.'

Maggie grinned, seemingly happy to have found some-one with a willing ear to mouth off to. 'But there are some bonuses. Apparently we discovered old Mr Morris didn't actually need that Viagra he's been requesting.'

Dan turned to her, eyes wide, 'No . . .'

Maggie was delighted with his disbelieving response. 'Oh yes. No problem in the hydraulics department at all, as it turns out. Which is just as well, because with his blood pressure, even one of those little blue pills would probably have finished him off and he was hell-bent on convincing Dr Bruce to prescribe some.'

'Wouldn't have taken much to persuade Henry, would it?' Dan commented bitterly, apparently still furious to discover that Henry's last golfing jolly had been funded by their local drug rep. The vehemence loaded into his words took Holly by surprise and she looked up, just in time to catch Dan's look of utter disdain in Henry's direction.

'Quite,' said Maggie with feeling.

It was as though Holly had accidentally stumbled onto the set of some prime-time drama this morning. There seemed to be more sub-plots and historical feuds to untangle than the idyllic setting had actually prepared her for. If anything, thought Holly, the pressure cooker of such a small working community made the tension worse than at the hospital.

'Anyway,' Maggie carried on, 'according to the nurses, it turns out poor Mr Morris just couldn't get it up for his missus. But then, I've met his vile missus and her weepy bunions on many occasions, so you can't really blame the old fart.'

Dan snorted into his cup of tea, inhaling the hot liquid painfully up his nose. 'Maggie!' he protested, shocked into hiccupy laughter. 'It's one thing to think disrespectful thoughts about one's patients, it's quite another to ... Oh hell, who am I kidding? If we can't find a little light relief somewhere ...'

The tiny bubble of their hilarity was burst the second that George, the Senior Partner, walked into the lounge. Dan's eyes were still watering with tears of laughter and Maggie was casually dabbing spilt tea from his tie. Jade had been in the process of whispering some tiny pearls of her wisdom into Henry's willing ear and Jason was trying to convince Julia to sample his 'health shake'. To judge from the expression on George's face, he may as well have walked into an orgy.

He cleared his throat, averting his gaze endearingly. He could be such an old fuddy-duddy at times, according to Dan, but Holly was convinced there simply wasn't a bad bone in his body. Always keen to see the best in people, there were those, according to Grace, who took complete advantage of his good nature.

George fidgeted for a moment, polishing his glasses on his shirt tails. Desperate as they were to discover what was so important they were missing their lunch-break, it only took a moment for silence to fall. George blinked at them all myopically. 'Thank you for, er, taking the time to be here. I know you've got to have some time to eat, but, er, I wanted to share a little news with you all.' He paused awkwardly, waiting for the words to find him. 'It's been no secret that I had hoped that my eldest son Peter would come down to

Somerset and join The Practice. After all, there's been a Dr Kingsley in this Practice for three generations and, whilst I'm obviously very proud of the surgery he's performing up in Edinburgh, there is a great privilege to be had in being part of a community . . .'

Holly tried hard to stay engaged with George's speech about the honour of contributing to their patients' lives, but it was unbelievably hot in the lounge, with them all packed in there and it seemed to be the same call to arms he had proclaimed at her interview. She could see the others around her quietly tuning out too and she felt quite sorry for George. Public speaking was obviously not his forte, but she mentally urged him to get to the point before he lost his audience all together.

According to Grace, or The Oracle of Larkford, as Holly was beginning to consider her, Peter was a patronising, arrogant son of a bitch and, if he had in fact agreed to come back to Larkford, then all their working lives would be affected.

'But sadly,' George continued, 'it is not to be and Peter assures me that he will not be changing his plans. With that in mind,' he paused and looked around the room for dramatic effect, 'I have decided to take early retirement and intend to do so, two months from today. So then, you shall all have to manage without a Kingsley at the helm. Although, since most of you frequent my Teddy's pub on occasion, I'm sure we'll not lose touch.'

The silence in the room became a little strained as George was obviously hoping for a reaction, but it was taking a moment for the penny to drop and for everyone to compute what he was saying.

Holly, for one, frowned in intense concentration, replaying his words over and over in her mind. Was this guy for real? He'd hired her himself – his main pitch to her had been about family and continuity of care and moving into a more stable working environment ... She had planned her life around this job! She swallowed hard and looked around her. Was she the only one in the dark about this plan?

But no, Dan was looking similarly wrong-footed and the gentle hubbub of conversation was fast rising to a chaotic level of discussion.

Poor George was trying to quieten them down, as questions were bandied back and forth about the future of The Practice and who would be stepping into his shoes.

Holly looked over at Julia Channing and felt instantly unnerved by the calculating and conceited look on her face. Was this already a done deal? Was Julia Channing going to be her new boss? Because if so, Holly decided, then her wonderful new job was on a decidedly shaky footing.

George clapped his hands for silence but then stumbled a little over his words, suddenly in a hurry to be out of the limelight. 'And of course, we shall have to decide which of our esteemed Partners should become the Senior Partner in my absence. I'm sure several of you would like to throw your hat into the ring and we have two months to decide, so no hurry there.'

The room exhaled as one with a groan, obviously foreseeing two months of pitching and competing and back-stabbing, in all likelihood. Holly watched Dan stare across at Henry Bruce, smooth and unruffled in his pin-striped suit. Julia, on the other hand, kept her eyes firmly on George and remained convincingly (albeit superficially) serene.

Crap, thought Holly, as the tension in the room escalated. This was clearly going to be a three-way race that could get very ugly.

'Oh and, on an unrelated issue, since we're all gathered together,' George called over the bedlam, 'I'd like you all to join me in congratulating Julia Channing on her new project, Doctor In The House, which I believe starts filming next month and will be aired in the summer. So, to Julia!'

Julia quietly murmured her thanks, as Henry Bruce's acolytes abandoned him and swarmed around her with congratulations. 'I'd like to know when she thinks she's got time to go swanning off being a TV star,' Grace mumbled, one eye as always on the complicated schedule.

Taffy and Dan sat in silence for a moment, as Maggie and Lucy pounced on Grace to find out the inside line.

'So, that's put the cat amongst the pigeons,' said Taffy eventually.

'Yup,' managed Dan monosyllabically.

'You know her better than me, mate, but I'm guessing that the fragrant Dr Channing would be a bitch from hell as Senior Partner?'

'Yup.'

'And Henry is basically a used-car salesman with a medical degree, who's rather fond of his prescription pad?'

'Yup.'

Holly sat quietly taking it all in, feeling as though she was eavesdropping, but gaining valuable insight into the battle ahead. She felt a wave of nausea ripple through her and swallowed hard. Three choices for the job. Two of which would probably make her life hell. Hell, they'd probably just fire her and be done with it! There was only one thing she could do – throw her support behind Dan Carter and make sure he was the outstanding and obvious choice.

'Taffy? You still got that vodka stashed in the vaccination fridge?' Dan murmured eventually, as he rose to his feet.

'Summit meeting in my sodding office then, mate,' he said despondently. 'Think we'll need a liquid lunch, don't you?'

'Bloody hell, Dan,' Holly cursed under her breath as they left. It certainly looked as though Dan Carter had no intention of making that easy for her!

Chapter 7

Holly hunched on Lizzie's doorstep that evening, a chill wind whipping around her ankles, cursing Lizzie for refusing to have a doorbell 'for aesthetic reasons' and feeling decidedly anti-social.

She craved a little head space to corral her thoughts into line before seeing Milo, quietly hoping that this Partnership thing would turn out to be a storm in a teacup, rather than a life-changing tsunami.

Just as Holly was about to completely lose the last remnants of her sense of humour, the heavy wooden door was pulled open by Lizzie's endlessly patient husband, Will.

'Come in, come in. Sorry, chicken, you look freezing out there! We really need to get a sodding doorbell – most people just give up and leave!' Will ushered Holly over the threshold and scooped her into an enormous bear hug, landing kisses of welcome on each of her chilled cheeks.

'Thank God, you've brought more wine. Lizzie's been, er, cooking with the rest,' said Will, tossing her coat over the end of the bannisters, with little or no regard to his wife's perfect interior décor. 'Come on through, we'll get one of these bad boys open and sit you on the Aga to defrost for a bit!' Will flung an arm around Holly's shoulders as they made their way through Farrow & Ball hued rooms, every wall and surface adorned with framed shots of the family – all three children in fabulous clothes, doing fabulous things, looking fabulously happy. If Holly didn't love Lizzie and Will quite so very much, it might almost have been a little nauseating.

'Thanks for picking up the boys. Things got a bit hectic at work,' she said, leaning into Will's solid frame, his chunky jumper making him look like a slightly chubby Swiss ski instructor.

'No problem,' he said and then lowered his voice conspiratorially, 'Now it's only fair to warn you that Lizzie's insisted on cooking tonight. And I've seen what's for supper so you'll be wanting to tuck into the crisps.'

Holly could feel the tensions of her afternoon slowly releasing and she even managed a smile. It had always been a standing joke that Lizzie couldn't cook for toffee. Well, to be more precise, everything she did cook turned to toffee. Or a brown, sticky, often unidentifiable substance anyway. Their student flat share had been one long exercise in compromise. Namely, Holly did the cooking and Lizzie did the washing up. Although, to be fair, she wasn't actually that great with a Brillo pad either.

Lizzie was leaning against the Aga as they walked into the kitchen and Holly was struck as always, by how closely Lizzie's life resembled one long lifestyle photo-shoot. A huge saucepan was bubbling behind her, and she cradled a large goblet of wine in one hand and her daughter Lily on her hip with the other. Oblivious to her toddler's attempts to sneak a slurp of the good stuff, Lizzie leaned forward to kiss Holly on both cheeks enthusiastically. 'You're late, so I've started without you.'

Holly caught hold of Lily as she lunged in for a cuddle, beautiful chestnut hair cut into a severe but wonderfully stylish bob and pink cheeks proclaiming her health and vitality. Next to her Holly felt like a used teabag.

Lily pressed into Holly for a proper cuddle, clearly unworried about sullying Holly's more relaxed style of dressing. With Lizzie, all the kids knew the rules – small sticky hands did not go well with cashmere and suede. Lizzie's boys ran past with the twins in hot pursuit, barely stopping to wave and grin at their mother. At least someone was having a good day.

Moments later, the scrabbling of paws on polished oak floorboards announced the arrival of Eric, the Labradoodle. Eric's unruly blonde curls looked more and more like Lizzie's every day, only serving to add to the notion that life in this house ran to a colour scheme; without doubt, a very stylish palette today, in shades of caramel and cream.

Eric nudged at Holly's hand, pressing himself against her legs until she crouched down to scruff his ears affectionately. 'Hello my gorgeous boy.' She released Lily to scoot off and join the boys and Eric sat beautifully and attentively at Holly's feet, fixing her with his big chocolatey eyes.

'Oh Eric! Stop being such a tart,' said Lizzie, flicking a perfectly ironed tea towel in his direction. She waggled her empty wine glass at Will, who was hurriedly cracking open a few bags of Kettle Chips. 'Fill me up, Buttercup, would you? Oh, and get Holly one of those dreadful elderflowery things she likes.'

They moved about the kitchen with the ease of three people who had known each other for years. They might no longer be students together, but the occasional photo of them looking fabulously knackered and naïve could still be spotted amongst the *Larkford Life* interiors, assuming you knew where to look.

Holly also knew that those same pictures made Milo feel uncomfortable, as though he were still an outsider to their little group. He did try to join in, but often his jokes somehow fell wide of the mark; his 'witty' repartee being that bit too close to the bone and lacking the layer of affection that might soften its impact. Still, Holly appreciated the fact that he persevered. It gave her hope that this fresh start might yet be successful. And, as long as they both kept trying, they were surely moving in the right direction?

She tried to ignore the little pangs of jealousy, as she watched Will affectionately stroke the small of Lizzie's back as he walked by. Lizzie and Will seemed to have forged a marriage that was based upon a mutual respect and a shared sense of humour – both of which felt sadly lacking in her own these days. Sometimes Lizzie's relationship gave Holly hope for what a partnership should look and feel like. Other days – today possibly – she just felt a little envious of her friends' obvious happiness.

Before Lizzie and Will's wedding, Holly had often felt like she was learning to cook from a recipe book with no pictures. She had simply no idea what she was aiming for. And now, because of Lizzie and Will, that same cookbook came with full colour photographs and a three-dimensional demonstration of what love should look, taste and sound like. Or rather, what love *could* be like. Because it was becoming increasingly obvious that, in life, as on *Bake Off*, not everyone following the same recipe would end up with the same result.

'Supper's nearly ready,' said Lizzie moments later, stirring her bubbling concoction, whilst simultaneously clamping down her fringe to prevent steam-frizz. Mary Berry she was not. 'Shall we give Milo a ring?'

'What? To warn him?' deadpanned Will.

'To see what time he'll be here,' clarified Lizzie, some-what missing the joke. 'Or will he be keeping us waiting and making an entrance later as per usual?' Her tone was light but there was no missing the judgement in her words. Lizzie made no secret of the fact that she hated Milo's power games; she hated to see Holly being bossed around and diminished, even if Holly herself didn't always appear to notice it was happening.

'And I've told the kids they can stay up and watch a movie, as long as they're in their PJs, okay?' said Lizzie. Holly hesitated, quietly thinking that an evening cuddled up on the sofa munching popcorn was probably exactly what the boys needed. Life hadn't exactly been a bed of roses for them recently: too many changes all happening at once. But then, she found herself mentally rehearsing the argument with Milo, who had incredibly strict ideas about bedtime routines for someone who was so rarely around to partici-pate in them. 'They've had a long day . . .' she prevaricated, wondering how much energy she had left in the tank and where to focus it.

Lizzie pulled a face, as though she could read Holly's mind. 'Come on, Holls, blame me if you must, but let them stay up and watch a movie. It is Friday night.' She bustled about the kitchen, throwing a tray of dairy-free snacks together for the children. Holly appreciated little things like that more than Lizzie would ever know.

Lizzie waited until Will left the room in search of more wine and then wheeled round to focus on Holly properly, 'What's going on? You look shocking.'

Her comment caught Holly on the hop, the warmth of the kitchen having finally allowed her to relax for a moment. 'What? You don't like my doctoring outfit?' She plucked at the ageing fabric of her best and favourite work dress and struck a pose, not letting on that Lizzie's comment had stung a little bit on delivery.

'I didn't mean the dress – although you're right, it *is* awful – but I suppose it'll do for the NHS. I actually meant *you* ... Have you lost weight?' she accused, narrowing her gaze appraisingly. 'Have you been on a diet without me?'

Holly shrugged. 'Nah. Panic not.' She knew how competitive Lizzie could get when it came to diets. 'It's probably just my sheepdog bra – optical illusion.'

Lizzie looked blank. 'I don't get it.'

'You know,' said Holly, pushing her shoulders back for comic effect, 'the sheepdog bra – it rounds them up and points them in the right direction!'

Lizzie simply looked bemused, her own perfect A cups always enclosed in wisps of delicate silk and lace. Proper supportive underwear was like drought and famine to Lizzie – it happened to other people, not her, and she didn't really like to think about it.

Lizzie's binocular vision for fashion and interiors often gave the impression that she was as deep as the proverbial puddle, but underneath all that, she could be an amazing ally and friend. Once you'd got past the obligatory 'pep talk' of course. Holly slumped a little, the effort of being peppy suddenly taking its toll. 'I actually really need to talk to you about ...'

'Here!' Lizzie interrupted. 'Let's get some eye-liner on you and you'll soon feel brighter.' She ferreted around in a very smart shopping bag, complete with interlocking C's and a black grosgrain ribbon. 'I've tons of freebies, so you can have these.' She passed Holly a lipstick and mascara that probably cost more than the entire contents of Holly's make-up bag.

'I'm not sure make-up's the answer this time, actually, Lizzie.'

Lizzie looked shocked; Holly's comment bordering on the sacrilegious.

Will reappeared in the doorway and shook his head. 'Leave her alone, Lizzie. Not everyone needs six coats of mascara just to leave the house. Although I do seem to recall a certain student Holly wearing buckets of the stuff. Looked amazing, as I recall.'

'Yes, yes, Holly has sickeningly long eyelashes and all the boys in Bristol knew it.' Lizzie's voice had a slight edge that made Holly look up in surprise, catching her friend off-guard. Lizzie coloured slightly and then moved to make amends, 'Well, maybe you don't need the mascara, you lucky sod, but a bit of lippy would give you a lift. My gran used to say that she couldn't drive without her lippy on.'

'Hmm,' said Will, 'but the jury's still out on whether she should be driving at all. I'm still convinced Specsavers might be more help than Chanel!'

Holly laughed and gratefully took the proffered lipstick, just happy to have dodged the mascara bullet. After all, how was Lizzie to know the reason that she'd ditched her beloved mascara obsession.

Holly could never bring herself to confess that Milo joked mascara made her look like Bambi, or sometimes a camel, depending on his mood. Although on his more scathing days, Alice Cooper's love child had also been mentioned. Needless to say, her fondness for the mascara wand had rather worn off after that one! She smoothed the lipstick into place with her little finger, the action coming back to her instantly, except this time it was Chanel Hydrating Crème, not Rimmel's £2.99 Apricot Blush.

Lizzie smiled contentedly, her work done, seemingly oblivious that Holly's problems might be more than skin-deep.

'The thing is . . .' Holly began, wondering where to start and deciding just to rip off the Band-Aid, 'there's a chance I might be out of a job . . .'

Will and Lizzie, to their credit, rallied immediately. Pulling up chairs to the scrubbed pine kitchen table, they demolished two bags of Kettle Chips and another bottle of Pinot before Holly had even finished filling them in.

'I mean, I'm trying not to take it personally that within two days of my arrival the Senior Partner who employed me is retiring.' Holly gave a slightly strangled laugh to make it clear that she was taking it all in her stride. Or trying to, at least.

'Maybe that's the reason they wanted an extra GP in the first place?' Will said, trying to be the rational voice of reason.

'Well, maybe that *is* why they needed me, but the first I heard of it was when he announced it to The Practice as a whole and suddenly there's factions and cliques and leadership squabbles. The whole afternoon has been a crap shoot.' Holly sighed. 'I can't help feeling a bit misled really, but then, why *should* they tell me? I'm new and I'm junior. It's just made me feel a bit unsettled. After all, I've moved house, moved the kids, my whole life really, for a job that seemed steady and safe. What if the new Senior Partner, whoever it turns out to be, thinks that I'm superfluous to requirements? I don't even have a proper contract yet.'

Holly shrugged unhappily, as she fought to swallow down

the lump in her throat that had been lurking ever since she heard the announcement. 'I mean, please don't get me wrong. I love this town. I adore being nearer you guys and seeing more of you. But I think we all know that Milo's not going to be a happy bunny if the whole relocation turns out to be for nothing.'

There was an uncomfortable silence for a moment; nobody could disagree with that understatement and yet none of them knew what to say.

Will stood up and stirred at their supper disconsolately. 'Speaking of which, will His Lordship be much longer? I can pop this on life support, but I don't know how long it'll survive. Professional opinion, Holly? IV fluids? Class A drugs?' He waggled the Worcestershire Sauce at her questioningly. They all knew full well that Lizzie's 'family recipes' were probably the reason her whole family were so damn skinny, but nevertheless, they did occasionally allow themselves to hope.

Lizzie sighed. 'Your husband can be a real pain in the backside, Holly, did you know that?'

'It hadn't entirely escaped my notice,' she said drily, 'but please be nice. He really is making an effort. And guys? Don't mention the job thing yet, will you? I need to get my head around it first, work out what I want to do. I mean, I love Milo, I do, but he's not really known for keeping his cool in a crisis, is he?'

Will put his arm around her shoulders and squeezed. 'Of course we'll be nice, *won't* we, Lizzie? And who knows, maybe he'll surprise us all and be wonderfully supportive ... And we're here for you, Holly, whatever you decide to do.' He gave Lizzie a stern look as he stressed the word 'whatever' and carried on, 'Of course, if we knew what you see in the man, it might make it easier to understand ...'

Lizzie gave a filthy laugh and hopped up on to the kitchen counter, swinging her legs like a teenager. 'Oh I think we all know what Holly saw in Professor Dreamy, don't we?'

Will looked blank.

Lizzie passed him his wine and waggled her eyebrows. 'Don't you remember? Miss Innocent Graham here had quite the thing for older men. There was her epic crush on that gorgeous ethics lecturer — oh the irony! And then that orthopaedic consultant with the enormous eyebrows ... Unrequited love, if I recall? And then of course,' she swooned dramatically, 'one night in Casualty, just as the clock struck midnight, enter Milo Payne ...'

Holly blushed furiously. 'Don't be daft. It was nothing like that!' Only it was exactly like that and Holly knew it. She also knew that the adage to marry in haste and repent at leisure had never had such a resounding endorsement.

She knew, in her heart of hearts, that she would have been well advised to get to know Milo a little better, rather than spending the vast majority of their courtship fooling around in bed. But it simply hadn't felt like an option at the time. Sex with Milo had been a complete revelation for Holly. After the student fumblings of her flings at med school, suddenly here was a man who knew his way around the bedroom and it wasn't long before Holly had been putty in his hands.

She thought back to her second year of residency and to the night they had met, when Milo had come into Casualty, his finger bleeding from a nasty glass cut. She remembered how he'd quietly convinced her to go out for a drink with him after her shift, even though she'd been working for eighteen hours straight. The attraction had been instant. He just knew what he wanted and he made it happen. There was no bluster, no arrogance, just complete self-assurance.

It was the first time she'd properly gone out with someone a few years older than her, rather than simply harbouring an unrequited crush; someone who knew exactly what they wanted out of life and was prepared to put in the effort to achieve it. It had been quite the aphrodisiac.

Back then, Holly thought she had found that rare and elusive beast – a steady, thoughtful man, who also happened to be a demon in the sack. She remembered thinking, as she walked down the aisle towards him, that he really was the whole package, almost too good to be true.

If she'd known then, what she knew now . . .

Holly sighed, thinking that she probably wouldn't be quite so quick to say 'I do'.

Eric curled up against Holly's leg, as if sensing her spiralling mood, pressing his little furry body into her, tail tattooing a steady beat on the flagstone floor. Holly stroked his ears distractedly, grateful for his unconditional support. 'I wish we could have a dog,' she sighed. 'It would be amazing for the boys and Ben really responds to him, have you noticed?'

Will draped the tea towel over his shoulder and sat back against the counter beside Lizzie, his hand gently massaging the small of her back. 'Why don't you, then? You could have a little one, couldn't you? Now your hours are more regular? It wouldn't need that much exercise.'

Holly shrugged uncomfortably, suddenly wishing she hadn't brought it up.

'Failing that,' Will joked, 'you could just share this one.'

'Ooh yes,' Lizzie cried, suddenly animated, 'then we can have him on timeshare! Oh, come one, Holls, it'll be great. Go on! Be honest, you know I didn't really think this dog business through – I don't have enough time to give him all the attention he needs. But I *do* have time for half a dog and so do you! And he already prefers you anyway ... And he loves staying at yours. We can just become one of those big, modern, dysfunctional families!'

'You mean we aren't already?' Will said wryly.

But Lizzie was on a roll, clapping her hands excitedly and leaping down from the worktop. 'How could you say no – just look at his little fluffy face! Plus, it would be really good for all the kids ...'

'Alright, Lizzie, give the girl a chance to breathe. Obviously Holly needs to talk to Milo about it first. She can't just come home with a timeshare puppy, no matter what loopy scheme you two cook up.'

Holly fidgeted a little, as that's exactly what she'd been planning to do. Firstly, because she could probably keep a Shetland pony in the spare bedroom and Milo wouldn't notice and secondly, because of The Other Problem – the elephant in the room – the detail that Holly was almost too embarrassed to admit to. Somehow, inadvertently and without any prior knowledge, she had married a man who didn't like dogs!

What kind of a person didn't like dogs? More to the point, what kind of a person sat and listened to his fiancée going on and on about her plans for the future – the kids, the dogs, the country practice – and never said a word? Not once.

Yet another indication that Holly should have done more due diligence before saying 'I do'.

Lizzie, suspecting strongly that Milo's aversion to dogs had more to do with not wanting to lose any more of Holly's attention, for once kept quiet. She could see her friend wavering and was silently cheering her on to make the right decision.

She had her own suspicions about why Holly and Milo's marriage was falling apart, although she was obviously madly biased in her friend's favour. She knew that Holly had been drawn in by Milo's strong, capable, caveman routine, but now it just seemed to her that Milo wanted to control Holly's every move. To Lizzie's discerning eye, he seemed to resent Holly's return to work, he openly begrudged all the time she spent with the boys and he missed no opportunity to put her down. As Holly's friend and champion, Lizzie found it hard to keep quiet.

Holly started attacking another packet of crisps, in grave danger of pinging them everywhere. Eric was instantly alert, summoned by the rustle of packaging, and was soon wedged in next to Holly, his head on her lap, chomping on a crisp delightedly. Even at eighteen months, he was still a big baby really.

'You'll spoil him,' Lizzie warned.

'Isn't that going to be my job, as part-time parent? To spoil him rotten and then hand him back?' Holly grinned, offering him another crisp and cuddling in to his blonde fur, smoothing his silky ears and revelling in the look of total adoration in his deep chocolatey eyes.

His little body wiggled insistently, the tail literally wagging the dog. In a moment of intense joy, he sprang up, desperate to find a place on Holly's lap.

She gently pushed his nose out of her face, as Lizzie fell about laughing at her attempts to get him down. 'Eric,' chided Lizzie sternly, 'we've talked about this. No tongues! You'll get the whole town talking. Again.'

Holly laughed like a drain, the tension in her chest from their conversation evaporating. She gave in and pulled Eric's wriggling body into her arms for a cuddle. 'Let's just say that the more men I meet, the more I love your dog.'

'Our dog,' protested Lizzie. 'And not all men . . . just, you know, yours . . .'

Chapter 8

A firm, confident knock at the front door echoed through the house.

'He arrives!' said Will dramatically, with a wink at the girls, before heading through to the hall to let Milo in.

Milo erupted into the room with his cashmere scarf swaddled around his neck. 'Hello, Gorgeous!' he said, giving Holly a lingering kiss on the lips. 'Don't you look glamorous!' He pulled Holly into his side, tucking an arm around her shoulders. 'I was only saying to Holly this morning that she should ditch her ratty old make-up and start afresh.' He smoothed her cheek with his thumb, a look of intense adoration on his face. 'But then if you've got a face like this, you really don't need it, do you?' He smiled over at Will, in an all-boys-together gesture of solidarity. 'Of course, I probably wasn't quite that tactful! I never quite get it right, do I, Holls?'

While Milo gushed on, greeting Lizzie and praising the 'tantalising' aromas emanating from the stove, Holly found herself mentally crossing her fingers. Milo on good form was charming and witty and even Lizzie had been known to soften in the spotlight of his attentions.

'Are the boys all settled, or do I have time to say

goodnight?' Milo asked, as though it were the most natural thing in the world.

Sheer relief coursed through Holly, as she watched everyone laughing and chatting as though from a distance. She sipped at her drink and let the conversation ebb and flow around her. Her husband was nothing if not enigmatic, but his abrupt mood changes these days still made her feel as though she were constantly on a cliff-edge. Maybe, she wondered, this was what losing the plot felt like? After all, they did say that madness was hereditary and, come to think of it, Great-Aunt Phyllis had certainly been two sandwiches short of a picnic.

'Is that bouillabaisse, Lizzie?' Milo enquired, as they all sat around the table a short while later. 'Lord, that's ambitious. You are clever for giving it a go. I'm not sure I'd know where to start!'

Lizzie shrugged nonchalantly, as though she whipped up French cuisine every night of the week.

'Holly's idea of a culinary adventure is adding tomato puree to the Bolognese, isn't it, darling?' he joked, totally missing the filthy look that Lizzie shot his way.

Will stood up with a ladle and reached out for Milo's bowl. 'I'll be Mother then, shall I?' he said, quietly and deliberately dishing up an enormous helping for Milo and distinctly more petite portions for everyone else.

'Sweet Jesus,' mumbled Holly, as she and Will bravely sipped at their spoons, 'it's a good job you're pretty, Lizzie.'

Lizzie grinned and poured herself another glass of wine. 'It'll be fine. You do fuss so, you two. It's got all the right ingredients in it ...'

'But not necessarily in the right order,' replied Will,

as he gamely tried to chew and swallow some mystery seafood.

Tilting his head to one side, Will finally swallowed and caught Holly's eye. The two of them collapsed with laughter as they tried and failed to find something positive to say.

'You are rotten, you two, ganging up on me. I'll never get any better if I don't practise! I mean, how bad can it actually be?' Lizzie exclaimed.

As Holly clutched her stomach in laughter, leaning happily against Will's shoulder for support, Milo stretched across the table and deftly moved Holly's wine glass out of her reach with a look of disdain. Holly didn't notice, but Lizzie did and she promptly moved it back, as though the two of them were playing a surreal game of chess.

Lizzie stared at him, challenging him to make the next move.

For a moment, the derision was written clear on his face, before he shrugged and sat back, a winning smile taking its place.

'Do you know, Lizzie,' Milo said smoothly, as though nothing had happened, 'I think that this is far and away the best bouillabaisse I have ever eaten outside of France!'

Lizzie frowned, unaccustomed to his lightning changes of mood and unsure what to make of the compliment. 'Milo, have you ever eaten bouillabaisse outside of France before?' she asked suspiciously.

He just smiled enigmatically and raised his glass, before leaning back in to the conversation with a joke. Holly and Will, already on a hair trigger for the giggles, were soon caught up in his funny anecdote about the mad librarian in Bath. Resting his arm around Holly's shoulders, she nestled into him instinctively. Only Lizzie sat back, watching the evening unfold, with a nebulous sense that she was missing something.

Later, as Lizzie attempted to load the dishwasher without Eric trying to climb in and act as Pre-wash, Holly plonked more plates down beside her.

'Nice to see Milo on form,' said Lizzie, quietly fishing.

'It is,' Holly agreed, pushing aside the spiralling thoughts that tormented her. Would they need to move yet again before she'd even finished unpacking? She was only too aware that redundancy was such a career-killer on a doctor's CV. And with the boys only just starting to get settled . . . She sighed deeply: soul-searching would have to wait. It was yet another luxury she didn't have time for.

Lizzie gave her hand a squeeze. 'Penny for them . . .'

Holly smiled. 'Where would I be without you?'

'Mistress to that dodgy ethics professor, with a shaggy perm and questionable taste in clothes? So not that different really . . . but without a timeshare puppy obviously.'

Holly leaned in and kissed Lizzie on the cheek in a spontaneous gesture of gratitude. For all her foibles, Lizzie was the best friend she'd ever had. 'Then I guess I owe you one.'

Lizzie drained her glass. 'Oh darling, at this point we really should stop counting!'

A plaintive wail from upstairs got Holly's instant attention. When Ben kicked off in the night, there was always a small but distinct window of opportunity to get him settled again, or they were in for a long one.

'I'll come and help,' said Lizzie, noting that Will and Milo seemed to be having a pleasant conversation for once and wanting to leave them to it.

*

With Ben cradled back to sleep in her arms, Holly perched on the end of Lizzie's bed. She brushed Ben's fringe from his eyes and savoured the moment of peace.

With him asleep and his little starfish hands relaxed against her, Ben's fight against the world was on hold. All the tension in his little body was gone and Holly held him to her, murmuring sweet nothings.

'Holly? You do know you're going to have to tell Milo about your job?' said Lizzie, gently but firmly.

'I know,' said Holly. 'I just think I need a bit more information first.'

'Or you could tell him tonight, while he's in a good mood? Then you two can make a plan together over the weekend. Either way,' she persisted.

Holly didn't reply and Ben snuggled closer into her arms. In that moment, Holly didn't really trust herself to speak. Everything she was doing, all the choices she was making were about making the best life for her boys that she could possibly manage. And little boys needed their dads. Everybody knew that. Everybody told her that. All the bloody time. She'd tried to tell herself that there were better male role models out there, but Milo was their father and, faced with that incontrovertible truth, her arguments sounded hollow and unconvincing even to herself. It wasn't particularly helpful either, that despite everything, she did still love him and yearned for their earlier days together, when life had seemed so simple.

A volley of laughter came from downstairs, the sound so unusual that Lizzie and Holly both looked at each other in amazement.

'Bloody hell, Milo really is pulling out all the stops tonight,' said Lizzie. 'How badly is he on the back foot this time? Has he found himself a new little postgrad to play with?' Her tone was scathing and it instantly made Holly feel all prickly and defensive.

Her silence was loud in the room and Lizzie sighed dramatically. 'Sorry. Bit tactless. Too soon?'

'Definitely too soon. And I would have thought you'd be pleased he was making an effort?' Holly managed tightly.

'I am, I am,' said Lizzie apologetically. 'I just worry about you, Holls. All this talk of him making an effort ... Should it really require such an effort to be pleasant to your lovely wife? And, be honest, Milo on buoyant form normally means he's fucked up something. How many compliments has he been throwing your way this evening?'

'Cynic.'

'Realist,' Lizzie countered firmly. 'I could go on ...'

'Please don't, though,' said Holly with feeling 'I know you two butt heads occasionally, but really I just need you to support me on this.'

She normally valued Lizzie's objective input, even when it came to her marriage, but she couldn't cope with any Milo-bashing tonight. He was obviously doing his best and that ought to be enough, even if she sometimes wondered deep down whether it was all an act. He certainly seemed able to switch it on and off like a tap.

Holly was only too aware that she had a blind spot where Milo was concerned: her boys. She did try to trust her instincts, to stay on balance, even when Milo seemed to do his level best to distort her recollection of events. But over-riding everything was the desire to keep her family together, despite the little voice that whispered that things weren't quite right. The trouble was, she had no idea what to do to make them better.

She felt paralysed by doubt, caught in a vicious circle that made her feel passive and weak. The responsibility of making the wrong decision was utterly overwhelming: at this point, doing nothing actually felt like the proactive choice.

Lizzie sat down beside Holly on the bed and pressed a set of keys into her hand. 'I've been thinking and I want you to have these, Holly. Just in case you need a bolthole any time. Phone – don't phone – just turn up if you need to . . .' Her tone brooked no argument, but Holly was still shocked.

'I'm not a battered wife on the run, Lizzie!'

'I didn't say you were. I just gave you a set of keys in case you ever needed them.' Lizzie squeezed her hand tightly.

Had Lizzie spotted the fear in her eyes and misinterpreted it?

Because Holly *was* afraid; it terrified her now to realise how completely she had surrendered her independence when she became a mother. Sharing parenthood of their lovely boys was surely a tighter bind than any marriage vows or mortgages.

She'd been completely prepared for the sleepless nights and the stretch marks, not to mention the overwhelming love she would feel for her babies – but somehow, amongst all the hormones and nipple cream, nobody had thought to forewarn her that she was now inextricably linked to Milo for the rest of her life: no matter how much he'd changed and whether she liked it or not.

Lizzie, true friend that she was, sensed Holly's mood and didn't push the issue. Having found the opportunity to make her point, she changed tack. 'Besides – you'll need those keys when you come to pick up Eric!'

Holly smiled. She couldn't deny that the prospect of a time-share puppy was extraordinarily appealing, although heaven knows how many arguments that arrangement might provoke at home . . .

Lizzie fidgeted uncomfortably beside her and sighed. 'Right, enough of all that touchy feely bollocks! We really ought to go back downstairs you know.' She stood up and pulled distractedly at the crotch of her skin-tight jeans.

Holly realised, and not for the first time, how lucky she was to have a friend who could be supportive in the moment, but never felt the need to dwell on the drama. Right now, Holly was just grateful for the opening to talk about something else, 'Erm, Lizzie? You've gone all squirmy. You okay?'

Lizzie just laughed. 'It's alright, Dr Graham, I'm not hitting you up for some Canesten! I just tried a new minty shower gel – smells gorgeous by the way – but I have to be honest, it's made my lady bits go all tingly.'

Holly shook her head, well used to these bizarre occurrences. Lizzie was forever experimenting with toiletries, hair dye and make-up. Obviously some with better results than others.

Lizzie squirmed again and gave a little jiggle. Holly just grinned. '*That* tingly, huh? Well, maybe I should get some for myself!'

Lizzie's filthy laugh lifted Holly's spirits even more. She laid Ben back into his little camp bed and carefully tucked the house keys into her pocket. She didn't need them of course. In all likelihood would never need them. But somehow, knowing that Lizzie was worried enough to get them cut, gave her a perverse little boost. At least she wasn't imagining everything!

At the top of the stairs, Lizzie caught her arm. 'Don't wait, Holly. Perseverance isn't always a good thing. You should just tell him you're not happy,' Lizzie insisted, her head tilted to one side in the universal sign of compassion and looking even more like Eric than usual.

Holly paused for a moment, as she considered the possibility, rejecting it almost instantly. The mental picture of the four of them together – her family – foremost in her mind. 'I am, though,' she said, a touch defensively, 'I *am* happy – most of the time. Between the boys and work and, well, you guys ... I'd say, eight days out of ten, I'm perfectly fine.'

Lizzie gently elbowed her in the ribs. 'Listen to yourself. This isn't a bloody Whiskers advert!'

Holly laughed, but the strain never left her face. 'I do know I have to talk to him and obviously we need to make some changes. And don't worry, I will. But in all honesty, I need to wait until I've got myself a little more balanced,' she shrugged and then flashed Lizzie a smile, 'otherwise I'm not entirely sure I'd have the restraint to stop, once I got started.'

Holly swallowed hard. It was all very well joking about these things, but she knew that the day was coming when she couldn't put it off any more. She was just hoping to be in a slightly stronger frame of mind by then. And preferably not unemployed.

'Did you have a nice time tonight, Holls?' Milo asked as they walked through Larkford on their way home later that night. 'It was good to see you relax a bit. I do know your job isn't your average nine 'til five and we all realise how hard you work. You're quite something to live up to!' He kissed her gently on the top of her head and, for a moment, it was just like old times. When Milo decided to be charming, there was no one more attentive or sweet.

Holly breathed out slowly, her shoulders dropping back into their rightful place. Her breath clouded in front her, the spring night still chilly, and she nestled into her coat. The twins were happily bundled into the Beast, with layers of blankets keeping them snuggly as they slept. The rest of the evening had passed in a blur of funny stories and casual banter. Holly couldn't remember the last time the four of them had had such a relaxed and enjoyable evening. Even Lizzie had stopped glaring at Milo after a while, his silly stories winning her around to a casual détente.

Walking along, with the stars scattered across the night sky and the echoes of the evening's laughter still sounding in her head, it was so easy to remember why she fell in love with him.

'Aren't they beautiful when they're so sleepy and peaceful?' she murmured, enjoying the warmth of Milo's hand on her own as she pushed the pram.

He leaned in closer, his breath warm and familiar on her cheek, gazing at their boys with an almost quizzical expression. He gave a little sigh. 'You know, I think I might prefer them like this . . .'

Holly looked at him sharply, wondering whether he was in fact making a sweet paternal joke about his noisy little boys or whether he truly meant it. She was disconcerted to find that she honestly couldn't tell.

'Shall I make us a snack while you put the boys to bed?' Milo offered. 'I'm starving.' He held up a placatory hand. 'I know, I know, I'm not supposed to speak ill of the best friend, but that fish stew was shocking.'

They shared a knowing smile and Holly gently laughed, trying to relax back into her earlier cosiness. 'I think we've all agreed that cooking is not really Lizzie's forte!'

'You will notice that I still ate it, though.' Milo said, helping Holly lift the Beast around a lamppost. 'I do get that it's important to make an effort with your friends. And frankly if eating that stew doesn't show you that I'm trying, then nothing will!'

It was as close as Milo was ever likely to get to an apology and Holly breathed more easily, just from knowing that the latest storm had passed.

They walked in companionable silence for a while, Holly wondering whether it was worth fracturing their fragile détente by mentioning work. The warm smile he gave her and the languorous feeling in her tired muscles, made her think that that particular conversation could definitely wait.

Bundling through the door, they each took a twin upstairs and Holly began to stealthily sneak them into bed. She sighed, tired but content, and delighted that the evening had gone so well. In a funny way, she was grateful to Lizzie for her pep talk, no matter how bluntly phrased it had been. She could always count on Lizzie to give her the unvarnished truth and something to think about!

Switching on the night-light, she whispered more good-nights to the boys and made her way back down to the kitchen, where Milo had been rummaging in the fridge. The cold, detached tone of his voice stopped her in her tracks.

'Didn't you forget something? Go back upstairs, Holly, and wipe that muck off your face!' he said, his voice dripping with contempt, as he absent-mindedly sliced some Brie onto a cracker.

Her hand fluttered to her lips, to the make-up she'd completely forgotten, and in a heartbeat, Holly felt like Alice down the rabbit-hole all over again.

For all that Holly was determined to give her boys a stable and loving family life, was it really worth the price that living with Milo would surely cost?

Chapter 9

Dan Carter pulled off his tie as he walked into the heaving bar of The Kingsley Arms, nodding hello to various patients as he passed. The warm fug of beer and bodies lent the pub a comforting aroma that immediately made Dan feel more relaxed. Taffy forged ahead, determined to get a few rounds in, after the interminable bickering that had broken out following George's announcement.

Teddy Kingsley spotted them from the other end of the polished oak bar and waved them over. 'You both look wrecked,' he commented, lifting down pint glasses from the shelf behind his head.

'Strategy meeting,' grumbled Taffy, pulling up a stool and pushing a second one over to Dan with his foot. 'Went on a bit.'

Teddy grinned and tossed him a packet of pork scratchings. 'I guess Dad dropped his little bombshell then? As if you haven't all been waiting for the day . . .' As the black sheep of the family, who had dared to choose fine cuisine over first aid, Teddy had been amused to watch his father dither over the timing of his retirement for the last few years.

'Did he say who's going to step into his shoes, since obviously the Prodigal Son has chosen not to return?

Although the Publican Son does do a nice fatted calf!' He waved his hand at the specials board, all lovingly crafted by Teddy every day. 'The kitchen's technically closed, but if you guys are hungry, I can knock something up for you?'

'Nah,' said Taffy, his mouth full of pork scratchings, 'I'm good. Just a few pints of cider, please, Ted. Line 'em up.'

Teddy carefully manoeuvred four pints of cider onto the bar. 'That should keep you two going. It's last orders in a bit.'

'Cider?' Dan queried. 'Haven't you got the early shift?'

Taffy shrugged, his first pint already half gone. 'Hence the cider. It's basically apple juice.'

Dan laughed and took a sip, the tart bite of the apples making him shudder. 'You know, Taffy, for a GP, your take on nutrition is a little sketchy at times.'

'Ah yes, but everything's in full working order and I don't want to rock the boat. If it ain't broke, don't fix it.' He jokingly flexed his considerable muscles and grinned. Despite being fair-haired, the hours Taffy spent outdoors each week, training for the local rugby team, meant that his face and arms were lightly tanned all year round. He was a picture of health and vitality and, with his upbeat, sociable personality, it was little wonder he was such a hit with the ladies.

Dan watched his friend drain the first glass and push it aside. There was no doubting Taffy's claim, as his work-hard, play-hard lifestyle seemed to be suiting him. Lots of rugby, lots of girls, lots of fun. And it was clear that Taffy wasn't the one having trouble sleeping.

Dan checked his watch and felt the familiar cramp of panic at the thought of yet another sleepless night ahead. He'd become used to taunting himself through the small hours of each night, 'If I get to sleep now, I can have five hours' sleep. That's enough. That's fine. I can cope with five hours . . . If

I get to sleep now, I can have four hours ... If I get to sleep *right now*, I could still have three hours ...'

It had become such an ingrained habit, that even here in the pub, Dan was mentally tallying up how much sleep he could fit in before the next shift.

For all Dan's bravado, Taffy wasn't stupid. He could see that Dan was struggling again and he was torn between respecting Dan's wishes not to discuss it and stepping in to help his mate. Technically, *technically*, he should really mention this to George. There was an unwritten Practice rule that if one of the team was in trouble, George wanted to know about it. 'If I don't know, I can't help,' he would say. But with the debate for Senior Partner thrown wide open, Taffy could see that this may not be the best time to play by the rules.

Since Teddy was distracted at the other end of the bar, he decided to take a more oblique approach. 'Haven't seen you too much this week. What's new?'

Dan slid his sleeve down to cover his watch face and shrugged. 'Same old, same old. Too much work, not enough time. Was actually planning on taking a little break, to be honest, just to get away and do something physical. Burn off some tension, you know. But now George's thrown down the gauntlet, I think it's probably better to stick around, don't you?'

'You mean keep an eye on Julia and smarmy Bruce?'

'Wouldn't you?' Dan raised one eyebrow. There was certainly some truth in Taffy's words. He couldn't exactly protect his position from halfway up a cliff face in Anglesey.

Dan rubbed at his eyes with the heel of his hand, as he often did when searching for the right words. 'It's not as though the whole team's going to split up into sides, but there will be an element of campaigning and I'm not sure I want Julia to get a head start, to be frank. If she hasn't already with her new TV show.'

Taffy nodded in agreement, struggling to keep his attention on Dan, while three local girls perched on the other tall bar stools in tiny little skirts. The pretty little blonde toying with her glass had a cracking pair of legs, he could see, as the fabric rode up her thighs. Dan gave him a resigned nudge. 'You ought to go over.'

Taffy cast one more lingering glance, as the girl struggled to keep her balance on the edge of the stool and a little more thigh was tantalisingly exposed. 'Nah, not tonight. There's always another day,' he said with the supreme confidence of knowing that there always would be. 'Besides, they're no match for the rather delectable Dr Graham, are they?'

Dan raised an eyebrow. 'The rather delectable, rather married, Dr Graham, you mean?'

Taffy shrugged, happy that Dan was at least trying to engage in their conversation rather than brooding into his pint. 'I'm just saying, you kept a bit quiet about that one, didn't you?'

'What's to keep quiet about? I did tell you she was lovely. But I can promise you that neither one of us would be her cup of tea. She likes nerdy guys and there's also something else . . . oh yes, she's Married!'

'I know, I know,' said Taffy, 'but since she's also gorgeous, a boy can dream, can't he?'

They were interrupted in their conversation by the arrival of the three girls, who had apparently already clocked his admiring glances. A lithe brunette threw them a smile, before holding out an over-manicured hand. 'I'm Ashley,' she said. 'This is Lindy and this is Jenny.'

Taffy put down his drink. If he was totally honest, he couldn't remember their names already, but in all likelihood, he knew that wouldn't matter. 'I'm Taffy. This is Dan. Aren't you girls cold?'

The girls chatted away to Taffy, acutely aware from their initial introduction that Dan's interest and attention lay elsewhere.

Dan's dark good looks and athletic physique were always enough to pique the girls' interest when they went out in the evenings, but to Taffy's ongoing dismay, Dan would insist on having proper conversations with them. He actually wanted to get to know every girl he spoke to and talk about movies and politics and travel. All very well if you're out shopping for a girlfriend, but Taffy was of the opinion that if his friend cut loose a little, he might be a bit more chilled out in general.

Taffy was keeping an eye on Dan, whilst enjoying a little friendly banter with Ashley. Half his mind was trying to work out how to ditch the more brazen Ashley and Lindy. He was far more interested in quiet little Jenny, still wobbling on her bar stool and flushing adorably every time he looked her way.

The other half, arguably his better half, was worried about Dan. He knew perfectly well that Dan hadn't told him the whole story about why he was off his game this week. He took in Dan's pale face, taut jaw and tight, white grip on the pint glass. There was a faint pulse at his temple and he didn't look good.

'Hey!' said Ashley suddenly. 'I just realised, I know you two from the paper!' Her voice was higher than before and her body language suggested she was determined to win their undivided attention. 'You were the doctors at that big crash the other week!' She grabbed Taffy's arm excitedly. 'You were both, like, heroes or something – saving all those kids!'

Taffy watched Dan flinch, eyes flashing wide with alarm. Ashley yabbered on, fawning a little and gushing to her friends all about the mini-bus crash that Taffy and Dan had attended.

Dan stood up abruptly, pushing his stool back so hard it toppled. He drained his glass, ignoring the full one awaiting his attention, voice strained, 'I think I'll call it a night actually, Taff.'

The bell for last orders rang loudly and suddenly right beside them and the glass shattered in Dan's grip, the last dregs of cider running over the cuts in his hand. 'Shit!'

Taffy stood quickly, filled with concern. It was all he'd needed to see, to convince himself he was right.

'Come and have a quick fag with me before you go,' Taffy said, getting to his feet. There wasn't much he could do tonight, but at least now he knew what had been bugging poor Dan for the last few weeks.

Despite the lateness of the hour, there were still a few souls wandering around the Market Place. In only a few hours, this central square would be bursting with market stalls selling everything from gourmet sausages to bundles of dishcloths. The buildings along the older, south side of the square all huddled and leaned together like old women, their pinafores a muted rainbow of pink, blue and cream. This was the main tourist photo of Larkford market: the ancient buildings, each painted a different tasteful shade, with the stunning architecture of the church looming up behind them.

Perched on the wall beside the pub, Taffy expertly lit up two cigarettes and passed one across to Dan, ignoring his protests by claiming they were medicinal. Taking a deep drag, Taffy chose his words with care. 'Bad shit the other night, wasn't it. Still keeps creeping up on me.'

Beside him, Taffy felt Dan stiffen. There was no point in pretending that he didn't know exactly which night Taffy was referring to. Even in a reasonably large town like Larkford, big pile-ups like that one didn't happen very often. Was it luck that the two GPs had been some of the first to arrive on the scene? At the time, and for the passengers of the mini-bus, it must surely have felt like it. After all, they had been able to do so much to help, whilst waiting for the paramedics.

Taffy pulled his coat closer around him as a shiver ran involuntarily up his spine. He watched Dan closely, under the yellow haze of the distant street lamp. He too was obviously feeling a chill and Taffy watched, as Dan stuffed his trembling hand deep into his jacket pocket, still wrapped loosely in a paper napkin to staunch the blood. The other held a cigarette that was quietly burning itself to extinction. His voice, when he spoke, came out in a broken croak, 'I still can't believe that lad didn't make it. We did everything right. He was wearing a seat belt . . .'

His voice petered out and Taffy nodded in agreement. 'We did, you know. We did everything right.' A heavy sigh escaped his chest. 'And somehow, knowing that everyone else made it still doesn't seem enough does it?'

Dan hunched his shoulders further and the two men looked out over the Market Place, carefully avoiding each other's gaze. 'He was just a kid, Taff. It's so fucking pointless.' His voice was hoarse and Taffy could hear Dan's teeth chatter. He knew only too well it wasn't the cold, but he couldn't let the subject drop. They'd been here before.

'I can't get it out of my head either to be honest, mate.

All those flashing lights and the bus going up like that ...
I keep wondering what would have happened if we hadn't
got everyone out in time ...' His soft Welsh lilt had a gentle
hypnotism that often made people open up to him.

Dan was no exception. In the dark, with no one watching
and Taffy beside him, the big man gave in to the drowning
pull of his fear. 'It's like fucking Basra all over again. I just
can't ... it just won't ... I keep seeing ...' And then his hands
were out of his pockets and dashing away the tears that were
threatening, as all his strength wasn't enough to hold them
back.

Taffy flung a supportive arm around his broad shoulders before Dan could crumple completely, as he muttered
incoherently. Little snippets about the horrific crash seemed
to have merged in his mind with the violent tour of duty he'd
served in Iraq. Coming back a shattered shell of a man, he'd
worked so hard to overcome the demons that haunted him,
but with this one fatal accident, he was thrown back four
years in one heartbeat.

He was sitting outside a pub in Larkford, but in his mind's
eye, he was continually reliving that one day. The day that
American missile had accidentally slammed into a school
in Basra, not half a mile from where Dan stood. The day
that he and his team had spent eighteen hours pulling tiny,
broken bodies out of the rubble and doing everything he
could to save them, as their wailing parents surrounded him,
alternately blaming him and begging for his help. By his
own admission, Dan had wept that night, along with braver
and stronger men than him. Some days it felt as though the
memories would never leave and some days he asked himself why he would want them to. He wanted to remember
mankind at its lowest ebb, so he could do everything in his

limited power to make sure no child ever died on his watch again.

'Why the fuck do I spend my life pulling kids out of wreckage?' he asked Taffy, his voice suddenly tight and clear. 'What's the point of all this training, if I can't even keep the kids alive?'

Taffy knew there was no point reasoning with him, pointing out that there were twelve teenagers on that mini-bus and they'd saved all but one, some of them against all odds. Because Dan wasn't talking about the kids in the mini-bus on the A36. Every time, he was back in Basra, pulling more broken children from the chaos and failing time and time again to mend their shattered bodies.

Taffy leaned over and gently removed the burnt out cigarette butt from Dan's fingers. 'I can't help thinking that holiday might be a good idea anyway, Dan. Go climb a mountain or hike someplace. Burn it off, like you said. Or go back and see Chris. Nothing official, but maybe have a chat?'

Going back to see Chris was the best suggestion that Taffy could come up with. He himself was certainly out of his depth when it came to helping Dan, but the army counsellor had been amazing when it first turned out that Dan had brought back more than sand in every pocket as a souvenir from Iraq. PTSD – post-traumatic stress disorder – wasn't the everyday case load for a rural GP, but it had become Chris Rogers' speciality.

You could acknowledge the symptoms in theory of course, the flashbacks, the fear, the insomnia and panic attacks. You could throw as many pills at it as you liked, but there wasn't really a cure. It would always be lurking under the surface, waiting for a trigger to set the panic in motion again.

*

The door to the pub burst open suddenly and their quiet enclave was flooded with light from the bar. Teddy Kingsley stood in the doorway, his voice high and strangled with panic, 'Dan? Taffy? Quickly – I need you!'

Teddy knocked a chair flying as he leapt aside to let the others come running into the bar, where one of the girls they'd been chatting to earlier now lay unconscious on the floor.

'What happened?' Dan quickly knelt down beside the young woman, whose face was strangely swollen and distorted.

'I don't really know,' said Teddy, running a hand through his hair in despair. 'She was all friendly and chatty one minute, her mates popped to the ladies' and then suddenly her face started swelling up and her voice went all strange.'

Teddy hovered uncertainly, clearly squeamish, as Dan too seemed to freeze in a moment of indecision. The only activity was the sound of Taffy scrabbling through the girl's handbag. 'Dan, is she breathing?' prompted Taffy, to no reply. He looked up sharply. Dan was shaking his head as if trying to jump-start his brain into action.

Taffy elbowed his mate aside, quickly starting to do a fast once-over of the girl's vitals, before pulling up the woman's skirt to expose her thigh and deftly swinging an EpiPen into the flesh with a click.

Her friends appeared moments later, with shrill screams and shrieks at the scene that confronted them. 'Oh my God! Lindy? Is she going to be alright?' squawked Ashley.

Taffy calmly assessed the situation and settled his gaze on Jenny, the only one in the room who seemed to be keeping her head. 'Jenny, can you call me an emergency ambulance?

Tell them it's an Anaphylactic Shock. Cause unknown. Am guessing 26-, maybe 27-year-old female, right? Weight maybe 130lbs. I've given 0.3mg of adrenalin if they ask.' He withdrew the needle after counting to ten and then began to rub at the puncture mark to ease the bruising. The possibility of bruising was actually the least of Taffy's worries in that moment, but he had to do something while he gave the adrenalin chance to do its work.

Lindy's breathing was barely more than a shallow grating now, as she struggled to pull air through her swollen throat, her lips and tongue all puffed out grotesquely.

Taffy rummaged through the girl's bag for a second EpiPen, wishing that the girl had the foresight to carry a spare. If the ambulance didn't get here quickly, he'd be forced to perform an emergency tracheotomy. It was all very well seeing these things on the television, but Taffy was the first to admit that a bottle of vodka and the tube from a Bic biro were not the ideal trach supplies. He looked over at Dan. 'Run to the surgery, would you, mate? Bring me a sterile trach kit and another shot of adrenalin? 0.5ml should do it.'

Dan nodded blindly, stumbling to his feet, his pallor in contrast to the livid red urticarial rash climbing over their patient's face.

Not waiting for a reply, Taffy began checking her vitals again, willing her to respond.

He turned to the girls. 'This is Lindy, right? Do you know if she's allergic to anything? Is she local?'

Once again, it was quiet little Jenny who proved the most useful. Ashley was whimpering on a nearby bar stool and Teddy appeared to be throwing up in the gents' after watching the EpiPen administered – hardly a chip off the old block then.

'Peanuts and shellfish,' she managed. 'Is she going to be okay? They said the ambulance might be ten minutes.'

'She'll be fine,' said Taffy reassuringly with a composure he certainly did not feel. He hoped to God that Dan could get back in time and that he wasn't somewhere outside, locked in his own personal breakdown.

Dan meanwhile was sprinting through the lanes of Larkford, jolted out of his stupor by the fresh cool air on his face and burning off the jolt of his own panicked adrenalin surge by pushing his body as hard as he could. There would be plenty of time for recriminations and assessments later. In the meantime all he could focus on was getting this kit to their patient before it became redundant.

A light drizzle plastered his hair to his forehead but Dan kept running, pushing harder and harder until his lungs screamed for a break. A little pain was a small price to pay in his opinion. Partnership or no, he needed to get his head together before somebody lost their life to his personal dramas.

He barged back into the pub with all the kit, just in time to see Taffy pulling down bottles of vodka. 'I've got this,' said Dan with authority, covering his embarrassment with brisk efficiency and giving Taffy a reassuring nod.

Dan rolled the girl on to her side, injecting the adrenaline into the large muscle of her bottom. Objectively, he couldn't help but notice that their patient was clearly in excellent shape. Perhaps she was some kind of athlete.

He calmly withdrew the needle, automatically checking his watch and knowing it was their last chance before a more invasive intervention would be called for. In a moment, the trach tray was ready, scalpel and tubes all pre-sterilised and sealed. Dan swallowed hard. He wanted to give the girl just a few more seconds for her body to respond to the mega-dose of adrenalin he'd given her, before he made a decision which, although saving her life, would leave a beautiful young woman essentially scarred for the rest of it.

'Come on,' he willed her urgently, checking her vitals over and over again. Her skin was becoming clammy and cold, only warm where the vicious weals of bright red nettle rash disfigured her pale skin.

Taffy crouched down beside him, watching him like a hawk for any sign of nerves or tremor. 'Dan, do you want me to take this?' he said quietly. 'Don't let's wait too long.'

Dan shook his head, one hand firmly measuring Lindy's pulse, stethoscope pressed to her chest. 'Just one sec,' he said, concentrating intently, listening for the sounds of her breath. Slowly he exhaled. 'Taff? How long on the ambulance?'

'Five minutes, at least,' he replied.

Dan shook his head again, trying to differentiate between the blip in heart rate that the adrenalin had caused and whether there wasn't just a small improvement in Lindy's breathing. Her body juddered with the effort of every single breath, but Dan knew that the injections should be enough.

'One more sec,' he said, breathing deeply and holding her hand in his own, monitoring every change in her without distraction. A slow easy smile spread across his face as he felt her hand instinctively return the pressure from his own and her eyelids flickered open.

Startled by the vivid green colour of her eyes, Dan leaned back a little. She dragged another breath into her battered lungs and attempted a lopsided smile. 'Am I okay?' she rasped, before coughing hard and reflexively curling into a ball.

Dan checked all her vitals once again and debated the need

for an IV. She'd probably be fine now the initial reaction had abated, but a course of hydrocortisone was a sensible precaution; as was a night in hospital if the swelling didn't start to calm down soon.

He brushed her bobbed dark hair from her forehead to assess the swelling and saw her watching his every move.

'Thanks, Doc,' she managed.

'My pleasure,' he replied, his own adrenalin rush leaving him crashing and exhausted. 'I'd give the peanuts a miss next time, though.'

'Not my best look,' she agreed.

He didn't have the heart to tell her she looked like Quasimodo, albeit an obviously pretty, feisty Quasimodo at that.

'Ambulance is here,' called Jenny from the front door, her voice tremulous with relief.

With the hustle and bustle of handing over notes, agreeing on the cause of the anaphylaxis and making Lindy comfortable on the stretcher, there was no real chance for Dan to say any more to his patient. He closed the door as the ambulance pulled away and ripped off his latex gloves. The high of the drama left him wiped but jangled at the same time.

'Jog home?' suggested Taffy, knowing exactly what Dan needed to settle himself after what had just happened.

'Cool,' said Dan, wondering at what point his friend would come out and say what was really on both their minds. He cleared his throat and set out at a swift pace, Taffy comfortably keeping step beside him. 'Thanks, Taff. I owe you one.'

Taffy said nothing, he just clamped a hand on Dan's shoulder before picking up the pace and jogging the long way back to Dan's house through the pouring rain.

Chapter 10

Julia looked down at her shredded cuticles and mentally reprimanded herself to get a grip. It was yet another sign of weakness she would struggle to hide. Even as she castigated herself for her lack of control, she felt the dense, metallic taste of blood fill her mouth, where her teeth had compulsively torn at the inside of her lip.

Friday night and here she was, scrolling through her contacts, looking for company. She reached T by the time she was forced to admit the truth – there was not one friend listed in her phone that was going to make her feel better. Not through any fault of their own of course, but because Julia had created a little world where nobody knew of her troubles and therefore nobody could be blamed for their lack of support. Hers was a world of smoke and mirrors – a carefully crafted edifice of lies and half-truths – specially designed to dodge prying questions and well-meaning sympathy.

Julia hated sympathy.

Even as a child, the compassionate head tilts of her friends' mothers as they oh-so-casually asked how things were at home, had driven her to distraction. Sympathy made Julia feel weak: weak and vulnerable, to be precise, and that was not something she would allow any more. Wasn't that half the joy of being an adult? The ability to selectively edit one's past until it fit with the idea of how one's present should look?

She glanced up for a moment, habitually running through the mental checklist of her life. Looking around her beautiful home, her gaze flitting across the mantelpiece where an array of photographs charted her recent travels, Julia slowly exhaled. Images of herself in Hawaii, Patagonia and Borneo soothed her anxiety. Every image had been carefully selected for the story it told. Not the common or garden holiday anecdotes of 'oh, wasn't it hysterical when the waiter thought I ordered the octopus head', but because every image reinforced the brand message of success, beauty and perfection that Julia strived so hard to project.

Julia didn't really need the photos. Everything about her home screamed affluent and tasteful. There was no chaos or clutter to mar the physical perfection or sophisticated palette. Not a cushion or orchid out of place, nor even a cosy dent in the sofa cushions that might suggest casual relaxation.

No, Julia habitually sat in the leather Eames chair in the corner, looking out over the little oasis she had created for herself. The chair represented her freedom and was the one item of furniture in the room to look careworn from use. It had been her first purchase when she bought this house. Saved for, longed for and adored.

Julia ran her hand down the side of the glass of wine beside her, fingertips trailing through the condensation. As she circled the stem, she managed a smile. This was her own personal Everest. Every night, Julia Channing would pour herself a glass of wine. Every night she would leave it untouched, before pouring it down the sink at bedtime.

The shrink that had told her that addictive personalities

were hereditary certainly had a lot to answer for. So now, instead of savouring the occasional drink, Julia would test her resolve. After all, she would reason, any fool can ignore something that isn't there.

This way, Julia could prove to herself that she had total control – this was her test, her nightly challenge, to prove again and again, the strength of her own free will. She needed the constant reassurance that history would not be repeating itself, that she at least could conquer the treacherous pull of her DNA.

She opened her leather-bound notebook and set to work. This was no time to drop the ball – not when she was so close to achieving her professional ambitions. The TV show had long been her secret dream and she cursed George Kingsley for deciding to up and leave now. She wanted the TV slot, but she *needed* the validation of becoming Senior Partner and now her focus would be split.

She smoothed her hand over the clean page in front of her and quickly slashed two hard lines with her pen to give her four sections. Strengths, Weaknesses, Opportunities, Threats – everyone may laugh at her business-like approach to medicine, but at least she knew how to evaluate her own performance.

Tapping her pen against her newly whitened teeth – she had no desire to appear on national television looking anything other than polished – she quickly began to fill in each quadrant. She quickly filled the Strengths box, no interest in false modesty there, and paused as she considered those Threats against her. Her mind immediately going to Dan Carter and taking her focus with it.

She was so sorely tempted to call him. She hated herself for still knowing his number off by heart, but Julia's mind didn't know how to forget. It was both a blessing and a curse. She remembered all the wonderful and all the ghastly times in equal, precise detail. Even with the passage of time, she knew she had behaved appallingly to Dan, had pushed him away just as he was getting closer. Even as she'd been so vile to him, so thoughtless and disrespectful of his feelings, a part of her had been hoping that he'd call her on it. That he would be the one to see past her hard, brittle exterior to the girl beneath. The girl that loved him. The girl that was terrified by the prospect of being in thrall to another person – vulnerable yet again. But no.

Even now, knowing that this partnership battle would set them against each other, part of Julia still wanted to talk to him, check he was okay. She had noticed him struggling recently and had wondered if the flashbacks were tormenting him again. The stress of George's announcement could easily be enough to tip him over the edge. So now she had a choice to make. Even though they were no longer together, she couldn't change the way she felt about him, and he might be in need of support. On the other hand, there was the Partnership.

Julia watched another bead of condensation carve a path down the glass of wine, conflicting scenes playing out in her head. She ran the smooth barrel of her ink pen through her fingers as she analysed scenarios, putting aside her residual feelings for Dan and taking comfort in logic.

She shook her head lightly as her brain spat out its duly considered conclusion. Dan Carter had other friends. He didn't need her. He certainly didn't want her. Let him go to them for support. This promotion was hers for the taking and she wasn't going to let Touchy-Feely-Dan pip her to the post. It was bad enough that he'd ruined all her plans for their future by breaking up with her; he wasn't going to ruin her Plan B as well. All she had to do was stay focused.

Her pen flew across the page as she filled in her quadrants. This, at least, was something she could do on her own.

Her phone trilled beside her and Julia sighed with resentment at the interruption, as she saw the word 'Dad' flash up on the screen. As she answered, she knew only too well what his first words would be, before he'd even said hello.

'Call me back, Joo. I'm on the mobile. This is costing a fortune.'

Julia listened to dead air, as her father had already hung up, and mentally prepared herself for yet another stressful discussion. She breathed slowly and calmly in an effort to keep her cool as she dialled his mobile. 'Hi, Dad, how are you both?' she asked, quietly crossing her fingers and hoping that today would be that rare and elusive thing – a good day.

She heard the tremulous tone in her father's voice as he spoke, even though he was clearly trying to disguise it, and her eyes prickled with unshed tears.

'I just don't know what more I can do for her at the moment, Joo. I've been into the doctor's every day this week, trying to get her into an NHS programme, but they keep saying the same thing . . .'

Julia sighed. 'That it has to be court-ordered, or with the patient's consent,' she finished tiredly. She wondered how many times it was possible to go over the same ground, with her mother determined to deny that she had a problem. 'How much is she drinking now?'

Julia's father cleared his throat. 'I thought we were making progress, Joo, I really did. And then I found out she's been hiding three bottles of vodka in the back of the airing cupboard. I mean, how desperate do you have to be to drink lukewarm vodka?' The disgust and exhaustion was obvious with every word and Julia dropped her forehead into her hand. 'I need your help, Joo.'

'Okay, let me see what I can do. I'll look into the private programmes again, but Dad, the last one set me back nearly twenty grand and she was drinking again inside a week. I just can't afford to keep writing cheques like that.'

'I know, love, I do. But on what I earn? It's bad enough doing the night shift at Tesco so I can be here during the day, but then trying to stay awake to keep an eye on your mother . . .'

And your wife, interrupted Julia silently, wondering why she only ever had any ownership of this dysfunctional family when there were bills to be paid.

'I'll do what I can, you know that,' she replied evenly, struggling not to lose her temper and ask how the sodding vodka had got into the house in the first place.

'Or we could still come and move in with you?' he replied. 'We could sell the bungalow and make a fresh start in Larkford. I'd love to see you more, Joo . . .'

Julia swallowed the sudden rush of bile in her throat at the thought of her mother's drunken outbursts shattering her own carefully constructed world in Larkford. She'd worked too hard for too long to get away from their claustrophobically toxic house, for her parents to simply up and follow her here.

'We've talked about this, Dad. I don't think you both moving here is the answer . . . but I'm up for a big promotion here soon and I'm hoping that will help.'

'Yes, well, we both know you're very busy. What's it going to cost, though? I bet they want more money off you, don't they?'

It was astonishing to Julia that her father was always so protective of his daughter's finances, when the biggest drain on them was, and always had been, her own parents. Maybe that explained it? He wasn't looking out for her, just protecting his own little cash cow.

'If I'm going to be Senior Partner, I will have to invest to hold the majority shareholding, Dad, but it'll help in the long term.' She hated the slightly supplicating whiny tone in her voice, as if she were actually trying to justify her own investment.

'Hmm,' said her dad, with no sign of pride in the potential promotion. 'It's the short term I'm worried about! Just don't forget your mother when you're doing your sums.'

As if I could, thought Julia. 'I'm doing my best,' she said quietly, before making her excuses and getting off the phone.

She looked at the sheet of analysis in front of her and calmly added a line to the Weaknesses box in neat, tight script. 'I will never escape them,' she wrote.

She put aside her notebook and picked up the glass of wine. As she walked into the kitchen, she could feel her stomach churning. The longing to make herself sick was there, as always, niggling away at the back of her mind, promising relief. Slowly, with total control, Julia poured away the glass of wine and pulled on a pair of rubber gloves. She opened the cupboard under the sink and began to clean the already immaculate kitchen.

Julia methodically and slowly arranged the kitchen exactly as she liked it. After years of chaos and uncertainty, she wanted to believe that she had enough self-control not to let one little phone call knock her completely off her stride.

*

Even on a good day, Julia could appreciate that she was no picnic to live with. And on evenings like this, when the niggle of loneliness and self-doubt had managed to find a foothold in her mind, she could easily understand how it had come to this. Midnight on a Friday and she was alone. Scrubbing a spotless floor and making plans to take a bath with her favourite medical text.

If she was honest, she would grudgingly admit that she even found herself wearing at times. It was something to do with the indefatigable nature of her personality – there was, quite literally no down time. If she wasn't working, working out or keeping her house to a virtually unsustainable standard of cleanliness, then she would be playing chess, or doing puzzles or devouring medical journals. Her mind needed sustenance and distraction the way her body needed oxygen.

She knew it wasn't normal. She knew it was exhausting – not just for her, but for those around her. But she also knew it wasn't her fault.

Obviously, it was one thing to rationally say that and quite another to wholeheartedly believe it.

To Julia's mind, her mother's therapy in rehab had damaged their little family far more than it had helped. As an adult and even as a child, Julia had always known that her parents had struggled with her intellectual abilities. They simply weren't able to relate to their ferociously, precociously gifted daughter. Knowing they resented her constant questions and her insatiable thirst for knowledge had somehow always been part of the deal.

Hearing her mother's unfiltered opinions when drunk had been relatively easy to dismiss. Hearing the blame being laid at her feet had been hurtful but in some way understandable.

Drunk people liked to lash out at those they loved, didn't they?

But hearing those same opinions being meted out by her mother at the rehab clinic had been so much worse. Decades' worth of spite and blame pouring forth, suddenly gaining credibility when viewed through the medium of family counselling sessions? Well, that had been harder to justify or ignore.

Julia had previously thought that knowing her mother's true feelings about her might have been a price worth paying for sobriety; a small price, in fact, for a chance to rebuild their shattered family. But when her mother had relapsed only weeks later, was apparently drinking yet again, those blaming taunts were like fresh barbs in Julia's psyche over and over again.

Airing all those demons had simply made it harder.

Harder to care, harder to get involved and certainly harder to write a cheque for yet another round of rehab that was destined to fail. If the very definition of insanity was doing the same thing over and over again and expecting a different result, then by this measure, and certainly where her mother was concerned, Julia was downright certifiable.

Nevertheless, Julia pulled off the rubber gloves and picked up her cheque book. She wrote out the cheque carefully, signing it precisely in her small cramped handwriting. At this point, she had stopped paying out of loyalty or gratitude, had passed through paying out of guilt and now settled, more brutally, on a desire to just get this sorted and get on already. After all, she had a TV show to make and a partnership battle to win.

Chapter 11

Holly paused at the corner of the Market Place to compose herself and whistle off a quick text to Lizzie. She knew it was a bit adolescent, but she'd been so excited about coming to Elsie's house this morning that she'd resorted to an early morning phone call to Lizzie about what to wear. In hindsight, it had probably been a mistake to download some of Elsie's more famous films last night, but she'd craved distraction from her own demons and what better way than utterly absorbing classic movies? It had been an even bigger mistake to stay up, completely enthralled, until 3 a.m. Now, not only was she star struck but also exhausted and feeling ridiculously overdressed in a rather short skirt.

Lizzie had sworn blind that she could carry it off, and since Lizzie had never been widely recognised for her tact, Holly felt that she could always bank on getting an honest opinion. Some might even say too honest, thought Holly, remembering the bikini shopping expedition last summer that had ended in tears and the purchase of the all-encompassing, hoover-action Miraclesuit. But she had to concede that Lizzie had a point – it may have taken some serious leverage to get the bloody thing on, but it did things to her figure that had only previously been thought possible with the aid of general anaesthetic – or possibly a nasty bout of salmonella.

This morning however, the chill spring breeze swirling through the valley was only serving to make Holly feel exposed and decidedly vulnerable with every gust. She was quietly glad she'd rebelled against Lizzie's advice and stuck a pair of opaque tights on. Okay, so it slightly ruined the look, but it was worth it to avoid the worry about constantly flashing her knickers.

Of course, she'd forgotten to account for the fact that – to go anywhere in Larkford – you had to allow twenty minutes extra for chatting. Seemingly nobody in this town ever just walked past each other with a cheery hello; there was always stopping and chatting. Often quite a lot of chatting. Holly wondered how anybody got anything done around here and it was taking quite some getting used to.

Last weekend, it had taken her over an hour to walk a forty-minute loop with the twins.

Today, she'd stopped at the Spar to buy some tights without holes and lost half an hour.

Of course, that had partially been her own fault. Mrs Fry, the lovely organist from the church had been in the queue in front her, letting out volley after volley of rattling coughs.

The words had been out of Holly's mouth before she could stop herself – are you okay? – it was a rookie mistake.

Any doctor will tell you, that in *any* situation – at a drinks party, a funeral, the supermarket – you should never, *ever*, ask this question, unless you have: (a) a genuine interest in the answer; (b) some legal liability for their health; or (c) a freely available exit route planned.

After what felt like hours of listening to the minutiae of Mrs Fry's ongoing battle with phlegm, Holly had only been saved by Mrs Fry's other ongoing complaint – a bladder the size of a peanut. Whilst she sympathised with the old lady's incontinence, Holly had also felt guiltily relieved as Mrs Fry had hared off to the ladies. She hadn't liked to point out that all that coughing was probably doing wonders in strengthening those pesky pelvic floor muscles!

'Right,' muttered Holly under her breath, smoothing down her skirt yet again, as she reached Elsie's house. 'I am a doctor, she is my patient. It does not matter that she has won an Oscar or that she has quite possibly seen Sean Connery in his birthday suit . . . I am calm and professional and . . . shit, really quite late!'

She knocked on the glossy green door of Number 42, jumping as another intrusive gust of wind whooshed up her skirt, and glanced through the sash window to the side. The house was an absolute gem and Holly tried not to think about how much something like this would cost. Since renting the house in Orchard Lane, Holly had become obsessed with local property prices and how much she would have to squirrel away just to get a foot on the property ladder in such a desirable area.

Holly heard the sharp staccato beat of very high heels on a polished stone floor and the heavy front door was yanked open with force.

'You're late!' said Elsie imperiously, fixing her with an uncompromising stare. Leaving the door open, Elsie walked back into the house, her hand trailing along each piece of furniture as she did so, whether for support or simply to remind herself that they were all still there, Holly wasn't sure.

After hesitating for a moment on the doorstep, Holly stepped inside and followed, apologies on her lips, emerging from the dark hallway into a beautifully bright and sunny morning room at the back of the house. Elsie had laid out morning tea on a tray and there was a small toast rack of perfect brown triangles, jam and butter in tiny ramekins. The old lady had settled herself into a high-backed armchair and she waved carelessly at Holly to take a seat.

'Ms Townsend, you didn't need to go to all this trouble!' exclaimed Holly, sliding obligingly into the appointed chair. Deprived of even a cup of coffee, as she had discarded outfit after outfit as unsuitable, Holly now felt light-headed and hollow. She flushed, 'I'm so sorry to be late. I was rather, um, unavoidably detained.'

Elsie soundlessly poured her a cup of tea, adding a splash of milk, and holding it out for Holly to take. She nervously eyed the delicate porcelain cup that looked as fragile as a doll's tea set in her hands. Holly gratefully took a sip, and carefully placed it on the table beside her, before she could possibly break it.

'Well,' Elsie said eventually, 'firstly, it's Elsie and secondly, I rather like morning tea and since Dan Carter thinks I need to have a babysitter, I thought we could enjoy the whole thing.' She waved a hand regally. 'We can always tick the boxes on your dreadful little forms later.'

She passed Holly a plate with a perfectly toasted crumpet, dripping with butter. 'Now eat up and you can tell me all about the latest scandal. I imagine your arrival has set a few pulses racing at The Practice, to say the very least?'

Holly busied herself taking a bite of crumpet, wondering how on earth to respond.

'Ah, the blushes rather give you away, my darling. You really need to work on your poker face or you'll give the local gossips a field day. Is it the glorious Dr Carter who's caught your attention then?' enquired Elsie innocently, nibbling gently at a corner of toast.

'Elsie,' Holly remonstrated. 'I've known Dan Carter since forever and besides, you seem to be forgetting that I'm married.'

Elsie shrugged lightly. 'Married, yes. Dead? No. So drink your tea and when you've finished you can tell me all about your glorious morning romp?'

Holly nearly choked on her crumpet. 'My what?'

'My dear girl,' Elsie smiled at her benevolently, 'I wasn't born yesterday and it's perfectly clear to me that you're either running late after a lovely session of morning nookie or you've recently been flirting with someone out of bounds.' This last was delivered in a stage whisper, laced with delighted merriment. 'Now, my late husband, Arthur – not the last one, the one before – he was always up for a morning tumble. I'm more of an afternoon person myself,' she said thoughtfully, trailing off mid-sentence. 'Anyway, you've clearly been having a lovely time and I'm terribly bored, my darling, so I thought the least you could do was entertain me.'

Holly swallowed the last crumbs of the crumpet and licked her sticky fingers, earning a raised eyebrow from Elsie and causing the blood to rush to Holly's cheeks again.

'I'm sorry to disappoint you, Elsie. I feel terribly pedestrian even saying it now, but I was late because the twins wouldn't get dressed and then I had a little wardrobe malfunction myself.'

'Ah of course ... *la vie domestique*! So draining, no? But then all the more reason to find passion in your work?'

Holly couldn't help but smile. Elsie was so delightfully, deliberately eccentric. She also seemed determined to converse as though they had known each other for ages. Holly admitted defeat, under Elsie's enquiring gaze. 'If you must know, the only feathers I've managed to ruffle at The Practice seem to be Dr Channing's. I don't think she's terribly pleased with me.'

'Of course she won't be,' Elsie replied gleefully. 'She's beautiful and clearly very intelligent, but she has a very brittle quality, don't you think? All terribly ice maiden and by all accounts, a total bitch.'

'Elsie!' said Holly, shocked but also trying not to laugh.

Elsie waved away her protests. 'Let's call a spade a spade at least. She is not a very kind woman. An excellent doctor, no doubt, but she comes with baggage that one, I promise you. Now you, on the other hand,' Elsie looked at Holly appraisingly, 'you come with baggage of a different kind.'

Holly slowly drained her teacup, suddenly wrong-footed by the turn of conversation. She'd come here to assess Elsie for goodness' sake, not for a session of psychoanalysis.

'I can assure you that my life is terribly mundane and there are no fabulous skeletons tucked away anywhere.' Holly mentally discounted Milo's issues as she spoke, but it was clear she wasn't fooling anyone.

'We'll see,' said Elsie. 'Perhaps that's something I can help you with? A wife should always have two things, in my opinion, Holly Graham: some running-away money and someone who admires them from afar. I suspect that those two things alone, might give you a little more confidence in both your abilities and your attractiveness.'

Holly said nothing, her mind running in confusing loops as Elsie's words carried a certain resonance. She could certainly identify with the need for financial independence from Milo, even if the notion of an admirer seemed a little ridiculous.

It was as though Elsie was reading her mind, as she leaned forward and took Holly's hand. 'I'm too old and too nosey to stand on ceremony, Holly. I know, I know, we've barely met, but please – let me help you a little, while you're so sweetly helping me. There simply isn't time to make all one's own mistakes in life, so please do feel free to learn from mine.

'Cheating husbands are my speciality. And when it comes to money? Well, let's just say that I do know what I'm talking about,' she said firmly, gazing around her stunningly decorated room. 'All of this, you see, came from Husband Number Four, after Husband Number Three cleaned me out. All my movie money, all my life savings . . . All quite, quite gone. That was Arthur, he of the morning glory, but I will say this,' she gave Holly a frank stare, 'he may have been a useless bastard with money, but by God, he made me happy.'

Holly could have sworn that Elsie winked at her lasciviously, but when she looked again she was sipping tea, one little finger outstretched, as if butter wouldn't melt.

Holly tucked her hair back behind her ears and watched her patient. Dan had sent her here to assess Elsie for dementia and Alzheimer's. Maybe it was Dan who was losing the plot, because from where Holly was sitting, Elsie looked as sharp as a tack. She fumbled in her bag, completely unnerved, and took out her notebook, where she was supposed to write down all her observations about Elsie to add to her evaluation file.

'Ah!' said Elsie, clearly disappointed. 'I see we've moved on to the professional part of our visit. No matter. There's plenty of time for us, Holly. I'm always here when you need me.

'But, you know, Holly, I'm sure Dr Carter does know what he's talking about, but I really don't think I *am* losing my marbles. Que sera, sera,' she sighed. 'Maybe there are benefits to this Alzheimer's business anyway? You know, always meeting new people, hiding your own Easter eggs . . .'

For all her witty comments, Elsie seemed to have

withdrawn into herself a little at the sight of the forms and Holly felt bad for cutting her off mid-flow. She couldn't account for how Elsie was making her feel. It was as though Elsie had 20:20 vision where Holly's life was concerned and Holly didn't feel quite strong enough to hear any more home truths this morning; not after last night.

'Let's just get this bit done, Elsie, and then we can have another cup of tea.'

Holly ticked her way through the boxes, without a word. She could see without asking that Elsie was perfectly able to dress and feed herself, she could probably stand up for herself too, if anyone gave her any of this Alzheimer's nonsense. Holly noted again Dan's scribbled note about her nocturnal wanderings and tried to rouse Elsie from her slump.

'So, no more daffodils in the Market Place?' Holly smiled at her, feeling awful for having brought the pall of reality down on her lovely morning tea party.

'No,' Elsie sighed. 'Nobody really liked the daffodils.' Her sad face made Holly feel even worse, until the flicker of mischief flashed briefly in Elsie's beautiful eyes. 'I shall have to think of something a little more entertaining next time.'

Holly grinned. 'Maybe we could have a little outing one morning?'

Elsie sipped her tea and looked wistful. 'Now that would be nice. I only really go out for hospital appointments and funerals these days. Well, and the occasional dinner party of course, but I suspect we could have fun together you and I. It would probably do you good to be led astray a little.'

Holly had accepted one last refill and then ducked away to use the loo before heading back to work. There was something about Elsie that she couldn't put her finger on. She was lively, she was fun and she was certainly insightful, but there was a sadness to her that Holly couldn't place. She was already looking forward to getting to know Elsie better. Another perk of local practice, she thought as she headed down the hallway to find the smallest room. Pushing open the door, Holly couldn't help but laugh out loud. The smallest room in Elsie's house happened to be illuminated by a crystal chandelier and the loo roll holder appeared to be Elsie's Oscar statuette. The irreverence of the gesture had Elsie written all over it.

After washing her hands, still with a smile on her face, Holly had somehow managed to take a wrong turn out of the loo, though, because instead of arriving back with Elsie in the morning room, she walked into a stunning kitchen extension instead.

The units were made from limed oak and the worktops from jet-black granite, but it wasn't the fixtures and fittings that caught Holly's attention. 'Oh shit,' she muttered, as her gaze took in the chaos and the smile slipped from her lips. On every surface, there were cups, vases and jam jars filled with milk. Even an egg cup or two had been pressed into service.

Elsie appeared at Holly's elbow and rolled her eyes. 'Such a bore, isn't it?'

'Hmm?' said Holly succinctly.

'Well, the milkman says that I'm to rinse the bottles and put them back out for him to collect. But I can't possibly drink all that milk in one day, so I've had to adapt.'

Holly watched her flitting around the kitchen, tidying the jars and bottles into rows. She felt suddenly wretched to find that Dan Carter might not be so wide of the mark after all.

'I think you should probably keep the milk in the fridge, Elsie,' she said gently. 'And I'm sure the milkman wouldn't mind if you only put the bottle out once you'd finished.'

Elsie fluttered her fingers at Holly, 'I can't possibly keep it all in the fridge, silly girl.' She swung open the door of the enormous refrigerator. 'That's where I keep my make-up.'

Holly's phone buzzed in her pocket and she knew it was Grace wondering where on earth she'd got to. There was probably a room full of patients waiting to be seen, but Holly still felt awful about leaving Elsie alone. She'd helped her tidy away the milk and organise the fridge to leave a little space for food, but she wasn't really sure what to do next. Holly knew she should probably put in a full report to Dan, but she and Jason had been asked to do a week's evaluation and it was only day two. Where was the harm in waiting? And at least it was Dan she'd be reporting to, who was certainly the more human of the doctors when it came to making judgement calls. Holly sighed, rather wishing she'd just stayed and had tea and left none the wiser. You certainly couldn't help having a certain admiration for Elsie and she didn't want to see her unhappy.

It was exactly this scenario that Henry Bruce had warned her about, wasn't it? Becoming emotionally involved with one's patients could only cloud objective judgement. Simply put, did Holly like Elsie too much to write the report that needed to be written? She sighed, torn with indecision.

Elsie laid her head against Holly's shoulder as they stood, putting the finishing touches to the new fridge layout. 'I love my home. Don't you? I think it sums up everything I've ever been and everywhere I've ever gone. My life is here.' She turned to cup Holly's face with her hand, reaching to do so. 'You do understand that, don't you, my darling girl? You understand what I'm asking of you?'

Chapter 12

Holly logged into her computer and checked her afternoon schedule. It was all very well George insisting that The Practice offer Saturday clinics, but Holly couldn't help noticing that, even in the scant few weeks until his retirement, George wasn't actually down to do any of them. Having said that, with just Dan, herself and one of the nurses working this afternoon, the atmosphere in the building was noticeably calmer.

Even just the clip-clopping of Julia's heels, or Henry's none-too-discreet lifts, had the capacity to set Holly's nerves a little on edge already. It was like the warning music that started up in movies to put you on your guard.

She could hear the low murmur of Dan's voice through the wall, his easy bedside manner something to aspire to. She took a sip of water, marshalling her thoughts away from Elsie Townsend, and walked through to the waiting room.

'Stevie Roberts,' she said, immediately struck by the young boy's appearance. He was scrawny and pale, looking much younger than his seven years. 'Hi Stevie, Mr Roberts. I'm Dr Graham, come on through with me and we can have a chat.'

She noticed that the boy was almost green and was carrying an empty Tupperware container just in case. Occasionally he would dab at his mouth with a bloody tissue. Settling him up on the treatment bed, she could see that his little skinny legs were strangely mottled.

His eyes bugged out a little, which might suggest a thyroid problem, but for some reason Holly's mind had immediately gone in another, more unlikely direction. She had half a mind to call Dan in for a second opinion. She'd had a patient in Reading once, who'd lived solely on croissants and Nutella, who had then presented with similar symptoms. Or perhaps she was leaping to conclusions and the poor lad had an absorption problem ...

Was it possible that she'd gone from miniature cucumber sandwiches at Elsie's, to a seven-year-old boy with scurvy in mere minutes?

Welcome to Middle England, she thought. She quietly checked all his vitals, murmuring reassuringly as she did so.

She'd noted the boy's address when she opened up his file: the Pickwick Estate.

When people mentioned the Pickwick Estate in Larkford, they tended to do so with a certain grimace and a tilt of the head. The Pickwick Estate was Larkford's dirty little secret, never mentioned in any tourist guide, tucked away behind the small industrial estate that also housed the bus depot and the tile warehouse.

Out of sight and out of mind for most of the local residents, unless they happened to have their car broken into or their wallet snatched, when all eyes suddenly turned to the residents of Dickens Drive. There was no dressing it up with fancy literary names – this was social housing at its most basic. And, since half the residents could probably only muster a reading age of nine or ten, the fancy street names meant little more to them than the A36.

Holly knew from her interview that it was a source of continual aggravation to both Dan and George that there wasn't more being done to help the residents there.

Lizzie actually had a theory that the council were actively trying to persuade the tenants to move elsewhere, for the land must surely be worth a fortune now for its development opportunities. Instead, the four-storey sixties blocks crouched there in a grid pattern, with only the odd tree to break up the concreted expanse, where the residents' children kicked a football around. Hardly local planning's finest hour.

Dan had asked Holly to support his plans to make the health education of Larkford's children a priority. He wanted to restart the series of workshops he had run in the local school, focusing on diet and exercise for the younger ones, and sex education and alcohol awareness for the seniors. The school had been amazingly supportive the first time round, but some of the parents had complained and that was the end of that. Seeing this poor lad, made Holly think that the restart was long overdue.

She perched in front of the boy on a stool and gently palpated his calf muscles. Stevie pulled his leg away and began to cry quietly. 'It 'urts when you do that,' he whimpered in his strong Somerset accent.

'Talk to me about what you have for breakfast then, Stevie . . .' Holly said as she softly counted the boy's pulse rate under her breath.

Stevie immediately looked wary and glanced nervously over at his father, who was quietly sitting by the desk, fiddling with his mobile. Holly was astonished at the total lack of interest he was exhibiting in his son's medical exam. She was rather more accustomed to the helicopter mothers, who hovered around, endlessly peppering questions during an examination.

Since his father didn't actually seem to be paying any attention at all, Stevie clearly felt a little bolder and spoke up, 'My teacher at school said I 'ad to come in and see you, coz my legs 'urt when I run and all the other boys are bigger than me. I get two pieces of toast at the Breakfast Club though – coz I'm little.'

'Well, I'm really glad you did come in today, Stevie. Let's see what we can do to make you feel a bit better, shall we?' Holly reassured him. 'And well done your clever teacher for sorting it out. Now, after you've had some toast at the Breakfast Club at school, what do you have then, for the rest of the day?'

Stevie outlined his lunch of chips and beans, and the occasional egg in the school canteen, with the odd Mars bar thrown in for good measure. 'That sounds a lot like my boys' favourite lunch,' said Holly gently, 'but sometimes they like to have a really big glass of orange juice with it. Do you like orange juice, Stevie?'

Stevie shook his head again. 'I like orange lollies though.' He grinned widely and Holly tried not to show her shocked reaction at the state of poor Stevie's gums. Bloody and sore, there were gaps where his little milk teeth had fallen out early, since his rotten gums were too spongy to cope.

After they'd quickly established that supper at home consisted of a Nutella sandwich on white bread, Holly was quite convinced by her tentative diagnosis. She turned to Stevie's father. 'Mr Roberts? We need to take a little blood from Stevie to send off to the lab. It won't hurt,' she reassured Stevie, noticing him stiffen, 'but it will give us a much better idea of how to treat him. The most important thing, Mr

Roberts, is that we talk about Stevie's diet and make sure that he's getting enough vitamins and minerals to keep him healthy.'

'You try buying fancy food on what me and Cathy earn,' he answered defensively.

'Well, that's something we can explore with the Health Visitor once the test results are back,' Holly replied, wanting this lad's father to take the situation seriously.

'Health Visitor? What's that, some kind of social worker?'

'No, no. Just one of our team who will help Stevie, and you and Cathy, learn about economical ways to improve his diet.' Spotting immediately that Mr Roberts was none too enamoured with this plan of action, Holly changed tack. 'Stevie is severely malnourished, Mr Roberts. He's a very poorly little boy.'

'Just as well I brought him in then,' said Mr Roberts. Barely into his twenties, the father looked just as peaky and underfed as his son, acne pitting his complexion. 'Can't you just give him some medicine? His prescriptions are free, aren't they?'

Holly sighed. 'Obviously we can give him some supplements of key vitamins to help him recover, but he needs a good diet every day to get him well.' Holly's eyes flickered to the clock on the desk. 'If you'd both like to come with me, we'll see if Jade is available to do some of the tests now and have a chat with you about meal planning. Perhaps you could call Stevie's mum and she could come down and join you?'

Stevie shook his head. 'Mummy's asleep in the day.'

'Okay,' said Holly calmly, her mind immediately leaping to assumptions of wild partying, drugs and alcohol.

Stevie chattered on blithely as they gathered up his coat and his just-in-case bowl. 'She works all night, sleeps in the mornings when I'm at school and goes to college on Thursdays. My mummy's going to be a Sec-ret-ury,' he sounded out proudly. 'She's only a cleaner at the moment, but she says it's a shit job and I should work hard at school.' He gave her another devastating grin and Holly felt a hot wave of middle-class guilt wash over her.

'Thanks, Doc,' Mr Roberts managed, determinedly avoiding her gaze. 'It's been a bit tricky since I got laid off,' he muttered defensively and guided his son towards the Nurses' desk, ruffling his hair affectionately.

Holly began to second-guess herself, wondering whether Mr Roberts' odd behaviour had more to do with embarrassment than the lack of interest she'd simply assumed.

'Jadey-wadey!' exclaimed Stevie in delight when he saw Jade, minuscule uniform straining at the bust. 'Are you going to do my blood zam?'

Holly paused at the Nurses' desk, watching Jade scoop up young Stevie and promise him a sticker if he was good.

'How does Stevie know Jade?' she asked Mr Roberts in surprise.

'Jade?' he said. 'Oh, she lives in the flat next door. Been neighbours all our lives.'

Holly was then forced to re-evaluate her opinions for the third time that day. It wasn't terribly PC, but if Jade had managed to get all her nursing qualifications whilst growing up on the Pickwick Estate, Holly had a whole new respect for her. Putting aside the indecently short skirt, Holly felt that anyone motivated enough to work so hard in such tricky circumstances had to really, really want it.

Holly was beginning to wonder when she'd stop peeling back the layers of this little town. It was surprising her and challenging her assumptions daily.

Larkford was so much more than the sum of its parts and Holly decided it was the perfect antidote to the pessimistic and judgemental thoughts that had been plaguing her more and more of late. It was actually rather refreshing to have one's eyes opened again.

Afternoon clinic finally finished some three hours later and Holly was on her way to grab a quick glass of water when she spotted the noticeboard. The *Larkford Gazette* article about Dan's Friday night rescue was now sellotaped to the wall. Under the headline, 'Peanut Tragedy Averted', ran two photos – the rather professional one of Dan making him look intense and brooding. The other photo was clearly a family snap of a young, laughing woman, with sleek bobbed hair and wide shining eyes.

Holly couldn't help but laugh at speech bubbles now drawn, coming out of the girl's mouth saying: 'Dr Dan, my hero, I wuv you, kissy kissy kissy . . .'

The handwriting looked an awful lot like Taffy's.

She also noted that under the 'Worried about alcohol?' poster, that same hand had written . . . 'Then worry no more – The Kingsley Arms is now open at lunchtime too . . .'

She wandered into the office and found the man himself sitting at Grace's desk. 'I've just been admiring your notice-board, Dr Jones.'

He looked up and smiled innocently. 'My noticeboard?'

Holly gave him a sideways look. 'You have distinctive penmanship. The little swirls on your y's?'

'Oops,' Taffy mumbled. 'Sorry,' he added, looking anything but contrite.

'What are you up to anyway?' asked Holly with a smile. 'If

you don't mind me saying, you look highly suspicious there, Dr Jones.'

Taffy clicked on the screen-saver and stood up quickly from Grace's desk, perching on the edge to give Holly his undivided attention. He was wearing a peculiar tweed jacket and carried a pair of tortoiseshell glasses tucked into his breast pocket. He grinned and waggled his eyebrows, which seemed somehow bushier than usual. 'Do I look mysterious and debonair?'

'Erm . . .'

'Handsome and alluring?'

'We-ll . . .'

Taffy struck a pose against the desk, one luxuriant eyebrow firmly wedged up into his hairline. 'Masculine and mystifying? Don't keep me in suspenders, Graham. Give me the truth – I can handle it.'

Holly wrinkled her nose as she tried to alight on the perfect description, trying not to laugh. 'The truth? Crikey! Well, to be honest, you either look like you're in the early stages of a stroke, or you've got really bad wind. Were you aiming for something different?'

Taffy caught up her hand and landed an enormous kiss on the inside of her wrist. 'Ah – the truth – she is a fickle mistress.' Holly couldn't help but notice that he was still holding her hand as he ran an assessing eye over her body, before appraising her like a vintage Claret. 'Yes, yes, full bodied, supple though. I'm getting blackcurrant and a hint of scepticism too. Excellent depth of flavour, great legs – that's a proper wine term you know, Graham – smooth, yet playful. Yes, a cheeky, bold little number, I think.'

Holly was speechless for a moment, until Taffy accidentally knocked the mouse and the computer screen beside him sprang into life. 'How To Fake It As A Wine Connoisseur' read the title, along with a list of adjectives and phrases.

'Is there something you'd like to share with the group there, Taffy?' managed Holly, laughing, as she prayed for her heart rate to calm down. Surely, Taffy could feel her pulse racing against his fingers, where he still, bizarrely, continued to gently hold her wrist, throwing her completely. Whereas only moments before she'd been happy, confident to banter a little and join in the fun, now she found herself speechless.

'A vintage year, I think,' said Taffy, his voice suddenly quiet and intimate. He ran his thumb in small circles along the delicate skin at Holly's wrist and held her gaze, no longer joking around, but looking into her eyes intently. 'Definitely one to be savoured, don't you think?'

The air stilled in the office as Holly's mind lunged around uselessly for a witty comeback, not entirely convinced that this last comment was still part of Taffy's dodgy wine persona. 'What . . . ? Who . . . ?' she managed eloquently, no longer sure what game they were playing.

'Right now? Just me,' replied Taffy, looking for all the world as though he was about to lean in and kiss her.

Holly's pulse beat a quickening tattoo against Taffy's muscular yet gentle grip, as she willed her mind to calm.

The office door swung open with a whoosh of cold air. It was enough to pull Holly to her senses. She reclaimed her wrist reluctantly, catching the flare in Taffy's eyes as she did so.

'Brilliant!' said Dan loudly, making them both flinch a little. 'I see you've introduced Holly to Reginald Fortesque Esquire – wine buff, petanque champion and amiable raconteur. What do you think of Taffy's alter ego, Holls?'

Taffy recovered more quickly than she did, adopting a

mock Etonian accent and dislodging his eyebrow from its elevated position. 'Of course, my darling, I use wine all the time when I am cooking. Sometimes, yes sometimes, I even add it to the food.'

'He's fabulous fun,' continued Dan. 'Any night out with Reggie here always ends well, doesn't it, Taff? Give me five to get changed and then Holly can meet Professor Ludo Gartner too. Then we'll be off, okay?' Dan disappeared from view leaving Holly feeling oddly deflated. The earlier tension in the room, that had felt so pleasing and intoxicating, now had the bitter twist of leftover wine.

'I had no idea you were such an aficionado in the wine department,' said Holly quietly, purely for want of anything better to say.

Taffy shrugged. 'I know what I like, Holly. The trick is to always ignore what it says on the label.'

There was a moment's pause when Holly wished that, as in many other areas of her life right now, people came with subtitles and subtext clearly explained. She didn't want to think what label Taffy might apply to her particular vintage.

'Who's Professor Ludo What's-his-face?' she asked suddenly.

'Ah, well.' Taffy looked uncomfortable. 'You're either going to think we're quite mad or tragically entertaining . . . The thing is, a while ago, Dan was feeling a bit down and he didn't want to go out. Ever. So, I made up these two older guys – quite successful, terribly confident, bit of a caricature, and we dressed up as them and went to a party in Bristol. Best party ever.

'Anyway, long story short, it's become a thing we do. We get to completely let our hair down and let off steam – we get to say outrageous things and just have a very silly, extremely childish time. And, mainly, well, it seems to help Dan too. He gets to step outside his head for a little while. That's the real win.'

Holly looked at Taffy in his bonkers tweed ensemble, his eyes full of warmth and fun.

Taffy squirmed a bit under her gaze. 'Go on – you can say it – you think we're too old to play silly buggers.'

'Actually,' said Holly with an affectionate smile, 'I was just thinking how lucky Dan is to have a friend like you. And that, next time, if I'm not intruding – maybe I could come too?'

Taffy/Reggie – she wasn't sure who – leaned forward and scooped up the weight of her hair from the nape of her neck. His warm breath fanned her cheek as he stayed in character, polished vowels and all. 'I think you would have to come as a struggling Russian violinist. Katerina Shovoffski perhaps?' His eyes twinkled pure merriment. 'I am longing to hear your nocturnes and perhaps a little adagio, a slow pas de deux?'

This time there was no mistaking the double entendre in Taffy's words, but his lightness of tone and the grin on his face left Holly feeling comfortable, that this could just as easily be the welcoming hand of friendship, as a mischievous flirtation.

'Ah, but then, I am forgetting, no doubt the beautiful Katerina would tell me to Shovoffski?' Taffy gave her a gentle nudge.

Holly shook her head and groaned at his terrible pun, as Dan came back in, wearing pleated slacks and a purple cravat. 'You old boys have fun this evening, then,' Holly said.

'But ov course,' said Dan in a comedy German accent that was so appalling, Holly couldn't believe anyone fell for it. 'Vot else would we do at the Annual Bristol Vintners' Convention?'

Taffy picked up an ivory-handled cane from beside the desk and twirled it in his fingers. 'Go work on your violin, Katerina, and maybe next time you too can try out Dr Jones' Patented Cure of Distraction.'

It didn't seem terribly likely, thought Holly, as the door swung closed behind them, that Dr Jones' panacea would be quite so effective when distracting her from her own wayward thoughts – particularly the X-rated ones pertaining to the good doctor himself.

Chapter 13

As nine o'clock rolled around on Sunday morning, Holly tried to get dressed, as the twins emptied her underwear drawer with intense concentration, fuelled by scrambled eggs and with the energy of the Duracell bunnies. She ignored the flashes of rose-coloured silk and wisps of creamy lace that the boys were tossing around her bedroom delightedly and rescued only a pretty camisole to cover the simple t-shirt bra that formed the mainstay of her weekend wardrobe these days.

The boys had quite the selection to play with, as Milo's obsession with expensive undies meant that Holly always knew what she was getting for Christmas. Obviously, she'd tried discussing present ideas with him on many occasions. Even none-too-subtle pointers that, since having two babies come out the sunroof, she wasn't really up for prancing around in wispy thongs that didn't even cover her C-section scar. French knickers? Lovely. Sexy silky camisole? Fantastic. But no, Milo wasn't a man to take suggestions. These days, he wasn't a man to compromise full stop. He liked his world to be the way he wanted it to be, the way it had always been, as he tried to control all the players as if they were characters in his latest book.

Tom toddled over to her and threw his arms tightly around her legs, before she scooped him up for a cuddle. He grinned at her delightedly, pulling at her top as he always did, as he pressed his tiny body against her. 'Mmmm, squidgy Mummy,' he breathed.

Holly shook her head with a smile. There was no point correcting him and, while the twins found her new, softer figure the perfect cuddle spot, she knew that Milo despaired of ever having his sleek, perfectly groomed wife back. In all honesty, the very fact that this bothered him quite as much as it did, gave Holly additional incentive to avoid jumping on the Weight Watchers bandwagon with all the other mums. In fact, even just thinking about it made her fancy a defiant chocolate Hobnob or three.

Logically, she knew that the constant stress and exhaustion were contributing just as much as the Hobnobs to her stubborn little cortisol muffin-top. Constantly on the verge of Fight or Flight, the stress hormones were flooding her system and storing up the podge for emergencies ... Holly sighed, thinking that maybe she knew a little too much about how the human body worked – it rather took the mystery out of life.

She could hear Milo now, singing in the shower, and she hurriedly pulled on her jeans before the water stopped and before he emerged as always, still honed and perfect, with his lightly stubbled chin and searching for his trendy media specs.

Since the boys were still happily entertaining themselves with La Perla bras as jaunty deerstalkers, she pulled out what remained of her eyeliner and quickly smudged a charcoal line around her eyes. Blinking hard as she poked herself in the eye, Holly decided that a shopping trip to Boots was in order,

as what remained of her sorry excuse for make-up was fast becoming a health hazard.

Tom pulled himself on to her lap and stroked her cheek adoringly. 'Pretty Mummy. We go swings?' he asked.

'We'll see, but we have to go to the supermarket first. And you two have to be good, okay? What do you think, Ben? Do you want to go on the big swing today?'

Only on a Sunday could she really take her time to enjoy these leisurely moments, because the rest of the week was spent dashing to get everyone dressed and fed and at Nursery before morning surgery began at 8:00. Of course, due to the perversity of parenthood, the faster you needed everybody to move, the longer everything took, with many a morning completely derailed by a last-minute tantrum. Every morning seemed to be spent constantly clock-watching, making sure she stayed on schedule. It made her feel happier to know that, even with a cleaner and her lovely husband Will, Lizzie's mornings were also chaos.

Lizzie claimed, in fact, that jungle warfare was no match for the drama that took place in their kitchen between seven and eight every weekday morning. Yet she still managed to hold on to her prestigious Editorship and her sense of humour, and Will's business seemed to be thriving – well, enough to pay for a cleaner anyway!

Eventually the door to the bathroom flew open with a billow of steam and a hit of eucalyptus from Milo's potent shower gel. He smiled when he saw the boys, running up and down the landing, still swathed in Holly's lingerie. 'Well it's about time your scanties had an outing, isn't it, Holls?' He tucked the towel tightly around his taut waist. 'Although that wasn't exactly what I had in mind when I bought them.'

He walked over to her and slid his hand around her middle, the camisole riding up slightly. 'Why don't you pop the boys in front of the TV for a bit, hmm? It has to be my turn to have you all to myself?' he said, kissing her lightly on the side of her neck.

He pulled her back against him, the towel damp and cold on the back of her legs. There was no mistaking his intention.

She wavered, trying not to dwell on the enormous list of things she had to do this morning or the outing she'd planned with the twins. It had been weeks since they'd made love and, if she was honest, she missed the intimacy, the release from herself.

It was hard enough fighting her own exhaustion, but tiptoeing around Milo's mood-swings was like living in an emotional minefield. She knew though, that she ought to make an effort, try to reconnect. Obligation just didn't seem the perfect catalyst for reigniting their exuberant sex life of old.

It didn't help that Tom's hearing was seemingly set on a hair trigger these days. At the slightest squeak of a mattress spring in the night, he was awake and crying. It could have become a shared joke, a challenge even, to fool around somewhere different, but no ... It had simply become something else for Milo to get mouthy and resentful about.

How was she supposed to flick a switch, she wondered, and feel turned on by a man who, she increasingly found, she sometimes didn't actually like very much?

But in that moment, her rebellious body had no interest in all the petty slights and grievances that she stored up about her husband. She leaned back into him, a gentle moan escaping her, as his lips touched the sensitive part of her collarbone. He certainly knew what she liked. She breathed

in deeply, content to let her body find its own path back, secretly relieved there was still something there, even if it was only in the bedroom.

'Come on, Holls, a bit of exercise will do you good. You can do the house later,' he persisted, believing in his own back-handed way that she still needed convincing. His hands gave a gentle squeeze to the softness of her waist and Holly stilled instantly, his words effectively dousing the warm flickers of lust that had begun to grow within her.

She didn't move for a moment, swallowing down instead the frustrated cry that was building in her throat. The boys were still tearing around on the landing, but her world seemed to slow down around her, as her mind and her libido went to war.

She needn't have worried about making a decision though, because from the corner of her eye, she watched in slow motion as Ben tripped forward across the landing, his foot caught in the hem of the camisole he was using as a cape. He tumbled to the carpet with a thud, his cries instantly shattering Holly's immobility.

'Oh for fuck's sake!' cursed Milo, exasperated, pushing Holly away from him and storming across the bedroom. He didn't even look at her, as he threw his sopping towel to the floor and pulled on his boxers.

Holly scooped up her crying child and pressed gentle kisses to his forehead, soothing him with the gentle rocking that he loved.

Over the top of Ben's tousled head, Holly watched Milo put on his watch and tap the face three times, just as he always did, his movements jerky and agitated. It was a constant source of amazement to her in fact, that someone with a touch of the OCD could actually be such a slob. Milo slid

into his usual writer's ensemble of skinny v-neck and jeans, wrapping a long knit scarf around his neck several times. 'I'll be at the library all morning then,' he said, without looking at her and went downstairs, leaving a trail of destruction in his wake.

'Daddy messy,' announced Tom solemnly, standing quietly and looking around the bedroom.

'Daddy thoughtless pig,' murmured Holly under her breath, wondering how long she could leave that towel on the bedroom floor before it smothered the remains of her libido entirely.

Holly and the boys arrived in the kitchen a few minutes later, just in time to see Milo dump his coffee cup in the sink. 'Have a good morning, yeah?' he said, kissing the top of her head distractedly as he walked past, his mind having clearly shifted into work mode. He gathered up his papers from the kitchen table and went to open the back door, touching the handle repeatedly without turning it.

Holly dropped the overflowing laundry basket to the floor and watched, fighting the urge to interrupt his routine. She let him get to eight, knowing that his compulsive mind needed ten touches of the doorknob to find its peace. 'Milo?' she said, her face a picture of innocence. 'We'll see you for lunch later?'

She watched the subtle twitch in his face as he nodded, then turned back to the doorknob. Holly shepherded the twins into their respective high chairs and took in the scene of devastation on the kitchen worktop. The last of the milk dribbled lazily across the dark granite surface, wending its way between the crumbs and the butter and the discarded crusts from Milo's morning toast.

Six, seven, eight ... 'Oh and Milo? Don't forget to phone your mother back will you? She's already called three times this morning.'

His hand shook slightly now as it hovered above the door-knob and Holly felt a twinge of guilt for messing with his head. She may have laughed herself stupid when Lizzie had pointed out that no man had ever been murdered whilst hoo-vering the sitting room, but it still felt a little petty to exploit such an easy target.

He paced at the door now, clearly agitated, and took a deep breath. 'Fine, fine.' He paused warily. 'Anything else?'

Holly shook her head and the boys gave him toothy grins from between mouthfuls of dry Cheerios.

Five, six, seven ... 'Have a lovely day, darling,' Holly couldn't resist, smothering a smile, before scooping up the laundry and heading to the utility room, where Milo's run-ning kit lay sweaty and discarded on the floor, and Holly could really begin to enjoy her 'Day Off'.

Holly threw a huge bag of pasta into her trolley and prayed that none of her patients would judge her if they saw that, when it came to nutrition, it was probably a case of 'Do as I say, not do as I do.'

She sped around the supermarket as if she were against the clock. In a way of course she was – the gentle jostling as the twins sat side by side in the trolley could quickly escalate to full blown elbows-at-dawn if she wasn't careful.

Holly made sure that, on the surface at least, their weekly shop was the epitome of perfect health: Smiley Faces and fish fingers buried beneath a veritable avalanche of cherry toma-toes and avocados and bananas.

She popped in a few cans of Pedigree Chum for Eric's

planned sleepover later in the week, already looking forward to the prospect of some rewarding company, snuggled up on the sofa beside her. She still couldn't quite believe that Milo hadn't batted an eyelid at the proposal, seemingly content enough with the explanation that Lizzie needed help with dog-sitting as she was working long hours right now. Occasionally Milo would have a moan about Holly 'being taken advantage of' but, frankly, he was so self-involved at the moment, Holly suspected that Eric could move in permanently and it would take Milo several weeks to notice.

She slid a multipack of illicit Curly Wurlys down the side of her trolley and was just thinking that they might yet make it round before one or both of the twins descended into meltdown.

Holly adopted a dash-and-grab approach to supermarket shopping, cursing herself for her lack of organisation and wishing she'd booked an internet delivery. Somehow the ability to plan ahead, though, had rather deserted Holly since the move. Although now, she had to make sure that Tom's little eyes were never given the opportunity to focus on all the goodies he was missing out on, just to keep his brother's little digestive system happy. Speed was of the essence.

The checkout was in sight and Holly was just rewarding herself by wedging a few bottles of Pinot and a huge bag of pistachios in the trolley when her plan fell apart.

'Good morning to you, Dr Graham,' trilled Cassie Holland, Larkford's social conscience and epitome of political correctness, who was blocking the aisle and showing no intention of moving. Her son Tarquin was slumped miserably in the trolley. 'You're just the person I needed to see. Could you be an angel and tell my Tarka that wheat-derived glucose

syrups are not the healthy choice for a growing boy. When
I think of all the processing ... Do, please, back me up, Dr
Graham.'

Holly ground to a halt, unsure of how to respond to this
request. She was all up for talking to her boys as though
they were people not puppies and you would never catch her
talking in a baby voice, but Cassie seemed to have taken the
notion a little too far. Indeed since Tarquin was barely three,
the need for a thorough explanation of food manufacturing
processes seemed to be stretching the imagination a little.

Cassie held up two packets, making no effort at all to move
aside. She shook them a little when Holly didn't immediately
answer and her eyes slid across to examine Holly's trolley as
if she couldn't help herself.

'Well? Could you explain to Tarka for me? Should we go
for cereal with no additives and use our own runny honey?
Or are we better to try the one with organic glucose syrup?'

Cassie was still blocking the aisle, her feet firmly planted
and her poncho flaring out to make her look even more formidable than usual. It was clear that Holly was going to have
to offer some form of opinion.

'Either's good, to be honest, Cassie. They're both reput-
able brands. Keep it simple and you can't go wrong, I say.'
Holly smiled and squeezed past on her way to the checkout,
relieved to have got away so lightly. She may have only lived
in Larkford a short while, but already she'd been Cassie'd
more times than she cared to admit. Holly's heart sank as
Cassie nipped in behind her in the queue and loomed alongside the twins, keen to chat.

Looking distinctly unsatisfied at Holly's blatant lack of
interest in her oatmeal dilemma, Cassie gave her a sympathetic look. 'It's so hard getting our little men to make the

right choices about their diet, isn't it? I mean, our household is completely organic, but we still have to be their guiding light, don't we?'

Her beady eyes fell on the three bottles of Pinot Grigio, wedged in place with a large bottle of bleach and some out-of-season asparagus from feck-knows-where and her jaw tightened. 'Obviously not everyone can lead by example, and when you're working you have to cut corners somewhere.'

Swallowing her instant dislike for anyone who referred to their son as a Little Man, Holly took a calming breath. She could see that Cassie was trying very hard indeed to be supportive. She was trying even harder not to leap upon Holly's un-organic, un-green, un-recycled trolley-full and rip it limb from limb. In fact she was trying so hard that Cassie's face had taken on an uncomfortable squirrelly look as if she were holding in some particularly offensive wind.

Tom tugged on Holly's sleeve. 'Scooze-me, Mummy,' he said, sounding like a particularly eloquent Jersey cow. 'Choccie snack for Tom?' He held up a bar of Dairy Milk pilfered from Holly's nemesis and weekly undoing, the checkout display.

Holly took a deep breath and gently took it from his clutching fingers. 'No, darling. No chocolate. Would make Ben poorly.' Normally she would have been on the ball to avoid this, fully prepared with a game, a joke or a snack to distract them, but obviously her attention had been elsewhere and now she was paying the price.

Tom's eyes welled up and his little legs began to work furiously to be free of the trolley. 'Tom like choccie!' His tiny face began to turn purple and his wails became increasingly distraught.

Cassie made no move to step aside and Holly could have

sworn that there was more than a hint of smug satisfaction to her sympathetic smile. 'So hard,' she murmured.

Holly gave up all pretence of politeness, swallowed a selection of swear words, and turned her back on Cassie. She was actually annoyed with herself these days, disgusted even, wondering where her fighting spirit had gone. It seemed that she'd become so accustomed to editing her opinions at work, and then at home, that the habit now seemed to have spilled over into her own time. In fact, she'd become so practised at rephrasing her opinions to make them more palatable, that she was in grave danger of either losing the ability to stand up for herself completely or losing her temper in an entirely unprofessional outburst.

She took another deep breath, hoping today wouldn't be *that* day, and made do with cursing under her breath all those sanctimonious women, who thought that working for a living made you a bad parent. Surely she would be an even worse parent, if she let her children struggle by on the pittance that Milo brought in every month. You can't fund an organic idyll on tuppence in loose change after all.

Holly quickly unloaded her shopping to be scanned, as Tom grizzled in resentment in the trolley. Marion on the check-out, bless her heart, had assessed the situation in a heartbeat. She leaned over and took a packet of crisps from the till display. 'Is Ben alright with these?' she queried and Holly nodded gratefully. Once each child was munching quietly, she stacked the shopping through, wondering at how Marion knew to quickly pack the illicit goodies into bags before anything else.

'Marion, did I ever tell you, you're an angel?' Holly smiled.

'Once or twice,' she whispered conspiratorially, 'but to be

honest I can never hear it enough. Besides, life's hard as it is without inviting the aggravation in – don't give that Cassie the satisfaction, I say. Anyway, I'm just grateful you haven't gone over to the internet shopping, like so many of the mums round here. I know it's easier with the little ones, but we do miss their business.'

Holly said nothing. Only thirty seconds before, she'd been cursing herself for not being more organised and getting their life delivered in a van like everyone else. Now she felt as though shopping locally was one more thing on her list of Things To Do To Fit In With The Locals.

'Anyway, must dash. I've got the mother-in-law coming for lunch . . .' She let that one trail off, and gave a brief wave to both Marion and Cassie before quickly slipping the boys out of their trolley harness and into the Beast, which was now festooned with bags of shopping. 'Bye . . . and thank you,' she called, as she made her escape into the morning sunshine.

She almost collided with the Major as he made his regular Sunday visit to collect his newspapers. 'Oh God, Major, I'm so sorry. Are you alright?'

'I'm fine, darling girl. Just fine. Although that pram seems to have the better of you there, if you don't mind my saying? Actually, you're just the gel who could help, if you've got a mo?'

Tom and Ben were elbowing each other in the pram and fighting over who got to carry the loo roll. Their squawks of disagreement growing ever louder, Holly was a bit distracted. 'I'm sorry, Major, what did you say?'

'Well, I was rather hoping you'd take a quick look at my leg?' The Major began to unbutton his coat and the four-pack of four-ply came flying over the pram's canopy, bouncing squarely off the Major's tweed cap. 'But then maybe you're a little busy . . .' He backed away and headed for the supermarket.

'But if it's urgent,' called Holly after his retreating back, 'you can call the Out-of-Hours, or I'm in tomorrow morning . . .' But the Major was gone and Holly shrugged. It was apparently a standing joke in Larkford that the Major had never yet been seen at The Practice. He seemed to manage all life's little ailments with supermarket remedies and accosting the medical staff about town. Holly hated to think how he'd handle a prostate problem, should the need ever arise.

Holly retrieved the loo roll and wedged it on top of the other bags as the boys played tug of war with Ben's left shoe. 'Right,' she said firmly, 'you two obviously need to let off some steam. Who's up for a play at the park?'

The giggles that greeted that suggestion lifted Holly's spirits enormously and she turned towards the church and the parkland that lay beyond, sheltered in a beautiful oasis of green, chattering to the boys as they walked.

'Morning Reverend, morning Dibley,' said Holly cheerfully, as they passed each other on the pavement.

'Good morning, Dr Graham,' replied Reverend Taylor, her face splitting into wreaths of smiles as she watched the young twins squabbling, 'and may I say what a jaunty hat your young man is wearing there.'

The Reverend reached down into the pram, Dibley the terrier circling her heels enthusiastically, and emerged with an enormous pair of pants. Huge pants, covered in little rosebuds and still bearing a price tag from the supermarket. 'Some of Marion's new range, by the looks of things, and possibly not the right size, if I may be so bold.'

Holly's face turned puce as the Reverend passed her the pants. Bad enough that her children had clearly turned to crime, but to be caught by the bloody vicar was just too much! She was about to launch into a lengthy explanation, when she noticed the vicar was still smiling.

'Only last week, young Dibley here decided to help himself to the sausage rolls, so I'm sure that Marion will be equally forgiving.' She gave Holly a wink and crouched down in front of the pram. 'Now you boys know that taking things is wrong, don't you. So you shall have to have the same punishment that I gave Dibley. Three good deeds. Each.'

The boys nodded solemnly and Holly mouthed 'thank you' when the Reverend stood back up.

'Unfortunately, one of Dibley's earlier good deeds appears to have been impregnating the Hampton's pedigree lurcher bitch. So, if you know anyone in the market for a puppy? Bit Heinz 57, but adorable little things ...'

Holly and the Reverend fell into step, as they walked towards the park, both with the express intention of wearing out their small charges. For Reverend Taylor, it was the only way to get through the morning service. For Holly, it was the only way to get through lunch with her mother-in-law. Well, that and the Pinot Grigio.

Chapter 14

'You look tired, Holly.'

Holly forced a smile as she finished the washing up. 'Probably.' The unspoken response hanging in the air.

'Well, I suppose it's inevitable really. Normally I'd say you need a few days in the sun, but then you always have had that slightly pasty complexion. Can't really be a sun worshipper can you? Not with your skin. You know, the kind of skin that ages badly, so actually it's probably not the best idea. Still, you do look awfully peaky.'

Holly breathed deeply. 'Yes, you've mentioned that before, Jean. But thanks anyway.'

'Well,' mused Jean, clearly too self-absorbed to appreciate the sarcasm, 'you could always make a bit more of an effort. Maybe get up a bit earlier and pop on some of that wonderful fake tan they do nowadays? Might give you a bit of a lift when you look in the mirror, mightn't it?'

'Indeed it might, Jean. But in all honesty, if I get up any earlier there's really no point going to bed at all.'

'Mm, what? I was just thinking about Milo, darling, really. I mean, you might not care what you look like, but it doesn't reflect terribly well on him, does it? After all,' she laughed girlishly, 'we're none of us getting any younger.'

Holly's grip on the Wedgwood bowl tightened as she dried it. It was hideously ugly and completely impractical since it refused to fit into the dishwasher, but Milo still insisted on using it every time his mother came to visit. Apparently Jean needed regular reassurance that her wedding gift to them was still in use.

Holly put down the bowl before she could do someone – Jean – a grievous injury with it and went back to the kitchen table where she'd set up the boys with some blocks of paint and huge sheets of paper. They were busy smearing paint over the paper, their aprons and basically everything within reach. Holly couldn't help but laugh at their innocent pleasure. 'Right, you two. Five more minutes and then it's bath-time.' She picked up a brush and was soon immersed in their little world, putting aside her anger about Jean's comments or the fact Milo hadn't bothered to play with his sons all day. No wonder I'm a crappy wife, she thought distractedly, as she painted around Tom's hand, I'm a mother first and a doctor second. When, she wondered, had being the perfect wife slipped so far down the pecking order?

'Don't talk,' whispered the voice down the telephone later that evening. 'Just listen.'

Holly tried not to laugh, as she recognised Lizzie's voice. She held the phone tightly pressed to her ear as she surveyed the damage to the sitting room. She may well have spent half the morning tidying up in anticipation of Jean's visit, but now, with newspapers and empty glasses scattered everywhere, she wished she hadn't bothered. Next time, she decided, she was going to have a bubble bath instead.

'In a minute, you can make all the right noises, but for now, I'm a patient in distress and you need to come out and do a home visit. Well, actually, I thought we could do a pub visit, because if I don't get out of this house in the next half hour, I bloody well will be a patient in distress!'

'And does it hurt if you press it?' enquired Holly, in her best doctoring voice, still trying not to laugh. 'Is there anyone there who can help you?'

'There's too many people here, since you ask, and none of them are helping – unless the idea is to drive me to an early grave or the bottom of the gin bottle,' replied Lizzie indignantly. 'I don't know what I was thinking, having his parents over this close to Easter. Now I'll have to live through it all again!'

Holly could hear the chaos at the other end of the line as Lizzie's three children fought over the Wii controls and her husband and his parents fought over pretty much anything and everything.

'How quickly can you get out?' whispered Lizzie, as the voices clamouring for their mother to act as referee came closer.

'Where are you?' asked Holly, forgetting herself for a moment and earning a curiously sharp stare from Milo, who was setting up the board for another game of backgammon with his mother and ignoring the fact that his sons were desperate for his attention.

'I'm in the sodding laundry cupboard. Where else would I be on a Sunday evening to get a little peace and quiet? Shit! I've been compromised. Pub. Seven o'clock,' and without waiting for an answer, Lizzie rang off.

'I'll be there as soon as I can,' said Holly to a dead line, in her most professional tone and hung up too.

'Let me guess?' said Jean, a little the worse for wear after consuming rather large quantities of Milo's experimental vodka jelly. Keen to encourage her son in his epicurean experiments, she'd tucked right in, proclaiming him on a par with Heston Blumenthal. Holly was pretty sure that even Heston could knock up a quick Spag Bol midweek though, if he pushed himself to it, but Milo preferred to preserve his energy for party pieces and shied away from what he called 'hum-drum' cooking and everyone else in the world called food. 'You've been called out to work? And on a Sunday?'

'Yes,' said Holly simply, too excited by the prospect of a spontaneous Sunday evening outing to be bothered by Jean's disapproval.

Jean turned to her son and sniffed, 'And I suppose you're to put the little ones to bed, are you?' She shook her head in dismay. 'It's no wonder you can't get on with your new book, Milo, with these kinds of pulls on your time.'

If Holly hadn't been keen to escape after an afternoon of listening to her mother-in-law on her soapbox, she was now. 'Well, if that's all settled then, I'll just leave you to it.' She knelt down on the floor and snuggled the twins, who were already bathed and in their pyjamas. 'Just ten more minutes, okay? Then Daddy and Granny will tuck you into bed.' Jean sniffed again and the devil appeared on Holly's shoulder. 'And Granny will read you a *really* long bedtime story.' Holly kissed their smooth, perfect cheeks and couldn't resist another squeeze, before she scooped up her work bag and left.

Leaning against the wall outside, Holly was a little shocked at herself. She couldn't quite believe she'd done a runner on a Sunday night. She also knew that Milo didn't believe it either. For some reason though, tonight, she didn't actually care.

By the time Holly had walked through the Market Place, she felt better about her decision, mainly because, with every shop window she walked past, she thought about what she would have bought if they had a little money. Two proper incomes, say, instead of relying on her wages for everything. And what she might have been able to afford if Milo didn't consider things like the boys' childcare to be 'her' expenses.

She'd worked herself up into a state of moral indignation by the time she arrived at the pub, her feet freezing in ancient Uggs. Her resentment had only been exacerbated by spotting a pair of glorious chocolate leather boots in the window of the Boutique on The Square. They looked warm and comfortable and very, very expensive.

'God, I needed this,' said Holly in greeting, finding her friend ensconced in an armchair by the fire with two G&Ts on the table and an ecstatic Labradoodle at her feet. She pulled off her coat, scruffing Eric's ears and relishing the beat of his over-excited tail against her legs, before sinking down beside Lizzie, who also appeared to have devilment on her mind this evening.

'Get stuck into that and I'll get us another round. Then maybe some chips while we have a natter? How does that sound?'

Holly swallowed a mouthful and shook her head a little as the Bombay Sapphire left a burning trail down her throat. 'Sounds heaven,' she managed, as her eyes watered. She looked up to see Taffy and Teddy, huddled together at the bar, watching her indulgently.

Without saying a word, Teddy filled a long glass of water and walked over, placing it on the table with a wink. 'Take it easy there, Dr Graham. I don't want any brawling this evening from you two. Now, did I hear it was chips you ladies were after?'

'Ooh yes please,' said Lizzie, 'with lots of mayo for dipping.'

Teddy smiled and walked away and Holly said nothing, mainly because she had just realised that she had come out to the pub in her ancient skinny jeans, a grandad cardigan and with a biro holding up her hair. No wonder Teddy was offering them absorbent food – he thought she was only one step away from becoming the village nutter!

As if reading her mind, Lizzie slid down in her armchair and gave Holly the once over. 'Nice outfit, by the way. What happened there?'

Holly shrugged. 'I think it was one of those now-or-never type moments. Besides if you really had got a ruptured appendix, I wouldn't have popped upstairs to put on some lippy, now, would I?'

Lizzie grinned. 'I imagine that would rather depend on whose appendix was rupturing. For instance, if the glorious Dr Jones over there needed medical attention, I dare say I'd manage some eyeliner. Why *is* he staring at you, by the way?'

Holly cradled her drink in her hands, building up the courage to take another mouthful. 'He isn't and don't stare.' Holly paused for a moment, fighting the urge to smile. 'Is he?'

Lizzie nodded and leaned in close. 'What have you been up to, to make you go all pink, Holly Graham?'

'Nothing. It's just that he's lovely and he's been helping me settle in at work and he made me a really nice cup of coffee the other morning and ... oh, shit, do you think I might have given him the wrong idea?'

'Jesus, Holl! I was only teasing and that was, like, 27 "and"s in one sentence there. Is there something you want to talk about?'

'No,' said Holly firmly, catching hold of herself. 'Don't be silly, of course there's nothing to talk about. I'm married.'

'Hmm. Well that didn't seem to stop your husband ogling every blonde on campus. No one would blame you for having a little flirt with the dishy doctor, you know. And you have to admit that Taffy Jones ticks an awful lots of boxes . . .'

'So does Milo,' insisted Holly loyally, but even to her own ears, her voice sounded hollow and unconvincing. 'And what's the point in having principles if you don't live by them. Otherwise, otherwise,' she said vehemently, 'we're all one step away from being like Henry Bruce!'

'Alright. Steady. Point taken,' said Lizzie quietly, draining her drink without even flinching. 'Dare I ask how His Lordship has taken the news about the ructions at work?'

Holly said nothing.

'Holls? You are going to have to tell him, you know. Especially if there's a chance, however small, that you might be out of a job.'

'I know. You're right. But to be honest?' Holly sipped her drink. 'Between you and me, I just can't deal with his drama at the moment. So there's no point mentioning it really, not until I know more. And the more I think about it, I was probably right and this partnership debacle might just be a storm in a teacup. I know they're all at each other's throats now, but it'll all be sorted in a week, I reckon.

'You've worked with Julia Channing, haven't you, Lizzie? I mean, she seems a right piece of work and Henry Bruce is just a bit, well, slimy for my taste. So it's an obvious choice isn't it? Dan Carter. And he supported my application, so there's probably nothing to worry about and I'm just over-reacting.'

Holly looked up to see her friend watching her sceptically. Lizzie wasn't a journalist for nothing. She had the ability to turn you in knots, get you questioning yourself and blurting out every secret you'd ever held, just by sitting quietly, saying nothing and letting you hang yourself.

'What?' said Holly eventually. 'Lizzie, if you know something, please tell me. I'm going quietly bonkers over this. I need this job. Milo can kid himself as much as he likes, but when your Head of Department puts you on unpaid leave for improper conduct, they're not really expecting you to come back, are they? And I know I promised we'd have a fresh start when we moved here, but I just don't know that I can.'

'Lizzie, he still swears blind that it was all innocent, that the girl just misinterpreted something he said. But, I'm not stupid,' Holly said darkly. 'There's no smoke without fire and the University wouldn't put him on leave if there was nothing to it. Would they?'

Lizzie just shrugged. They'd been around this particular roundabout more than once before, with Holly alternately supporting or vilifying her husband. 'Do you want me to make some calls, go on a fishing expedition? I can be discreet. Or you could actually just ask him. Put him on the spot.'

Holly wrinkled her nose. 'If I told you there's no point, because I wouldn't believe whatever he said, I know what you'd say next.'

Lizzie leaned forward in her chair and grasped Holly's hand. 'Run. Run. Run away. Which is actually what I *thought* you were doing when you applied for the job here, to be fair. I didn't think for a minute that you'd bring him with you!'

'I didn't bring him for me,' Holly said matter-of-factly. 'He's their dad. How can I tell those two boys that I left their father based on a rumour? Seriously? I know what it's like to have no dad, remember. I can't do that to them.'

'Holly, you must see that this is different. Your dad loved and adored you and he died. Milo is only interested in Milo. You must see that? He is never going to change, no matter how much you want him to. Does he even appreciate that you've given him a second chance or is he back to taking you for granted and ignoring the boys already.'

Holly's lack of reply was answer enough.

'Right,' said Lizzie, driven to frustration at seeing her gutsy, animated, eloquent friend reduced to this. 'I'm getting in another round and then you can tell me all about the delicious Dr Jones. There's no harm in window shopping, is there?'

Holly twisted in her chair to see Taffy still propping up the bar. He and Teddy were in deep conversation, but he turned as she looked, as if he could feel her eyes on him. He smiled gently and gave a tiny nod, before turning back to Teddy. Shit, thought Holly as her stomach somersaulted and she clung on to her principles, what the hell do I do now?

The two girls passed a couple of happily relaxed hours putting the world to rights. Husbands, children, work, wardrobes – they skipped about like butterflies through each other's lives. In the way of friends that have seen each other through a few ups and downs, there was a kind of shorthand to their conversation that would certainly have bemused anyone attempting to listen in.

Best friends since university, neither of them could remember what life had been like before they'd had each other to laugh with, to moan to and, above all, to rely upon for unconditional support. Holly valued Lizzie's outspoken opinions and irreverent wit, but also knew how fragile Lizzie could be, beneath the perfectly honed veneer of the career, the curls and the confidence. Lizzie meanwhile, did everything she could think of to counteract the damage Milo was doing to Holly's self-esteem and to find any opportunity for the funny, feisty side of her friend to shine through.

And of course Eric, their newly time-shared-puppy, would become the glue that held them both together. He clearly loved them both with all the passion in his little doggy heart and his trademark howl, a gentle, loving woo-oo-oo, had always been reserved only for Holly and Lizzie. Holly claimed that he was trying to say I Love You, but Lizzie had always been adamant that he was actually trying to recreate Eric Clapton's hit classic, 'Layla'. To Lizzie's mind, it was only logical that he should be named after his rock hero, although most of the town would comment from time to time, that Eric was an unusual moniker for a dog. Holly didn't care either way. She would have adored him no matter what.

'Did I tell you we went for Archie's interview at Charring-ton?' Lizzie said, twirling the stick in her G&T, and name-dropping the exclusive prep school for boys nearby. 'Three hours of aptitude tests for a five-year-old! Honestly, the whole thing was a farce. I thought we were doing okay, despite the fact that we had the gall to turn up without a double-barrelled surname . . .'

Holly started laughing, amused and fascinated in equal measure. 'I'm sure you could have fudged that one.'

'No,' said Lizzie with feeling. 'It's Will's cock-eyed idea anyway. I'm very much take us as we are, or leave us, thank you very much.'

'And which is it? What was it like?'

'Well, to be honest, Holls, I think it's become rather clear that Archie's not quite the academic elite they're looking for.

The little boy before us had a portfolio of his work, for Christ's sake. They were talking about the motivation of Christopher Robin when he goes looking for Winnie the Pooh!'

'And Archie?' asked Holly tentatively.

Lizzie grinned. 'Well, what's there to say? He's five. He can't read, he can't write and he wants to be a dinosaur . . .'

Holly clapped her hand over her mouth to prevent a spray of gin. 'So probably not Charrington for you, then? What about Jack?'

'Nah, we've cancelled Jack's visit. If Archie's interview didn't convince me, then all the glamorous mummies at pick-up would have. Who wants to live under that kind of pressure?' Lizzie habitually chose to ignore the fact that she was, in fact, one of those glamorous mummies and would still outshine most women, even if she chose to turn up in a bin bag.

'Speaking of mothers on the rampage, I forgot to tell you,' said Holly, 'I got Cassie-d in the supermarket earlier on. She was going on about oatmeal and nutrition and there I was with a trolley full of Curly Wurlys and plonk. Then Tom started kicking off because I wouldn't let him have chocolate in the house.'

'Well, you're damned either way really, aren't you? If you have the blasted stuff in the house, it's unfair on Ben. If you don't, it's unfair on Tom. How's he doing at the moment? He looked a bit blue at Nursery on Friday.'

'Oh Lizzie, I don't know where to start with that one.' She started shredding the paper napkin in her hands. 'I ordered some extra tests for him when we moved – you know, hearing, allergies, bloods, the works . . . I am just so fed up of people telling me not to worry, when clearly there's something to worry about.'

Lizzie was silent for a moment. 'And did they show any-thing, these extra tests? Anything you can work with?'

'Nope,' said Holly, her tired voice cracking with impotent frustration, as she ditched the mangled napkin and tangled her fingers in Eric's fur. 'According to every test we've done, he's a healthy little boy with a dairy allergy and delayed social development. The health visitor thinks he's not bad enough to count as autistic and I have to say, I agree with her. Otherwise he'd be bad all the time, wouldn't he? But he's not. He's fine for days on end. I took him for his hearing test last week and we had the most wonderful time going into Bath, just the two of us. So, then you start thinking, is he jealous of Tom? Does he just hate Nursery that much? Is it because I'm back at work full time?' She swallowed hard. 'I'm telling you, Lizzie, you could drive yourself properly mental with it all.'

'Shit,' said Lizzie with feeling. 'You poor soul. Obviously, I knew things weren't great, but I honestly hadn't thought it all through. You have to stop second-guessing yourself though, or you'll lose sight of the bigger picture. He's such a gorgeous little boy. Please tell me that Milo is being support-ive about this at least?'

There was an uncomfortable silence for a moment. Holly took a slug of her drink, swallowed hard and gave a slightly bitter laugh. 'Not so as you'd notice, no. In an ideal world, I need Milo more involved, his mother less involved and a nice juicy lottery win so I can stay home with my boys.'

Lizzie's eyes widened in shock. 'You don't mean that? After all the times we've talked about how important it is to work, to have our own identities ... Holly? Seriously? Remember how you said you didn't want to become one of those hollow-eyed, devastated women who come into your surgery when their kids leave home, all asking for anti-depressants. It's got to be worth a few sacrifices now . . . Hasn't it?'

Holly looked up. 'You're right, you're right, of course. And I really shouldn't drink gin. It always makes me teary, but yes . . . all those ideals are great until your baby's not very well. Then, it all means shit, doesn't it? And you'd trade any of it, to know that your little boy could walk into a room, look someone in the eye, talk to someone other than his twin, heck, talking at all would be progress . . .'

They sat quietly for a moment, as the air around them settled and Holly took a juddering breath. 'I just need to find my normal again, Lizzie. And do you know what Jean said to me this evening? She said that if I stopped thinking about the boys and my job all the time, and put on a nice frock occasionally, my husband might not be so miserable! Can you believe it?'

Lizzie nodded and scrunched up her perfect little nose. 'Don't hate me, but I can actually. In fact, I seem to remember my mum saying roughly the same thing after Jack was born. And although I can't bear to admit it, Holls, in my case she kind of had a point. I was so totally focused on the kids and my job that Will had almost become a lodger. I was just so tired and resentful and I didn't give him any care or attention at all.'

Holly picked at the remains of the deliciously salty chips they had devoured between them. 'So what we're really saying here, is that I need to make a bit more effort?'

'Oh no, no, no . . . Don't you misunderstand me here, Graham, that is not what I said and I'm *not* talking about all day every day. A few tweaks, maybe . . .

'But since you seem so bloody determined to stick to those

principles of yours, against all better judgement, might I add, and stay the course with Milo, it's got to be worth a go. You never know, you might even enjoy it. Just get your hair cut, put on a nice dress and go out for supper with your husband. I'll even babysit if you like,' she grinned, 'and it'll give me an excuse to get away from mine.'

Holly grinned. 'Well, I suppose I could use a trim.' She mentally flicked through her wardrobe. 'But I either need a new dress or a smaller body. You wouldn't think that last half stone would make such a difference when it comes to, you know, zipping things up. But honestly, I can't face going to Weight Watchers again. Not after last time, when half the women there were only going because someone from The Practice had told them to lose weight.'

'Haircut then,' said Lizzie, 'and maybe a few more chips while we work out the details of this diet.'

Holly laughed until the gin and tonic came out of her nose, which set Lizzie off again and soon had everyone in the bar staring at them. But not everyone was staring because they were making fools of themselves. Teddy was delighted to have a bit of life in the place on a Sunday night and two pretty ladies having a fine old time certainly did that. The Major was staring because, when Lizzie sat back in her chair, her jeans slid up to reveal a pair of perfect ankles and Taffy was staring because he couldn't tear his gaze away from the sight of Holly, relaxed, laughing and having fun. It was a sight he'd quite like to get used to.

Chapter 15

The next morning, Holly rubbed at her aching temples and silently cursed Lizzie, Bombay Sapphire and her own lack of willpower. Karma was a bitch, she decided. True, she should have known better than to stay up late on a school night, let alone to bank on Milo being able to get the twins into bed at the appointed hour. And that third drink had obviously been a mistake, as she clearly couldn't handle her liquor any more. The same could not be said for Lizzie, who'd moved on to a bottle of red, around the time that Holly had switched to mugs of tea, Cadbury's Mini Eggs and paracetamol.

'You looked like you were having fun last night,' said Taffy, as he hung up his jacket and found his schedule for the morning. 'How's the head?'

Holly groaned. 'Don't ask. Just kill me now. Preferably quietly.' She refilled her coffee mug and turned away from his sympathetic gaze. There was altogether too much affection in his eyes and it sent little shivers down Holly's spine that had absolutely no place being there. On the other hand, perhaps she had picked up a nasty bug and was destined to spend the next few days tucked up in bed with a fever and a Lemsip, she thought hopefully.

Holly shook her head at her own stupidity, instantly regretting the sudden movement. How ridiculous was her conscience to try and project an actual, physical illness, rather than admitting the simple truths?

She was sleep deprived, hung-over and unnerved.

It was that simple.

The reasons she was feeling unnerved however, were a little more complicated.

She sat back against the worktop in the doctors' lounge and watched Taffy assemble his coffee – three sugars, two spoonfuls of Nescafé and a huge slug of cream from the fridge. He was basically a teenager . . .

'What? I'm hungry,' Taffy protested, as he noticed the expression on her face. 'And don't judge until you've tried it.' He held out the mug to Holly. 'Go on. It's my patented hangover cure, so I wouldn't be so quick to dismiss it, if I were you.'

Holly took a tentative sip, half expecting the Mini Eggs to make an encore appearance, but to her surprise, Taffy's sickly concoction was like a hug in a mug. 'Well,' she prevaricated, unwilling to succumb so easily, 'it's no bacon sandwich . . .'

Taffy just grinned, pulled out another mug and began to cook up a second batch. 'Drink it, it's yours. Now, by way of thanks, you can tell me what you and Lizzie were gossiping about last night? You can be honest. I'm not shy. It was my new jeans, wasn't it?' he said, his face completely dead-pan.

Holly couldn't help but laugh, having noted with some amusement last night, the entirely shredded and shabby appearance of what was clearly a very well-loved bit of denim. 'You've got me,' she said. 'In fact, Lizzie will probably be calling you later to set up a photo shoot for the magazine.' Holly tried not to think about how the soft, worn denim had sculpted Taffy's thighs so perfectly that Lizzie had even tried to get a snapshot on her iPhone.

'Don't mock the afflicted,' he said, trying to look offended and failing. 'We can't all roll out of bed looking gorgeous, Dr Graham.' He gave her a cheeky grin and left the room, leaving Holly floundering for a witty response. He couldn't possibly mean her, could he?

Perhaps he was due for his annual sight test, Holly decided in the end. It made a lot more sense than the alternative.

After a few hours of ministering to the sick, the malingering and the generally deranged, Holly was beginning to question the idea that General Practice would be an easier proposition than her shifts at the hospital. True, the atmosphere was more conducive to intimate revelations, but the stories were not so different. It seemed to Holly as though maybe she was actually seeing the same patients, just earlier on in their stories, before 'Doctor' wasn't enough and an upgrade to 'Hospital' was required.

Taffy's Tincture had worked wonders and Holly couldn't deny that having him around was making her new job that bit more fun. It was the one thing she'd been worried about when going into General Practice – the dark and wonderful sense of humour at the hospital had kept them all going through some tricky times. It had built up their sense of camaraderie and Blitz-spirit and Holly had adored it.

She'd already seen that Dan and Taffy approached medicine in much the same way. Thankfully the rest of the team seemed to follow their lead – with the notable exception of Julia Channing and Henry Bruce.

Even George Kingsley had turned out to be a bit of a hoot. Although, to be fair, Holly wasn't entirely sure that it was intentional. Only this morning, she'd popped through to his consulting rooms to find him playing duck with some cervical dilators. He seemed to be even clumsier than she was – in his embarrassment, he'd knocked a huge pot of tongue depressors flying.

According to Grace, in the last week alone, he'd broken an anatomical model of a knee joint and nearly injected himself with insulin by mistake – apparently he fiddled when he was nervous or distracted.

By all the evidence then, Holly reckoned he must be pretty nervous and distracted about his retirement plans.

Holly poked her head around the waiting room door. 'Martin Lane? If you'd like to follow me?' Holly held open the door to her consulting room and guided him through. He looked fragile and emaciated and Holly pulled a chair around so it was closer for him.

Even so, pale and struggling, Martin looked defeated by the distance to the chair.

'So, Martin, what's been going on with you? I gather you've lost about a stone in the last few weeks?' Holly leaned in closer, guiltily thinking that, after a morning of ear infections and thrush, it was quite nice to have a more challenging case.

Martin nodded. 'I've been really under the weather, Dr Graham. At first we thought we'd got the flu from the grandkids, but they all got better and I didn't.'

'When you say the flu,' said Holly sympathetically, her eyes ranging over him, searching for visual clues, 'what symptoms did you have?'

Martin rubbed at his forehead. 'Well, the little ones were all coughing and sneezing, but I just had really aching joints, splitting headache, exhausted . . .' His words trailed off as if the effort of talking alone had indeed exhausted him. 'I've been off work, off my food, off my game generally really.'

Holly quietly made notes as Martin spoke. 'Okay, but you did get your flu jab this year, didn't you?'

'Just goes to show it's a waste of time, doesn't it?'

'Obviously there are different kinds of flu, Martin, but what you're describing is so generalised, we could be looking at almost anything. Has there been anything else unusual? Any other illness in the family? Any change in routine?'

Martin shrugged, reluctant to admit the extent of his illness. He blinked hard to get the tears from his eyes. 'Sorry to be a bit weepy about all this, Doctor. It's been a miserable couple of weeks, with no sleep and feeling so wretched and now I daren't even cuddle the new grandson in case I'm contagious . . .' His voice petered out and Holly discreetly handed him a tissue.

It seemed that most of Holly's time here had been spent dispensing tissues to crying patients. Most people seemed to wait until they were at their wits' end before booking themselves in for an appointment. With so many concoctions available over the counter, Holly realised that it was inevitable really. Most people, after all, weren't in a desperate hurry to spend ages sitting in a germ-filled waiting room. Except, ironically, the Worried Well. The WW, as Taffy would say, were terribly suggestible and one bad episode of Horizon or Panorama could have the waiting room packed to the gills.

Holly let Martin chat on as she methodically checked his temperature, ears, throat and blood pressure. She felt around for swollen glands and tried her best not to show her shock at the extent of the swelling around Martin's lymph glands in his armpit and at the side of his neck.

She could see from his file that Martin's father had recently passed away from leukaemia and he'd been in a couple of times, asking for something to help him sleep. She offered up a silent prayer that this was not going to be a case of history repeating itself. He obviously wasn't a young man, but he'd apparently been in reasonable health and Holly hoped that he might dodge ticking the statistical boxes for a little while yet.

Holly leaned forward in her chair, elbows on her knees, brain crunching data. 'Think for me, Martin. Have you had a sore throat? An earache?'

Martin shook his head. 'I was absolutely fine, helping out the youngest with her new business and then bam – I was knocked for six. Thought it might be the early starts, you know? I've got out of the habit of getting up early.'

Holly stood up and pulled a roll of paper over the treatment bed and helped Martin to his feet. 'Well, let's get you comfortable lying down and we can discuss what happens next. You know, one of us could have visited you at home, Martin. You only had to ask.'

'I didn't want to be a bother,' Martin replied.

Holly quickly and expertly drew enough blood to send off to the lab, hoping that Grace wouldn't give her stick for doing what was technically a job for the nursing team. But she couldn't see the point in making Martin wander around the building when he was clearly struggling. As Holly held down a ball of cotton wool on the inside of Martin's arm, Martin himself was chattering away about his Fiona's wonderful new enterprise and how proud he was that she was so dedicated.

Holly turned Martin's arm to and fro in the light, leaning in to examine his skin amongst the dense black hair that seemingly covered him from head to foot. 'Martin?' she said slowly. 'When did these lumps appear?'

Martin looked down at his arm. 'Oh about a month ago, the first one. It was like a little ganglion, you know. I had to stop the wife from bashing it with a bible! And then, the others, slowly since then. Fiona made me stop picking up the heavy boxes after that. Obviously not as fit as I used to be.'

Holly pulled the overhead light down and examined the lumps that ran from Martin's wrist to elbow, some pearly pink, some purple, others openly weeping. She racked her brains as a germ of an idea stayed stubbornly out of reach. 'We'll send all the blood off, Martin and I think I'll give you something topical for these too, in the meantime. Can you really think for me, Martin, did anything happen before the lumps began?'

'Only helping Fiona out, like I said.'

Holly printed out a prescription for some topical ointment and shook her head with frustration, knowing that the answer was in there somewhere. 'I'll call you when the results come in and if anything changes, I want you to come straight back in, okay?'

Martin nodded and stepped down from the bed. 'And if you want a few flowers to brighten up the waiting room, I'm sure Fiona would love to help. She's a wonder with a floral arrangement, my girl. She'll be the best florist for miles around soon.'

Holly felt all the cogs of her brain click into place. 'Martin, sit down. You've got sporotrichosis. You pricked yourself on a rose thorn, didn't you? When you were helping your daughter?'

Martin looked perplexed. 'You know, you're right. I did. But what's that got to do with this? It was weeks ago.' He looked down at his arm and ran his fingers over the lump on his thumb, which was now a deep purple.

Holly breathed a sigh of relief and then tore up Martin's earlier prescription. 'There's mould spores on rose thorns that can cause some really nasty infections if they get under your skin. If you don't catch them early, it can actually get pretty serious, Martin. So, we'll still get the bloods checked and I'm going to speak to a colleague about whether we need to refer you, but in the meantime I want you to use this potassium iodide and I think an anti-fungal wouldn't go astray here either.'

Holly talked Martin through his proposed course of treatment and other developments to keep an eye out for. The last thing they needed was for this to develop into a nasty cellulitis. All the while, in her head, Holly kept thanking the gods that Martin was a chatty fellow, or she may have missed this one completely.

Score one for General Practice, thought Holly, as she saw Martin through to the Pharmacy. A little squiggle of excitement in her stomach reminded Holly how much she loved her work – the challenge, the puzzle, knowing she'd made a difference. Knowing now, more than ever, that she'd made the right decision.

'You look like the cat that's got the cream,' said Grace, as Holly perched on her desk after a long morning surgery.

Holly shrugged. 'A lucky catch, that's all.'

Grace nodded. 'Some days you win … I have to say Holly, George and I are thrilled at how well you're settling in. Seems like you've been here for ages. I know he's worried about how his little team are going to cope when he's gone. Let's his heart rule his head, that one. But between you and me, with this partnership fandango, I rather hoped he would stay true to form. But, he's got a bee in his bonnet about being fair and open-minded.

'He's never been a big supporter of Big Business when it comes to medicine – rather likes the personal touch – so it's obvious to anyone who knows him that Dan's his natural successor. But obviously Julia and Henry deserve their bite at the cherry too.' Grace sighed. 'If only Dan were on top form, then it wouldn't even be an issue.'

Holly sat quietly, wondering whether Grace was supposed to be letting any of this slip. Not that Holly didn't want to know, she was practically on tenterhooks, but she didn't want Grace to regret confiding in her later.

But Grace carried on, seemingly relieved to be sharing her concerns. 'There's no doubt in my mind at all that Dan's the superior GP, Holly. Henry would probably be happier in private practice to be honest. He does love his perks that one. And Julia, well . . . I always get the feeling she misunderstood the meaning of "Critical Care". Not the most empathetic of souls, is she? She would have made the perfect surgeon, don't you think?'

Holly laughed, as Grace's comment was unerringly accurate. Julia *would* make the perfect surgeon. Clearly ridiculously intelligent and dedicated to finding solutions, Julia was very black and white. Find problem. Fix problem. Go home. Avoid talking to your patient in any depth at all wherever possible. It was so bloody obvious, now that Grace had articulated the thought, that Holly wondered how she'd missed it before. 'Grace, you're so right. She's clearly missed her calling.'

Grace shrugged. 'Missed, bodged, flunked . . .'

Holly leaned in, intrigued. 'And?'

Grace looked flummoxed for a moment, as if she'd spoken out of turn. 'We-ll, I don't think I'm breaking any confidences, when I say that Julia came to us from Barnards teaching hospital. She was on Professor Wyley's surgical rotation but she left, suddenly, decided surgery wasn't for her after all.'

'Wow,' said Holly quietly, thinking that this little morsel of information might go some way to explaining Julia's patronising attitude. Even though Julia herself was now a GP, it was clearly her second choice, so maybe she thought that it was for everyone else too? Holly blushed a little as she realised that, when working at the hospital had clashed so badly with family life, General Practice had been her own fall-back position as well. It was a weird sensation, finding that she had something in common with Julia Channing. It wasn't necessarily something she wanted to advertise though, if she was honest, because the similarities ended right there. Holly was rather proud to become a GP and she firmly believed that George Kingsley was right, being a GP *was* a noble calling – they were, as he often said, the infantrymen fighting on the frontlines of family health. Or something like that. Holly decided that she really ought to listen to George more, next time he was giving them all one of his pep-talks, rather than tuning out as she often did.

Holly realised with a start that she'd done it again, that Grace had carried on talking and Holly had dropped the thread of the conversation completely.

'. . . and Dan Carter is exactly what this practice needs. But, you know, George isn't blind. Hell, even I can see that he's struggling again and I know Taffy's doing his best to get Dan to talk to someone but . . . Well, let's just hope he can get himself back on track in time. Don't you think?'

Holly didn't actually know what to think. How could she have zoned out and missed the most important confidence that Grace had shared with her? She could blame the late night, or the Bombay Sapphire, but she basically had to admit that her concentration skills needed one hell of a polish. 'Dan seems so together at work, though,' she hedged uneasily.

Grace sighed. 'It's not an easy thing to recover from though, is it?'

Holly nodded thoughtfully, her mind running on – Heartbreak? Drugs? Alcohol? But luckily Grace was on a roll. 'And there's not so many folk in Somerset with PTSD is there? We can't just send him along to a meeting now, can we? Hi, my name's Dan and going to Iraq ruined my life? Poor bloke. And he really is one of the good ones, Holly. We'd be lucky to have him as our boss, even with the flashbacks.'

Holly was stunned. Speechless. Suddenly, lots of little snippets of conversation all made sense. She tried not to feel hurt that neither Lizzie nor Dan had chosen to confide in her about this. If he'd been struggling for ages, as he obviously had, maybe she could have done more to help. Grace was chattering on, obviously believing that Holly's friendship with Lizzie and history with Dan meant she wasn't telling her anything she didn't already know. It was all Holly could do to keep her face from betraying her surprise.

'Does everyone at The Practice know about Dan then?' she asked tentatively.

'Oh no, just one or two of us. Dan's a very private person, as you know. He'd hate the idea of people talking about him.' Grace suddenly looked uncomfortable. 'But obviously, we need to discuss it a little don't we, if we're going to help him. And on that front, where I was heading actually, I wanted to ask you if you could take over a few of Dan's more, well, emotional cases for a while. You've probably already noticed that your patient list is basically all the ones that nobody else wanted, so I thought it might work for you and for Dan.' Grace had the decency to look a bit sheepish at that little admission. 'Give him some headspace and let him work on the simple stuff and give you a few more challenging cases in the process. What do you think?'

Holly felt like a ping-pong ball bouncing back and forth. She wasn't sure her brain could cope with much more information. Her new job – her dream job actually – was turning out to be made of smoke and mirrors. 'That sounds like a good idea all round,' she managed.

Grace swivelled in her chair and took one of Holly's hands in hers, her kind expression almost bringing Holly to the verge of tears. 'I know there's been a lot going on in the last few days, and that you must be wondering what on earth you've got yourself into, but it's not as bad as you're imagining, Holly. You've already got quite the fan club round here, I promise you. Stick with us. Rumour has it, you've got Elsie Townsend singing your praises and you've even had the Major accosting you for a car park consultation already – so that just proves it – you're officially accepted. Just beware the grapevine, okay? Otherwise Sunday night drinks with your colleagues could easily be misinterpreted.' Grace gave her a smile and got up from her desk.

'But,' said Holly, wrong-footed yet again, 'I was with Lizzie.'

'I know,' said Grace gently, 'but the way I heard it, a certain male doctor couldn't keep his eyes off you all evening. He's a very sweet lad, that Taffy Jones, but he's never short of a girlfriend, if you know what I mean. Bees round a honey pot springs to mind. But then,' she finished with a sideways glance, 'I'm sure I'm not telling you anything you don't already know.'

Holly nearly laughed out loud, forcibly struck by the irony of Grace's parting comment. With every day that passed, the list of Things That Holly Didn't Know seemed to be growing exponentially longer.

Chapter 16

Holly meandered through the graveyard at the back of the church early the next morning, coffee in hand. She couldn't quite face the cheery chitchat in Hattie's Deli this morning, just needing a few moments peace and quiet, a few moments all to herself.

She breathed out slowly and felt the first tendrils of sunshine brushing her face. She closed her eyes, turning toward the early morning sun. The graveyard was like a quiet oasis, tucked away beyond the bustle of the Market Place and even the thrum of traffic was swallowed up by the warm stone of the church. An angry little robin with delusions of grandeur startled her by hopping down suddenly in front of her, scolding her indignantly.

'Sorry,' whispered Holly, stepping carefully back on to the path and trying not to laugh as the little bird recovered from its huff and flitted upwards to rest in the branches of the ancient yew hedge. 'Have you got a nest up there?' she asked, intrigued by the feisty little bird's behaviour. She watched in fascination as it fluttered down, gathered a beakful of mossy twigs and disappeared into the upper branches of the hedge with a bob of its tail.

She perched on the little wooden bench that was tucked

into this remote corner and looked around her. This sure beat the socks off rush hour in Reading. The boys were at Nursery, Milo was undoubtedly still asleep, but somehow Holly had managed to find a little window before work just to 'be'.

She noted with lazy interest the seagulls swooping overhead, wondering why she'd never noticed them before. There were red swathes of cloud dusting the tops of the woodland across the valley and there was a heavy warmth in the air that reminded Holly of childhood holidays in Italy. It may still be early in the year, but a few days of pleasant weather would make a very welcome change. She sipped slowly at her steaming cup, wondering why she didn't do this more often. It was one thing to get up early to heat up the GHDs (something she could never quite be arsed to do); it was quite another proposition to have a little sanity break like this. She sighed contentedly and closed her eyes.

The sudden shifting of the bench beside her and a gentle cough made her start, sloshing hot coffee over her toes. 'Shit!' she blurted, caught unawares.

'Morning, Dr Graham, hope I didn't disturb you?' asked the Major with a wry smile. He handed her a beautifully pressed linen handkerchief and indicated with a nod of the head that she should mop her sodden feet. Holly looked aghast at the very suggestion. The handkerchief was a study in physical perfection, bright white, sharp creases and a monogram, for Christ's sake!

'Oh Major, no it's fine, really.' She plucked the ubiquitous packet of baby wipes from her handbag instead.

The Major laughed. 'No lectures from you about being more environmentally friendly then, Dr Graham?' He gave the word 'environmentally' an additional few syllables that Holly had previously been unaware of. 'I knew I liked you.

Cassie Holland has got one or two backs up around here.
And I don't know what she's so het up about – I recycle my
whisky bottles, don't you know.' He gave Holly a wink and
then waved a hand at her coffee cup. 'Should we get you a
new one of those? It rather looked as if that caffeine may have
been the only thing keeping you awake just now.'

'Honestly, Major, it's not a problem.' She looked around
the beautifully tended graveyard, some of the stones so
eroded and covered in moss that it was impossible to decipher
the sentiments etched there. 'It's just so tranquil here. I was
just grabbing a quiet five minutes with my face in the sun.'

'Well then, enjoy it while you can. Smell that?' He waved
a hand in the air. 'That's the calm before the storm that is.
Why do you think the seagulls have come this far in land?
See, red sky in the morning?'

'Shepherd's warning,' Holly remembered. 'Well, at least
we've had a few minutes sunshine now.'

She paused, giving the Major an opportunity to chip in,
as he always seemed to, with whatever was ailing him this
week. She genuinely didn't understand why he never came
to The Practice, but she hoped that, with a little practice and
patience of her own, she would learn to handle his random
requests with grace.

When he remained silent, Holly looked at him more
closely, taking in the wistful gaze, and noticing for the first
time the bundle of freshly cut forsythia. He ran the linen
handkerchief through his fingers. It was actually the fact that
he wasn't talking that made Holly suspect that something
really was amiss.

'Major?' she said gently, resting her hand on his tweed
sleeve. 'You know you can always talk to me. About anything. And you don't need to come to The Practice.'

She waited, watching as the feisty little robin began chittering at a stray neighbourhood cat who had dared to amble by.

The Major cleared his throat. 'It's just rather embarrassing, at my age, to be talking about personal things with a young lady such as yourself.'

Holly smiled. So that was the problem. Embarrassment. 'Major, I can promise you that nothing about the human body can shock me any more. You wouldn't believe the things I've seen, the things I've extracted . . .' she gave a little involuntary shiver. 'I might be able to help, if you talk to me.'

The Major blew his nose heartily into his hanky and placed it in his jacket pocket, looking pointedly in the other direction. 'I'm a bit lonely,' he blurted, his voice gruff with emotion. He pointed to the beautifully carved headstone in front of them and Holly registered the name properly for the first time Lady Verity Waverly.

She left her hand on his sleeve and leaned in a little closer, instinctively wanting to give the old boy comfort, but knowing that a bear hug was out of the question, professionally speaking. The dates on the headstone showed that it was less than two years since the Major's wife had passed away. After a lifetime together, how long should it take for the pain to go away? Judging by the anguish on the Major's face, two years wasn't nearly long enough.

'Oh Major, you poor thing. I can't imagine what it's like to lose the love of your life.'

The Major harrumphed for a moment; it actually looked as though he was laughing and Holly felt a moment's confusion. 'Oh you dear sweet girl, Verity wasn't the love of my life; that particular honour is reserved for my spaniels. Verity was a right royal pain in the backside, but she was also a

fabulous wife and an excellent sparring partner. Nowadays,'
he sniffed, 'I have to be so polite to everyone.'

Holly couldn't say she'd actually noticed the polite part,
always thinking that the Major acted rather too entitled and
bossy for her taste, but she carried on undeterred. 'Well,
maybe you could get some friends together and have a good
old bicker with each other?'

The Major was instantly dismissive. 'My dear girl, gentlemen don't bicker. We have discussions and disagreements,
but there's nothing like the intimacy of quarrelling with
someone you love, is there?'

Holly shrugged. 'You might be getting advice from the
wrong person then, Major. I can't stand arguments – will
actively go out of my way to avoid them.'

'Ah, I see, bit of a doormat, are you? Didn't take you for a
spineless ninny, but then looks can be deceiving, I suppose.'

Holly bristled slightly, trying to keep her composure.
'Surely there's lots of lovely ladies in Larkford, who'd be
delighted to spend some time with you. Granted, they may
not all be up for a squabble on the first date, but is there no
one who's caught your eye? I'm sure Verity wouldn't want
you to be lonely.'

'Bah. And that just shows how little you know about my
wife. Magnificent she was. Hell of a woman.' He gave her
a sideways glance and a smile tugged at the corners of his
moustache. 'Of course, you'd probably have called her terrifying, but we settled for indomitable. Good woman. Lousy
bridge player. Best of friends.' He dabbed at his face with the
handkerchief again.

'She sounds a little like Julia Channing,' Holly quipped,
before cursing herself for speaking out of turn. First rule of
living in a small community: never bad-mouth anyone.

The Major really did smile then, tucking his hanky away once more and picking up his bundle of forsythia. 'Now there's a hell of a woman. I've a lot of time for Julia. She may be a bit brittle sometimes and, true, you never know which way the wind is blowing with her, but ... Well, let's just say that she's saved me more often than I care to think. That Meningitis outbreak a few years ago, when they were vaccinating the whole town? It was Julia Channing who came and sought me out – knew I wouldn't go to The Practice, you know? Probably more than her job was worth to treat someone who wasn't registered ... And again when I had those dodgy scallops on my boat, it was Julia who phoned the local doctor in France for me ... Wonderful lass.' He sighed. 'She was a sweetheart with my Verity at the end too.'

Holly wanted to say, Are you sure? Are we talking about the same Julia Channing? The mismatch between the woman she worked with and the woman the Major was describing was just too large. So much for first impressions, thought Holly; she was suddenly reframing Julia in a whole new light.

'And last Christmas,' carried on the Major, 'she came round for a piece of cake and a cuppa on Christmas Day. Knew I'd be on my own. She's a good girl, that one.'

Holly checked her watch and stood up slowly. 'You know, Major? If it's strong women you like, why don't you chat to Marion Gains? If there's someone for you in Larkford, Marion will know who it is. She's practically an Oracle.'

The Major stood up beside her. 'Perhaps I shall. I shall certainly give the matter some thought. It's been lovely to chat with you, Dr Graham. I think you'll fit in here rather splendidly. I might even take your advice. Perhaps you would do me the honour of taking mine, with regards to Julia Channing. Don't judge a book by its cover, will you? We all come with baggage, Holly, if I may call you Holly?'

Before she could reply, he was off, reverently laying down his offering at Verity's headstone, before marching towards the Market Place without even a backwards glance.

Holly smiled and dropped her coffee cup into the bin. Since when did it become embarrassing to admit to being lonely, she wondered. And if even the confident and gregarious Major was afflicted, she wondered how many other souls amongst them felt the same way. She waved at the robin stalking her as she left the graveyard, but two thoughts jostled for position in her mind.

Did one necessarily have to be single to be lonely? And was Julia Channing actually much nicer than she let on?

Refreshed and renewed by her mini sanity saver, Holly felt much happier about facing the day ahead of her. It was just as well she'd had a little boost, because the test results waiting when she got in spelled disaster for one of their patients.

'Holly, have you got a few minutes?' asked Dan, poking his head around her door. 'I could really use a second pair of hands on this one.' He came into the room and sank down on the chair opposite Holly. He looked pretty stressed and Holly could see there was a faint tremor in his hand, as he held the buff patient file on his lap.

'No problem,' said Holly, clicking save on the referral letter she was typing. It didn't matter how many times Grace told her she could just dictate them, Holly was still more comfortable thinking on paper. These letters didn't need to be eloquently crafted, but having been at the hospital end of this very equation, Holly knew that the right personal information, phrased in the right way, could often make a significant difference to waiting times.

From that perspective, what was five minutes more of her time, compared to weeks of additional worry for her patients?

'Still typing your own referrals, I see,' said Dan.

'I know you all think I'm mad, but it's important to me,' Holly replied. 'Don't start telling me all about GP time ratios again.'

'I wasn't going to,' Dan said. 'In fact, I'm beginning to wonder whether we should all be following your lead. You're the one with hospital background, after all. And anyway, it's actually your fluffy-bunny sensibilities I need this afternoon.'

He opened the buff folder and pulled out a print-out sheet from the MRI scanning department in Bath. He passed it to Holly without comment.

Holly didn't need any. The tumour was unmistakable, showing white hot against the hazier outlines. 'Well, that's not good,' she said, mentally calculating scale. 'That has to be an inch across. Any secondaries?'

Dan silently passed her a second page.

Holly took a moment to check she was seeing everything; it was so easy for the eye to be drawn to the bigger growths, but sometimes it was the smaller, more aggressively mutating ones that would prove more devastating.

'So,' she said eventually, 'are we providing familial support, or Macmillan referrals ... I presume they'll get the news from the consultant direct.'

'Normally, yes,' said Dan, 'but we need to be a little bit careful with this one. Kid gloves so to speak, so the consultant has asked if we can break the initial news and then he'll see them in the morning. Shirley, our lovely Macmillan nurse was going to come and hold my hand, but Mr Jeffries is on his last legs and she's needed there really.'

The request was unspoken and Holly felt quite panicked. This bit of her job never got any easier. At least, by leaving the hospital, she never had to break the news of a fatality any more – that was guaranteed to give her sleepless nights for ages.

'And the kid gloves?'

Dan shook his head. 'It's Lance. From the deli?'

'Oh no,' cried Holly, involuntarily. 'How bloody cruel.'

Lance was all of thirty-two years old and he ran the deli with his gorgeous wife, Hattie. After four rounds of IVF, Hattie was finally, ecstatically pregnant. But Holly had seen her only the other day for a blood pressure check, so she knew from her file that the IVF had been necessary after years of unexplained miscarriages. The last thing they wanted to do was to trigger another one.

'I need a bit of help on this one,' said Dan apologetically. 'I hope you don't mind, but Julia is not known for her sensitivity when it comes to pregnancy. She claims that pregnancy isn't an illness and therefore shouldn't be something we deal with, but I think the whole thing kind of freaks her out. I know it sounds weird for a doctor, but she's actually kind of squeamish. That's why we needed you.'

'Okay then,' said Holly, Julia edging ever closer to human on the spectrum in Holly's mind. 'I'm not saying I'll be any good at this one, but at least I know Hattie. She was one of the first people to welcome us here actually.' Holly felt herself getting a little choked up. She tried to pull herself together, but when she looked up, Dan's eyes were decidedly moist too.

'Are you sure we're the best people to be handling this?

Surely, the distance and anonymity of an oncologist might make it all feel a bit less real?' Holly wondered out loud.

Dan shrugged. 'We've been through hell and back with them here, trying to get Hattie through each pregnancy. Not to mention the fact that Lance and I have known each other for ever. Let's just stick to the basics, tell them the news and I'll go to Bath with them tomorrow. Just in case they have any questions.'

'Do you normally do that?' asked Holly, pressing her hand to her chest, beyond impressed.

'Sometimes. Not all the time obviously, but this isn't just anyone, is it?'

Holly pushed back her chair, handing Dan the print-outs. 'So you do the talking, I'll do the hand-holding?'

'I suspect that we'll both be doing a little of each.' He took Holly's hand in his, squeezed it and then let go. 'Thanks for this, Holly.'

Holly was about to say 'my pleasure' but the words fell to sawdust in her mouth. 'No one should do this alone,' she said instead and she meant it.

Holly pulled open the door to Dan's room, where Grace had already escorted Hattie and Lance and organised a jug of water.

The news at this point felt like a mere formality. The stricken look on Hattie's face said it all. They weren't stupid and the minute glasses of water and two doctors arrived, their worst fears began to be realised.

Holly felt clumsy and ill-informed as Dan outlined the diagnosis. She held Hattie's hand in her own, rubbing her thumb in circles, as she might to soothe one of her boys after a nightmare. But Hattie's nightmare was only just beginning.

After a few minutes, both Lance and Hattie were beginning to look overwhelmed. 'There's just so much to take in,' said Hattie bewildered.

Lance had yet to say a word, he just listened with an intensity that suggested his life depended on it.

Holly pulled a piece of paper from Dan's desk and scribbled her phone number on it. 'I know Dan will answer all your questions and guide you through your options tomorrow, but, Hattie, please do phone me if there's anything you want to talk through, anything that's not making sense.'

Hattie choked up further then. 'You can't go round giving out your home number, Holly, you'll have all the nutters on the phone.'

Holly rubbed her shoulder. 'Well, you don't seem that nutty to me. Keep it. If you need me, I'm there.'

Dan hung back, talking quietly with Lance, as Holly made sure that Hattie was feeling alright. 'Let's just check your BP to be on the safe side. And if you can get some sleep tonight, then you and the baby will both be better for it.'

'I knew, you know, Holly. As soon as we found that lump. I knew it would come to this. I tried keeping busy, sticking my head in the sand, but there was just this feeling that wouldn't go away. How could we get so lucky as to have this little bean on the way ...'

Holly wrote down the BP readings and looked Hattie in the eye. 'We'll get you both the best care in the county. You won't be on your own through this, Hattie. And Shirley will be around tomorrow, from Macmillan, and she's wonderful.'

'You're not bad yourself, Holly. Thank you for telling us here. I hate those impersonal doctors that make you feel like a number not a person. And you giving me your number ...'

'Use it,' said Holly. 'I wasn't just being polite. I know you don't know me very well yet, but I very rarely make offers, or threats, that I don't carry through on.'

'That's why your boys are so good,' said Hattie, hiccupping through her tears. 'They know their boundaries.'

'Doesn't work so well on husbands, though,' said Holly with a wry smile, as she gave Hattie a gentle hug.

Why did it always work like this, thought Holly, and not for the first time. Bad things did happen to good people and yet some of the worst old reprobates she knew were still in the running for a telegram from the Queen. It was almost enough to make her question her every belief.

Chapter 17

'Dan? Have you got a minute?' Jason appeared in the door-way the next morning, in his off-duty ensemble of tracksuit and trainers. His face was flushed and he was walking rather strangely. The front door had barely been unlocked ten minutes, but already the waiting room was filling up and the phones were ringing off the hook. There seemed to be a couple of viruses doing the rounds and the patients would insist on coming in and sharing their lurgies around, rather than simply taking it easy at home for twenty-four hours.

Taffy was perched on the end of Dan's desk, making short work of a bacon sandwich.

'Literally a minute though, and then you can both sod off. I've got a roomful of malingerers awaiting my undivided attention in ooh, about 15 minutes. I didn't think you were in this morning, Jason.'

'Not 'til later, really, but I've got myself in a bit of trouble and I need your help.' Jason sat down gingerly. 'You guys have to promise not to tell anyone though – it's kind of embarrassing.'

Taffy grinned, wondering what (or possibly who), Jason had been up to. 'My lips are sealed, but I could do with a laugh. Come on – out with it. What have you done?'

Jason gingerly rolled down his tracksuit trousers, wincing as the fabric caught on the strips of wax covering one leg to the thigh. He shrugged, embarrassed. 'I've got a big triathlon at the weekend and I read somewhere that professional cyclists always have smooth legs – you know, less drag. So I was thinking that if I used one of those leg waxing kits ...'

Taffy gave the reddened skin a gleeful poke. 'And how many did you manage to get off before you panicked and came in here?'

'One,' admitted Jason rather pathetically. 'It *really* hurt!'

Dan took in the sorry sight and squashed the urge to slip out his camera, delighted to have a reprieve from his morning of pointing out that 90 per cent of sore throats go away on their own without antibiotics.

'Are you supposed to put them all on in one go?' he asked, intrigued.

'Dunno,' Jason shrugged sulkily. 'It was a spur of the moment kind of thing.'

Dan grabbed one corner of a wax strip and pulled. The strip snagged slightly, so Dan pulled harder, making Jason's eyes bulge. It clearly wasn't the right technique.

'Against the grain,' Jason groaned, 'I think you're supposed to pull against the grain.'

'Come on, let me have a go. It's not rocket science,' Taffy interrupted. He grabbed the other end of the strip, changing direction and pulled even harder. The wax strip came away, along with a forest of leg hair and what remained of Jason's dignity as he yowled like a little girl.

'Can't I have an injection or something? There's eight more to go! You could give me some lidocaine or something? Surely?'

'Nah – don't be a baby. The girls do this all the time. How bad can it be?' Taffy laughed.

'Yeah,' said Jason grumpily, rubbing the scarlet patch on his leg, 'but they also manage to have babies, which I gather is like pushing a watermelon through your nostril. They have to be wired differently, mate.'

Dan stepped in with the element of surprise as he ripped off the second strip and Jason swore loudly.

Moments later, a gentle knock at the door and Holly's voice from the hallway, 'Erm … Morning. Is everything okay in there?'

Jason looked at Dan and Taffy beseechingly, 'Don't let her in …'

Dan patted his leg. 'I think it's time we called in the experts now, Jase. And Holly's a good sort – she won't tell.' He got up and let Holly in with the warning, 'Not a word to anyone, okay?'

Holly shook her head and clapped her hand over her mouth, as she took in the view. Jason's leg was now erupting into angry weals where the two strips of wax had been removed and two very hairy caterpillars of wax were lying discarded on the treatment bed.

'Honestly, guys! How long have these strips been on?'

Jason checked his watch. 'About two hours now.' His voice got a little higher. 'The little fuckers just won't come off!'

Holly bent double at this, clutching at her sides as she tried and failed to stop laughing. 'But why?'

Jason tried to explain about his cycling race but Holly only shook her head. 'They shave them, Jase. With a razor.' She ran a hand gently over the reddened skin. 'We need to get these off.'

'I can't do it,' said Jason. 'I take one look and lose my

nerve. And look what a bloody mess Dan and Taffy have made of it.'

'I'm a doctor, Jason, not a sodding beautician,' remonstrated Taffy huffily.

'Okay then,' said Holly, grinning. 'It looks like it's my turn.' She rolled up her sleeves and cracked her knuckles, watching Jason flinch. 'Or, you know, you could just go home and sit in a hot bath until they fall right off?'

The three men looked at each other in sheer disbelief. 'A bath? That's all it takes?' managed Jason.

'That's all it takes,' she confirmed.

'But how did you ... ?'

'This is not my first time,' said Holly, attempting to waggle her eyebrows but giving in to the laughter instead.

Dan watched as Holly took pity on Jason and sponged down his legs with a warm flannel, easing the wax strips away.

'He says it's for a triathlon, but I reckon he's getting all spruced up for the Spring Swim,' Taffy said to Holly, holding out the bowl of warm water for another dip. 'You are coming, aren't you?'

Holly bit her lip as she eased off another wax strip with concentration. 'I don't know, maybe?'

'Sorry, Holly, but maybe's not good enough,' said Dan, distractedly opening up his files for the morning. 'I should have said, it's a three-line whip. Everyone on parade I'm afraid.'

Taffy swotted at him with the other damp flannel. 'Well, don't make it sound so tempting will you? Jesus!'

Dan looked sheepish. 'Sorry. Taff's right though, actually. We all go every year and it's brilliant.'

'Properly good fun,' interjected Jason, who was beginning to recover from his dented pride.

'Bring Milo and the kids and some hot chocolate – lots of towels. You can't go wrong. George is even Master of Ceremonies this year,' Dan said.

'Seriously though,' Taffy carried on, 'it's such a laugh. All the grannies and the little ones, all in together. It's my favourite Larkford event of the year.'

Jason sniggered, 'You mean compared to the fête, the Hallowe'en parade and the WI cake sale? It's hardly a riot a minute around here, is it?'

Taffy shook his head. 'Now you're just making me feel old. So be quiet and concentrate on your lovely smooth bits.'

Holly's smirk did not go un-noticed.

Dan gave her a nudge. 'Do come, Holly. If nothing else, it's really good for the partners to see you getting involved in the community.'

Holly nodded. 'I'll crank up the water wings and we'll be there.'

'You need water wings?' said Jason, slow on the uptake as ever.

Taffy cuffed him round the back of the head, prompting Jason to immediately try to rescue his 'do. 'For her kids, you wally.'

Jason shrugged, pouting a little about his ruffled hair. 'Well, I didn't know, did I? Some grown-ups can't swim.'

'And some have no common sense,' cut in Dan with a wry grin, 'but we gave you a job anyway. Now, if you've all quite finished turning my room into a beauty parlour, I've a delightful morning ahead of me . . .'

He stood up to shoo them out. 'Oh Taffs, looks like I've got one of yours on my list this morning, Karen Dobbs?'

Taffy let out a belly laugh. 'Well good luck with that then, mate. You're very welcome to work your magic there. I've all but given up. She's a heart-sink patient that one.'

Dan knew immediately what he meant. There were a handful of 'regulars' at The Practice that literally made your heart sink the minute they walked in the room. Often, they seemed to have spent far too long on WebMD and were only too quick to tell you if they felt their proposed course of treatment was too lenient, too aggressive, or flat out wrong.

'There's not a lot you can do to help that one, until she decides to help herself, to be honest,' said Taffy.

'We'll get out of your way and leave you to it,' said Holly, helping Jason to his feet. 'Have a fun morning,' she said with a grin as she walked out of the room, several pencils seemingly holding up her hairdo and tripping slightly as she went.

Dan turned to Taffy, smiling. 'For such a clumsy person, she does a remarkably good job of staying upright, don't you think?'

Taffy said nothing for a moment, just watching her go. 'For such a clumsy person, she does a remarkably good job at most things.' He wandered back to his office, thoughts clearly elsewhere. He didn't even crack a smile about the patient that came out of the loo with her skirt tucked in her knickers and that worried Dan most of all.

'So, Karen? What can I do for you this morning?' Dan asked moments later, as his patient attempted to settle herself into the chair in front him. Politely put, she was Rubenesque, but Dan had a feeling that the British Medical Council might be a bit blunter.

'Well, Dr Carter, my kinesiology lady says my candida levels are very high again. And I have been having a few issues down there, so I wanted your thoughts really.' Karen pulled a print-out from her vast patent handbag and Dan tried to keep an open expression on his face, even though as promised, his heart was sinking. 'This says that a one-off course of flucka ... floocka ...'

'Fluconazole?' suggested Dan slowly.

'Yes, that's right! Fancy you knowing that. Well, this fluconazole works wonders apparently.'

'Well, yes it does and it is very powerful medication too. Had you given any more thought to what you discussed with Dr Jones last time? Trying to lose some weight? Avoiding sugary foods, alcohol, yeast and mushrooms?'

Karen folded her rather pudgy hands in her lap and looked a bit put out. 'I know you doctors like to blame everything on my weight, Dr Carter. But not everything is down to that, you know. I have very heavy bones and a rather slow metabolism, as I mentioned before.'

Dan took a calming sip of his coffee, before realising it was stone cold and grimacing. He tapped his pen on the desk and scrolled down the screen to double check. Yes, he was right. Karen had been in roughly twenty times in the last year – often requesting a different doctor and seemingly always with some new ailment or malady and never with any intention of following the advice she'd been given.

'How have you been getting on with the walking programme? Has that helped with the swollen ankles at all? And you have been remembering to elevate them at night?'

Karen shifted in her seat. 'Well, obviously I do it when I can.'

'And how often would that be?'

'Once a week, maybe once a fortnight when I'm busy.'

The silence hung in the room and Dan scrolled back further and saw Taffy's own unique annotations. TEETH, he'd noted down, when Karen had come in about feeling tired. Again, obviously that had nothing to do with the extra six stones in weight she was lugging around everywhere she went. Tried Everything Else; Try Homeopathy. Dan sighed, making a mental note to thank Taffy later for foisting the alternative health brigade on him.

'Well,' said Dan diplomatically. 'I'd like you to really give the low-sugar diet another go and try and do a bit more walking and then we'll review in a month or so. You haven't any other symptoms to speak of, no itching or rashes?'

Karen shook her head, clearly disappointed not to have a little green piece of paper, after making the effort to come in to the doctor's. She stood up, with considerable effort, and headed for the door.

Dan's eyes flickered to the clock, noticing that he was one patient in and already running late if he wanted to accompany Lance and Hattie to their appointment in Bath.

'Oh there was just one other thing, Doctor,' Karen said, hovering by the chair and looking embarrassed. 'It's been terribly painful having sex recently and my Gary says he might have felt a lump. Do you think that's something I should be worried about?'

A small vein in Dan's forehead slowly pulsed and the calm expression on his face became a little more forced. Why did they always do this? Waste their appointed time talking about trivialities and save the big stuff for when their hands were on the doorknob. 'Sit down, Karen,' he said gently, deliberately turning away from the clock. 'Now, tell me all about it.'

Chapter 18

It only took Holly a moment to realise that two clichés she'd routinely discounted were actually bang on the money – you never did hear anything good about yourself by eavesdropping and blood really was thicker than water.

Holly shrank back against the wall outside Dan's office and tried to stop her thoughts spiralling. She'd only stopped by at the end of the day to give Dan some local stats about male cancers and some promising research taking place in the States, that might, just might help Lance. Only minutes before, she'd imagined another sleepless night looming, worrying about Lance and Hattie and their baby. Now, it seemed she would have something a little closer to home preoccupying her thoughts into the wee small hours.

Inside the office, Dan and Lizzie were locked in a heated argument, the edited highlights of which made Holly feel as though her chocolate muffin was about to make an encore appearance and eclipsed every other thought in her head.

'For fuck's sake, Lizzie! Just let it drop, will you. I can't magically snap my fingers and be kicking up my heels without a care in the world. I'm getting counselling. I'm being a good little patient. You can't just wish PTSD away, you know.'

'But Dan – come on – you have to get yourself in a better place than this. You're a wreck. Even if everyone else around here is too polite to comment, I'm not. You look like shit. You look distracted and edgy – not the most comforting look for a GP, I might add. You said you wanted Senior Partner more than anything. So, what happened to everything we talked about?' said Lizzie, her voice rising in frustration.

'Well you lied to me, didn't you?' he retorted.

'White lies, Dan. White lies. And nobody got hurt did they? I said I'd find you moral support and she's here. You said you needed to feel supported at work and I brought you Holly. People don't come more supportive than Holly. Jesus Christ, you could be a murderer on death row and she'd find a way to hold your hand while she looked for the silver lining!'

There was an extended pause and Holly had to fight every instinct in her body, which was flooding with adrenalin and strongly urging fight or flight. She felt completely unprepared and ill-equipped to cope with this. It was sheer strength of will that kept Holly rooted to the spot, trying to buy herself some thinking time. It wasn't so much the acerbic words pouring out of Lizzie's mouth that were so hurtful; it was the cutting tone of her voice that made Holly feel so used and abused. That, and the feeling of being completely blindsided by someone you counted as a friend – a best friend.

Obviously Dan too had registered the scornful dismissal as he leapt to Holly's defence. 'Would you listen to yourself there, Lizzie? This is your best friend that you're talking about. She's uprooted her entire family to move here. She's walked into a job that has fuck-all security – you know I couldn't tell her what was going on here. But you could. And damn it all, Lizzie, you promised you would!'

'Well if I had, she wouldn't have come, now, would she?' Lizzie shot back, a sullen vicious bite in her words that was normally reserved for the bottom of the third bottle of wine.

For all that Lizzie said, Holly was no clueless Pollyanna. She could see the flaws in her nearest and dearest with perfect clarity – when she chose to. But she also knew that she herself wasn't perfect and therefore made a conscious effort to cut everyone else some slack. She was only too aware that you never really knew what was going on behind closed doors.

Truth be told, moving to Larkford had given Holly more insight into the reality of Lizzie's world than she'd ever had before. Lizzie's constant quest for perfection on every level was enough to make Holly feel tired just thinking about it. Working for a glossy magazine was one thing, but Lizzie seemed determined, driven even, to live the dream.

Yes, Lizzie was beautiful, indulged and ambitious, but until now, Holly had never thought that made her a bad person. She questioned Lizzie's priorities sometimes – didn't all friends do that from time to time? – but she had never imagined such a chasm could develop between their moral viewpoints.

Her own moral compass was swinging indignantly at this point: her wounded feelings yelping for an explanation or an apology and in shock from the ambush; but her fairer voice of reason was quietly and insistently pointing out that the sheer volume of Lizzie's alcohol consumption of late, suggested all was not picture-perfect beneath the surface.

Holly tried not to think of herself as an enabler, but she was also well aware that confronting Lizzie about her drinking would have only one possible outcome. End of friendship. So she'd held her tongue and bided her time. She could see now that had been a mistake. But Lizzie simply didn't *do* criticism. More precisely, Lizzie couldn't *take* criticism – she was more than happy to dish it out, though.

Holly found herself straining to hear Dan's reply, forced out as it was through gritted teeth. 'You should have told her, Lizzie. You've put her and me in an impossible situation. George is off. Any idiot could tell you I'm not up to the job of running this place and then what? Did you think about what would happen to her for a minute?'

'Of course I did, but forgive me if I put my own cousin's needs first. You needed the new doctor to be on your side, yes? She is. You needed someone who'd fit right in, yes? She has. You needed someone pliable and people-pleasing and just a little bit needy? Ta da! I'd say you're welcome, but I can't help noticing that you've never once said thank you.'

'Thank you for what? For misleading and manipulating your best friend for me? For promising you'd tell her how the ground really lies here before she accepted the job and then not saying a word? Of course, I love that you were looking out for me, but I never, ever would have wanted you to do it at this price.'

Holly could hear Lizzie tapping her feet, as she always did when she was put on the spot. Perhaps, Holly wondered dispiritedly, the guilt was finally starting to kick in. Her own rage was now simmering on a slow heat, as she wrangled her emotions under control. She still felt poleaxed – almost as if this were a bad dream – but the bitter taste of betrayal, strangely metallic in her mouth, and the tiny crescents in her palms, where her nails had taken the butt of her restraint, were all too real.

'Look, I don't see what you're getting so het up about.

This is Holly we're talking about. I was doing her a favour. Milo was chasing skirt – again – and she was schlepping away all hours at the hospital. This is an improvement for her! Best friend on tap, great colleagues, fab place to live. Okay, so she screwed it all up by bringing twat face with her, but still ... Even with cheating husband in tow and no future job security, this *has* to be better than where she was before.' Lizzie was clearly making an effort to win Dan around, as she changed gears and layered reason and compassion into her next words. 'Surely you can see that, Dan? I really have done her a favour. And you honestly aren't thinking straight if you think coming clean up front would have been the best approach. My cousin needed my help. You, Dan, needed my help. What was I going to do?'

'Erm, had you considered honesty? You really can't see it, can you?' Dan said slowly, incredulously. 'You've lied to me. You've lied to Holly. You've manipulated both of us.'

Holly heard the screech of wood on polished flooring, as Dan pushed back his chair and stood up, but her mind was too distracted to translate. It was only when the door jerked open and they stood face to face, equally aghast, that Holly's brain kicked in.

'Evening, Dan,' she managed calmly. 'Evening, Lizzie. Isn't there something you wanted to tell me?'

There was an ugly pause as every person in the room wished they were somewhere else.

Dan looked especially mortified. 'Holly,' he began, 'I don't know what to say ...'

Holly took a shuddering breath. 'Then that makes two of us.'

She watched him struggle to find a way to express himself,

one hand firmly gripping the hair at the nape of his neck. So many half-heard conversations and snippets of information suddenly made so much more sense. Without the charisma and aura of professionalism, Dan simply looked like a broken man. It was hard to lay the blame entirely at his feet, when he clearly had so much else going on.

Holly even knew that there was an element of truth in Lizzie's hurtful words too. Moving to Larkford *had* been an improvement for her, a lifestyle choice. But was that really Lizzie's call to make?

Dan reached out and touched Holly's shoulder, breaking her train of thought and making her jump. 'Everything's up in the air right now, Holly, but I need you to know, I've got your back. Whoever makes Senior Partner, there's bound to be a reshuffle, but you have my support, for what it's worth.' He flashed Lizzie a look filled with anger and frustration. 'And that is what Lizzie was supposed to tell you. We only hand out short-term contracts to all new employees, just to check that we get the fit right. But it does rather leave you vulnerable, Holly.'

'So what happened to, it's a mere formality, rolling terms . . . All the spiel trotted out at the interview? Was all of it bullshit?' Holly demanded.

'It was the party line. George wasn't sure of his plans, we needed to stay flexible . . . But again, from my point of view, I stand by every word.' He managed an uncomfortable laugh. 'I just need to make sure I get the job.'

Holly looked at him, his right hand trembling and a sheen of sweat on his forehead. This conversation clearly wasn't doing him any good and she almost felt sorry for him. After all, with him looking such a train wreck, what were the chances he would beat suave, sophisticated Henry Bruce or the wildly ambitious Julia Channing – no matter how many fluffy bunny under-layers she seemed to be hiding?

'Dan. Go home,' said Holly gently. 'Have something to eat and go to bed. I'm not convinced this is really your battle. I'll lock up.'

Dan hesitated, looking from Lizzie to Holly as if evaluating whether it was safe to leave them alone together.

'I really am truly sorry, Holly.'

'I know,' she said quietly. 'Now go home.'

It was some indicator of his state of mind that he did so without question.

The minute the door closed behind him, Holly walked around and sat in his chair.

Lizzie hadn't moved, she was still sitting down with her feet propped up, a splayed open bag of Kettle Chips forming the basis of her impromptu get together with Dan. She didn't look in the least bit remorseful.

'So,' said Holly. 'I'm sure you've lots to tell me, so why don't we start with the truth?'

Lizzie rolled her eyes and Holly felt her pulse rate ratchet up another couple of notches. 'Oh don't be so melodramatic, Holly!' Lizzie leaned forward and pushed the Kettle Chips across the desk.

Holly felt like throwing them on the floor and grinding them into the carpet with her heel, the sour spasms of hurt only fanning the flames of her anger.

'You know, I'm not sure it actually *is* melodramatic to discover you've been used as a pawn in someone else's chess game. In fact, I think melodrama might be an under-reaction at this point – did you stop to think for a moment about me? The boys? Milo?'

Lizzie batted Holly's words away with her hand. 'Like you really care how this affects Milo? You were down here like a shot, whether he wanted to or not.'

Holly watched Lizzie talk as though she were a total stranger. All the pep talks about being the sole breadwinner and earning the right to choose were obviously part of Operation Gullible Fool.

'Did you want me here at all, Lizzie?' Holly asked quietly.

Lizzie rolled her eyes again and Holly wanted to shake her. 'Again with the drama – of course I wanted you here, you daft eejit. Would I have gone to all this trouble to find you a job if I didn't?'

'Is that all you've got to say? No apology? Nothing?'

Lizzie shrugged. 'You know I don't do apologies. Let's just put it behind us and move on. You know I'm right, Holls, you have to trust me on this one.' Lizzie leaned back further in her chair, her body language that of someone who knows victory is assured.

'But I don't,' Holly realised in that moment, 'I don't trust you. Not after this. And the worst thing is, that I've been replaying every conversation we've had since I got here and it's all lies.' Holly shook her head in disbelief. 'Big fat lies!'

'White lies,' Lizzie immediately cut in.

'Really?' Holly asked, her voice dripping with an overwhelming current of disdain. 'Was it a white lie when we had supper at your house and you feigned surprise that George was retiring? Was it a white lie when you pretended that Dan was "just a bit tired"? Or maybe when you encouraged me to sign a twelve-month tenancy on my house, for the "security"?'

'Oh Holly, where's the harm? You're here, I'm here, Dan's getting some help – although it's too little, too late in my opinion ... You know, he's really got to get his head in the game because Julia's TV thing is looking really lucrative and ...'

Holly was out of her seat and halfway to the door, before Lizzie finally gave up.

'Sit down and have a drink? Let's have a proper girl's night, yeah? I've got some gossip that will have you looking at your patients in a whole new light.'

Holly stopped, suddenly realising what she'd always chosen to ignore. Her friend was a gossip. Quite a malicious cruel gossip, by all accounts. It was something that was easy to ignore while bathed in the light of her friendship and patronage – but now Holly had experienced a small taste of life on the other side of Lizzie's sharp tongue.

'You may be my oldest friend, Lizzie, but you haven't been a very good one, have you? Startling lack of apology aside, along with your complete lack of awareness that you have done Anything Wrong.' Holly's voice had started so calmly, but was now rising to a crescendo. 'I'm not sure I actually like you very much. And from how you were talking about me just now, I'm not convinced that you like me very much either.'

Lizzie didn't say a word. So accustomed to having Holly fall into line, she had obviously assumed that today would be the same. 'You don't mean that,' she eventually said defiantly.

'You know,' said Holly, 'despite being – now what was it? – "pliable, people-pleasing and just a little bit needy", I do know my own mind. And right now, with friends like you, who needs enemies. I think you'd better leave, so I can lock up.'

*

As Holly went through the motions of bath and bedtime with the twins that evening, she struggled to hold herself together. She could try and talk to Milo about it, of course, but then she'd have to tell him the full story.

Besides, she didn't actually need to have the conversation to know what he'd say. He thought that Lizzie was a complete narcissist and always had done. The irony was not lost on Holly that Lizzie believed Milo guilty of exactly the same thing.

In this scenario, Milo would tell her to walk away. His scathing comments about Lizzie were often trotted out, particularly on those occasions when Holly needed reassurance after a sarcastic dig or unfeeling jibe made her feel fragile. He could just never understand why she always went back for more.

As she snuggled down under the Fireman Sam duvet cover to read *Going On A Bear Hunt* for the umpteenth time, Holly revelled in the warmth and security of that moment. Right now, these two boys felt like the only honest thing in her life.

Somehow, she realised, she had managed to populate her adult world with self-involved, self-admiring egotists. What on earth did that say about her own mental health? Was she really not worthy of the leading role in her own life story?

Even as she tucked the twins into bed, little trousers and t-shirts all laid out for an early start, her mind was running on, searching for a handle on the situation.

'One more day and then it's the weekend,' Holly murmured, looking down at their little sleeping bodies. Ben lay still, perfectly neat, his covers perfectly smooth.

Tom, on the other hand, was immediately spread out like a starfish – thumb in his mouth, the other hand down his pants. In his mid-blue pyjamas, and with that blissed out expression on his face, Holly knew that Lizzie would be making her habitual masturbating-smurf-joke about now. She sighed, wondering how to explain to the boys that 'Auntie' Lizzie might not be around to play for a bit.

Holly suddenly realised what that meant. In cases like this – who got custody of the dog?

She felt her eyes well up yet again and cursed herself for minding so much.

She really had done a number on herself – handing out the responsibility for her own happiness left, right and centre. Between Milo and Lizzie, Holly felt as though she'd surrendered her own vote.

She slid down against the wall and watched her boys sleep.

Tomorrow was another day, she decided.

To borrow the cliché for a moment – tomorrow was the first day of the rest of her life. It was time that she rediscovered what it felt like to take control, to live honestly and be true to herself. She was a doctor and a mother and a person in her own right.

If only she knew where to start.

Chapter 19

Dan limped to the end of his highly unsatisfactory run. It didn't seem to matter how hard he pushed himself that evening, running hadn't helped and he headed to the benches in the park to stretch out his legs as he always did. He was vaguely distracted for a moment by the sight of someone else looping through the parkland, skin-tight Lycra running gear highlighting every curve of her perfectly toned physique. He squinted into the distance as she powered effortlessly up the slopes to the running trail and gave him a flawless view of her pert derrière.

It certainly didn't help him calm his heart rate back down to normal levels.

Now, if he'd been Taffy Jones he realised, he'd have run a second lap of the trail, just to get her phone number. He even contemplated it for a moment, before giving in to the fact that he was exhausted, grumpy and frankly longing for this day to end. Maybe if he had a lovely girlfriend waiting for him at home, it might help him cope with everything, but he doubted it. The flashbacks were haunting him almost every night now, the possible consequences of George's announcement were weighing on his mind and now, to top it all off, he had the image of Holly's stricken face seared into his mind's eye.

Guilt was a vile emotion, he decided. He'd known Lizzie for a very long time, known how she operated. Lizzie's promises were solid and reliable, unless they happened to clash with her personal view of the situation. Then she could be surprisingly ruthless. Dan was busy kicking himself for not breaking the rules and telling Holly himself, but he also knew it had suited him to delegate. After all, what could he possibly have said? Holly, do please come and relocate your whole family to Larkford, but The Practice is set for a big upheaval and I can't promise how long you'll have a job for? If I get promoted, you'll be fine, but then I've got mental health issues and might not be up to the job. What do you think – start Monday?

Dan sighed heavily, the weight of responsibility tightening the muscles in his shoulders. Had he known, on some level, that Lizzie had her own agenda, he wondered. There were times when he'd certainly suspected she wasn't finding the whole motherhood thing as rewarding as she'd hoped, seemingly stunned on occasion by the mundanity of life with the under-5's. And Lizzie never had been one to do things by halves. Just because she was a mother now, it didn't make her less ambitious on the career front.

It was subtle, yet obvious once he started looking. Without any willingness to compromise, Lizzie's load was simply too great for one person to bear. Too proud to openly ask for help, Lizzie appeared to have chosen gin over counselling and her only agenda had been to get Holly on her doorstep. Holly, it seemed was to be the panacea for all Lizzie's issues.

If he was honest, Dan didn't quite get the dynamic of their friendship, but then what did he know? Perhaps it was hugely satisfying for Holly to have someone pointing out all her sartorial faults and taking the piss out of her husband, whilst simultaneously holding her hand and being sympathetic?

Maybe Lizzie derived enormous pleasure from seeing her competent friend struggle with the self-same parenting dilemmas, only with less style? Dan shook his head, he'd never understand women, he decided.

But he did know this. The Holly he'd met back in the day had been feisty and opinionated, dancing on tables and debating the issues 'til the wee small hours. It had been somewhat of a shock to meet her at the interview. Post-Milo-Holly was exactly as Lizzie had described – filtered – Holly Lite. As a doctor she was wonderful, as an ally she was perfect, but she would be no match for Classic Holly – almost as though she'd become a mere imitation, an edited version, of her former self.

Dan yanked roughly on his ankle, stretching his quads to screaming point, as the image of Holly's face flashed into his mind, shock and pain twisting her features. She'd trusted him. She'd trusted Lizzie. And now who would she turn to?

'Dr Carter? Dan?' Gentle pressure on his arm startled Dan from his reverie and he found himself looking down into intense green eyes that seemed somehow familiar. 'Are you okay?'

Even bouncing lightly in her runners, the girl only came up to his chest. She was like a china doll – her sleek black bob skimming her jawline and her luminous eyes huge in her pale face. It was a face worthy of Walt Disney.

'I'm fine,' Dan replied automatically, running through his mental Rolodex to try and place her. He felt pretty confident it was her backside he'd seen powering up the hillside earlier and that thought alone was enough to fluster him.

The girl smiled. 'Hang on, you might recognise me more like this . . .' She blew out her cheeks, puffed up her lips and rolled her eyes.

Dan couldn't help but laugh. 'Kingsley Arms. Peanuts one: Belinda Grey nil. Am I right?'

She seemed delighted that he remembered, colour high-lighting those perfect cheekbones. 'How was your run?'

'Not the best,' Dan admitted ruefully. 'Rather unsatisfying really. How are you feeling though, after your run-in with the dreaded legume?'

'Pretty good actually, all things considered. Thank God you and Dr Jones were there. I gather my friends all went to pieces and were spectacularly useless. Which is reassuring, obviously.'

Dan didn't like to burst her bubble that he'd rather gone to pieces too, but she seemed to be taking the whole thing in good humour so he let the moment pass. Doing his best to ignore the gentle hand on his arm that had yet to go away, Dan tried to keep things professional. 'There's a DVD at The Practice, I think. How to use an EpiPen. Why don't you borrow it and make your friends watch it. Just in case.'

'Good idea. And why don't you let me buy you a drink to say thank you for saving my life. It looks like your run's going nowhere tonight.'

Dan took in her open expression, the taut little body and the insistent pressure of her touch on his burning skin. He wished for a second that he was more like Taffy. Taffy wouldn't start having ethical debates with himself, he would simply say yes.

Belinda didn't miss a trick. 'If I promise not to put you in a compromising doctor/patient situation, can I buy you a drink?' Her eyes sparkled and danced and she was clearly teasing him.

They fell into step as they walked through the park, heading for the lights of The Kingsley Arms.

'Are you training for something or just keeping fit?' Belinda asked.

'I was wondering about doing the Bath Half Marathon, if we can manage the hills. I normally train with Taffy,' he explained. 'It's our sanity saver, actually.'

'I can imagine,' she empathised. 'I guess your job is pretty stressful sometimes.'

'Yup,' said Dan with feeling, wanting to change the subject instantly and wondering why he'd brought it up. 'Maybe you could give us some tips about training routes round here. We keep ending up at The Kingsley Arms.'

She grinned. 'Well it *is* very important to keep hydrated! But, joking aside, there's actually a Larkford Harriers meeting every Thursday if you guys want to come along. The more the merrier, but I will warn you that some of the team take it all quite seriously.'

'How seriously? Are we talking lycra onesies and Vaseline on the nipples?' he grinned.

'Worse,' she whispered, looking from side to side conspiratorially. 'Some of them are . . . tri-athletes.'

Dan snorted with laughter. The fad for triathlons had swept through the county over the last few years, as the latest marker for a blooming mid-life crisis. All the podgy dads in the town had become quite competitive about getting into shape, obsessively measuring start times, heart rates and protein intake, only to end up at The Practice, with shin splints, sprains and slipped discs. It hadn't stopped them training and trying to recapture their lost youth, but they were certainly

more regular visitors at The Practice than they always used
to be.

'Not sure Taffy and I are quite committed enough to the
cause, Belinda.'

'Lindy, please.'

'And what do you do, Lindy, when you're not running
or tackling illicit peanuts, if that's not too much of a clichéd
question?'

'I'm a teacher.'

Dan gave her a quizzical look. 'You're a teacher? You don't
look old enough to be a teacher.'

Lindy laughed. 'I'll take that as a compliment. I think. But
yes, I *am* a teacher. I'm actually Deputy Head of the Sixth
Form unit in town. So, not just fluffy bunny songs either.'
She said this with the slightly tired inflection of someone
who had gone through this subject a million times before.
Just because she looked petite, young and approachable didn't
automatically make her a Kindergarten teacher.

'What do you teach, then? Geography? History? English?'

'Biology and Chemistry actually. Well, and Biochemistry
too.'

Dan looked impressed despite himself. And then a little
embarrassed as he realised what a Neanderthal that probably made him look in Lindy's eyes. You girl teach science?
Og . . .

Lindy just raised one of those perfectly shaped eyebrows
again and didn't say a word.

By the time they reached the pub, they were chatting easily
and Dan was trying to remember why he'd thought this was
a bad idea. Maybe it was time he stopped smarting over the
whole Julia Channing fiasco and got himself back in the

game. They went straight for the bar to find Taffy in deep conversation with the Major about his bunions. 'Save me . . .' mouthed Taffy whilst the Major attempted to do up his shoelaces again.

As they tactfully rescued Taffy, Dan watched Lindy with a smile. Pretty, confident, clever – certainly more socially adept than himself. Dan could feel Lindy's charms working their magic on his fragile mood.

They ordered some drinks and propped up the bar. 'Taffs, Lindy has very kindly invited us to join the Larkford Harriers for our training.'

'The Harriers?' Taffy queried, pulling a face. 'I thought they were all a bunch of . . . well, I believe tri-athletes is the socially acceptable term?'

Lindy's throaty laugh had both men's attention. 'Not all of us. There's a few marathon runners and time-wasters for good measure.'

'And which are you?' Dan asked with interest.

'Well, I like to think of myself as a time-waster, but I just can't deny it. I love to run. Marathons preferably, but I'm just as happy on Claverton Down with a good soundtrack.' She took a delicate sip of her drink and tried to conceal a smile. 'So tell me then, Half Marathon Boys. How's the training really going?'

Taffy just laughed and ordered another pint leaving Dan to formulate a sensible reply. 'Well, to be honest, it's not really. Bit hit and miss, you know? But we're both pretty fit, so I don't suppose it'll take too long to get in shape. We've got months.'

Lindy shook her head. 'Typical bloke. Have you been to Bath lately? All the hills? You'll be lucky to even finish without a decent training programme.' They appeared to

have hit upon Lindy's pet topic of conversation. She listed
out the most common injuries caused by lack of preparation
and was about to start demonstrating a few stretches when
Dan stopped her.

'We'll be fine and even if we do injure ourselves, at least
we know the right people,' he said, aiming for gentle humour
and falling wide of the mark.

She flushed, embarrassed by what she clearly took to be a
snub. 'I was only offering to help.'

Dan watched a whisper of colour warm her cheeks and
he had to resist the urge to pull her towards him. He was
suddenly desperate to know whether the wafts of orange and
jasmine that were tormenting him came from the nape of her
neck, where her neat little bob signposted the pale, delicate
skin he was longing to kiss.

'I'd actually like that very much,' he said huskily, stopping
to clear his throat and cursing himself for sounding like one
of the adolescents in her school.

Lindy bounced back with such speed that Dan was in
danger of losing track of the conversation altogether. Before
he knew it, Taffy had melted into the crowd and Lindy was
draining her glass. 'Shall we go somewhere quieter?'

'Erm . . . Great,' he managed, feeling as if he'd just finished
a loop on a rollercoaster and wondering if his day could get
any more confusing. This wasn't his usual territory. When it
came to meeting girls, Dan was a slow burner. This was all
feeling very fast, very Taffy and very much as though Lindy
was the one in the driving seat.

The silence was loaded and Dan rose to his feet, enjoying
the fact that he towered over Lindy and could scoop her to
him in one arm if he chose. She'd angled her head to look
up at him and her hair fell back, releasing another waft of

summery perfume. Her eyes were wide and her lips had a slight sheen that beckoned him down.

They barely made it to Dan's Land Rover in The Practice car park, before Lindy's fingers were entwined with his, petite and pale against the broadness of his own. It was a wonder they even got inside. Dan didn't even have chance to ask the age-old 'your place or mine,' before her hands were in his hair and her lips were on his, urgently seeking a response. She shifted in her seat and let the seatbelt pull back as she slid along the bench, one leg hooking easily over his thigh.

Dan pulled her to him and groaned as she kissed the side of his neck and the silky curtain of her hair brushed against his face, with its erotic jasmine scent, and one of her hands ran over his chest. 'Jesus,' he managed, thanking God that the car park was in pitch blackness.

She slid her thigh against his, rising slightly against the seat until they were locked together. He fumbled with his seatbelt, desperate to turn towards her and lifted her easily, with his big hands around her tiny waist. All thoughts were driven from his mind as she settled down against him with a sigh, as if the feeling of his desire against her was what she'd been searching for. Her hips moved gently, driving Dan past any thoughts of modesty and he found a way under the layers of Lycra until his hand brushed against the taut lace of her bra and the hard pressure of her nipples. She broke away from the kiss then and whimpered slightly in her throat as he dropped his head and pulled her breast into his mouth, fabric and all. His hot breath made her cry out, the attentions of his tongue through the layers of lace and fabric giving an extra frisson of desire.

'Take me home,' she breathed.

Dan stopped abruptly. 'Okay. Sure. I mean if that's what you want. I was thinking maybe dinner, but . . .'

Lindy nibbled very gently at his bottom lip and pressed her hips against him insistently. 'Your home,' she whispered. 'Your bed. Let's start with dessert.'

Dan took her face in his hands and his smile spoke volumes, as did the sudden leap of his erection against her. 'Are you sure?' he asked, hoping for a yes, but wanting to be sure. This wasn't exactly how he'd envisaged his first date in months, but it sure beat anything his own imagination had come up with.

She slithered around until she was sitting next to him, her wanton expression filling her eyes with light and her lips wide and full. She slid one hand up under his shorts. 'Just drive.'

It was a wonder that they reached Dan's cottage in one piece and they certainly didn't waste any time on drinks or conversation when they got there. Dan kicked the front door closed and followed Lindy through to the kitchen. She kicked off her trainers and with both hands on the edge of the kitchen table, she lifted herself onto the surface. She slipped out of her shorts in one swift movement and Dan thought he may actually have a heart attack. A glimpse of her soft creamy skin had him stripping off his shirt without a second thought. Lindy ran her hand over the firm outline of his stomach, tracing the smattering of hairs heading under his waistband.

'I thought you said you hadn't been training?' she murmured. Dan pulled her top over her head in one, her hair falling neatly back into its bob and revealing a tiny lace bra, cupping her delicate breasts. He sucked on her again, pushing the lace aside with his tongue and pulling her body against him.

'My God, I want you,' he groaned, hooking his fingers through the wisp of lace that stood between him and being inside her. Her hands now cradled him and his clothes were thrown aside. She deliberately, slowly, sucked on her thumb and made small circles around the tip of him, spreading his desire with her gentle persistence. He pulled away suddenly, unable to keep himself under control if she carried on this sublime teasing.

He dropped to his knees and pulled her to him, his hands grasping her hips until she was writhing in helpless anticipation. Her voice became breathless and she begged him to take her. Barely taking a moment to remember a condom, her hands guided him into her and they toppled back against the kitchen table. Her legs wrapped around him and pressed him in deeper until Dan could barely restrain himself. Only as she began to cry out did he let himself go and their two bodies worked together until they were blinded by lust and the waves of satisfaction that broke over them.

After a quick shower, which inevitably turned into Round Two, and a long glass of water, Dan leaned against the sink to catch his breath. Who knew? He would certainly never have foreseen the way this evening was going to pan out. Maybe Taffy had been right all along – what he needed was distraction. But even with Lindy wrapped around him in the shower, he'd struggled to stay in the moment, his treacherous thoughts constantly veering off into dangerous territory.

But then maybe, he thought, there were lots of ways that having someone new and all-consuming in his life could remedy even that? He looked at his watch and couldn't believe it was only half past nine. Maybe they could cook up some pasta, watch a movie?

He was already wondering what they might be able to do together at the weekend, as he padded back into the bedroom and found Lindy perched on the edge of the bed fully dressed in her running kit and shoes.

Dan raised an eyebrow. 'In need of more exercise? Let me find you a shirt or something?'

She bit her bottom lip and shrugged. 'Well, to be honest, I thought I'd kind of . . . you know . . .' She waved one hand around and looked a bit uncomfortable. 'I didn't want to leave without saying goodbye.'

Dan felt completely wrong-footed and his confusion must have been obvious.

'Shit,' said Lindy. 'You were thinking more . . .'

'More something, yeah. Like supper, or a movie, or a conversation . . .' Dan could feel himself getting defensive.

She shrugged again. 'Hey, Dan, it was great hooking up and maybe we can . . . you know . . . another time. Friend me on Facebook if you want. But I thought we were both on the same page here?'

'Sure,' he replied, wondering what the hell page that might be. He half expected a brief handshake might follow. 'Course, yeah . . . I was only saying that if you wanted some food or . . .'

'I'm good. Thanks.' Lindy slipped away, stopping briefly to kiss him on the cheek and Dan heard the front door slam moments later.

Okay, he thought, so this much is clear. I'm officially off my game. Dating has *really* changed. And I haven't a freaking clue what to do now.

Suddenly Taffy's recent obsession with Holly Graham made a lot more sense. In a world of 'hooking up' and the nausea-inducing rejection that ultimately involved, Dan could see why someone who embodied the concept of Something Real would be undeniably attractive.

He poured himself a bowl of cereal, suddenly ravenous. He couldn't deny the sex had been great. But – and he would never admit this to anyone – he felt a bit hollow. He actually quite liked the kind of sex where you woke up together the next morning. Where, if at all possible, you could remember their surname. And, if wishes were on offer, that he hadn't just had a one-night stand with one of his patients.

'Get a grip, Carter,' he admonished himself as he reached for a spoon and the TV remote.

Chapter 20

'Shit, fuck, wank, bugger, bugger, bugger ...' muttered Holly under her breath, the next evening, a whole day of being virtuous and clean-living having taken its toll. It wasn't natural to go all day without swearing, she decided, not when your day had included quite so many orifice-related incidents! Her world seemed to consist of bodily fluids and biscuits these days – although thankfully not yet at the same time.

Besides, she remembered reading somewhere that having a mantra to turn to in times of stress was positively beneficial. If pushed, she would probably admit that this Tourette's-style outburst wasn't exactly what the guru had in mind, but she did actually feel a little bit chirpier.

In her quest to remain calm, she'd spent most of the day avoiding people: Dan and his constant apologies in particular. She was still feeling blind-sided and bruised, and no amount of positive vibes were going to change that. Even her belief in karma was feeling dangerously shaky right now.

Maybe she was coming at this from the wrong angle after all? A moment's indecision nibbled at the back of her mind. Maybe Lizzie was actually the one who had the right approach?

Perhaps she should take up smoking, have a gin and a quick shag – preferably not with her husband – trample over everyone else's feelings and end the day with a bang? There was only so much virtuousness that one person could stomach and Holly had to admit she was reaching her critical limit. Any day now, she'd be oohing and aahing over floral aprons and offering to 'whip up a soufflé'!

She picked up her mobile to phone Lizzie, a plan on the tip of her tongue, before realising yet again that it wasn't an option any more. In all likelihood, she would only suffer the straight-to-voicemail, two-rings fate and end up feeling worse than ever.

She paused for a moment, vaguely weighing up the professional advisability of what suddenly seemed like a brilliant idea. 'Elsie? It's Holly Graham. I know this sounds a bit mad, but I need your advice. I'm in need of distraction.'

Elsie's throaty laugh could be heard echoing down the phone as Holly launched recklessly into her new theory, knowing that Elsie would almost certainly understand. 'You see, all the things I used to do when I wanted to let off steam, well, I can't do them any more. I need a new sin! The spontaneous weekend away, the shopping spree, the stay-up-all-night-drinking-Martinis, the fling, the flung, the fags, the dancing … All vetoed by two small people in stripy pyjamas and a bank balance that's lurching into the red as we speak. So I was wondering … help me out? I need to find a new vice to help me let off steam and I can't help thinking you might have all the answers …'

Half an hour later, two said small people in stripy pyjamas were tucked up on Elsie's sofa watching Bob the Builder and Holly was in Elsie's kitchen. 'You are sweet to invite us over, but it wasn't until I was knocking on your front door that it occurred to me, you might just have been being polite.'

Elsie raised her perfectly arched eyebrows. 'Holly, my darling, you should know by now, I'm too old to be polite. If I don't want to do something, I'm perfectly capable of saying so. In fact, it occurs to me that you girls these days all have the same problem. You spend half your lives doing stuff you don't want to do, simply because you feel that you should. So, there's your first notion – ban the word "should" from your vocabulary. Erase it. Ex-punge it,' she said with relish, dragging out the syllables. 'Obliterate it.' She took a long swig of her habitual Campari and soda.

She deftly mixed up a fresh round, passing Holly a drink that closely resembled something AB negative. Taking a tentative sip, Holly blinked hard. 'Jesus, Elsie! That's quite strong, you know.'

'I know,' said Elsie wickedly. 'Isn't it divine? Get a few of those inside you and you'll feel so much better.'

Elsie pushed a bowl of salted almonds across the table, which had clearly been repeatedly trotted out since the late 1990s. Obviously, in Elsie's world, nibbles were just for show.

Holly struggled to get past the bitter taste in her mouth and the burn in her throat. This concoction may be perfect for loosening inhibitions, but it tasted more like something from a chemistry lab. She swallowed gamely and blinked the tears from her eyes.

'Hmm,' said Elsie critically, watching her. 'Just how much of that are you going to drink out of politeness, before telling me you don't like it?'

'No, not at all. It's fine. A little unusual perhaps . . .'

'Dear God, Holly Graham, it's worse than I thought: have an opinion! Make a decision that doesn't involve tiptoeing around other people's feelings.' Elsie stood upright, her trim little feet planted in second position and her hands on her hips – even at shoulder height, she was formidable. There was a pause as Holly tried and failed to articulate a response.

Elsie's eyes sparkled with renewed energy at the prospect of a challenge. 'I dare you,' she said wickedly.

Holly slowly put down her glass, coolly placing it on the coaster. 'Okay then ... well then ... to be honest ... that's to say ...'

Elsie hooted with laughter. 'I'm not getting any younger over here, you know. Spill it, say it, be offensive, be brutal! Tell me what you *really* think.'

'It's vile,' said Holly quickly, as if she couldn't get the words out fast enough. 'Awful, hideous – the worst thing I've put in my mouth for a very long time. I don't know how you can bear to drink it. It tastes like de-icer.' She stopped as suddenly as she'd started, cheeks pink and a little out of breath. She looked, and felt, a little shocked at herself.

Elsie's face slowly crumpled sadly until a lone tear wove its way through the perfect mask of make-up. 'That cocktail was my father's recipe,' she gulped, shoulders heaving. 'I can't believe you just said that!'

Holly felt the bile of remorse surging into her throat and she rushed forward to take Elsie's hands. 'Oh my God, I'm so sorry. I don't know what I was thinking and you've been so kind to me and ...'

Holly's thoughts were waging war in her head, confused about what had just taken place. Hadn't Elsie dared her to be brutal and offensive only moments before? Hang on a minute. 'Elsie?' she said sternly, as if talking to a recalcitrant toddler. 'This hideous cocktail wasn't your father recipe at all, was it?'

Elsie looked up, her eyes still glistening but a broad smile on her face. 'Nope,' said Elsie. 'You can't trust me, I'm an actress, remember? The look on your face was absolutely priceless though. No courage in your convictions at all. But back to the lesson in hand: admit it – didn't it feel good to just let it all out? To say something for once that wasn't edited in your head?'

Holly nodded slowly, the adrenalin still pumping through her veins.

'So then, let's play a little game. Just say the first word that pops into your head, okay? No thinking. Or over-thinking. Toast?'

'Butter.'

'Elsie?'

'Trouble,' said Holly with a sideways glance and a smile.

'Larkford?'

'Home.'

'Ooh interesting. What about . . . Dan Carter?'

'Struggling.'

'No secret there,' said Elsie blithely. 'Milo?'

'Controlling.'

'Well, this is more illuminating than I had even hoped.'

'For me too,' murmured Holly under her breath.

'Lizzie?'

'Opinionated. No, that's not fair, I'm going to say . . . strong. No, selfish. Or driven, maybe?'

Elsie didn't comment, just raised an eyebrow, which some-how flustered Holly even more. She wasn't used to allowing uncensored thoughts out of her mouth.

'Taffy Jones?'

There was a long pause as words fought with each other for their freedom. Kind? Sweet? Funny? Gorgeous?

'Thoughtful,' she said eventually. Even though Holly could feel Elsie's eyes on her, she gave her head a little shake like an Etch a Sketch, willing the images to disappear just as easily.

'Well, that's all been very jolly. I think it's time we found out what you *really* like though, don't you, Holly?'

Elsie lined up a selection of drinks on the kitchen counter, each reflected in the polished granite to look somewhat Dali-esque. Holly found herself wanting to take a photograph, as the Martini glasses, wine glasses and shot tumblers all looked down at their own inverted doppelganger.

'So,' began Elsie, 'when you go to the pub, what do you drink?'

'Erm, wine?' ventured Holly. 'G&T, if I'm with Lizzie.'

Elsie gave her a hard look. 'Let me rephrase that, if you went to the pub, what would you *like* to drink?'

Holly looked at all the beautiful elegant drinks lined up in front of her. 'I used to like Martinis, but then it all got so complicated. With onions and olives and vodka and gin . . . I gave up, to be honest.'

Elsie nodded sagely. 'Good instincts there. Martinis used to be something special, didn't they? I blame James Bond. And Essex. Once they're ordering something in All Bar One in Chigwell, you know it's time to move on.' Elsie sighed. 'We seem to lose many a good cocktail to the hoi-polloi. The Cosmopolitan – now there was a drink to fall in love with. Ruined. And I do so miss a Caipirinha. There's nothing on earth like a proper Caipirinha on Ipanema beach at sunset . . .' She sighed wistfully and seemed a thousand miles away for a moment, possibly walking on Ipanema beach.

As Elsie disappeared off down memory lane, Holly looked at all the drinks before her. She sincerely hoped that Elsie wasn't expecting her to drink all of them, not with the boys on the sofa next door. She started taking tiny sips and arranging them into groups. Love. Like. Hate.

It was much, much easier than she had imagined. Her taste buds weren't clued in on Holly's quest to be acceptable. They really didn't give a stuff what anyone else thought. As she sipped at some ruby fruit concoction, Holly got an attack of the giggles.

Elsie tuned back in, delighted to see Holly making progress. 'What's so funny?'

Holly squared her shoulders and looked Elsie in the eye. 'I've just remembered. My name's Holly Graham ... and I like Vimto!'

'Bloody hell,' said Elsie quietly, with a twinkle, 'what have I done?'

There was no stopping Holly now. 'I like cider 'n' black or ginger ale when it's hot. I like whisky macs when it's cold. And I don't actually like gin and tonic or wine.' Holly clapped a hand over her mouth, as if she'd said something sacrilegious.

'They give me a headache,' She qualified apologetically.

Elsie pulled her into a surprisingly strong hug for one so delicate and petite, letting out a filthy laugh that wouldn't have been out of place in a working men's club.

'You see!' Elsie cried. 'I know it's baby steps, but you *do* have an opinion. You've just been, I don't know, trying to slide by in the shadows. What else?' she asked eagerly.

'I hate roast lamb,' said Holly without missing a beat. 'We have it every Sunday and I hate the way it tastes all fatty. I like getting up early and going to bed before the ten o'clock news and everybody else seems to like it the other way around. I loathe the fact that I can't parallel park – it makes me feel stupid and clumsy – but asking for lessons makes me feel worse. I can't bear documentaries – I don't care how fabulous the animal photography. I want to watch smart, clever, sophisticated drama – where I can't work out the plot before my cup of tea has gone cold. And I quite like my hair when it's curly, even though it's a bit frizzy and not very fashionable.' Holly's voice petered out as her consciousness caught up with her thoughts. 'In fact, I can't bear to waste another moment of my life holding hair straighteners and pretending that it doesn't smell like a blacksmith's yard.'

Holly turned to look at Elsie, whose hands were clasped together in excitement and pride.

'What do I do now?' Holly asked quietly.

Elsie smiled at her gently and gave a little shrug. 'You carry on, my darling girl. Every time you make a decision. I'm sure there's some psychobabble mumbo-jumbo book you can read, but I call it Personal Honesty and that was the only thing I took away from marriage number two. Be honest with yourself about what you really like and your motivations for choosing something you don't.

'Honestly, Holly, you wouldn't worry half as much about what other people think of you, if you realised how rarely they actually do.

'And now that all those nasty little *shoulds* are dead to you, you can really start thinking about what you really *want* to do. What you actually – if you stop and think about it – can't go another moment without doing.

'Find your passion, your drive, your bliss . . .' Elsie was on a roll, her arms flailing artistically, until she suddenly stopped and clasped Holly's hand. 'Better yet, think of it this way: how can you possibly ask for what you want, if you don't even know what it is yet!'

*

Half an hour later, having established that the twins were fast asleep on the sofa and with a cup of Earl Grey in her hand, Holly walked through to the kitchen to find Elsie tipping the remains of the cocktails over a sickly looking jasmine plant and stacking the dirty glasses in the refrigerator.

'Let me,' she said, pulling out a chair for Elsie and putting on the kettle. She logged away to check all Elsie's other appliances for stray crockery on her next visit and poured out another cup of tea, before perching at Elsie's kitchen counter, still trying to digest the earlier life lesson. Even just chatting casually here, Holly couldn't quite believe how often the word 'should' tripped off her tongue, how often she threw in a 'but' or made excuses for the people in her world.

By the time they were halfway down the chocolate digestives and the tea was cold in its pot, Elsie was trying to make Holly understand that her friendship with Lizzie wasn't broken, just a little fractured under the strain of being twisted so much in one direction.

'But, but, but, my arse,' declared Elsie eventually. 'Don't look so shocked. Lizzie is Lizzie and for now, she's sitting this round out and we're talking about you. You. What do *you* get from the friendship? Is she fun, supportive, kind?'

'She's all those things,' said Holly slowly, 'but she can also be a little controlling and maybe even a bit cruel sometimes. Like the other day, I'd spent hours getting ready and when I got there, she made all these comments about how I looked, what I was wearing and, you know, trying to be helpful, starting giving me tips on how to make a bit more effort. So I just let her go on. I couldn't bear to admit that I *had* made an effort. That was how I look when I've made an effort! And I liked how I looked. Well, I did when I left home anyway . . .'

'Why do you give her that power then, Holly? She can't make you feel inferior if you don't give her your consent. Why not say shut up? Bite me? Sod off?'

Holly laughed at the incongruity of the blaspheming coming from such an elegant, iconic senior citizen. 'I know, I know. It was just – easier?'

'In the short term, maybe,' said Elsie insightfully, 'but then the slights just keep on building until there's a blow-out.'

'Like last week? With the wine?'

'Indeed. Did you mean what you said to her?'

'That she drinks too much? Well, yeah. She's like a bloody fish. When she's happy, when she's sad, when she's tired, when she's not. Hey, it's Wednesday, let's open some wine! It was like the elephant in the room that nobody dared mention.'

'Or the goldfish,' quipped Elsie, 'the koi carp, if you will. But had you stopped to consider that it's her right to do that. And not forgetting that you don't actually like wine. Now, be honest, if she'd been drinking some vile Vimto and vodka concoction, would you have joined in a little more?'

'Not at four o'clock with a houseful of toddlers, no!' Holly paused for a moment, to access the new honesty she'd found. 'Okay, well maybe one, but no more until the children were in bed . . .' she admitted reluctantly.

'So, now we're finding our limits. Everyone has them – a different place they're prepared to draw the line. And Lizzie's life is all about Lizzie. I don't know her very well, but she doesn't strike me as the kind of person to put other people first. If she's helping you out, there's probably a hidden agenda,' said Elsie shrewdly. 'I dare say the same applies to your friendship. Maybe it's time to think about what *you* get out of the relationship?'

Holly was stumped for a moment, but Elsie carried on regardless, clearly adoring having a captive and attentive audience. 'Stop thinking about Lizzie, or Milo, or those adorable little rug-rats currently drooling on my chinoiserie. Think about you for a moment. You said you wanted to find a new sin. Well then, tell me, what do *you* want?'

'To be happy?' offered Holly apologetically after an extended pause.

'Hmmm. Too vague. And why the question in your voice? It's answers we're looking for. Goodness me, Holly Graham. Get some bloody gumption. If you could do anything, right now – no kids, no husband, no morning surgery – what would you do?' Elsie challenged her.

Holly sat there, slightly tipsy and completely dumb-founded, 'I honestly don't know,' she confessed. She could feel tears crowding into her throat, forcing her to swallow. She felt completely blind-sided, as if she'd suddenly put on glasses with the correct prescription. 'That's awful. I mean, how can I possibly . . . Oh, that's bad, isn't it? I should know what would make me happy.'

'Should?' queried Elsie with a sigh. 'Really?'

Holly shook her head, not even hearing Elsie's rebuke. 'How can I possibly ask for what I want, when I don't even know what it is,' she repeated Elsie's earlier statement as if it were the new Holy Grail and she was seeing clearly for the very first time. 'Shit,' she said succinctly and with feeling after a moment, before the nervous laughter bubbled into her voice. 'I'm trying to work out if that's lame or merely pathetic.'

'I'd say it's a little of both, sweetheart,' said Elsie with a smile, reaching out to take Holly's hand in her own. 'But it's also what you might want to call, a *start*.'

Chapter 21

Holly had begun to question her sanity as she'd pushed open the bathroom window earlier that morning and the cold air had rushed in. It was all very well agreeing to these things in theory, but she suspected that Larkford's Annual Wild Swim might prove to be a little more challenging in practice. She'd lost count of the number of patients and colleagues who had invited her and her family to join in and Grace had been very clear that, in terms of local camaraderie, the wild swim was definitely A Big Deal.

Talking to Elsie last night had therefore sealed the proverbial deal. Holly wanted to do this; she wanted the twins to do this – and just because Milo was dead set against it, shouldn't really make any difference. In the same way that she secretly let the boys climb trees, even though Milo had decreed otherwise.

She'd surveyed herself critically in the long mirror, tugging down her swimsuit to cover her bottom. Her trusty old Speedo was fine for ploughing up and down the pool at the local leisure centre, but it was hardly the ideal apparel for socialising with the entire community.

Holly had tentatively floated the notion of a wetsuit to Grace, but the feedback had been clear – wetsuits were only for the very young, the very old and the medically questionable.

Now, an hour later and shivering on the river bank, she watched the twins run around excitedly in theirs and tried not to feel envious. They shrieked happily in their little surf shoes and splashed at the edge while Holly kept them under close surveillance whilst attempting to blow up all four of their water-wings. 'Bloody, buggery things,' she muttered under her breath as they refused to inflate fully.

A voice at her shoulder made her jump and all the air came whistling out again. 'You're bright and early, Holly. Ready for a little pagan ritual?'

Holly, flushed and breathless from her exertions with the water wings, turned to find Taffy Jones beside her, a well-worn rugby shirt pulled on over his long baggy swim shorts. She huddled deeper into her padded coat. 'Pagan what now?'

'Well, technically it's the first day of Spring today, isn't it? That's what we're celebrating. Although, it crossed my mind that Mother Nature is having a cheeky laugh at our expense – the thermometer in my car says it's only eleven degrees. Bit brisk for my taste.'

Holly automatically righted Tom on his feet as he began to slip on the wet grass. 'Can't help being a bit jealous of the kids' wetsuits to be honest.'

'Well, at least you're not wearing one,' Taffy replied. 'Definite faux pas around here. You'll be getting loads of Brownie points anyway, just for turning up with the twins – they like newcomers who embrace the old traditions – even the bonkers ones.'

'Speaking of bonkers, no Reginald and Ludo this morning?' Holly grinned.

'Ooh no, we have to save those guys for very special

occasions or they lose their magic,' he replied seriously. 'No Milo this morning either?' Taffy's tone was casual, but he seemed inordinately interested in the answer.

Holly was at a loss for a reply for a moment. She really didn't want to let on about Milo's reaction to the invitation. He'd been rude and disrespectful about the locals, their loopy customs and what he called 'Holly's desperate need to be liked and fit in'. Privately, Holly thought that his extreme overreaction probably had more to do with Milo's aversion to all things 'nature' and his weakness as a swimmer, but he'd certainly lost no opportunity to undermine her confidence in the venture. He'd made it clear that if the twins were ill afterwards, it was her own lookout and his parting shot about her swimsuit this morning had left her feeling like a target for a Green Peace rescue mission.

Taffy didn't seem to miss a trick as he took in the emotions flitting across her face. Instead of waiting for her to reply and further incriminate her husband's character, he simply took the limp armband from her grasp and inflated it with one slow steady puff. As he crouched down beside her, he called out to the boys, 'Okay then, who wants to play hovercrafts?'

Soon they were both busy kitting out the boys and the awkwardness passed. Grace and Lucy ambled over to join them, Grace bearing a huge picnic basket and armfuls of towels. George Kingsley was wandering around with his beloved Nikon and snapped a few joyfully huddled photos, pre-swim and shivering on the river bank, their faces glowing with expectation and excitement.

'I'm a bit nervous actually,' Holly confided to Grace. 'So, since you've talked me into this pagan madness, can you fill me in on the plan?'

Grace beamed. 'I'm so pleased you came. I know it

probably doesn't seem like much to you, but to us ... Did
you know that this is the 65th Annual Spring Swim at the
river club? I guess we all feel privileged to still have a river
swimming club here – not many places do any more, you
know. We were one of the first and we're one of the last.
There's an amazing photo on the wall of The Kingsley Arms
of everyone here about forty years ago, with all the ladies
in their flowery swim hats. It's rather special actually.' She
squeezed Holly's sleeve happily. 'Shall we get over to the start
and we can hear the speeches?'

Making sure she had both squirming little boys clasped
tightly on each hip, Holly followed the group to the slop-
ing part of the river bank, where a small dais had been
erected. George Kingsley put down his camera and picked
up the loudhailer. 'Well, good morning to you all. It's
such a treat to see so many of you here – young and old.
It's the first day of Spring!' Some wag in the crowd let rip
with a huge Woo-Hoo and everyone fell about laughing.
There was such a feeling of bonhomie and anticipation
buzzing through the crowd, that Holly didn't miss a beat
when Taffy scooped one of the boys out of her arms and
lifted him effortlessly onto his shoulders for a better view.
George's welcome speech reminded them all of the history
of the Swim and how traditions like this kept communities
alive. He urged them to take part in the raffle that had
quickly been hustled together – a way of raising some funds
for Hattie and Lance while he underwent treatment. Holly
felt quite choked up actually, as she realised that she was
truly a part of this rather special event, rather than simply a
bystander. A place in this wonderful community was hers
for the asking.

'So then, ladies and gents, when you're ready, Spring has

sprung!' George blew sharply on a whistle and the hardier swimmers amongst them waded straight into the chilly water without hesitation. Holly was about to plop Tom down on the ground so she could take off her coat, when it hit her. It was Ben who was perched up on Taffy's shoulders. Ben who was cheering and shrieking in excitement whilst holding on to Taffy's hair for dear life, a huge smile illuminating his little face. Taffy looked over at her, his eyes dancing, and she felt a tiny shiver at the back of her neck that had nothing to do with the temperature.

'Let the madness begin, eh, Holls?' he said. He swung Ben down into his arms to check that the armbands were still firmly attached. 'Do you want a hand?'

'Erm . . .' mumbled Holly, still rather thrown by the ease with which Taffy had clearly bonded with her tricky little boy. 'Pick a twin and make sure he doesn't drown?' she ventured, still convinced he would plump for Tom as the easier option. She was loving the fact that he was prepared to help her with her madcap parenting. Twins were great but it didn't take a health and safety expert to point out that a one-to-one ratio was an absolute must for small children at the Spring Swim. Grace had volunteered to fill Milo's conspicuously empty shoes, but with a wave and a smile she had disappeared into the crowd once she clocked that Taffy had it covered.

To Holly's continuing surprise, it was Ben that Taffy scooped up yet again, blowing a raspberry on his tummy that Holly would never have dared attempt. 'I think I'll take . . .' he blew another raspberry to further shrieks of delight, '. . . this one!' He raised an eyebrow at Holly and quietly murmured an aside, 'If that's okay with you? I will be properly careful though, I promise.'

Holly swallowed hard, overcome by an unfamiliar emotion. She struggled to put her finger on it, as she mutely
nodded her head. Supported, that was it. She felt supported.
Not alone, or lonely, or out of her depth.

She watched as Taffy encouraged the boys to join in the
cheers for the first brave swimmers. It was as though he
instinctively knew how important it was to her that the boys
enjoy experiences like this one. How special it was for her
to be a small part of a community that cared about the past
as well as the future and whose idea of a family event hadn't
changed for half a century.

The adrenalin was pumping through her veins now, as
they waited patiently for their turn. 'Are you ready, boys?'
she grinned excitedly. 'It's going to be chilly.' She shrugged
off her down jacket and felt Taffy's eyes skimming her body,
lingering where her baggy t-shirt clung to her swimsuit and
taking no small amount of pleasure in the two high spots of
colour that appeared on his cheeks.

'Looking good there, Dr Graham,' he murmured quietly,
as they were pushed together by the others waiting.

'Not so bad yourself, Dr Jones,' she replied, trying not to
stare at his muscular abs and the fine smattering of hair on
his well-honed chest.

Luckily their turn had come, plunging into the shallows
of the meandering river and heading for one of the natural
pools that made this stretch of river a perfect oasis. Although
the air was cold, the water itself was by no means arctic and
they lowered the twins into the river. Residents young and
old piled in around them, spreading out into little cliques
in places, but mostly jumbled together like pick and mix –
Werther's Originals alongside young bouncing jelly beans.

Screams of laughter and shock at the cold water filled the

air as adults and children alike splashed each other gleefully. It seemed as though the only residents who hadn't made the effort to come were the bedridden and the snooty – it didn't take a rocket scientist to work out which category Milo fell into. Even the supermarket, shops and pub had closed temporarily so that the staff could join in.

Certainly, the sight of Police Chief Inspector Davis in his stripy bathing suit would stick with Holly for years to come and she couldn't help thinking what a bloody good sport he was, as he ducked handfuls of water thrown his way by the odd young troublemaker. The Major seemed to be getting some rather intensive swimming tips from Marion Gains, who was one of the river club's regulars, and was obviously loving every minute. Holly could have sworn she even saw Julia Channing in a floral swim hat down at the far end of the weir.

She watched the twins as they bobbed happily, warm in their little suits, and delighted by the cooing attentions of every granny who swam by. Taffy, to his enormous credit, hadn't stopped watching them for a second and Holly found herself feeling a little overwhelmed by the whole spectacle. He reached over and brushed a soggy curl from her face. 'Having fun?'

'Far more than one might imagine.'

He grinned. 'Yep, cold water, lots of people, early start – you wouldn't think it's a winning combination.'

Holly privately thought that it might just be a magic formula for happiness and acceptance but she wisely kept her ramblings to herself. She watched as an athletic teenager came flying from the tyre swing into the deepest part of the river and surfaced without his shorts. She snorted childishly with laughter.

Taffy leaned in closer. 'It's not normally a naturist swim, honestly. But if you felt the urge to join in, I'm sure that no one would object.'

Holly splashed him, her eyes widening at his intimate tone. Sure, there was a certain familiarity in their relationship. Somehow, he had become her surrogate partner this morning after all, but there was something in his voice that made Holly realise that, for all her protestations, Taffy's feelings for her were not purely of the platonic variety.

All she had to work out now, was how that made her feel. Watching him swing Ben around fearlessly in the water, she knew one thing for certain – Taffy Jones was one of the good guys. Whatever she chose to do, it had to be handled with care and affection. She had no desire to be the latest conquest on his list. It wasn't how she functioned. But likewise, she'd found a rather special friendship with Taffy and she had no desire to lose that while he worked through what could only be a passing fancy.

She started a little at the feel of his hand on her waist. Treading water, with everyone else around them, the intimacy of the gesture was somehow magnified. 'Shall we get the boys out for some hot chocolate, while they're still having fun? Probably best to finish on a high note and then they'll want to come again next year.'

'Good plan,' she smiled. 'Always leave them wanting more.'

The double entendre of her words only occurred to her, as she saw the flash in his eyes and the increased pressure of his hand that somehow felt perfectly natural brushing against her rib cage. She delighted in the boys' exuberant reactions to the promise of hot chocolate and cast one last look around the river, cementing the image in her memory as the moment she felt truly a part of this wonderful community.

Wading out of the water, there were volunteers wrapping everyone in towels and silver foil blankets, hot drinks pressed into their hands. The four of them found a tree stump to perch on, a child on each lap and steam from their drinks warming their hands and noses. A photographer from the *Larkford Gazette* snapped their moment of intimacy. Holly thought at the time that it was bound to be a fabulous photograph. She couldn't possibly foresee the furore it would cause at home when it made the front page under the caption, 'New Local Doc and Family Embracing Larkford's Spring Swim'. It certainly wouldn't have occurred to Milo that he could have been the one making his wife and children laugh like drains. But then, it had to be said, with Milo in the mix, they probably wouldn't be.

Chapter 22

Dan threw his wet gear into the boot of his car and stretched out the tension in his shoulders. He really was getting a little old for bombs and somersaults into the river, but he never could resist a challenge or a dare. He'd rather hoped to catch up with Taffy, have a bit of a chat, but Taffy seemed to be playing surrogate father to Holly's twins this morning. Dan genuinely couldn't see how this was going to end well for his friend. Despite being known for his skills with the opposite sex, Dan had never seen his friend like this before.

Speak of the devil, Dan looked up to see Taffy jogging across the river bank towards him. 'Feeling a little delicate, are we?' Taffy called out as he got closer. Perching on the edge of Dan's boot, he pinched Dan's towel to rub at his hair. 'Now, are we blaming the somersaults, or is there anything you'd like to tell me about a certain science teacher?'

Dan coloured immediately. To be honest, he hadn't really got his head around last night. He couldn't really complain though, could he? To Taffy The Player of all people? He'd basically been offered the Holy Grail – no strings attached, amazing sex with a beautiful girl. The problem being, of course, that he now felt a bit of a girl himself. A bit 'used and abused'.

'Nah, just pulled a shoulder, I think,' he said evasively.

'I have absolutely no sympathy, mate,' Taffy laughed, not missing a trick. 'If you spend the whole night doing unspeakable things to that gorgeous girl, you shouldn't really expect any.'

Dan attempted to shrug, but flinched as the pain spasmed through his shoulder.

Taffy sat down beside him and handed over his bottle of isotonic drink. 'Drink that and stop moaning, you big baby. And then I'm going to want details.'

Dan shook his head. 'No details.'

'Aw crap, that means you actually like this girl, doesn't it? When you go all cagey about privacy, it's game over. Can I at least ask whether she's as sporty in the sack as she is on the track? I heard she's got proper juice from my mate at the Harriers.'

Dan raised one eyebrow. 'Your mate at the Harriers? You mean Brian the equipment guy? Yeah. I'm sure he's the font of all knowledge.'

Taffy took back his drink and stood up. 'Well, if you're going to be snooty . . .'

'Look, Lindy's great – the full package really – and we had an amazing evening. We just, well, let's just say we're looking for different things.'

Taffy groaned sympathetically. 'Got all clingy, did she?'

'Not so's you'd notice, no.'

Dan's abrupt tone and his obvious discomfort conveyed the situation more clearly than anything he might have said.

'Oh,' said Taffy quietly. 'Bad luck, mate. To be honest, I probably should have warned you. She does have that reputation. I didn't realise you were thinking "relationship" – I just thought a decent shag would do you good!'

'Jesus, Taffy. Easy on the tact there – you don't want anyone accusing you of political correctness. Anyway, the sex was more than decent. Although, by the sound of it, she's had plenty of practice.' He sighed. 'I just couldn't get my head in the game. Too much whizzing around up here.'

Taffy perched beside Dan on the tailgate of the car and let out a deep breath. 'Don't worry about it, honestly. It happens to all of us and you'd been knocking back the cider a bit so . . .'

Dan's laugh was short and a little bitter. 'There's nothing wrong with the hydraulics. Just my stupid brain. Couldn't stop thinking about other things. There she is – gorgeous by the way – doing the nasty and I couldn't stop thinking that I'd really fancy a sandwich!'

Taffy grinned. 'What kind of sandwich? Are we talking roast beef, horseradish and a little rocket?'

'Nope,' said Dan disgustedly. 'Not even a fancy sandwich – just cheese and that pickle that Julia used to buy with the little sultanas in it. I'm a disgrace to my gender, Taffs, I really am. And then, next thing you know, she's dressed and off, leaving me feeling like . . .'

Taffy took back his drink and drained the bottle, tossing it over his shoulder into the chaos of Dan's car. The very fact that Dan didn't bat an eyelid was further evidence of his wobbly state of mind. 'Now don't bite my head off, but are you sure that thinking about Julia's chutney, of all things, might not have been a Freudian what's-his-face? You know, you were actually wishing you were in bed with Julia? And, as for the rest, stop kidding yourself. You're a Serial Monogamist. Always have been.'

'And leopards never change their spots?'

'Well, I wouldn't say that . . . I'm practically a reformed character these days.'

Dan gazed out over the river bank, letting Taffy waffle on. He wanted to listen, but just as last night, his mind took him off on its own little safari.

Dan leaned back and sighed. 'Taffs, with all due respect, mate, shut up about Holly for thirty seconds would you. I've had a bit of an epiphany.'

'Crikey mate, alright. Don't panic, we can get you a cream for that,' Taffy dead-panned.

Dan just shook his head. 'Seriously, for two minutes, I kind of need to talk to you.'

Taffy pulled a remorseful face. 'Okay then, start with the juicy stuff and we can go from there.'

'Not about Lindy. I need to talk to you about The Practice, actually. I need an opinion. I'm thinking of stepping out of the race for Senior Partner. It's just too much grief and hassle. Julia's building up some cliquey support and, frankly, doing my head in with her new split-personality. I have no idea from one day to the next whether she's going to be Jekyll or Hyde. And I just can't work out Henry's deal, with all his wheeler-dealing. I'm just starting to wonder if it's all worth it. Besides, it's not like I'm in great shape at the moment, is it?'

Taffy couldn't deny that he'd spent most of the week wondering whether Dan would show up for work and whether he'd be safe and capable when he got there. 'I do get what you're thinking, but aren't you overcomplicating this? Isn't it just a blip? You'll go to Hereford this week, Chris'll work his voodoo magic and you'll be fine again. Then, I reckon, you'd really regret pulling out. And we'd all have to live with the consequences,' he ended darkly.

'Maybe. Maybe not . . .'

They both sat in silence watching a group of joggers

stretching out on the trail on the opposite river bank. One or two were dressed in lycra body suits, their neon trainers glistening against the soggy ground. Their warm-up seemed to last forever and then they set off, as a pack, not speaking, just running. Dan pulled a Mars bar out of his pocket and took a huge mouthful, before offering it to Taffy.

'D'you think there's a chance we're not taking this marathon training thing seriously enough?' he asked, heading off on a tangent.

'Wha–?' mumbled Taffy, mouth full of chocolatey nougat.

'Well, all the Harriers have a special diet, according to Lindy. Low GI, high carb, lots of lean protein, no booze . . .'

Taffy swallowed hard. 'I would honestly rather have a stroke halfway round than eat an egg-white omelette and give up a healthy ale or two.' He patted his firm, muscled, but decidedly un-chiselled abs. 'Don't want to make the ladies feel uncomfortable by being intimidating.'

Dan snorted with laughter. 'Okay, Romeo. But seriously, what do you think about me stepping down? You're in kind of a unique position, you know. You know all the goings-on, who's up to what, but you're not tied in and blinkered like the rest of us.'

Taffy could see that Dan had a point, although he'd never stopped to consider it that way. He spent so many shifts at The Practice now, it had started to feel like home. It was the other shifts dotted around the county that actually felt weird. 'Well, to be honest, I think you're all mental in your own way. I'm not sure your flashback thing is any worse than Julia's desire to control everyone and everything around her. And Henry Bruce? Well, if you ask me, he's not exactly on the straight and level. Can't put my finger on why, but he always seems so fucking shifty, you know?'

Dan did know. Henry unnerved him. He was so quick to stick out his hand for a perk, a bonus, anything extra to his already generous package. 'He's not quite cricket, is he?' Dan said, remembering one of his dad's old sayings.

'If you mean, there's every chance he's a bit bent, with his hand in the till, then yeah. So if you look at the options, I'd say The Practice would be better off with a caring, compassionate doctor, who's a little too emotionally invested, than a control-freak or a blagger.'

Dan laughed and ran his hand back through his hair, grateful for Taffy's loyalty and straight talking. 'If you put it like that, I'd be mad to opt out. But we're quietly ignoring the elephant in the room here, Taff. What if Chris can't get me settled again. What if I keep having problems and it affects my patients. What if somebody dies on my watch because I couldn't get it together in time and . . .'

'Easy there, Cinderella!' Taffy put out a steadying hand to Dan's shoulder. 'Playing "What if" will send you bonkers quicker than anything else. What if Julia's cost-cutting means someone doesn't get the right meds? What if Henry's so busy taking back-handers and perks from the drug-reps that he blows all the money on a gold-plated stethoscope? What if Holly decides that husband of hers is a loser and moves in with me? What if? What if? What if?'

Dan smoothed his thumbnail against his bottom lip, as he thought about what Taffy had said. 'So putting aside for one tiny moment your obsession with the delectable Dr Graham, you reckon it's best to shut up and stay put?'

'Yup. Don't get me wrong, I'm not disagreeing that you've gone a bit mental again lately. But it doesn't make you the worst option, not by a long shot.'

'Christ, is this what it's come down to then? Two blokes

on a river bank. One's the best of a bad bunch at work and the other's in love with a married woman who hasn't noticed he exists.'

'Actually,' said Taffy quietly, 'I think she's starting to. I gave her an Orange Club the other day and she called me an angel. And she let me help with the kids today. God knows where that tosser Milo is, but he's hardly proving to be Husband of the Year, is he?'

Dan said nothing, just looked out across the undulating grass, the group of runners like tiny ants on the horizon by now. The silence extended until he replied awkwardly, 'Hmmm. Not sure that means as much as you want it to though, Taff.'

'Point taken. But it's only a matter of time, isn't it? How can she want to be married to a tosser called Milo, who writes books about Ancient Norse myths, for Christ's sake?'

'Yes, but he was called Milo when she married him and that didn't seem to stop her. And he's been writing those god-awful books for years, and it didn't stop her getting pregnant with his twins. And ... well, maybe you need to accept that she actually loves him. Even though, we can both agree, he is a monumental twat and you would clearly be a better choice.'

'Thanks, mate,' said Taffy, a little choked up. 'I'm sure it's only because I can't have her that I fancy her so much. It's not like I'm in love with her or anything, is it? Not like you and the limber Miss Grey?' He sighed. 'Jesus, I could murder a cigarette.'

'How's that going – giving up the fags?' Dan asked. 'Still trying that nicotine gum?'

'Nah. I gave up on that – it's shite, isn't it? All I've got to show for the whole enterprise is an achey jaw from all the chewing and a strangely compelling addiction to scratchcards.'

'What? From the gum?' Dan queried, confused.

'No, you div, from trying to buy something other than fags every time I go into the petrol station.'

Dan swatted him on the back of his head and jumped to his feet. 'And you call me a nutter? Alright then, Gobby. Therapy's over. Shall we catch up with the others? I gather Teddy's doing bacon butties for all the swimmers at the pub.'

'Seriously,' said Taffy, leaping to his feet. 'I've been listening to you waffle on and all this time, there was bacon.' He gave Dan a wink.

Dan slammed the boot shut and locked the car. He smacked a hand onto Taffy's shoulder as they headed into town, thanking his lucky stars he had a mate like Taffy, who instinctively knew how to strike a balance between soppy and supportive. He simply didn't know how he'd manage without him.

'You know that t-shirt makes you look like a prat, don't you, mate?' said Dan, unable to communicate his affection any other way.

'Yeah,' Taffy countered with a grin, falling easily into their usual banter and bumping his shoulder, 'but at least *I* can change my t-shirt.'

Swinging by The Kingsley Arms on the promise of bacon and a restorative beverage or two, Dan was surprised to see Elsie standing forlornly in the car park with an empty dog lead swinging from her hand. 'Oh shit,' he muttered to Taffy, heading over to help.

'Morning, Elsie. How are you?' Dan said, trying to

remain positive and upbeat, because he knew how much it infuriated her to be patronised.

'I've lost the blasted dog again,' she replied, looking perplexed rather than angry. 'Must have slipped his leash and taken himself off for a walk.' She ran the red leather lead nervously through her hands and looked around, as if expecting the dog to materialise any moment.

'What kind of dog is it?' Taffy asked, always up to help.

'He's a little wire-haired Dachshund called Terry,' she replied distractedly, trying to whistle, but failing as her lips were blue from standing in the cold.

'Terry!' Taffy shouted, making them all jump, and whistling loudly through his fingers. 'Terry!'

'He's called Terry because he's always so terribly behaved,' Elsie confided.

'Sweet,' Dan said. 'I hadn't actually realised you had a dog.'

'Mmm?' said Elsie. 'What did you say?'

'I said, I hadn't realised you had a dog,' Dan repeated.

'Oh, I haven't,' Elsie said, wandering off down the car park and jingling the lead.

Taffy stopped whistling and his face coloured. 'Am I calling for an imaginary dog?' he asked, disbelievingly.

'Yup,' said Dan. 'Shame really, I thought Elsie was just having a little rough spell with all her blood pressure meds, but it looks like she really is losing the plot a bit.'

'Shifty bastard, dementia,' agreed Taffy. 'There's just no real measure to begin with, is there? I mean, is she actually batty or is she just eccentric?'

'Let's assume for now, that she's cold and needs some company. Any objections if I get her to join us for lunch?'

'Fine by me, as long as I don't have to go on imaginary

poop patrol and you get her to tell those fabulous stories about when she was famous.'

'She still is famous, Taffy. She's just famous for actually doing something, rather than having big boobs and living in Chelsea. Her fame actually means something. I mean, there's a sodding Oscar in the downstairs loo!'

'Seriously?'

'Seriously – she uses it to hold the spare loo roll. I think she's a hoot and I can't pretend I won't be gutted if she's going a bit gaga.'

They caught up with Elsie and reassured her that they could keep looking for Terry once she'd warmed up a bit. Dan guided her into the warmth of the pub and settled her down at a corner table.

'Well, aren't you a darling,' she said. 'I can't remember the last time I dined out with two such gorgeous young men. No, no bacon for me thank you, Dr Carter. A girl has to watch her figure, you know. Just a large glass of white and some olives please.'

Dan didn't argue, but made a point of ordering Elsie a bowl of leek and potato soup to warm her through. She may be struggling with reality today, but she wasn't getting tiddly on his watch.

Teddy wrote down the order and looked over at Taffy roaring with laughter at one of Elsie's shocking anecdotes. 'Did she find her dog then?' he asked, leaning around from behind the bar to check the floor.

Dan shook his head sadly. 'There is no dog, Teddy. I think she may have got a little confused, that's all.'

'No dog?'

'No dog.'

'Ah. Okay. She seemed pretty sure, but then I suppose she

is an actress, isn't she? Shame we've all got to get old, isn't it. Even Dad's losing the plot a bit, I reckon. This whole retirement business has him really stressed out and he's driving Peter nuts phoning him in Edinburgh all the time.' Teddy stopped abruptly, suddenly realising he may have spoken out of turn.

Dan smiled. 'It would be much easier for him if Peter picked up the reins, I know. It might actually be easier for everyone the way things are going at work.'

Teddy nodded. 'Stethoscopes at dawn, I gather.'

'Something like that.'

The pub door whooshed open and Grace appeared in the doorway, apparently with half a hedgerow in her hair. In her arms was a filthy, muddy, but undeniably smug-looking Dachshund.

'You angel! Grace, you've found him.' Elsie held out the red lead and Grace gratefully plonked the wriggling bundle on the floor, making sure that the lead was firmly attached first. When Terry wagged his tail, his entire body wiggled and he butted his head against Elsie's leg delightedly. She handed him a packet of crisps from the table and Terry stuck his head into the bag ecstatically, until the crisp packet was up to his middle and wagging in time with his tail.

'But?' said Dan and Taffy as one.

Grace dropped into Dan's chair and he pulled up another without a word. 'He'd been round the back of the pub again, looking for leftovers. Found him trying to mate with half a salami.'

Elsie chuckled and scruffed the crazy fur along his back. 'I don't know what I would say to Mrs Grover if I lost him again. She's sweet enough to let him come to visit while she's at work.'

Grace smiled indulgently. 'Actually, I think you're technically doing her a favour, dog-sitting every day. But, yes, let's not lose him again this week at least.'

Elsie reached down and scooped Terry up on to her lap, ignoring the streaks of mud being spread over her expensive dress. 'It's not your fault you have to live up to your name, is it, darling? We should rechristen him, I think. Any ideas?'

'Stinky?' suggested Taffy, with a sharp look at Dan.

'Roger?' Dan put forward, as Terry took a liking to Elsie's leg.

Grace spluttered and Elsie chuckled wickedly. 'I think we need something a little more positive for a role model, don't you? How about Hector? That's rather aristocratic.'

'Or Cuddles?' said Grace. 'Give him something to aim for?'

'Hector? Hector?' Elsie warbled, trying to get his attention.

'Drinks?' interrupted Teddy, arriving with a laden tray. He placed all the glasses on the table and picked up the shredded crisp packet without comment. 'No dog, eh?' he said under his breath to Dan. 'You'll be starting rumours that she's lost the plot, if you're not careful.'

'It's her neighbour's,' Dan replied. 'I hadn't realised she was dog-sitting.'

'Still better to get your facts straight. You know what the rumour mill is like round here. People will believe anything really. Even the idea of a teacher and a doctor going at it in a steamy Land Rover.' He gave Dan a wink and returned to the bar, while Dan's face coloured and he found himself unable to join in the conversation for quite some time.

As the day passed happily, with the help of vast quantities of bacon and several pints of local scrumpy, The Kingsley Arms became quite the gathering point. By lunchtime so many tables were pulled together that it looked like a private party. An American couple passing through had to be persuaded by Teddy that they were in fact open for business and of course they could come on in.

Dan returned to the table from getting in the latest round, to find that Terry/Hector had sickened himself with titbits and was now lying across Taffy's lap having his tummy gently massaged, until a burst of flatulence relieved his discomfort and he was back for seconds.

There was a lull in the conversation and Dan suddenly felt on the spot. 'Did I miss something?'

Elsie smiled wickedly. 'Not at all, I was just getting the juicy gossip from Taffy. Although, to be honest, we all knew. You can *always* tell who's been up shagging all night. It brings such a bloom to the skin.'

'Elsie!' Dan protested, but she laughed at his discomfort.

'Alas, the bloom has faded off this rose,' she said, patting her own cheek for emphasis. 'Doesn't mean I can't enjoy life vicariously though, does it?' She leaned forward and clasped Dan's hand. 'Was it absolutely fabulous, darling? You do have such enormous hands, so I'd always wondered.'

'Elsie!' the table chorused.

She held up a hand to silence them and three diamond tennis bracelets slid down her slender wrists. 'Alright, alright. But how else can a woman of a certain age get her own back, when she stands accused of looking for an imaginary dog? Hmm?'

Dan looked mortified. 'Oh Elsie, I'm so sorry.'

She laughed in delight. 'I was almost disappointed when Grace found him to be honest, we could have had fun with that one all day.'

Chapter 23

Holly fumbled for her door keys, as she attempted to balance the huge bag of wet swim-kit on the pram. The twins were fast asleep, exhausted by their exploits and stuffed full of bacon. Given the choice, she'd have stayed at the pub all day, chatting to all the locals and getting to know them as people, not patients. She still couldn't quite believe how quickly she felt at home or how welcoming everyone had been. There'd been a table set up in the corner of the family bar with colouring crayons and nibbles for the children, which meant that Holly had finally got to meet some of the parents from Nursery too.

It was a shame really that Milo had been ringing her mobile every twenty minutes or so, demanding to know when they'd be home. He'd made such a song and dance about weekends being family time, you would have thought it would have occurred to him to come along! Or, for that matter, for him to be at home now.

Holly carefully manoeuvred the fully laden Beast into the hallway and left the twins to their siesta. The house echoed with emptiness and Holly had to fight the rising tide of her temper. She'd left the Post-Swim Party in mid-flow, against all her better judgement, to come home to an empty house.

He hadn't even left a note or sent her a text. It was Classic Milo.

Before they'd left Reading and made all sorts of promises to each other about fresh starts, Holly had made it clear how she felt about this kind of manipulation. He didn't like her having a social life – not, as he claimed, because he wanted to have time with her – but because he couldn't bear the idea of Holly having a friendship circle that excluded him. He had been forever turning up at the hospital to collect her on nights when he knew full well there were birthday drinks planned, or the occasional team curry. The fact that he never thought to collect her on days when it was pouring it down or snowing, made his excuses seem all the more unlikely.

Holly told herself, and not for the first time, that she was a fool to think he would change his personality along with his postcode. She made herself a mug of tea and curled into the corner of the sofa, trying to reason with the indignant part of her brain. She could hear the gentle snores from the hallway that meant the twins were still out for the count and the heavy atmosphere in the house was almost stifling. If she wasn't so exhausted herself, she'd push the bloody pram all the way back into town – anything for some adult company and distraction.

But Holly knew that constantly distracting herself from the issues at play was just sticking on a Band Aid. It was about time she was brave enough to address what was going on around her.

She started counting on her fingers as she tried to impose order on the nebulous arguments circulating in her fatigued mind.

So, for all her big ideals about moving on and letting go, it turned out she was still furious with Lizzie – and Dan too, for that matter. But Lizzie, her oldest friend, her best friend allegedly, had flat out lied to her. Not once, but over and over again. And, since there was nobody else to hear, it didn't matter if Holly confessed that the grain of truth in Lizzie's horrible words was scratching much deeper than she'd care to admit.

Holly wasn't stupid. She knew she wasn't herself these days, was perfectly aware that she had lost her voice. Even Elsie hadn't missed that one. So Holly knew she was becoming a doormat. She just didn't like hearing it.

It hurt more than she could possibly have imagined, hearing someone you loved and respected outlining all your worst faults and then using them against you, using them to manipulate you. Falling out with Lizzie felt so much worse than finding out Milo had been suspended for inappropriate conduct.

And Lizzie wasn't the only guilty party here. Logically, whilst she knew Dan's intentions might have been better, he had actually misled her too. He could have been upfront with her about her job. He could actually have been upfront with her about his health issues too . . .

But then, she reasoned, did he really know her well enough to open up to her to that degree? Maybe she should cut him some slack. It wasn't as though he didn't have his hands full . . .

Holly was all for being reasonable. She liked to look at situations from both sides of the argument. But reason could only take her so far on this one, when her emotions were feeling so bruised, battered and betrayed.

With friends like these, who needed enemies, she thought yet again.

She sipped at her tea and swallowed hard. Elsie's words

from last night had really struck a chord with her and sitting here quietly, she gave herself permission to explore the questions that Elsie had posed. How could she ask for what she wanted, when she didn't even know what it was.

She certainly knew what she didn't want – did that count?

And she must have been kidding herself to think that Milo's recent efforts would be sustainable. Sooner or later, she had known he would revert to type and there'd be another drama to contend with. Whether or not one chose to believe Milo's exculpatory stories about his open friendly manner with his students being misinterpreted, on some level, Holly knew he liked to play games. Sexy, flirty, power games. After all, didn't he toy with her sometimes – manipulating her words, twisting her logic until she couldn't think straight?

She honestly didn't know what she believed any more. She wasn't convinced that she actually cared. The one thing she did know, was that she had wanted the twins to have their father around. But what use was that, when he failed to engage with them on any level? Was it time to admit she was wrong?

The twins had had more attention and fun with Taffy this morning than they'd had from Milo in weeks . . .

Just the thought of Taffy Jones was enough to throw Holly's thoughts into total disarray all over again. It didn't take a genius to see that the twins hadn't been the only ones to enjoy his attention this morning.

Holly's mind ran in circles, tempted by the promise of new possibilities. Elsie Townsend certainly had a lot to answer for.

The front door slammed so hard that every other door in the house opened with a puff of irritation. Holly started, pink with guilt about where her thoughts had been heading.

Within seconds the boys were awake and crying, sprung from a deep sleep and with no idea where they were. Holly watched in amazement as Milo walked straight past his sobbing offspring and into the sitting room. 'Where the hell were you?' he demanded.

'I might ask you the same question,' she threw back, as she pushed past him to unclip the boys and reassure them they were at home. Without stopping to wait for an answer, Holly took them into the kitchen to sort out little bowls and beakers for their snack. It was only when they were busy squishing fat juicy sultanas between their fingers did she look up to find Milo languidly leaning against the doorframe watching her.

'I asked you where you were. Could you give the childishness a rest for thirty seconds and answer me.' His voice was cold and hard, but his body was studiously relaxed. For the first time, Holly felt a flicker of unease. He'd always been possessive but he'd never actually frightened her with his intense moods.

His mother always claimed he had an artistic temperament, but as far as Holly could tell, it was just an excuse to be a moody selfish bastard – although obviously she didn't say that to Jean. Or to Milo for that matter.

'We were at the Spring Swim with the team from work. You know, the one you didn't want to come to? And then they had activities for the kids afterwards.' Holly wasn't entirely sure why she was fudging the truth a little. Somehow, the words were out before she could stop them and then confessing to a blissfully relaxing morning at the pub didn't seem terribly clever.

He grunted. 'Well, I gave up on you in the end. Apparently you're too busy now to bother about family lunches. All that fuss about spending time together and then you're out the front door at every opportunity. I had lunch at Mum's in the end – didn't seem like you were worth waiting for.'

Holly raised an eyebrow. The double meaning of his last snide comment hung in the air. The inherent truth in his statement was strangely liberating.

'Probably not,' she replied, wiping up Ben's spilled juice, feeling lighter in that moment than she had in days. Making the choice *not* to take the bait, *not* to be coerced into an argument she didn't want, was a revelation. A small act of defiance on her part felt like the first step in the right direction. Finally.

'Mum sends her love anyway,' he carried on, his eyes flashing.

'How lovely,' countered Holly, although she doubted very much that was the case.

'She wondered how you were coping with the house. Said you seemed a bit snowed under last weekend.' He shrugged now, a little sullen from being deprived of Holly's usual reaction. 'Probably didn't help that I couldn't find any clean socks this morning.' He hitched up a trouser leg. 'Had to go barefoot. Mum says she's got a few tips to help, if you can't cope with the laundry and the house now you're working full-time.'

Holly laughed. She couldn't help herself. It had started as a biting comment, but somehow translated en route from brain to lip.

'Come with me,' she said, still smiling, as she opened the door to the utility. 'As it turns out, I have a few tips too.'

Milo shuffled behind, nonplussed by his wife's unusual behaviour. They both knew only too well how this conversation would normally have ended and it wasn't pressed together in the laundry room.

'Here, let me introduce you. Milo – this is the washing machine. Washing machine – meet Milo. Be nice to him, it's his first visit, but he's going to be coming back regularly, so it's best that you get along.' She gestured towards the machine as though she were perched on the bonnet of a Porsche 911 at the Earls Court Motor Show.

'Holly, for Christ's sake, stop being so bloody fatuous! I was just pointing out that I didn't have any clean socks.'

'I know you were,' replied Holly calmly, 'and this is where all the magic happens. I'll leave you two to get acquainted, shall I?' She passed the bottle of Fairy Non-Bio to her open-mouthed husband and walked out of the room. She couldn't quite resist the spring in her step or the smile on her face.

In fact, it was only a shame that Elsie couldn't be here to share it – the long overdue moment when Holly rediscovered her voice.

Chapter 24

Holly tried to listen carefully, mindful that her attention was liable to wander this morning. She had too much going on in her head and the pressure that was building behind her temples was becoming unbearable. She closed one eye and then the other, trying to assess whether the blurring of her vision was due to the headache or simple exhaustion; she was predominantly powered by jelly babies and caffeine today.

'Don't you think, Dr Graham?' demanded her patient. 'Dr Graham, are you even listening to me?' Margot James swelled with righteous indignation. She tapped her fingers briskly on the desk top and glared at Holly with ill-disguised fury. 'What's the point in my coming to see you and answering all of your intrusive questions, if you're not even listening to the answers?'

Holly smiled weakly, aiming for reassuring, fearing instead that it made her look slightly wet and ineffectual. 'Margot, of course I heard what you were saying,' Holly replied, guiltily. It was only a white lie, she reasoned. She had, of course, heard the first few stanzas of why-I-find-it-so-stressful-going-to-Tescos and had manfully hung on in for the reprise of nobody-understands-me-and-my-life's-so-difficult, but the pain in her head, the rain on the windows and Margot's spoiled voice droning on . . . well, maybe her attention had lapsed a little.

But Margot was the embodiment of Taffy's much-maligned Worried Well. Even though they had been spooked by something they'd read in the newspaper, or more recently an innocent symptom googled . . . Well, they still needed calm reassurance and sensitive handling, and also a certain wary vigilance. After all, just because a patient had been exaggerating in the past, cried wolf to get attention, didn't mean there wasn't a genuine problem today. It was Holly's job to look for the wolf.

Although she wasn't quite sure how, 'What can I do for you, Margot?' counted as intrusive questioning, Holly gamely carried on. 'It's been a while since we looked at your blood sugars and I notice you've a family history of diabetes, Margot. If you feel that the exhaustion is becoming worse, we should probably book you in for a Glucose Tolerance Test. You'll need to see the nurse and fast before the test, so try and do it on a day when you've a quiet morning. Then I'll give you a call with the results, how does that sound?'

Slightly mollified, Margot collected up her belongings. 'It would be nice to have some peace of mind, Dr Graham, I don't mind telling you. I keep reading all these articles that tell me I should be in my prime.'

Holly stood up to open the door, sensing that Margot was about to launch into another monologue. '*Should* is a dangerous word, Margot. Try and think about what you'd *like* to do and prioritise that instead for a bit, if you feel that you're flagging.'

'Hmm,' said Margot, dithering in the doorway, unwilling to relinquish her captive audience. 'I think it might be time you took your own advice there, Dr Graham. You won't mind me saying, I know, but you really do look terrible. And I'd do something about that squint if I were you. Makes it look as though you're not really listening, you know?'

Holly saw Margot back through to the reception area and checked her watch – ten minutes until her next appointment. Technically she *should* be opening up her post and dealing with emails, but the insidious pressure from that toxic word again, galvanised the fuck-it attitude that had been lurking all week.

She headed for the doctors' lounge and the promise of a decent cup of coffee. Financial stringencies at home meant that her beloved tins of Illy had recently been replaced by some granular filth that tasted of washing-up water and looked startlingly similar.

A quick break for some caffeine and paracetamol, she decided, would actually make her a better doctor. Certainly more so than a ship-shape inbox.

She walked into the room, to find the lounge unusually quiet and the only company in the form of Julia Channing. Holly swallowed hard and plastered on a smile, because she thought she should, and then promptly let her face relax, as she remembered she wasn't playing that game any more. 'Hi, Julia,' she said instead, rubbing at her temples. 'I'm making coffee, do you want one?'

Julia looked up from her iPhone, surprise etched on her face. 'Um, yes I'd love one actually – I just thought I should deal with these emails first.'

Holly tentatively sniffed the milk from the fridge. 'I've given up on *should*,' she said candidly. 'I'm giving myself a bit of a holiday from feeling stretched in all directions. In fact, this cup of coffee right here is the first step in today's tiny rebellion.'

Julia gaped a little, wrong-footed by the wind change in Holly's demeanour. Well accustomed by now to Holly's annoying chirpiness and upbeat, can-do attitude, she found herself unwillingly defrosting.

'You're actually the second person this week to tell me that,' Julia said, slipping her phone into her pocket. 'Does it work? Do you suddenly feel liberated and energised?'

Holly considered that for a moment, unwilling to admit that she was swinging erratically between feeling decadent and guilty for making the change. Surely at work she should be keeping up appearances? She added milk to Julia's coffee and handed it over, annoyed with herself for how often that poisonous little word kept popping into her head. 'Actually, to be honest, I'm finding it much harder than I thought I would. I hadn't realised how often I was bossing myself around, making myself do things because I ought to, rather than because I wanted to. It is a bit liberating, but also bloody depressing.'

Holly shrugged and popped out two paracetamol. 'I mean it's never as though we use it for ourselves, is it? I should go home and put my feet up – I'm knackered and I have a splitting headache. But we both know I won't. But ask me to cover Dr Bruce's shift this evening and you can bet I will, because that's what I should do if I want to keep my job, right?'

Julia sipped at her coffee and perched on the edge of the table. 'You know, if you give an inch with Dr Bruce, he'll take a mile. Don't let him intimidate you, Holly. If we're being frank with one another, it's all too easy to give the male doctors superior status in The Practice, but the only one who has it is George. Henry, Dan and myself are all on equal footing.'

Holly flushed red, mentally kicking herself for having dropped her guard. 'I didn't mean . . .'

'I know you didn't,' Julia cut in. 'It was a friendly word of advice, that's all.' She paused and drank her coffee. 'I know that friendliness isn't my go-to setting, but I'm not all bad, Holly. I have been known to be almost human at times. I just, well, I just like to get on and do my job. As well as I can on any given day.'

There was a moment of quiet contemplation on both sides, as they drank their coffee in silence. Holly swallowed the compulsion to fill the void with chatter, as she normally would. She'd always hated the idea of someone finding her so boring that they had literally nothing to say to her. Or of her being so socially inept that she couldn't even maintain a civilised conversation. Instead, for once, she just let the moment be.

She felt Julia's eyes upon her but didn't look up, savouring instead the peace and quiet.

'You're not so bad to chat to, Holly Graham,' said Julia suddenly. 'I always pegged you for one of those women who never stop talking, even when they've nothing to say. I even assumed you'd be one of those mothers that whipped out photos of their babies at every conversational lull. But when I'm wrong, I'm wrong.'

Holly grinned suddenly, almost excitably. 'You know I *was* tempted. Knowing as I do, your fondness for baby pictures,' she said ironically, 'but you know, I just couldn't be arsed all of a sudden. Maybe you were right, maybe this is going to be enormously liberating.'

Julia's brow furrowed in confusion. 'You mean the baby chit-chat is part of your "should"?'

'I know – who knew?' smiled Holly. 'Maybe, I thought that mums who return to work have to prove that they're missing their children all the time. Otherwise, we're just, you know, monsters . . .'

'I couldn't do it,' said Julia matter-of-factly, as she absent-mindedly plaited her long blonde hair over one shoulder. 'Have kids I mean, not the working mum thing. I couldn't even consider it. Babies are just so needy, aren't they?'

'Yup. Needy, clingy and demanding. That's why they have the big eyes, you know, to make us all fall in love with them. Then we don't mind so much when they pee in your hair at 3 a.m.!'

'In your hair?' cried Julia, aghast, clutching at the immaculate plait.

'And that's just the tip of the iceberg.' Holly grinned wickedly. 'The tales I could tell you would have your tubes tying themselves in knots. There is no group in the world that pays as much attention to contraception as New Mums. And then, of course, the love thing over-rides all that and all they remember are those big blue eyes.'

Holly stopped suddenly, clapping her hand over her mouth in shock, suddenly aware that she was talking to one of her superiors at work and not Lizzie. 'That's to say, what I mean is . . .'

'What you *should* have said . . . ?' interrupted Julia, amusement lurking in her voice. 'Please don't apologise on my account. It's actually rather refreshing to hear someone straying away from the Official Party Line that parenting is the be all and end all. In my experience, everyone who has ever had a baby in the history of the world, feels it incumbent upon them to share the glad tidings and rope me in too. I

wondered at one point whether they were all on commission – you know, bring another member into the cult? Now,
I wonder if they just want me to feel the same pain . . .' Julia
trailed off for a moment. 'Oh and to share the joys of motherhood etcetera,' she finished ironically.

'Well, there are some perks,' said Holly, trying to recover
her equilibrium. 'The Parent and Child parking spaces are
huge. Seriously, even I can reverse into them first time.'

Julia smiled, one eyebrow raised. 'So that's your Golf
parked diagonally in the car park, is it? I might have
known.'

'Do you know,' said Holly slowly, 'I feel like this is the first
proper conversation we've had.'

'It's certainly the first honest one,' rejoined Julia. 'You're
not half as unbearably smug and bouncy as I thought you
were!'

Holly's eyes widened slightly, along with her smile. 'And
when you're not being intimidating and patronising, you're
actually quite nice to chat to. Even if I do secretly hate you
for your teeny tiny waist and immaculate wardrobe.'

Julia brushed the spotless sleeve of her jacket and grinned.
'Well, I publicly hate you for constantly eating chocolate biscuits and never getting spots. And because all the men here
think you're funny and want to take care of you.'

'Well, I hate the fact that I look like such a victim, that I
need taking care of.'

'Hmm, well I'm a duck. All calm above the surface and
legs paddling madly underneath. And I don't like people very
much.'

'A duck, eh? Well, then, I would have to be a giant squid.
Too many hands, all full, flailing out of control . . .'

Julia sniggered at the mental picture and then sighed.

'Well, for all that, duck or squid, at least we're both delicious. Or at least, we are to the Chinese.'

'I love that you hate all that about me,' said Holly quietly, honesty colouring her cheeks. 'I can't remember the last time I actually said what I was thinking without running it through the filters first. Engage Brain Before Opening Mouth, you know?'

'If it makes you feel any better, I actually have to check that I'm not being too nice or friendly when I open my mouth, or before you know it, I'm looking at baby photos and being invited to coffee mornings. It's quite hard work being aloof, but now you know all the reasons I can't stand the whole perky ponytail perspective, I can be nice. To you, I mean. Just occasionally. And don't read anything into it. We're too different to be friends, and I might just have to fire you in a few weeks time. But still . . .'

Holly clinked her mug against Julia's. 'To fuck-it philosophy and ditching the shoulds. Oh and FYI, those heels you're wearing? The nurses call you Miss Whiplash when you wear them. Just saying.'

Julia grinned, the smile transforming the contours of her face until Holly was stunned by her good looks. 'I may just have to wear them more often then, don't you think? Right, now, stop slacking, Graham. Go and do some work. But at least you don't look like death any more. Bit of colour in your cheeks. Chip chop. I happen to know there's some infected acne heading your way. Saw it in the waiting room. Have fun now . . .'

Julia got up and left the doctors' lounge leaving Holly feeling rather buoyed. Her headache was fading and the caffeine had lifted her out of her slump, but she couldn't deny that the smile on her face was all down to Julia. Who knew?

Chapter 25

Julia pulled open the fridge in the doctors' lounge, hoping to squeeze in an early lunchtime. 'Where the hell is my lunch?' she burst out, with an uncharacteristic lack of composure. Her conversation with Holly earlier had left her feeling unbalanced and irritable: annoyed with herself for opening up and unnerved by the feelings that had been provoked.

She swung around, her high-heeled boots squeaking on the floor and eyed everyone in the room with distrust.

Taffy was tucking into an enormous sausage roll, Grace was nibbling a vast egg salad baguette and Jason appeared to be nibbling Laura's ear-lobes. Julia cleared her throat and tried to adopt a breezy tone. 'I don't suppose anyone's taken my lunch by accident? Little Tupperware bowl? Blue lid?'

Taffy waved his sausage roll in answer and Jason didn't bother to look up. Only Grace looked uncomfortable. 'Oh Grace, please don't tell me you've eaten my lunch. I have had a very trying morning and I really just wanted to sit down and eat my macrobiotic salad and take a few minutes without being moaned at.'

Julia felt she was on the verge of tears. It was almost as though every patient she'd seen this morning had been specially selected to wind her up. She could never get past the frustration with patients who couldn't do the simplest things to help themselves. Was it really so hard, as a diabetic for example, to stay off the fizzy pop and out of the hospital?

She sighed, any hope of a quiet lunch now gone. Anxiety always exacerbated her issues with food and it was only the thought of her perfectly prepared, calorie-counted, gluten-free salad that had offered her comfort. Without that, Julia felt hungry and panicked. It was much the same feeling that would overcome her if she tried to do a supermarket shop on an empty stomach – as though she wanted to sit in the middle aisle and weep, completely unable to make a decision about what she could eat.

Grace swallowed her mouthful of baguette, bought from the bakery over the road and rolling in mayonnaise. It was clearly delicious and decadent and seemed to require her undivided attention. 'Erm . . . Your salad? Was it in a square tub with a blue lid?'

'Ye–es,' replied Julia, forcing herself to be patient. 'Like I said.'

'It's just that I was cleaning the fridge out, like I do every morning. And there was a square pot, but it was just full of fungus stuff and a few soggy beansprouts. It must have been there for ages, because it smelt awful. I'm afraid I threw it out.'

Julia ground her foot into the floor, not really caring in that moment that she was behaving like a spoiled teenager. 'That was a soy, miso dressing and that was a very expensive macrobiotic selection of fresh shoots. I put it there this morning!'

'I'm so sorry, Julia. My mistake. You can share my sandwich, if you like?' Grace reluctantly held up the creamy egg baguette and Julia's eyes bulged.

'I do not eat mayonnaise!' she cried and barged out of the room, muttering under her breath. She picked up her bag and had slammed her way out of the building before the shame kicked in and she realised she had nowhere to go.

Julia glanced around the deserted Market Place and made a snap decision, stepping quickly inside the offices of Squire & Bates. She still felt shaken, but she'd walked three loops of the Market Place and at last, her thoughts settled. It wasn't that her visit to the local estate agent was a secret, she justified to herself, it was simply that she didn't want anyone to know what she was doing. And certainly not before she did.

Piers Bates was on his feet within moments, holding out a manicured hand. 'Dr Channing, hello. How are you? Please, please take a seat.'

She perched on the edge of the uncomfortably modern chrome and leather chair and wondered when estate agency had become such a trend-driven business. When she'd bought her little house in Larkford five years ago, these offices had been furnished with squishy sofas and uphol-stered chairs that made you feel completely at ease. Although obviously the circumstances had been rather different too, as back then she'd been caught up in the heady excitement of buying her first property. But here she was today, looking to sell, feeling uncomfortable and with no better options on the horizon.

'Rachel? Could you get Dr Channing a coffee? Coffee, Dr Channing, or would you prefer tea?' Piers' politeness bor-dered on the obsequious and Julia wasn't really in the mood to play along.

'Coffee's fine. I just need to have a quiet word about the

possibility of selling my house. And by quiet, obviously I mean confidential.'

'Of course, of course,' said Piers as he clicked away at the computer and pulled up her file.

Rachel, his assistant, appeared with two cups of Nescafé's finest and placed them down on the desk. 'You're not selling that lovely house of yours, Dr Channing? I hope you're not leaving us? I couldn't possibly go to one of the men for my check-ups, not when they're all so dishy, well, not Dr Kingsley obviously, although for an older chap, he's not bad looking is he? But I suppose I meant Dr Carter and Dr Jones really. I mean, what if it's your lady's appointment?' She mouthed the last two words in a comedy whisper, before grinning conspiratorially. 'I don't know how you lot get any work done over there, with those two . . .'

'Thank you, Rachel,' Piers cut in tersely, 'and perhaps this is a good moment to remind you of Dr Channing's request for confidentiality?'

Rachel blushed furiously. 'Of course.' She made her way back to her desk, duly chastised and Julia felt sorry for her. Okay, so she was a chatterbox, but it didn't immediately make her a gossip too, at least Julia fervently hoped not. Perhaps spontaneously dropping in wasn't exactly the best way of keeping things confidential.

'So,' Julia continued, 'I wanted to get some idea of value and to find out whether you had anyone on your books already who was looking for something similar. If I decide to go ahead, I'd be looking at a quick sale, no chain. Can you help?'

Piers smiled ingratiatingly, adjusting his silver cuff-links, and Julia suppressed a little shiver. 'Of course, Dr Channing, of course. As you may recall, the properties on

Blythe Street are always very much in demand on account of the views across the parkland from the bedrooms, but then I don't need to tell you that.' He tapped on the calculator on his desk and sucked for a moment on a Squire & Bates pencil before giving his professional opinion. 'I won't lie to you, Dr Channing; it's not the best time to sell. The market's fallen significantly since you bought and, depending on your mortgage situation, I'm afraid there's a real risk of negative equity.'

Julia tried to keep her face in neutral, but a tiny tic flickered in her eyelid. 'But do you have any prospective purchasers on file?'

'We do, we do, I'm just not sure that any of them would be prepared to match what you paid for it. Let's see now, two bedrooms, spacious garden, off-road parking ... it's a little gem.' He steepled his fingers together and tried to look sincere. 'Obviously, if you're determined to sell, Dr Channing, we can put together a marketing package for you, dip a toe in the commuter market, see if we can get a little bidding-war going, but I want to be upfront with you. It's a buyer's market at the moment.'

Julia nodded slowly, hearing her suspicions spoken out loud, even by the notoriously smooth Piers Bates, had rendered her incapable of speech. In the back of her mind, she'd always assumed that, if the worst came to the worst, she could just sell her house, release some capital, pay off her debts and give some money to her parents to keep them at arm's length. It hadn't crossed her mind until she'd actually begun to read the property pages that her mortgage might actually be worth more than her house.

'Are you free now?' Piers asked, clicking print on the computer and gathering up her property details from before.

'I've got a window and we could pop round and do a proper valuation, let you know where you stand and then we can take it from there? Just give me five minutes, okay?'

Julia stood up dumbly, trying to stop her mind whirring. A wave of nausea washed over her and she couldn't think clearly. So much for Plan B. She certainly didn't think her 'des-res' would be quite so desirable as a house-share with her parents. She simply nodded and picked up her bag. She managed a half-hearted wave to Rachel who was clearly eavesdropping whilst doing the filing.

Julia didn't know whether to blame or thank Holly Graham after their conversation earlier. After all it was Holly's notion of losing the 'shoulds' that had made her walk into Squire & Bates. She may not like what she'd found out about the likely value of her house, but at least now she knew.

And actually, now she started thinking about all the little *shoulds* that held such power over her, she was able to analyse them from a more objective perspective.

Why did she cling on to the notion of owning her own home? Her mortgage was enormous and gave her little flexibility. Why didn't she just sell up and rent something more modest?

She knew that she wasn't alone in this: a generation of Thatcher's children, brainwashed into believing that you were only a success once you owned your own bricks and mortar. It wasn't an optional indicator of success – it was carved in stone in their psyches; it was their right.

Reeling from the thoughts that exploded from this, her very own damascene moment, Julia couldn't help but smile. She may not want to advertise her decision, with the partnership battle looming, for fear of sending the wrong signals, but Julia felt a sense of relief. After all, if she was living in a rented one-bed flat, there would be no room for house-guests or lodgers, would there?

Put like that, Julia felt a fool for not thinking of it sooner.

She thought back to last night's cleaning frenzy, working on the bathroom grouting with an expensive interdental toothbrush bought specifically for that purpose. What a waste of an evening!

Julia checked herself there. Good God, where would this train stop? Would she soon be eating processed sugar and coming to work with no make-up on?

Even as that thought crossed her mind, she could feel the tightening mask of foundation pulling at her skin. What would it feel like to see the world without its frame of mas-caraed lashes?

She looked over at Piers, a little flushed and neatly assem-bling the tools of his trade and wondered what he thought when he looked at her. Did he see a glamorous, well-groomed professional or did he see someone so physically perfect that she was cold and aloof, as Dan had once said in anger?

It was a thought that often tormented Julia, as one by one, the slightly tubbier, frizzy haired girls of her acquaintance had married and settled down.

Yet here she was.

Not even forty and on the shelf.

Her body may be honed to perfection in the gym, but really what was the point when nobody ever got to see it?

Julia sighed. Even Holly, with those vile stretchy suede boots and her endearingly rumpled ponytail, seemed to attract men like flies. All the guys falling over themselves to make sure she has a snack because she's oh-so-tired looking after her picture-book twins. Even Holly, with her undoubted stretch marks and the faintest hint of a moustache, was undoubtedly getting more action than she was.

Maybe if she hadn't been so determined to maintain the façade of perfection around Dan, Julia thought, they might still be together now?

If, just for once, she'd enjoyed breakfast in bed, without worrying about crumbs? If they could have made love in the shower, without noticing the mildew?

If she had found a way to say 'fuck it!' would she still have Dan?

Rather than viewing Elsie Townsend as outspoken and eccentric, to be tolerated at best, should she in fact be venerated as the font of all knowledge? She was definitely on to something, Julia conceded.

Finally stepping out into the Market Place brought Julia up short, as it was suddenly buzzing with the lunchtime sandwich-grabbers. Piers had been prattling on with his spiel at her side, but her mind was still partially in her alternative universe.

Seeing Henry Bruce walking straight towards them, lifting slightly from his elevated shoes with each step, and with Jade hanging on to his arm, forced Julia's mind into focus, thinking fast.

'Shit! Just play along, would you, Piers?' she whispered urgently.

'Henry, Jade, you two look like you're on a mission,' Julia smiled determinedly.

Henry did a swift double-take when he saw who Julia was with, even more so when Julia tucked her arm possessively through Piers'.

'We're just popping out for some lunch at the deli,' Henry replied, conspicuously trying not to stare at Piers. After all, who was he to talk?

Jade, however, had no such compunction. 'So,' she said cheerily, 'how long have you two been dating then? You've done well to keep that quiet around here.'

Julia slowly exhaled. It was a sign of how bad things had become that she would rather let the town believe she was dating Slimy Bates, than let on to her financial predicament. Pride was obviously yet another luxury she couldn't afford any more.

'It's all quite recent actually,' said Piers truthfully. 'We're just seeing how it goes, aren't we, honey?' Never one to miss an opportunity, Piers leaned in and kissed Julia lingeringly on the lips, squeezing her bottom for good measure.

That obviously answered her earlier question then – not off-puttingly perfect, merely out of his league – he'd leapt like a salmon at the opportunity for a feel.

It was hard to say at that point who was more uncomfortable and Henry merely raised one perfect eyebrow. 'When you're done with your *appointment*, do come and have a word with me, Julia. It's important. I'll wait at the deli for you.'

'Okay,' she said, with no time to think up an excuse, all efforts being focused on other things. One, how to disguise the revulsion she felt for Henry Bruce, his smoothly manicured fingers having stroked the side of Jade's neck throughout the entire conversation. And two, how to keep her temper with Piers Bates who was clearly taking this scenario and running with it.

As Henry and Jade walked on, their heads bowed together in intense gossipy conversation, Julia stepped back.

She slowly removed her arm from Piers' and resisted the overwhelming urge to wipe her mouth. 'Shall we get this valuation done then?'

Piers walked along beside her, a discernible spring in his step. 'Now when you say valuation, do you mean valuation, or is that just a clever ploy to get me into your bedroom?'

Julia shuddered slightly. 'Let's stick with the numbers, Piers. I think that will be disappointing enough for one day, don't you?'

When Julia stepped into the deli half an hour later, Jade was gone and Henry was sipping at an espresso, the tiny cup incongruous in his large hands.

'I'm glad you came,' he said smoothly, signalling to the waitress for another for his guest. There was no sign of Hattie or Lance and for that, Julia was grateful.

'I wasn't sure I had a choice,' replied Julia coldly. The valuation on her house had not gone well.

She knew that there were people in Larkford who considered her and Henry Bruce to be cut from the same cloth. But just because they both took care of their appearance and didn't gush endlessly at the sight of a baby or a puppy, that did not make them soulmates.

She thought of his sweet wife, Tina, and wondered how he had the nerve to brazenly flaunt his affair around the town.

'So?' she prompted, eager to get this over with.

'Slow down, Julia,' he drawled. 'These things cannot be rushed. You and I need to talk.'

'I cannot think of anything we have in common to talk about.'

'Really? Nothing?' A small burst of spittle bloomed on his lip and Julia had to look away.

She looked back pretty quickly though, as his hand fastened on her arm.

'My enemy's enemy is my friend,' he said. 'Have you heard that expression?'

Julia said nothing.

'I just think that we should get our heads together, Julia. I can make you a very wealthy young lady – and goodness knows, it can't be cheap having mummy-dearest in and out of rehab. Not to mention that, if I were an aspiring Senior Partner, and I had just discovered that my house was worth tuppence ha'penny, and I had no money to buy in, I might not be quite so quick to rebuff the hand of friendship.'

Julia could feel the blood rush to her face. Who the hell did he think he was?

'Come on, Julia, stop being stubborn. Throw your support behind me and we can get Dan Carter out of the picture. Wouldn't that be satisfying, hmm? Can't be easy seeing him every day. So this would be a win all round. You do your TV show and work with me as your Senior Partner and I'll cut you in.' He leaned in close, his breath sickly sour from the espresso. 'There are so many opportunities here, Julia, and I hold the key to all of them.'

He waved for the bill and peeled several twenty-pound notes out of a silver money clip, tossing them on the table carelessly. 'Think about it, Julia. You can't buy in. It's me or Dan. Your romantic past or your financial future. It really should be an easy decision.'

Chapter 26

'So,' said Maggie the pharmacist, carefully wiping a section of the front desk, before perching on it daintily, 'what did you think of the Spring Swim then, Dr Graham?'

Holly couldn't help but smile. She'd downloaded some of the photos from the weekend onto her laptop last night and couldn't remember the boys both looking so happy. At the same time, that is. The coincidence of good moods had been running rather short of late. In fact, Holly's hard drive was crammed with photos of the twins, in which one would be happily smiling and the other grizzling miserably. It probably didn't need pointing out that the worst of the grizzlers was always Ben. But, to give Tom his dues, should the moon and tides align for Ben to be having a good day, Sod's Law would dictate that Tom would, of course, give in to the dreaded sulks.

Holly had been somewhat blindsided though, when the picture of Taffy and the three of them had opened on her screen. It was easily the best photograph of Holly and the boys that had ever been taken. All eyes open, everyone smiling, everyone looking relaxed and easy, cheeks flushed pink from the cold. And as for Holly herself? Well, if pressed to put aside her modesty, even Holly could see that she looked gorgeous in that picture – healthy, glowing and positively radiant. The conundrum, of course, lay in the fact that she could hardly print it out and pop it by her bed, or even save it as her screensaver. The twins' sparkling, excited smiles would have to be saved in a folder for clandestine viewing.

Holly wasn't stupid, though. She knew that if it had been anyone else from The Practice in that photo, it would already be in a frame on the sideboard.

Keeping it quiet, not showing Milo – that spoke volumes. In fact, Holly rather wished that the photo had come with its own volume knob. She could hardly hear herself think this morning for the cacophony in her head, the tattoo of Taffy, Taffy, Taffy beating in time with her pulse.

She'd been forced to revert to her tried and tested routine of denial and activity. Hence the coffee break with the girls at the front desk (distraction), rather than in the doctors' lounge with certain other doctors (denial). 'See,' she told herself. 'You've got this handled.'

Maggie chattered on about previous years; heat-waves and floods, flu outbreaks and dramas notwithstanding. 'Even me, Holly – and there's no need to look so shocked – I'm in that river once a year like clockwork. Of course,' she lowered her voice conspiratorially, 'I do send in a river sample to the Environment Agency every February. Three-week turn around, terribly efficient they are. And you'll be pleased to know that the water's top notch.'

Holly grinned. 'You really do think of everything, Maggie. I shall have to remember to come and get the update next year, before we all take the plunge.'

Maggie shrugged. 'It's just common sense really. Survival of the fittest, you know. Not that I need to tell you that – excellent skills there, Holly, getting Taffy to help out with the twins. Water safety ratios and all that.'

Holly could feel her face colouring and was forced to feign a cough.

Maggie's eyebrows rose, as she clearly didn't miss a trick. 'There's some lovely piccies of the day up on the town website. Quite a good one of you and the boys, I think.' said Maggie carefully, clearly fishing.

'I must have a look at those when I get chance,' replied Holly, keeping her tone as even as she could. She really didn't need Maggie to know that that image and the way it made her feel had already kept her awake all night. Just thinking about lost sleep made Holly yawn widely. 'Sorry,' she mumbled, 'bit tired.'

'Me too. In fact, I nearly didn't come into work this morning,' Maggie confided to Holly. Lucy swivelled round on her chair, as the ringing phones gradually calmed to a more manageable level, and Maggie squirted another blob of hand sanitiser into her palm and began to massage it in. 'I don't know what possessed me, but I stayed up late and watched that *Contagion* movie on DVD. I kind of over-looked the whole viral-epidemic storyline.'

Lucy shook her head, laughing, 'Oh Maggie! What were you thinking, you muppet, watching that? You know what you're like. Grace'll wet herself when you tell her.'

Maggie pulled a face. 'But it had Matt Damon *and* Jude Law in it. What was I supposed to do?'

'Well, when you put it like that, I can see that you had no choice really,' said Holly.

Lucy wandered over to the printer and collected all the referral letters she'd been typing up between phone calls. 'Well, if you're going for immersion therapy, you should watch *Outbreak* next, Maggie. It hasn't got Matt Damon, admittedly. But the little monkey is seriously cute.'

'Would that be the same monkey that spreads the flesh-eating virus then, Lucy?' Holly laughed, delighted with the change of topic.

'Well, obviously she'll have to overlook that bit. Aw, but he's got little fluffy cheeks, and these tiny little hands and ...'

'And a nasty case of Ebola?' said Maggie drily, causing Holly to accidentally snort instead of laughing and reducing Lucy to a giggling heap.

The bell on the front door jangled and Mr Hampton shuffled over to the reception desk. 'I'b gob an aboointbent bith Dr Badding,' he spluttered through his handkerchief.

'An appointment with Dr Channing you say?' replied Lucy cheerfully, trying to keep a straight face. She was well versed in translating those patients with a bunged up nose. 'Take a seat in the waiting room, Mr Hampton. She'll be right with you.'

Mr Hampton nodded miserably and headed for the doorway. He stopped and took a deep breath, his face contorting as he tried to fight the overwhelming urge.

'Maggie, look out! We've got a sneezer!' whispered Lucy gleefully, watching the stricken expression on Maggie's face as she hurried from the room once poor Mr Hampton began exploding. It was just as well all the staff got their flu jab every year, as it sometimes felt like they were working in a Petri dish of all the regional lurgies.

Holly heard the squirt of the Dettox spray as Maggie once again set to work, trying to keep her world both germ-free and shiny white. Maggie was such a card – who in their right mind would choose to work in a doctors' surgery if they were phobic about germs to that degree? Maggie had been put off her food for days when Taffy had introduced her to the concept of his five-second-rule. It was basically his firm belief that, if you drop your food and it was on the floor for less than five seconds, it's technically declared safe to eat. Holly noticed that Maggie hadn't been very enthusiastic about his regular offers of fancy biscuits ever since, although Holly couldn't claim any such reservations with eating his orange Clubs whenever they were offered . . .

Dear God, she thought, I'm eighteen again! Just thinking back to the hormonal tumult of emotions that had characterised almost every year of university – the epic crushes, the unendurable heartbreak, until the next object of desire hove into view . . . Holly gave herself a little shake. 'I am a married mother of two. Get with it, Graham. One nice photo does not fill a photo album,' she muttered under her breath as she waved goodbye to the fun in the office and went to collect her first patient of the day – nothing like a seeping boil to keep any sexual urges in check.

Maggie fell into step beside her. 'It's so lovely having some fresh life in the place, you know, Holly. We all spend so much time here, we get a bit like family sometimes, you know, a bit sibling-y and bicker-y.'

Holly smiled. 'I do love it here, Maggie. And it already feels like home. And as for you lot bickering – I don't buy it. If someone annoys you, don't you just have a little grump behind their back and be done with it?'

Maggie looked shocked at the very suggestion. 'Ooh no, not behind their back. This isn't a City practice. If someone's bitching about you here, Holly, they'll do it to your face.'

'I'm not necessarily sure that's better. Is it?'

Maggie shrugged. 'At least you know what you're up against. Well,' she continued darkly, 'with most folk. The jury's still out on Henry and Julia.'

Holly wasn't entirely sure whether a laugh was expected

at this point. Maggie's words had a ring of truth about them that negated any humour.

But Maggie wasn't finished yet, delighted to have a willing listener and keen to know everything, she cast another fly across the water. 'Of course, seeing young Taffy being such a sweetheart with your beautiful boys at the weekend ... well, let's just say he won't be short of offers now, will he? Always lovely to see a bloke that's happy to muck in and help with the kids. I dare say he owes you a thank you. With PR like that, I imagine the Taffy Jones fan club will have gained a few more members ...'

Holly swallowed hard, completely winded. She reached for a response but nothing was there. Her face drained of colour and a hard tight feeling settled in her chest. Who was she kidding? The very photo that had haunted her dreams and thrown her emotions into turmoil, would be the photo that secured young, fit and single Dr Jones his next hot date ... Holly felt the pressure of Maggie's hand on her shoulder.

'Just as I thought,' said Maggie gently. 'I'm not trying to interfere, my love. But sometimes forewarned is forearmed, isn't it? Like I said, if I've something to say, I'll say it to your face. And a lovely lass like you, with those two lovely boys? Just be careful, won't you?' Maggie gave her shoulder another squeeze and disappeared into her domain of stacked prescriptions and sanitisers.

Holly slid down onto one of the chairs lined up outside.

She felt extremely foolish and suddenly old beyond her years. 'Grow up, Graham,' she muttered. 'What did you think was going to happen, hmm?'

Chapter 27

Holly scrubbed her hands rigorously. Despite having worn the requisite latex gloves, she couldn't quite shake the feeling that her hands would never be clean again. It was ages since she'd seen a good old-fashioned case of pubic lice, which was just as well really because things that scuttled and crawled were Holly's bête noire. Even as a doctor, she'd practically thrown up the first time one of the twins had come home from nursery with 'little visitors', as the accompanying note had so delicately phrased it.

In fact, Holly only had to think about the little cretins scuttling through her boy's sandy locks and she wanted to throw up. How she'd endured the last consultation without heaving was a wonder in itself.

More to the point though, why was she having to lecture an upstanding lady in her fifties about casual sex and multiple partners? Had the world gone bonkers?

She also knew that, according to the latest medical journals, pubic lice were no longer a huge problem among the younger, more sexually active generation, because all the girls had grown up watching Samantha on *Sex in the City* and had waxed themselves into pre-pubescent smoothness.

Putting aside her concerns about the kind of guys that

found it a turn-on to be shagging someone with Barbie's genitalia, Holly couldn't help but worry. If Cynthia Jameson was still putting it about in her fifties, having been unceremoniously dumped by her husband of thirty years, was that what they all had to look forward to? Rather than spending their twilight years in the bosom of their families, were they all destined to be hitting the Viagra and shagging their way around the Bridge Club?

Holly shuddered. She wasn't sure what felt worse – the idea of four more decades being patronised by Milo, or the unrecognisable landscape of modern dating.

Lucy poked her head around the door. 'Sorry to interrupt, Holly, but your next patient's a no-show and there's a bloke waiting to see you. Says it's "personal" and he's happy to wait.' Lucy made air quotes with her fingers around the word personal and waggled her eyebrows. 'He's very charming though, and well fit. Is it your hubby? Are we finally allowed to meet him?'

Holly swallowed the uncharitable response that, if he was charming, it was very unlikely to be Milo. She turned off the tap and dried her hands, the sun streaming in through the frosted glass. 'I'll come out,' she said, following Lucy through to reception. Whilst she hadn't expected Milo to turn up at work, she would never have predicted that her visitor would be Will. A tired, grey-faced Will at that, huddled uncomfortably in the corner of the waiting room, looking as though he had the weight of the world on his shoulders.

'How long have I got free, Luce?' Holly asked quietly.

"Bout twenty-five minutes, if you need to pop out,' Lucy replied. 'Not the Magnificent Milo then?'

Holly gave her an odd look. 'No, just my friend's husband.

I will pop out, though. Won't be long. And Luce – the Magnificent Milo? Where did that come from?'

Lucy's face flooded crimson and she looked mortified. 'Holly, I'm so sorry, it was just a slip of the tongue ... Some of the doctors, well, I mean, Dr Carter sometimes ... Oh shit – can you just be an angel and forget I said anything?'

Holly shook her head and smiled. 'Don't worry, I won't tell Dan that you dropped him in it.' She pushed open the door to the waiting room, leaving Lucy mouthing mutely in the corridor. Try as she might, Holly couldn't be cross with Lucy or Dan – the Magnificent Milo had an edge of truth to it that made it properly funny. Not that she would admit that of course. To anyone.

'Holls.' Will sprang to his feet as soon as he saw her. 'I'm so sorry for bothering you at work, I just need five minutes if you've got them?'

In no time, they had picked up two coffees from the deli and were meandering their way through the town parkland. 'Come on then, Willeth, what's up? The designer stubble's looking a little unkempt and you've that crazy look about the eyes. You've got your Finals Face on, so spill ...'

Holly watched as Will psyched himself up. 'I need you to tell me what's going on with Lizzie?' he said abruptly. 'I hardly recognise my own wife at the moment. She says you two have fallen out, but I won't believe it until I hear it from you.'

'Oh,' said Holly quietly, 'well, she's not making that up, if that's what's worrying you.' She felt incredibly awkward. She'd known Will almost as long as she'd known Lizzie. She counted him as one of her best friends, but suddenly, without Lizzie in the picture, Holly felt uncomfortable telling tales about his wife's appalling behaviour. 'I really think it would be better if you talked to Lizzie about this.'

He turned to look at Holly, slopping hot coffee over his wrist but barely seeming to notice. 'You don't think I've tried?' He sighed. 'Honestly, Holls, I wouldn't put you in the middle of this, unless I thought it might make a difference. I'm worried about her, Holly. She's hardly eating, she's snapping at the kids, and every time I see her she has a drink in her hand. I don't know what's going on with you two, but Holls, for me, can you make amends?'

Holly shrugged, feeling thoroughly conflicted. Of course there was a certain loyalty to Will, not to mention concern for Lizzie, but the hurt and betrayal of Lizzie's actions still hurt like a fresh wound.

'Look,' Will tried again. 'Lizzie's great at putting on a public face, okay. She's all calmness and serenity on the surface, whilst it's a maelstrom underneath, yes? Well, she'd kill me for saying this, but she'd been miserable for ages. Wouldn't admit that she was struggling, wouldn't admit that things weren't great ... And then you moved here, Holly, and my wife was smiling and laughing again – not just for visitors, but, you know, singing in the shower ...' He trailed off looking lost.

Holly took a deep breath and tucked her arm through his, as she quietly recounted the conversation she'd overheard. 'So the thing is, Will, I want to help. I do. But I have to look out for myself a bit too. I'm more than just a pawn on Lizzie's chessboard. She's messed about with my life, my job, my marriage ... This move was a Big Deal to me. And it's all smoke and mirrors. I can't work out what's true and what's lies and ... And, oh shit, Will, I feel so manipulated.' She dashed away a rogue tear that was blurring her vision. 'I don't know how to let this go. It's just too big, you know?'

Will said nothing. The shock was etched on his face. Holly wasn't entirely sure what he'd been expecting when he sought her out – did he think they'd fallen out over a muffin recipe, for Christ's sake? Surely he'd realised that it would have taken something fairly seismic to shake the foundations of their friendship?

'Well, I can see why you're angry,' he said slowly, scuffing the ground with his feet. 'In fact, I can't work out why you're not screamingly apoplectic.' He risked a glance in her direction. 'I think I would be.'

Will didn't need to know all the dark thoughts she'd been harbouring over the last few days. Likewise, she didn't want to admit to herself that the Spring Swim and Taffy and Milo had conveniently filled her waking thoughts all weekend, until the drama with Lizzie had receded to an uncomfortable flickering in her peripheral vision. It was as though she knew there was something on her To Do list, but she couldn't quite remember what it was. After all, what would she have written? *'One. Find way to forgive oldest friend for manipulating me and not giving a shit about any personal consequences I might suffer. Two, ignore the fact that she hasn't apologised. Three . . .'*

Holly shrugged. 'Lizzie's a loose cannon at the moment, Will. She doesn't even seem to appreciate that she needs to apologise. She thinks I'm over-reacting. So . . . well, now you know.'

'And there's no chance that you could be the bigger person here? Phone her? I don't know, invite her out for coffee . . .'

Holly couldn't hide her surprise and her tone was sharper than she'd intended it to be. 'You *were* listening just now, Will? You did hear what she did?'

Will looked embarrassed and uncomfortable and Holly felt immediately guilty. 'I know you're worried about her, Will, but I just don't think that I'm the solution to the problem. And, as much as I hate to admit it, I'm worried about her too. But like I said, I can't risk becoming yet more collateral damage.'

Will sighed again, pulling the air from his boots. 'Oh Holls, don't talk to me about risks. I'm an actuary, remember? I know all about risks ... it's all I do every bloody day. I work out the odds for the worst-case scenario. I calculate the likelihood of death and divorce and fire and flood – but at no point did I see any numbers about the probability of my gorgeous wife turning into a back-stabbing fiend with her face in the gin! Please – Holls – I wouldn't ask if I wasn't desperate ...' He leaned into her shoulder for support as they ambled along, forcing a note of laughter into his voice as he confessed, 'You see, I didn't realise before, that Lizzie only actually listens to me, if my opinion happens to coincide with yours. And now we need you. I need your voice of reason, because I'm worried and out of my depth.'

As Will gently filled Holly in on what he had seen, and what had triggered his concern, his face turned slowly ashen. 'It doesn't sound good, does it?'

Holly shook her head, wincing, cross with herself for caring so much, despite everything that Lizzie had done lately. 'Lately' suddenly felt like a drop in the ocean, compared to their years of friendship. She felt sick, and so, so frightened of what would happen if nobody intervened.

'I'm just terrified, Holly, that she'll crash. Literally and metaphorically,' said Will. 'I'm not sure and I can't prove it, but I have a horrible feeling she was wasted when she picked the kids up last night and I couldn't bear it if ...' He choked up, unable to finish his sentence.

Holly drank her coffee, her eyes unseeing as she tried to

take everything in. 'Right,' she said finally, her logical mind kicking in, 'simple measures first. The car can go in for a service until we know what's going on, can't it? Then empty the wine cupboard. I'll get you some information on what to look out for and what to expect. And then we need to find a way to broach the subject.' She breathed out heavily, overwhelmed by the sense of duty that settled on her shoulders. Whatever her thoughts about Lizzie right now, Holly owed it to Will and the kids – her surrogate family – to step up. They could deal with the other stuff later.

'We?' queried Will, the hope evident in his voice. His shoulders were slumped and he looked up at Holly, almost defeated already by the task awaiting him. 'Are you sure, Holls?'

Holly shrugged and looked uncomfortable. 'Nope. I'm not sure. I'm not sure, but I am really worried and I'll help if I can. I'm not promising forgive and forget here, though okay? Lizzie and I still have some stuff to deal with. She can't treat me like that and expect me to be okay with it. But if you need me ...'

Holly batted away the feeling of obligation – this felt like one of those *shoulds* that defined what kind of person you were.

Will smiled, finally, the relief evident in his voice. He hugged Holly tightly. 'Thank you,' he whispered into her ear.

They'd come full circle back to The Practice and Holly knew she was running late. Her heart sank at the sight of Cassie Holland looming on the pavement in front of her with her phalanx of groupies with prams behind her.

Will naturally took Holly's hand and stepped into the road to give them space to pass.

Cassie's eyebrows shot up under her henna'd fringe. 'I

told you that new doctor was a dark horse.' Her voice carried clearly back to Holly and Will, as Cassie strode away. 'Someone should tell her, we've got no time for her city ways in our town. Did you see her at the weekend, all over Taffy Jones and now here she is with another one in tow. Have any of you even met this husband of hers? I'm beginning to think he doesn't exist.'

Will couldn't help but grin. 'You shameless hussy, Holly. Only here five minutes and already they've got your number!'

Holly just shook her head, only hoping that Will was so distracted that he wouldn't pick up on the Taffy Jones comment. Fat chance.

'So, that Taffy's a very handy rugby player from what I hear. Probably just the right build to sit on your painful husband, should you ever decide to upgrade.' He gave her a friendly nudge to show that he meant no harm by it, but they both knew that Will would be there with Pompoms and a Parade should the day ever arrive.

'I must get back, patients to see . . . Let's speak later, yes?'

Will gave her another hug, holding on just a fraction too long. 'To be honest, I was kind of hoping you'd laugh at me about all this and tell me not to be daft.'

'But I didn't do that.'

'No,' said Will, 'you didn't do that. So now, we have to decide. Who talks to Lizzie?'

Chapter 28

The usual post-lunch malaise in the doctors' lounge was made worse by the fact that the weather had warmed up but the heating was still switched on. Somehow, not one of the team working that day could figure out how to switch the new hi-tech system off and the stultifying heat was making everyone crabby and irritable.

Dan watched Taffy look at his watch yet again and sigh. 'If you're so impatient for your lunch-break to be over, I'm sure Grace can find you something to do.'

Taffy pulled a face and picked up another magazine. 'Dead around here today though.'

Dan stifled a grin. 'If by that you mean, isn't it quiet without Holly Graham to lust after, then yup – dead around here . . .'

Taffy just scowled. Not the best sign, in Dan's experience. There was an awkward pause and then Taffy looked over the top of *Woman's Weekly*. 'Have you seen her today? Holly, I mean.'

Dan shrugged, deliberately not wishing to fan the flames. 'She was in the office with Grace and Lucy earlier. They were having a right old natter.'

Taffy nodded. 'Settled in well, hasn't she? Holly, I mean.'

Dan gave his mate an odd look. 'I told you she'd be a good fit.'

'Hmmm, you're right there – she is quite fit. Holly, I mean.'

Dan leaned forward to rest his elbows on his knees. 'I know you mean Holly, you daft plank. You may think, by the way, that you're being terribly discreet and opaque, but you're like a teenager on heat. Any mention of the word "Holly" and you're practically leaping up and down.' Dan sniggered. 'Good job it's not Christmas or all those carols would have you going like Pavlov's dog!'

Taffy threw *Woman's Weekly* deftly at Dan, the recipe section arcing out mid-flight to whack Dan squarely on the jaw. 'Easy tiger,' Dan complained.

'Yeah, well, it's easy for you, isn't it?' Taffy protested. 'Mr Deep and Meaningful, you're used to having "feelings" – urgh – I don't know how you get through the fricking day with all that going on in your head!'

Dan sat back, rubbing his jaw, and trying to ignore an interesting recipe for Pistachio Pavlova. 'Are you honestly telling me that you've never had feelings for anyone before? I'm sorry, Taffs, but I don't believe it.'

Taffy shrugged. 'Suit yourself. But to be fair – you've known me for what, ten years? Ever seen me like this before?' There was a long pause as Dan scrolled through his memory banks. 'See? I am, to coin the technical phrase, completely buggered here, mate. She's got in my head.'

'Well, there you have it – she's in your head, not your bed. Anyone else, you'd have been there by now, wouldn't you? Holly's just forbidden fruit – you want her precisely because you know you can't have her. It's a caveman thing. Probably.'

'Probably.' Taffy sighed and then slapped Dan's hand as he leaned across and pinched one of the last few Hobnobs. 'You're a bit perkier this week, anyway. Maybe your hot date was exactly what the doctor ordered.'

Dan swallowed the last of the Hobnob and wiped his hands on his trousers. 'Nah, fun though. But it gave me a bit of a wake-up call to be honest, so I took myself off to see Chris – you know, the counsellor I used to see in Hereford. Went out for a pint and a chat, off the books, you know. He's a bit of a legend that guy.'

'And? Did he say you were a nut job? Did he offer you one of those nice linen jackets with the wraparound sleeves? Did he buy you a year's supply of Cadbury's Fruit and Nut bars? Did he . . .'

'Are you done?' cut in Dan drily.

'Yup,' replied Taffy sheepishly, 'but even you have to admit there's plenty of mileage for piss-taking built in with this one.'

'Well, you'll be pleased to know that he's calling it a "blip" rather than a relapse. Reckons I stopped treatment too early and got complacent.'

'Well, you are known for your complacency,' nodded Taffy, trying and failing to be serious.

'Can you believe he told me to reduce my stress levels and then, in the very next breath, he told me to get a girlfriend. Seems to me the two are mutually exclusive . . .'

Taffy nodded. 'Well, you are drawn to the high-maintenance models. And Julia was hardly an oasis of restful delight, was she? But he might have a point – you know, medically speaking – from an endorphins perspective.' Taffy flicked the end of his biscuit at Dan. 'Plenty of opportunities for exercise anyway . . .'

Dan just shook his head. 'Anyway, long story short, it's back to all the mindfulness bollocks and a weekly session with the head shrinker.'

Taffy slapped Dan on the shoulder, relieved beyond measure for his mate, but emotionally unequipped to handle it. 'Well, don't go too often, because as we already know . . .'

'I've got a teeny tiny head!' finished Dan. It was an old joke from when he'd had his first army buzz cut – suddenly divested of his lustrous locks, every person he'd met had been unable to resist commenting on his Far Side proportions.

'Speaking of doctor's orders to get a girlfriend,' Taffy said after a while, 'any news of the Lustful Lindy?'

Dan shrugged. 'She friended me on Facebook.' He looked uncomfortable, fiddling with his watch strap and not meeting Taffy's eye. 'We've spoken a couple of times and sometimes she texts me late at night when she's feeling, erm, in need of company,' said Dan glumly.

'And you're down about this because . . . ?' Taffy queried.

'Well, she's just after a shag, mate, isn't she? Although she calls it "hooking up".' He gave a theatrical shudder at the term. 'I guess what I'm saying, is that I want more than the whole Friends-With-Benefits thing.'

'Well get you – Germaine Greer eat your heart out!'

'It's not very cool for a bloke to turn down sex though, have you noticed?' Dan said quietly. 'But getting together just for a shag felt kind of hollow and, to be honest,' he finally looked up at Taffy, 'saying no feels more pro-active – a conscious choice. Makes me feel like I deserve something better, like maybe a conversation afterwards, or something in common.' His eyes briefly flickered across the room towards Julia.

'Did you read that in *Cosmo*?' asked Taffy gently, but any teasing on his part was simply to make Dan feel at ease. The expression on his face was one of pure respect.

Dan grinned suddenly, grateful as ever for their banter. 'Nope – I think it was *Red* actually.'

They both looked a little sheepishly at the heap of magazines on the coffee table. 'We really need to get some new magazines in the waiting room,' said Taffy.

'We really do,' agreed Dan, blushing slightly from his revelations, but somehow glad to get that off his chest.

Dan and Taffy relaxed back in companionable silence. The little groups dotted around the lounge seemed to have been hit by the same soporific wave, as only quiet murmurs could be heard. Outside the window though, Dan could hear raised voices. Well, technically, only one raised voice. George Kingsley appeared to be marching up and down the car park, struggling to get a decent connection on his BlackBerry. Whoever he was talking to, it was clearly enough to make George's blood pressure rise. Even from this distance, Dan could see his face was flushed red and he was waving his arms around for emphasis.

'Taffs? Any idea what's up with George?'

'Hmm? Well, apart from being old and a bit fuddy-duddy and wearing awful elasticated trousers?' Taffy replied, not looking up from his magazine.

Dan plucked *The People's Friend* from his friend's fingers. 'No, look! Do you think we should go out and see if he's okay? I've never even seen him use his BlackBerry before.'

Taffy leaned against the window to get a better view, the words 'unacceptable' and 'preposterous' echoing back to where they were sitting. 'Well, as of last week, he was still calling it his Blueberry and couldn't switch it on, but he seems to have got the hang of it now.'

They watched as George got into his car, slammed the door with gusto and sped off, gravel flying. For George, the be-cardiganed promoter of road safety and considerate driving, this was tantamount to sacrilege. 'Shit,' said Taffy. 'Any idea what that's all about?'

'Nope,' said Dan, feeling on edge and out of the loop. He checked his own phone for messages and emails, automatically looking across at Julia to check that she wasn't riled. Whatever it was, George was obviously keeping it to himself.

Taffy sighed and flicked through the pages of yet another magazine he had lifted from the waiting room. The copy of *Heat* was so well-thumbed and out of date as to be practically vintage, but for the purposes of Taffy's game, it was ideal. 'Okay then, putting aside your pitiful mental health, my pathetic love life and George's impending nervous breakdown, we've got five minutes; let's return to the crucial issues of the day.' He laid *Heat*'s photo spread of 'World's hottest actresses' down on the coffee table in front of Dan. 'You have to choose – Snog, Marry, Avoid.'

Dan glanced down at the women in question and began weighing up the relative merits of Angelina Jolie, Jennifer Aniston and Gwyneth Paltrow. 'You know, when you look at it like this, the whole Brad Pitt brooding look makes sense. It's no picnic when you've your pick of all these gorgeous women. I always thought he was a grumpy sod, which somehow seemed inexcusable when you've a garage full of Ducatis.'

Taffy laughed. 'Come on, Carter, you're losing your touch. Snog, Marry, Avoid? And stop wittering on about motorbikes.' He snagged the last Hobnob, leaving Dan with the rejects in the bottom of the biscuit tin.

Dan took the last intact Rich Tea and shrugged. 'Well, as much as she's beautiful, I'd have to avoid Gwyneth, wouldn't I? I'd go nuts sharing a meal with her. You know how I feel about faddy feeders. And from there, it's easy isn't? Jolie's quite fit, but you wouldn't introduce her to your mum, would you? She's definitely Snog, which means I would have to marry the delectable Ms Aniston. Not really a hardship.'

Dan flicked the page, happy to be back talking bollocks with his mate and steering clear of anything too emotional. He made a mental note to touch base with George later and then presented Taffy with his choice, deliberately taking the alternative approach. 'Right then, you get to choose The Queen, Mrs Middleton or Joan Collins?'

'You're not playing that horrible game again, are you?' interrupted Julia sniffily, having wandered over to try and force yet another window open. 'You do realise it's sexist and degrading and just another example of your emotional immaturity?'

'I do,' replied Taffy solemnly, 'but it's also a bit of fun to break up the day, relatively inoffensive and every other woman in the room can see that.'

Julia huffed and looked around for someone to back her up and clocked Holly walking into the doctors' lounge, zeroing in on the coffee machine and totally oblivious. 'Holly!' she called. 'Back me up here – Snog Marry Avoid – what do you think?'

Holly tore her gaze away from the beckoning caffeine and wandered over. 'Ooh, I love this game. Who are we doing?'

A slow smile spread across Taffy's face. 'Well, I'm having to go with Marry the Queen – she's got castles after all – then, at a push I'd have to say Snog Joan Collins – she's probably got skills – and that leaves Avoiding Mrs Middleton – who's bound to be unbearably smug now her grandson's going to be king and all that.'

'Eww ... snogging Joan Collins.' Holly gave a little shudder. 'She's old enough to be your mother! What happened to choosing from a list of hotties? Do you play it differently?'

'Nope,' said Taffy ruefully, 'but Dan decided to punish me for giving him the Brad Pitt Trinity.'

'Jolie, Aniston, Paltrow?' queried Holly. 'It is a tough one ...' she sympathised. 'My turn?'

Julia, whose silence had been growing ever more ominous, flounced away in disgust, muttering about the sisterhood and leaving Holly looking completely bemused. 'Did I say something wrong?'

'Don't worry about it, she's always in a grump about something these days. She's been pretty much unbearable ever since Dan broke up with her. Although, that's not strictly accurate, since she was pretty unbearable before they broke up too.'

'Harsh,' interjected Dan.

'But fair, mate, you have to admit it,' countered Taffy.

Holly just shook her head. 'Come on, less chat, more my turn.' She checked her watch. 'I've got three minutes until I have to go and lance a boil. I've a high glamour afternoon ahead. Hit me.'

Dan was there before Taffy could muster his thoughts. 'Based on what I've observed, I'm going to go controversial.' He turned to Taffy and grinned. 'What you may not know Taffs, is that Holly here has always had a thing for Boffins.'

'Not true,' protested Holly, blushing. 'You're basing that on one party, nearly a decade ago, when I was dating that physicist bloke from Oxford. What was his name, um ...?'

'Nigel,' supplied Dan. 'He was called Nigel and he wore tortoiseshell glasses and loved talking about planetary alignment. I always assumed he must have just bored you into bed to be honest, but then you went and married Milo and my worst fears were confirmed. Boffin lover!'

Dan realised he was going out of his way to prove to Holly that their friendship predated any of the latest dramas. He still couldn't quite believe what Lizzie had done and the guilt was yet another thing weighing heavily on his mind. He gave her a grin and was relieved to see that she seemed to be following his lead.

'How the hell did you remember all that? And anyway if I'm not mistaken, did you not have one of your identikit blondes on your arm as per usual? Katie? Sophie? Lucy? And judging by your gorgeous ex, nothing much has changed there either – all style, no substance.' Holly clapped her hands over her mouth in shock. 'I did not say that about Dr Channing, I mean, that's not what I meant about *her* . . .'

Taffy just grinned. 'It's alright, Holls, your secret's safe with us, and to be honest you're not that wide of the mark. I, however, am loving all this walk down memory lane. I thought you two barely knew each other.'

Holly shrugged. 'Well, we'd only met three, maybe four times before I came here. It's Lizzie who's got the real dirt on both of us.'

At the mention of Lizzie's name, there was an uncomfortable silence, Dan and Holly both looking away awkwardly. Luckily, thought Dan, Taffy seemed to be oblivious, apparently focused so strongly on the little row of freckles that scattered across Holly's collarbone.

'Four times, huh? Well, you both seem to have made quite an impression on each other. No youthful fireworks there?'

Taffy probed. He slapped his hand to his forehead. 'But then, what am I thinking, Dan's clearly lacking a bit intellectually for you, Holly, isn't he?'

'Taffy,' said Dan warningly, as Henry Bruce walked into the room and Holly's watch beeped the hour.

She leapt to her feet instantly. 'Right, work to do, boils to lance ... Think me up a challenge for later.' She paused and looked undecided for a moment and then blurted out suddenly. 'But don't make it too boffiny, will you. I think I've outgrown that particular phase.' She dashed from the room, eschewing the chance to grab a coffee in her quest to start her clinic on time.

'Well, credit where it's due,' said Dan slowly. 'She's very punctual.'

'Punctual?' said Taffy in total disbelief. 'That's your takeaway from that conversation, is it?'

Dan shrugged distractedly, trying to work out how he was going to make amends there. 'It's just a game, Taff.'

Taffy shook his head in sheer disbelief. 'Come on, Carter, even with your supermodel filter running – how can you not have noticed? She is properly gorgeous. And when you get to know her, she's kind of quirky and funny too. In fact, I've just decided that, since she's not only gorgeous but also fun, sweet and basically everything I've ever wanted in a woman, she should probably be mine.'

'Did we not just discuss this? Are you not forgetting the married bit?' Dan said patiently, used to his friend's flights of fancy.

'Yeah, I will admit, that does throw a bit of a spanner in the works, doesn't it? But you heard her – she thinks she's outgrown her Boffin phase. Maybe all's not rosy in the Graham garden, if you know what I mean.'

'Bad idea,' said Dan bluntly.

'Because I'm stepping on toes? Please say now if I am, Dan, after all you have known her longer ... But then do keep in mind this is me, your very bestest friend and you wouldn't want me to be unhappy now, would you?'

Dan shook his head. 'No toes stepped on, Taffy. On the other hand, she is married and she does work here and the milk tends to last longer than your crushes. This is going to get messy. Why not just give this one a miss, eh? Not least because Lizzie will string me up if I let you anywhere near her best mate.'

The idea of Lizzie standing up for Holly suddenly seemed laughable. In fact, the idea of Taffy giving Holly some of the care and attention she so clearly wasn't getting elsewhere, suddenly didn't seem so daft after all. Dan sighed, wondering when life had got so complicated.

Taffy sat staring at the doorway, where Holly had left only moments before. 'You're probably right,' he said quietly. There was a slightly awkward pause and then he took a deep breath. 'And it's all academic anyway, because she'd never take a guy like me seriously. Once a player, always a player, isn't it?'

Dan sighed and stood up tiredly. 'If I'm honest, Taffs, the fact that you're even considering pursuing a married woman with two small kids kind of proves my point.'

Privately, he was beginning to think that it might be time for both himself and Taffy to grow up a bit and find someone willing to take that leap of faith with. And really? What were the chances that both their dream women worked here at The Practice? One of them married and one of them very, very angry with him. Dan watched Julia struggling with another sash window and wondered, not for the first time, whether his ship had already sailed.

Chapter 29

The phones were ringing off the hook as Holly poked her head into reception to say goodbye. She was still trying to work out what to do about Will's request. Jean was taking the twins back to her house for tea so technically it was the perfect opportunity to pop by Lizzie's – casually, easily, like they used to. But Holly felt drained already and she wasn't sure she had the emotional energy to cope. The afternoon had passed in a blur of sobbing patients – some days it felt as though everyone was running on a hair trigger – crying with pain over a crippling migraine; crying with frustration over a lack of a clear diagnosis; crying with joy over a much-longed for pregnancy ... Holly hoped that Maggie got a good deal on Kleenex, the amount of tissues they got through!

Lucy and Grace were each on calls already, so Holly popped her bag on a chair and picked up the ringing phone. 'Larkford Practice, how may I help you?' Holly smiled as Grace mouthed 'thank you' across the room and took down a message for repeat prescriptions. She hung up and rotated her shoulders, still stiff from lugging the boys around in the river at the weekend. Just the thought of the weekend was enough to get Holly's thoughts racing again. She'd spent all morning avoiding Taffy, for fear of feeling embarrassed and uncomfortable and then, easy as you like, they'd been able to chat and play that silly Snog Marry Avoid game with no underlying tension at all. Admittedly, he'd been a little bit odd, staring at her neck like that. She self-consciously rubbed her hand along her collarbone, wondering whether she was walking around covered in porridge again.

And if you'd asked her this morning how she felt about Dan and Lizzie, she'd have said that she was bloody furious, out-raged, cheated, manipulated . . . well, let's just say she wouldn't have been short of adjectives. Nowhere on her list would the words compassion, understanding or empathy have been found. But somehow, here she was – comfortable with Taffy, understanding of Dan and just plain worried about Lizzie.

At this rate, Holly was concerned that she may actually be maturing!

The phone rang again and without thinking, Holly picked it up, 'Larkford Practice, how may I help?'

A sharp efficient voice pierced her distracted reverie. 'I need to speak to someone about getting a statement for the press. I don't suppose you have a PR department do you?'

'Erm . . . Can you hold the line one moment and I'll find out for you,' said Holly, feeling rather gauche and ill-informed. Catching Grace as she hung up the other line, Holly clasped her hand over the receiver, unsure which of the multitude of buttons on the phone console would be mute and which would simply disconnect her caller. 'Grace,' she whispered urgently, 'do we have a PR department?'

Grace shook her head. 'Nope. Oh come on, Holls, give it to me. It's probably just some survey again – they think we've got nothing better to do than comment on the rise of Prozac prescriptions or how many obese kiddies we've got on our list!' She took the phone, pulled a face at Holly and, using her best BBC announcer's voice, she said, 'Hello, this is Grace. I understand you have a PR enquiry?'

She wiggled a little, mouthing la-di-da at Holly and pushed her glasses down her nose a little, playing the PR dolly to a tee.

Holly and Lucy both watched, grinning, as Grace picked up a pencil and stuck it provocatively behind her ear.

Suddenly, the colour drained from her cheeks and Grace sank down into her chair, her face stricken with anxiety. 'And if I could just confirm which report you're referring to?' she managed, whipping the pencil out from behind her ear and scribbling on the back of an envelope. 'Of course we can get something for you. Tomorrow you say? No problem, let me just take down your details.'

Grace's movements were jerky and uncontrolled and Holly was concerned to see a small tear streaking down Grace's pale cheek. Grace laid the phone back in its cradle and typed in the code to divert their calls to the Out of Hours Clinic.

She swivelled in the chair and her eyes were tired and hollow. 'That was *The Times*,' she managed. 'They'd like a comment on the news that we're being rationalised.'

Lucy looked from Grace to Holly and then back again. 'Rationalised?'

'Closed down. Cut back. Terminated,' Grace said quietly. 'We've got three months and then all the local practices are going to merge into one big centralised medical centre. The Primary Care Trust announced it today. Job cuts to follow.' Grace took hold of Lucy's hand, a tremor making her fingers dither. 'We're all out of a job.'

'But,' interrupted Holly, more upset than she would care to admit to, at seeing cool, calm, sanguine Grace reduced to a dithering wreck, 'they can't just do that – can they?'

Grace shrugged. 'From what that journalist was saying, it looks as though they already have.' She swallowed hard. 'Apparently there's been a consultation period among key personnel for some time.'

Holly sat down then too. So hard in fact that she bruised her hip against the edge of the desk. Was it possible that George Kingsley had known this all along? Was it possible that she'd been duped by him too. 'Grace,' she asked carefully, 'who would be our key person? I mean, I presume that George is our representative with the Primary Care Trust, yes?'

Grace shook her head, eyes widening as the reality of the situation dawned. 'George stepped down last year as part of his pre-retirement planning. Said all the meetings and the paperwork were getting too much for him – Henry Bruce volunteered to step in.'

Lucy gasped, no flies on her ability to judge a situation. 'Well, we're all buggered then, aren't we? Let me guess who's heading up this Super Practice – any chance it's our very own Henry Bruce?'

Grace nodded, unable to formulate a sentence.

'What a little shit. He's sold us down the river, hasn't he?' Lucy's voice was rising now, her shock giving way to anger. 'And I bet we were supposed to be consulted too, weren't we, Grace?'

Grace swallowed hard. 'Yes,' she said quietly. 'In fact that's why the journalist called us. We're the only practice to have endorsed the decision apparently – "full staff support" the lady on the phone said.'

'But that's fraud!' cried Holly, trying to gather her wits about her. It was one thing for her to lose her job – last in, first out and all that – but for the rest of the team? This was their everything – not just their livelihood, but a cornerstone of the local community! What would people do if they had to travel thirty miles to see a doctor? 'This can't be right,' she insisted. 'Nobody who lived in the countryside would sanction such a short-sighted plan. It's some kind of madness.'

Grace dropped her head in her hands. 'Ah, but this plan came from Whitehall, didn't it?'

'Not a fricking clue about how we live then, have they?' raged Lucy.

Holly had been through something similar with hospital cutbacks in Reading. The madness of bureaucracy never ceased to amaze her. In the year that MRSA was at its peak, the powers that be had ruthlessly slashed nursing and sanitation budgets. The left hand never seemed to know what the right hand was dealing with.

Holly leaned over and clicked open a computer screen, scrolling down to find out what time Henry Bruce would be finished with patients. The entire afternoon and all of tomorrow was blocked out. Holiday. Allegedly.

'Grace,' said Holly, feeling impotent and foolish, 'I think we'd better have a staff meeting, don't you?'

In the end, with George being mysteriously AWOL, Henry 'on holiday' and feelings running high, it was a depleted and defeated little group that huddled together in The Kingsley Arms. The pub was practically empty this early in the week and it had been decided early on that the easy availability of wine and pork scratchings trumped any potential issues with privacy.

'Besides,' Dan had said, 'if this is running in *The Times* then the cat will be out of the bag soon enough anyway.'

Luckily, it was Teddy Kingsley's night off, so there was no awkwardness, as several bottles of wine and a Vimto for

Holly were quickly organised and a large table in the corner seconded.

Maggie was the first to speak up. 'Does anyone know what will happen to our jobs? Are we supposed to take redundancy or will we be offered something else?'

Grace shook her head. 'I don't know, Mags. The woman on the phone seemed to think that some staff might be relocated, but it just doesn't make sense. What I'd like to know is how long George has known about all this and kept it quiet.'

'And Henry Bruce,' Dan reminded her. 'This has got him written all over it. No wonder he's been looking so cheery the last few weeks. He was whistling in the car park yesterday!' he said with disgust.

'He wasn't whistling when he found that bloody great dent in his car the other week though, was he?' Taffy said darkly.

Holly flushed. 'Frankly, if I'd known then, what I know now, I'd have popped into reverse and had another go!'

Everyone turned to look at her in amazement. 'It was you?' said Maggie incredulously.

Holly shrugged. 'Hard to feel guilty now.' She looked up and felt Taffy's gaze upon her. If she didn't know better, she'd have thought he looked almost proud. If not proud, then certainly a little impressed. 'What?' she whispered and he grinned.

'Didn't know you were feisty, Graham. And obviously, by feisty I mean, prone to episodes of wanton vandalism.' He shook his head. 'It's always the quiet ones.' The smile he gave her made the air rush out of Holly's lungs as if she'd been flung around on the dodgems.

Honestly, she chastised herself, here they were, discussing the very future of The Practice, and suddenly all she could think about was that she wouldn't get to see Taffy Jones at work any more. It would probably have made her feel a lot less foolish, had she known that Taffy was thinking exactly the same thing about her.

Her mobile buzzed on the table in front of her and she saw Milo's name flash up on the screen. Perfect timing as always. 'Excuse me a minute,' she said and slipped away to take the call, leaving everyone at the table in heated debate.

'Hi, how're you getting on?' she asked, heading out into the car park. She knew she was in the pub for a meeting, but to Milo the background noise would sound more like a party. Without any cloud cover, the temperature had dropped quickly that evening and Holly started shivering.

'Well, I was just wondering when you'd be fetching the boys from Mum's, actually. She's phoned three times, you know.'

Holly took a soothing breath. 'But when I called before, to say I had to stay late, we discussed this, remember? You were going to pick them up and put them to bed at home?'

There was silence at the end of the line. 'I hardly think that's fair, Holly, and no, I don't remember. You have to understand that I can't just drop everything when I'm writing and you can't expect Mum to be an unpaid babysitter. When shall I tell her you'll be there?'

'Milo. I have to stay. There's some big stuff happening at work and I need to be here. I'll fill you in later. Just get in the car and go to your mum's. And by the way, I didn't ask her to have the boys for tea. She practically demanded it, something about not spending enough quality time with them. I think her mate Joyce has her grandkids every Wednesday and they've been getting competitive . . . Either way, all you have to do is pick them up and read them a bedtime story.'

The sigh that reverberated down the line made the hackles on the back of Holly's neck rise. 'Fine,' he said begrudgingly.

'I'll get them. But we really need to talk about this, because it's unacceptable to take Mum for granted like this, Holly. And, yes, we all know your new little job is terribly important, but you're not the only one with things to do ...' With that there was a definite clunk as he hung up the phone.

Holly found herself speechless, spluttering disjointed expletives as she tried to marshal her emotions. Was the world going mad around her?

She jumped at the sound of a small discreet cough and looked over to see Taffy approaching her. 'Brought your jacket,' he said. 'It's freezing out here.' He held open her coat for her in exactly the same way that her father had when she was small, shrugging her into the sleeves. She swallowed hard.

'That was very thoughtful, Taff,' she said quietly.

'You looked cold,' he said simply. 'You okay? Not too shaken up by all this?'

Holly managed a small smile. 'Just domestic stuff, you know.'

He shook his head. 'I don't really, to be honest. I only have to think about me, myself and I most of the time. I get a bit jealous when I see my sister and her bloke – they've got this amazing teamwork thing going on with their kids. Makes me feel about as deep as a puddle.' He leaned forward and unhooked the folded in collar of her jacket, smoothing it down onto Holly's shoulder.

'I think I'd probably be jealous of your sister's teamwork too,' Holly said quietly. 'Milo's more, well, Milo's more ... Let's say, he takes hands-off parenting to a whole new level.'

Taffy's brow furrowed. 'But your boys are amazing. I mean, obviously it's bloody hard work being a parent, but isn't the fun what makes it worthwhile?' He looked a bit embarrassed for a moment, before clearly throwing caution to the winds. 'I loved doing the Wild Swim with them. There really is nothing like a bear hug from a tired two-year-old, is there?'

'There really isn't,' Holly agreed. She watched the breeze ruffle Taffy's hair and saw the gentle affection in his eyes. She knew he had a reputation as a ladies' man, she knew that Maggie had warned her off, but somehow Holly couldn't compute that anyone who looked at her with such warmth and compassion could be anything but lovely.

'We should go back inside,' she said eventually, not trusting herself in that moment not to snuggle in against Taffy's ancient jumper and never leave.

'We should,' he agreed, making no effort to move. 'I hope you don't mind, Holly, but Dan talked to me about the whole Lizzie/Dan/job thing. He's so worried that you're furious with him. Although, if you ask me, they've both been pretty shabby to you.'

Holly shook her head. 'I guess I'm not the only one out of a job though now, am I? Puts things into perspective. And for what it's worth, I've loved living here – wouldn't have changed it. The town, the people,' she swallowed hard, unable to meet his gaze. 'It may not have lasted long, but it's given me an idea of how I'd like to live, you know.'

'I lived next door to the same family for six years in London and I never knew their name,' said Taffy. 'I bet Marion Gains could tell you what I eat for breakfast every day.'

It was just the silly mood breaker that Holly needed to get her emotions under control, 'Ooh, Taffy. You and Marion Gains – I had no idea. Now come on, Romeo, let's get back inside and kick some bureaucratic butt.'

*

As they got back to the table, debate was still raging about lay-offs and potential redundancy packages. Possibly because she'd already known that she had no real job security, or possibly because she genuinely liked the people she'd met since moving to Larkford, but Holly felt that she was coming at this from a different angle.

It was all very well for the medical staff to be worried about their jobs if The Practice closed down, but had anyone actually stopped to think about the patients? How on earth would the residents of Larkford cope without their doctors' surgery? It was a hellish trek into Bath to see a doctor and to fight with the notorious traffic wardens. The only other alternative was the purpose-built centre in Framley, where rumour had it, you never got to see the same doctor twice and you had to wait three days to get an appointment.

'I think we should make a plan,' announced Holly suddenly. 'We can't sit around waiting for someone else to act. We need to start thinking about the patients. None of you have even stopped to think about what will happen to people like Elsie, or the Major even, if they haven't got a friendly doctor on the doorstep.'

Dan cleared his throat uncomfortably, looking a little sheepish that he hadn't mentioned that earlier. 'Look, obviously we don't know everything at this point, but from the people I could get hold of just now, it seems we really are behind the curve. As far as I can tell, the plans to amalgamate all the smaller rural practices through a central surgery in Framley are pretty advanced. All the talk over the last few months about slashing each individual practice's budgets has just been designed to get all the GPs on the back foot. The plan seems to have been to let everyone work out how badly the cuts will affect them, and then the idea of a new mega-practice wouldn't seem quite so bad.'

There was an uncomfortable silence in the room that even the warm buzz of an excellent Bordeaux couldn't soften. 'Shit,' said Grace quietly.

'They really are a bunch of scheming bastards, aren't they?' said Taffy angrily, not stopping to question how much of his anger was fuelled by his own personal motivations for keeping The Practice open.

'Rather a clever approach, though, really. Get everyone riled up and then throw them an olive branch,' said Grace.

'It's not an olive branch so much as a bloody great prickly holly branch,' said Holly furiously, completely missing her own pun. 'Why does everyone assume that bigger and newer is necessarily better? What's wrong with the personal, local touch? Jesus, what could be more personal than your family's health? I tell you, what we need is our own plan. Play them at their own game.'

'Well you've got my vote,' said Dan as the others noisily concurred.

'You're pretty fired up about this, bearing in mind that you thought you were off,' said Taffy quietly to Holly under the heated discussion that was raging around them.

Holly looked at him and felt her heart sigh a little at what might have been. 'Well, with something like this, it's not just all about me, is it? Or you? Or Dan?'

'Or us?' he replied, momentarily brushing his hand against hers under the table.

Holly held his gaze and felt her eyes fill with tears. 'Or us,' she agreed, before being pulled back into conversation with Grace about the best way to bring Henry Bruce down a peg or two.

Chapter 30

Holly sat on the twins' bedroom floor, surrounded by Duplo and, in that moment, utterly content. Yes, it was 5 a.m. and yes, most sensible people were still in bed, but the dawn was just beginning to break and the birds were kicking off a choral arrangement that was worthy of Westminster Abbey.

Tom was building an intricate arrangement of chimneys and Ben was on unusually affectionate form, cuddling onto her lap and twiddling with her hair. It was almost worth surviving on four hours' sleep.

If only the same could be said for her discussion with Milo last night. He simply couldn't see why she was so upset. As far as he was concerned, Larkford was where they lived *at the moment*. He'd accidentally let slip that he'd already spoken to a rental agency back in Reading after the furore with Lizzie and Dan the week before. In Milo's words, 'Let them get on with it, Holly . . . It's not our battle. And by the sound of it, nobody's promising that you've still got a job, either way.'

Holly looked out across the rooftops of their little road to the hills and woodland beyond. She could just make out the church spire in the Market Place and the slanting roof of Elsie's Georgian townhouse nearby. Never having been struck by community spirit before, Holly was finding it a little overwhelming. Obviously, she needed to make sure that the boys were okay and that she had an income coming from somewhere, but there was also the drive to see things done properly. The very fact that Henry Bruce had resorted to such cloak and dagger tactics made alarm bells ring in her head. If she had to leave, then so be it, but she was damned if she was going to sit by and watch this community deprived, just to swell Henry Bruce's ever-expanding ego and bank account.

Holly picked up Ben's favourite book, *Too Hot To Hug*, about a little dragon who needed a cuddle and was soon deeply engrossed in the silly voices and actions that they adored. She probably only had half an hour before the chaos of the day would begin and she wanted to make the most of it.

Two hours later, the boys were washed, dressed and fed and watching *The Shiny Show*. Holly was jotting down campaign ideas in a Bob the Builder notebook, galvanised into action by the pile of Reading Rentals particulars she'd found on the coffee table by Milo's chair. Sure, it was a long shot, that by saving The Practice she might also save her job. But it was a shot worth taking, with no downside. Even if she personally lost, then at least Larkford might win.

She looked up as Milo appeared in the doorway, designer stubble newly trimmed and a bundle of papers under his arm. 'Is it a good idea for them to watch so much TV?' he asked, completely oblivious to his condescending tone.

Holly didn't bother to reply. After all, what could she possibly say? Even if she fought her corner about the last two hours of reading and playing and singing and eating and cuddling, Milo wouldn't hear her. It was easier to ignore him.

'Oh, and I've been thinking about what we talked about

last night. I don't want you getting all gung-ho about this Save The Practice nonsense, okay? You've had your fun here. Better to leave with a little grace and dignity, I always think.'

Holly nearly choked on her toast. Was he honestly forgetting his own emotional outbursts at the University when the Board had voted to put him 'on sabbatical'? The wheedling, cajoling phone calls to the Dean? Or the angry diatribes when the wheedling failed? Talk about rewriting history!

'So, anyway,' he carried on, 'I've got Mum to have the boys for the weekend and I'm taking you away for the night. We need some quiet time to talk all of this through and who knows, a little couple-time might be just what the doctor ordered.' He really did look terribly pleased with himself. 'So, it's all booked and sorted, and you don't need to do anything. I've found the perfect place – a spa! Just, well, let's focus on ourselves for a bit, okay?'

With that, he was gone. Holly was speechless. She didn't want to go away. She didn't want to be poked and prodded and pummelled by a stranger, or by her husband if she was completely honest with herself. She wanted to stay here and swim in the river, play with the boys in the woods and have brunch at the deli – to make the most of living in this gorgeous place while she had the chance. And if she couldn't do that, well then, she'd still rather march around the Market Place with a placard. Was he totally clueless? Didn't he know her at all?

Holly swept into action like a well-oiled machine as she glanced at the clock on the mantelpiece and saw the morning getting away from her. That was when her gaze fell on the photograph beside it. Milo and Holly on their honeymoon, wrapped in huge terry-towelling robes, blissful smiles from ear to ear . . . at a spa. The spa that *she* had chosen.

'Bugger!' she said under her breath. Maybe Milo didn't know her now, but he'd known her then. He just hadn't seemed to realise that she'd changed.

'Mummy said bugger!' came a little voice beside her. 'Bugger bugger bugger,' Tom chanted, delighted with himself and his new word.

She knew it was wrong, she knew she'd pay for it later, but Holly began to laugh. It was the kind of nervous, exhausted laughter that built and built, draining away all the tension of the last week. She wiped the tears from her eyes and cuddled the boys on to her lap.

'Bugger!' said the little voice into her shoulder once more.

By lunchtime, Holly was almost relieved when Grace popped into her room with a request. There was so much anger and bitterness in the air at The Practice this morning, it was almost toxic. Holly had given up trying to get a straight answer out of anyone, trying to separate fact from rumour, and just got on with her patient list. There would be plenty of time for Twenty Questions later.

'I've just been chatting with Elsie Townsend on the phone,' said Grace. 'She wanted an appointment for this afternoon, but she didn't sound great to be honest. You never know whether it's something or nothing with these old dears, but she wasn't herself at all. She even said please! Any chance you'd be an angel and call in during your lunch-break? I'll pick you up a baguette for when you get back?'

'No problem,' said Holly, logging out of her screen and pulling a fiver from her drawer. 'Can you get me one of those egg mayonnaise ones, with crispy bacon?' Holly couldn't understand it, but the thought of wearing a swimsuit in front of Milo was making her want to stuff her face. Not the logical approach to a romantic weekend away, she had to admit.

She picked up her jacket and made her way through the office, finding Julia Channing loitering in the car park, a guilty expression etched all over her face. Holly hadn't seen Julia since the bombshell had fallen, leaving it up to Dan to break the news this morning. The expression on Julia's face made Holly wonder, for Julia, how much of a surprise all this news actually was.

Holly settled for a simple, 'Morning.'

'Holly, hi,' said Julia, guiltily taking a long final drag on the hidden cigarette before grinding it out in the gravel. 'Don't let on you saw me smoking, will you? It's just, all this business with the PCT, you know? Stressful.'

Holly nodded, trying to recalibrate. 'Did you know?' she asked bluntly.

Julia shook her head. 'I knew Henry was up to something, but well – it's Henry – he always is. I can't believe George didn't tell us, though! I mean, he had us jumping through hoops to be the next Senior Partner! Of what?' She looked furious, gutted and really rather human. Cross, chain-smoking Julia was actually much nicer than aloof, perfect Julia, Holly realised.

Without really thinking about it, Holly wandered closer. 'I'm just doing a house call on Elsie Townsend, so I probably should crack on. I'm sorry about the partner thing . . .' she said awkwardly.

'I'll come,' announced Julia suddenly. 'I mean I know she's your patient and everything, but if you fancied the company . . .'

Holly couldn't pretend that the idea of company wasn't appealing. It was more a question of it being Julia's company that was on offer. She was really missing having Lizzie to talk to at the moment. Who else could she moan to about the job and the weekend away, without sounding like a spoiled brat?

'You don't need to, honestly. I can manage and you must have something better to do than . . .' Holly lost her momentum as she took in the expression on Julia's face. The hollow look in Julia's eyes that suggested she had followed Holly's train of thought to the letter. That and the red flush creeping across her collarbones.

Holly suddenly felt mean and small. She could see the effort it had cost Julia just to make the offer. Even the twins would tell her that she was breaking her number one rule – treat other people the way you would like to be treated. 'Julia, d'you know, actually I would love your company. I mean, I think you're bonkers for giving up your lunch hour, but I can't pretend I'm not grateful. Here,' she tossed across the extra large packet of chocolate Hobnobs she'd been planning to demolish, 'you can be in charge of rations.'

Julia caught them deftly, looking slightly wrong-footed. 'Well, okay then.'

They arrived at Elsie's to hear the strains of *La Traviata* burgeoning from the upstairs windows and the front door ajar. 'I'm in here,' called Elsie imperiously from the kitchen. Holly and Julia wandered through, to find Elsie putting on the kettle. She appeared to be wearing a satin tea dress of some kind, with a dressing gown over the top and some extra thick ski socks.

'Oh you darling girls, you didn't both need to come. As I said to Grace on the phone, I just needed a quiet chat with Dr Carter.'

Holly settled Elsie in one of the carver kitchen chairs and flicked the kettle to boil. 'What's up then, Elsie? I couldn't resist another visit so I've saved you the trip.' Holly had got the measure of her patient very early on. If you made out like she was doing you a favour, you got much more information.

'Well, it was just a bit of that nasty chest pain I get sometimes, so I came down here to make a coffee ... and here you are.' She looked pleased as punch to see them, watching Julia's reaction as she took in the exquisite kitchen. 'Why did you bring that one, though?' she asked Holly in a cringingly loud whisper.

Holly gave Julia an apologetic smile. 'Well, Julia didn't believe me, Elsie, when I said you kept your Oscar in the loo. Anyway, tell me a little bit more about this chest pain. Were you doing anything in particular when it happened?'

'Not really,' said Elsie shaking her head until her grey curls fluttered. Holly noted the one solitary Velcro roller still nestled in Elsie's silver hair and wondered how she could extract it without Elsie noticing. 'I was just coming down from the attic with my summer hats, I'd been trying on my clothes for the Season, and then ... pouf ... chest pain.'

Julia looked at her as though she were mad. 'Elsie,' she began in a lecturing voice, but Holly interrupted.

'Putting aside the whole climbing into the attic business,' she said gently, 'and the cup of coffee to soothe the chest pains idea – Elsie, we've talked about this – how are you feeling now?' Holly quietly and deftly checked Elsie's heart rate and blood pressure. All surprisingly good for someone in their eighties.

'Oh, I'm right as rain now,' Elsie replied. 'But it's a hell of a mess upstairs where I dropped everything. It's going to take me ages to get it all sorted.'

Holly stood up and opened the casket with the camomile tea that she'd spotted last time she was here. 'First a little something DE-caffeinated and then we'll see about upstairs.' She checked her watch. 'We're all yours until two o'clock, okay?'

Hobnobs duly opened and tea-that-tasted-like-wee duly served and Holly could see that both Elsie and Julia were beginning to relax in each other's company. Julia, because she'd stopped staring around with her mouth open, and Elsie, because she'd clocked that Julia's 'classic driving shoe' was a limited edition from JPTods.

Julia looked delighted at Elsie's compliments and Holly was struck once more by how a smile could transform Julia's features from aesthetically pleasing to downright stunning.

'When I was younger, I read in a magazine about the idea of buying classic things that don't go out of fashion – you know "Buy well, buy once" – and it kind of stuck,' Julia was confiding in Elsie.

'I know what you mean,' responded Elsie with enthusiasm. 'I have never understood these people who pride themselves on culling their wardrobes,' she shuddered at the concept. 'They're happy to exist with a handful of items they've picked up over the last six months. Why on earth would you knowingly, willingly, erase your own history? You wouldn't dream of throwing away a photo album in favour of this month's faddy magazine!' Elsie was becoming so worked up that Holly was about to intervene, when Julia laid a hand on Elsie's arm soothingly.

'They're probably the same people who walk into John Lewis or Oka and buy a whole room set – I'll have page 23 please – no imagination, you see. Isn't it nicer to surround yourself with milestones, tokens you've picked up along the way?'

'Ah the precious little things,' nodded Elsie, 'the ones you won't entrust to the removal men. The ones you swaddle like newborns in your car every time you move. That fleeting pleasure of buying something new is so fast, so unsatisfying anyway, so – so nothing – after the first day, compared to the lasting contentment of having your old favourites around you . . .' Elsie's eloquent musings petered out, as she was lost in thought.

'I guess it depends on where you're buying your clothes,' Holly said quietly, distractedly thinking of the pile of vile t-shirts she'd been hanging on to until she could afford to replace them.

Elsie gripped Holly's hand tightly, making Holly jump a little and slosh wee tea into her saucer. 'Ask yourself this, Holly Graham – do you want to be a blank canvas, to be painted over again and again, or do you want to be a lush, three-dimensional tapestry of your experiences?'

Holly looked a little panicked at being any more 3D than she already was, but she could acknowledge that Elsie had a point. Why else was her favourite dress from that boutique in Florence still hanging in her wardrobe, despite the fact that it would never ever fit again?

'Right,' said Elsie, with a burst of enthusiasm. 'Upstairs we go then. I can see I shall have my hands full with you two girls.' Elsie skittered off down the hallway in her ski socks with a swish of silk around her legs.

Holly and Julia looked at each other, shrugged and then followed. Whatever else this might be, it was a darned sight better than the stressful and miserable atmosphere back at

The Practice, with George closeted away in his office, shouting at people on the telephone and refusing to have a straight conversation with anyone.

'Elsie!' Holly cried, aghast, as she got to the hallway. 'What on earth do you think you're doing?'

'Isn't it wonderful?' replied Elsie with a grin, suspended as she was, halfway up the stairs. 'I don't know why everyone doesn't do it!' She hoisted herself up another couple of stairs by pulling on the banisters. The Stannah stair-lift buzzed majestically past her, bearing its load of neatly folded dry cleaning and what appeared to be a rather large bottle of Bombay Sapphire gin.

'But ...' ventured Holly, trying not to smile at the grim determination etched on Elsie's face, 'it's supposed to be a *mobility aid* – to give you *independence!*'

'And isn't it working well,' said Elsie gleefully. 'I'm feeling more independent already!'

Elsie had certainly not exaggerated the mess upstairs. It looked as though Vivienne Westwood and Karl Lagerfeld had decided to play dress up. Julia was silent in the face of the chaos, or possibly the labels, Holly wasn't sure. She settled Elsie onto the chaise-longue and swallowed any comments about Barbara Cartland.

Sitting on the end of the bed, Holly's brow furrowed. 'What were you doing again, Elsie?' There must have been thousands of pounds' worth of designer clothes flung around the room. Holly unthinkingly picked up a woven scarf from beside her and smoothed the fabric between her fingers. It felt like gossamer. No wonder Elsie never wanted to part with her clothes if they all felt like this.

Elsie certainly wouldn't have approved of Holly's maternity

bonfire when they'd moved house. Seeing all those stained, baggy trousers and tops in a heap had been a liberating moment for Holly until she dramatically threw on a match and they'd just ... smouldered. Not a natural fibre in sight.

She looked at the scarf in her hands, at the palette of tasteful shades woven into an undulating wave and sighed.

'Missoni,' said Julia knowledgeably from the doorway. 'You've got a good eye there, Holly.'

'Indeed,' said Elsie happily. 'Take it, take it, you must. It's yours.'

'Oh, no, I couldn't possibly ...' flustered Holly. 'I mean that's very sweet of you, but ... no ...' She reluctantly put the scarf down on the bed and sank to her knees to gather up coat hangers.

With Julia swinging into action as well, in no time at all, the contents of Elsie's wardrobe were restored to order and the multitude of Harrods hat boxes were repacked and stacked. The attic was closed up again and Holly worked on extracting a promise from Elsie that she would never go up there on her own again.

'I promise I won't unless I absolutely *need* to,' Elsie prevaricated and Holly gave up.

She kissed Elsie firmly on both powdered cheeks and looked her in the eye. 'I'm coming back tomorrow.'

'I should hope so too,' said Elsie with a smile. 'I should like to hear more about your campaign to Save The Practice.'

'How did you ... ?'

Elsie tapped her nose. 'I can't give away all my secrets, you know. But you might want Bob back.' She handed over the Bob the Builder notebook that had been tucked in Holly's back pocket. 'It's good to see you fighting for what you want, Holly. I'm rather thrilled that you've found out what that is.

'Now both of you,' she turned to include Julia in their conversation, 'you have to pick your battles, yes? You can't go wading into every little argument that comes your way. Pick your battles. Pick your moment. And you won't go far wrong.'

Holly smiled, enthralled as always by Elsie's wonderful approach to life. Holly and Julia watched as Elsie weaved her way through the hallway, stopping to pick up a small brass watering can, before carefully watering her orchid collection. Most days she remembered they were silk and didn't bother. Today wasn't one of those days.

Chapter 31

The next day, Holly woke early to the sound of birdsong and slipped quietly out of bed. Milo might sleep through Armageddon, but the twins were prone to wake at the slightest creak of the floorboards. Stealthily placing her feet at the sides of the stairs, she made it downstairs without incident or creaking, Ninja floorboard training as a teenager having come into its own since she became a mother. Pulling the door of the kitchen closed behind her, she revelled in the silence. Silence was often in very short supply in Holly's world and each moment had to be savoured.

Normally she'd be filling the toaster with crumpets and heating up milk for a latte, but after the extreme biscuit consumption earlier in the week, Holly had been determined to stick to a sensible diet of eating absolutely nothing, until she absolutely had to. It was odd that her entire approach to dieting was based on a line from a movie – 'when I feel like I'm about to faint, I eat a cube of cheese'. It also explained why so many New York Subway delays were due to young women blacking out on the platforms!

She settled down with a mug of strong black coffee and a huge sheet of paper. She'd woken up early because her brain was on overdrive. She'd felt motivated and driven to action

in a way that she hadn't for years. She knew that she was the
newcomer to The Practice, but she just couldn't help thinking that it was her very newness that was her greatest asset:
she could see what was going on with a more objective eye.

Putting aside the fact that she felt closer to some of her
new colleagues and patients than she did to her oldest friend
at the moment, Holly still had her head screwed on enough
to be analytical, at least when it came to the medical and
business decisions that were looming. And, if she were being
totally honest, she was really in the mood for a battle. For
someone who'd spent most of her adult life avoiding conflict
in any form, it was a rather liberating feeling.

Elsie's words, 'Pick your battles, pick your moments', were
all but engraved on her psyche, she'd revisited them so many
times. The banishment of *should* had obviously just been a
place to start.

Right, thought Holly, uncapping Ben's Big Blue Mega
Marker. She began to draw large round ovals on the paper,
forming one of her trademark Pebble Plans. The idea was to
write inside each pebble and then shade it in when the task
was complete. If your mind didn't work in a linear way and if
lists made you break out in a cold sweat, this was a winning
way to go.

Strangely enough, lying in bed, Holly had felt overwhelmed with a multitude of problems. With the pebbles
drawn out in front of her, she could quickly see that there
were only four:

Ben needed help. She wasn't sure what, but it was time to
start thinking outside the box. It did seem a little bonkers
for a GP to eschew the traditional medical path, but it hadn't
helped him so far, had it? Maybe it was time to go alternative? Sure, some of it was a little beardy-weirdy, but there

was no denying that some of it worked. Hell, if she needed to burn sage and dance naked at the full moon to help him get better, then at this point, she would.

For all that she decried her patients resorting to the internet for answers, she could perfectly understand their temptation this morning. Normally limiting any research she did to the British Medical Journal website, Holly suddenly wondered if she was the one missing a trick.

Holly could see, with the power of the Mega Marker in her hand, that there was a certain gung-ho attitude creeping into her thinking, but rather than shying away from it like normal, she decided to face it straight on.

Next: Lizzie. Yes, Lizzie was more of a challenge to diplomacy. Go for the polite, let's-pretend-nothing's-wrong approach and swallow all her resentment? Or opt for the more controversial, but possibly more cathartic, fisticuffs at dawn? Holly drained her coffee cup. Probably better to start with a frank discussion over lunch, she decided. She owed it to Will if nothing else. Surely it was better to try and mend some fences before it was too late?

Hmm, talking of mending fences, why couldn't she get more excited about her weekend with Milo? Why indeed, when he'd last been hit by the need for romantic gestures and had scattered the bed with rose petals, had she immediately thought about who would have to clear them up the next morning? Didn't he know that he'd have been better off just being sweet to her, or supportive, or even just helpful around the house?

Well, at least she'd stopped mainlining Hobnobs. And a spa weekend might be lovely. Milo was right – a little quality time would work wonders. And, if she could even drop a few pounds in advance, then all his little comments about her figure might not dent her ardour quite so much. Although, at a size 12, and having popped out two rather large babies, might one not reasonably expect a little more latitude on the bikini body?

Thoughts of bikini bodies took her immediately to issue number four. Or at least, via Taffy Jones in his swim trunks, to issue number four: The Practice. More specifically, saving The Practice. Job or no job, Holly felt driven to Do Something.

She had watched over the last few days as Dan and Julia and Grace had all run around in panic. Even Julia (and her endless and slightly anal lists) seemed to have lost her focus. Dan had spoken to every MP and every NHS bureaucrat he could think of. Julia had written wonderfully eloquent letters, packed to the gills with salient arguments – but to no avail.

The feedback was always the same. The consultation period is over. You've had your chance to comment. Your feedback was positive. The wheels are already in motion.

Hell, Taffy had even been threatened with a slander suit when he'd pointed out that their so-called PCT Representative had fraudulently filed fake responses and was about to net himself a hefty windfall as a result.

Holly switched to a new sheet of paper and chewed on the end of the Mega Marker. What the others were all too close to see was obvious to Holly. They needed a new approach, she thought, one that capitalised on Larkford's greatest treasure – the very people who lived there.

Then she slowly and deliberately crossed out the 't' – the people who live 'here' sounded much better to Holly, because it meant that she was one of them.

They needed some cracking PR and they needed it quickly, but it had to be personal.

The story needed to be real. They needed to feature the doctors, the characters in the local community and how they would be affected. After all, reality TV worked for a reason; it allowed viewers to identify with the people involved.

Holly wanted a story that provoked a response. Less 'Isn't that awful, darling, can you pass the Shreddies?'

More, 'This is the thin end of the wedge, what a lovely community – do you know, it could be our doctors closing next'.

Holly wanted the country to sit up and take notice. It was bad enough that they'd lost their voice with the PCT; she didn't intend to surrender it all together.

It was a wonder that Holly got through morning surgery without leaping about in her chair. She was longing to discuss her ideas with her colleagues, but nobody seemed to be available until afternoon surgery had finished. Undeterred and with her pebble plan rolled up in her handbag, Holly had placed several calls to recommended alternative therapists. She wasn't quite sure how the acupuncturist was intending to get Ben to sit still long enough to become a porcupine, but Willow (hmm, that was her name) seemed confident that she could.

On a roll, and perhaps over-caffeinated, she'd even picked up the phone to call Lizzie. Well, technically, she'd picked up the phone to call Lizzie seven times. The seventh time had been the charm, as she'd actually finished dialling. Pick your moments, pick your battles, she'd recited to herself as Lizzie's mobile rang out. Keeping it simple, Holly had opted for a simple, 'Why don't we have lunch?'

*

Holly walked into the deli and Hattie smiled from behind the counter. She looked tired and the strain was obviously beginning to tell because the normally laden display table only contained a handful of dishes. 'How's my new favourite doctor?' she said.

Holly grinned and held out her arms in demonstration. 'Look, no pram. I can actually sit down for once.'

Hattie came round to guide her to the one remaining table, which was happily nestled in a corner by the window. 'Come on then, before someone else nabs it. Sit down and have a look at the menu. I'm afraid the selection's a bit limited at the moment, but I wanted to open up on the days I can . . .' she trailed off.

Holly put one hand on her arm to stop her. 'Hey, it all looks delicious as always, Hats. You're a wonder in the kitchen and to think that you cooked all this with morning sickness. I can barely rustle up a bacon sandwich with a hangover.'

Hattie shrugged. 'It's not so bad any more and to be honest, I mainly feel sick at night. But I think that has more to do with it being quiet and missing Lance and not keeping my mind occupied.' She didn't need to tell Holly that this wasn't the only week that her lovely husband Lance would be away in hospital. Even in the unlikely best-case scenario, he would have to endure weeks of treatment.

A flurry of new arrivals, including Lizzie, meant that Hattie delivered two espressos and then left them to it, silence descending over their table for a second.

'Hattie's being terribly brave, isn't she?' Lizzie said eventually. As an ice-breaker, it was extremely well judged, because Lizzie knew that Holly was always very protective of her patients.

'She's amazing,' agreed Holly, 'and so determined to keep everything as normal as possible. She's getting a little bit fed up of people treating her as if she'll break, but then it seems so callous to talk about life's trivialities when Lance's life hangs in the balance.'

'I can probably manage some triviality,' said Lizzie wryly. 'Shall we order some food to go with it?'

Credit where credit was due, thought Holly. Lizzie seemed to be taking it slow. Holly had been concerned that Lizzie's narcissistic streak would mean that she'd bound in like Tigger, oblivious to the fragility of the situation.

Holly picked up the beautifully handwritten menu, taking in the selection of pasta dishes and salamis. Her stomach growled. It had only been a few days of total abstinence, but Holly liked to imagine that her trousers were a little looser and that, by the time her weekend away arrived, she would be able to pull off wearing one of her slinkier dresses from days gone by.

She smoothed her hands over her hips and crossed her legs easily – something she'd struggled to do in these tailored trousers only a few days ago. She felt an odd slithering sensation on her calf and looked down in curiosity, just in time to see her favourite black lace knickers slide out from her trouser leg and on to the floor. She leaned down quickly, her cheeks flaming with embarrassment, and balled them into her hand, but not before Lizzie could clock what had happened.

Eyes bright with mischief, Lizzie couldn't resist, 'Did you seriously just snap your pants elastic?'

'Worse!' whispered Holly, aghast. 'They're yesterday's knickers!' The atmosphere between them thawed a few more degrees.

'Jesus, Holl – did you get dressed in the dark or something?' Lizzie grinned broadly, well used to her friend's occasional bouts of distractedness. Holly's face was an instant giveaway and Lizzie knew, without pressing, that she probably had.

She took pity on Holly's obvious discomfort and leaned in. 'Did I mention that Eric's new obsession is underwear? He retrieves them from the laundry – dirty or clean, he's not fussy – and then leaves them on the stairs as an offering. Will came in from work last night and was convinced his luck was in . . . He just followed the knicker trail up to our bedroom.'

'And?' interrupted Holly, realising with a thud just how much she'd missed Eric and wondering when she could reasonably organise a visit.

'And was rather disappointed to find me on my knees scrubbing the loo!' said Lizzie.

'Not the ideal foreplay,' Holly agreed, 'unless it was a bloke.' She considered for a moment, as if weighing up her options, 'I could probably get turned on by a bloke cleaning *my* bathroom.'

Lizzie shook her head at Holly's logic. 'And that, my darling, is why you *seriously* need a cleaner.'

Hattie came back through from the kitchen, wiping the flour off her hands and looking pale and drawn. 'Right then, do you need a little longer or can I tempt you both with the Carbonara?'

'Oh my God, that sounds amazing,' groaned Holly apologetically, 'but really just a mixed salad for me please, Hats. I'm trying to give up carbs, but it's so much harder than I imagined.'

Hattie smiled tiredly. 'No worries. Even though carbs are

what makes life worth living, in my opinion. And I reckon that I can eat twice as many now I'm eating for two.'

Holly nodded. 'I know I did when I was having the twins, but then they're two now and I still can't zip my favourite jeans up.'

'Do you want my advice? Buy new jeans. You look amazing, your skin is glowing and half the town has a secret doctor fantasy going on . . .' Hattie took her menu. 'Trust me, life's far too short to be miserable.'

There was a moment's silence hanging in the air between them, as all three women were only too aware of the truth in that statement.

'How *is* Lance doing?' Holly asked gently, as she gratefully took another sip of her espresso, wincing at the bitter flavour and dismissing the urge to swap it for a cappuccino or add a handful of sugar cubes.

Hattie shrugged tiredly. 'He's doing pretty well all things considered. I'll pop in to Bath and see him again later, but the surgeon sounded really positive yesterday. He reckons it was all contained in the, well, you know,' she whispered, rather than say the word testicles.

Despite years as a doctor, Holly could still identify with patients that struggled to name bits of their body out loud. Only yesterday she'd had a confident, blousy woman confiding that she was having a bit of trouble with her 'gazebo'. It had taken a few minutes of very confusing conversation before Holly had established that the poor woman was suffering from an awful bout of thrush but too embarrassed to come out with it.

'Are you coping okay with the extra work and all the running in and out to Bath? It won't help anyone if you overdo it and end up on bed rest, you know. Tell me, Hats, what can I do to help? I'd offer to make you a casserole, if I didn't know how crappy it might taste compared to your wonderful cooking.'

Hattie grinned. 'Food's the one thing I'm not short of, thankfully. Although lovely Marion in the supermarket told me off about pre-natal nutrition when I kept going in to buy pickled onions and liquorice allsorts.'

'Go steady on the liquorice, it can give you high blood pressure, but otherwise I'd say, just follow your cravings. Your body knows what it's doing,' said Holly reassuringly.

'That's the other thing I just can't get my head around,' Hattie confided. 'How on earth does it know what to do? Is there like a tiny army of workmen poring over a set of blueprints in there? And I know Lance is desperate to know whether it's a boy or a girl, but my 20-week scan isn't for another month.'

Holly drained her cup. 'Do you think it would cheer him up? To know?'

Hattie nodded. 'He just wants to be part of it all, you know, running out in the middle of the night because I'm craving ice cream and fighting in Ikea about which crib to buy. Like normal couples do. And instead, we're making decisions about chemo and radiation and wondering whether he'll even get to meet the baby.' Hattie's face collapsed as she staggered to the end of her sentence and pressed her hand against the neat little bump under her apron.

Holly stood up and guided Hattie into her chair, thankful that all the other patrons were engrossed in their own conversations. At least for the moment. She crouched down and wrapped her arms around Hattie's shaking shoulders and made a quick decision. 'What time can you close up here? Could you be done by four?'

Hattie nodded against her shoulder, the tears making Holly's t-shirt cling to her skin.

'Then let me make a few calls, okay? And then you can drink a tonne of water and drive to Bath this afternoon. If I can possibly swing it, then you and Lance can see your baby today. How does that sound?'

Hattie's sobs got louder, even as she pushed away and looked up at Holly. 'Can you do that?'

'Let me try. The Head of Obstetrics is a mate from way back and I can't think of a better time to call in a favour, can you? I just need to check that Lance can get down to the ward, or that they can move the machine up to his room.'

Hattie wiped away her tears with the back of her hand and smiled weakly. 'That would be amazing, Holly. Thank you.'

Any hope that the rest of the customers in the deli hadn't been eavesdropping on every word disappeared in a moment, as they all hustled around to share in Hattie's small moment. But with the unimaginable challenges looming in her future, it was probably these small moments that would keep Hattie going.

Holly couldn't help but notice that Lizzie was distinctly off with her after that. She couldn't put her finger on exactly why – why on earth would Lizzie have a problem with Hattie having an ultrasound? It wasn't as though there was any chance that Lizzie was getting broody – not with her 'contraceptive children' as she called them.

On the surface, they were chatting like always. The odd story about the kids or what they were planning for the summer, but there was an exhausting undercurrent. Holly was picking her words carefully but Lizzie just seemed distant. If she'd been building up to an apology, it might have been okay, but Holly wasn't so naïve as to expect one. Lizzie didn't do 'sorry'. It would have implied a certain culpability on her part that she was never prepared to acknowledge. This character flaw was so well known amongst her nearest and dearest that Will had even referenced it in their wedding vows. No, with Lizzie, the best you could hope was that she would behave as if she were sorry.

It had been looking promising, but now, if anything the chasm between them seemed to be widening.

'So, best joke of the week so far – why did the dog refuse to go to the zoo?' Holly tried.

'Erm, I don't know, why did the dog refuse to go to the zoo?' Lizzie replied, rolling her eyes.

'Because it was a shih tzu!' said Holly, unable to keep a straight face. 'Oh come on, that's one of Taffy's best. He's on a mission to keep us all smiling while . . .'

Lizzie cut her off mid-sentence. 'Are you still crushing on Taffy Jones then?' she asked, the friendly tone of intimate confidences in place, but with a hint of scorn layered in for good measure.

Holly was lost for words for a moment; this didn't feel like a friendly compassionate arena, in which to disclose her innermost feelings. She shrugged. 'He's a lovely guy. You said so yourself. No harm in having a mate to chat to at work, is there?' She found herself getting defensive and cursed herself for being so easily wound up.

Lizzie raised an eyebrow sardonically. Before . . . well, before Lizzie had strangled their friendship, Holly would have thought that her friend was clever and witty with such a look on her face. Now, there was a curl to her lip that hinted at cruel enjoyment.

Lizzie cast a hand around the deli. 'You'll have to get in line, Holls. He's probably bedded half the girls in this town. Look, there's Debbie his Ex, and there's Lara, his previous Ex, and . . . Well, you get the picture.' Lizzie drained a glass of wine, that Holly hadn't even noticed her ordering.

'I'm beginning to,' said Holly slowly, not just referring to Taffy, and trying to evaluate how she was feeling right now. She'd made a promise to Will and she'd keep it, but nobody said it had to feel good.

Holly took a calming breath. 'Well, for all Taffy's womanising ways, he's been amazing about this whole closure thing. There's so much to do, so much support to rally. Hey,' she said, speaking without thinking, 'do you want to do something in your magazine about supporting The Practice? It's a local magazine after all – this has to be relevant . . .'

Holly stopped talking at the expression on Lizzie's face. 'Holly, I'm sure you're a brilliant doctor, but please don't pretend that you know how to run a magazine as well. Besides, I would have thought that the last thing you would want, was for me to get involved in your "professional life".' Lizzie made air quotes with her fingers. 'I've already had a gut full from Dan and your wonderful Taffy about how appallingly I've treated you. I'm not sure I can cope with any more.'

The silence sat pugnaciously between them. Words just wouldn't come for Holly, at least none that were polite enough for use in public.

'Do you know,' said Holly in the end, tucking a twenty-pound note under the edge of her plate. 'I think I need to leave.'

She picked up her bag and left the table.

'Bye, Holly! Lovely to see you,' called Hattie from behind the counter. 'Oh, and you too, Lizzie, of course.'

Holly caught the furious look on Lizzie's face as she pulled the door closed behind her.

Holly kept on walking. Pick your battles. Pick your moments.

But what was really quite strange, if she hadn't known better, was that Lizzie looked positively jealous. Jealous of what though? wondered Holly, racking her brains for an answer, before deciding that she must have the wrong end of the stick yet again. There were probably several thousand more realistic explanations. Right now though, Holly had a patient with blue legs to see and a meeting to chair.

What were the odds that Rachel Haldon had been buying cheap denim jeans off the market again, Holly thought, as she mentally changed gear and walked into The Practice for her afternoon clinic.

Chapter 32

Julia sighed as she rifled through the leaflets in her desk drawer. Unusually for her, she wasn't rushing this morning, checking her watch or her reflection. Since the crushing news from the Primary Care Trust, she couldn't seem to find any enthusiasm for anything. She'd tried calling the TV production company that produced *Doctors In The House* but had been routinely stonewalled. Eventually, she'd tracked down one of the interview panel on their mobile and they'd been characteristically blunt. They wanted to forge an ongoing relationship. In simple terms, no Practice, no starring role for Julia Channing.

In even simpler terms, no money either.

Her motivation had completely deserted her.

Last night, she'd even gone to bed without taking off her make-up. In Julia's ordered world, this was nothing short of Defcon 2 – the highest level of drama being saved for the days when she was so distressed by life, that she resorted to eating carbohydrates. Julia thrived on a controlled environment. It made her feel safe and secure.

Today, however, that security had blossomed into an unwelcome malaise and the cloying pull of defeat. Even perky Holly Graham seemed to be more driven to find a solution to the problem than she was. Julia was so exhausted, she couldn't see the wood for the trees. She wanted to be annoyed at Holly, for being so god-damned energetic in the face of such overwhelming opposition, but their recent conversations had actually given Julia a little taste of what it might be like to have a female friend. To be honest, she'd actually quite enjoyed it.

She knew, because her mother's shrink had told her so when she was twelve, that she was socially retarded. She didn't *do* friendship. All the confessionals and in-jokes and the unbearable neediness of it all . . . She shuddered. On the other hand, when she saw girls together, in cafés, jogging, just chatting comfortably, she always felt excluded. This friendship thing was obviously a big deal to some people, but for Julia there was one underlying stumbling block: she just didn't like people very much.

Well, she now amended that thought: she didn't like *most* people. Holly Graham and possibly bonkers old Elsie, might yet be the few exceptions to that rule. Julia assiduously ignored the image of Dan Carter that flashed into her mind.

She ignored the mobile phone vibrating yet again on her desk, knowing without looking that it could only mean yet another drama at home. Didn't she have enough to deal with here, for goodness' sake? All her carefully laid plans were slowly falling to pieces and, as much as it was easier to blame Dan, or George, or her parents, sometimes it just felt as though the universe was simply conspiring against her.

Thankfully, there was nothing like General Practice to focus the mind. She looked up as Mrs Brent and her little boy, who appeared to be picking his nose and munching the bogies, walked in. Taffy's definitions tickled the edge of her mind and she very nearly typed FLK and NFS into his notes, just stopping herself in time. Little Jimmy Brent may be a Funny Looking Kid and he probably was Normal For Swindon, but that didn't mean she should be anything less than professional.

'Right,' she said, trying to pull herself together, 'let's have another talk about sorting this constipation, shall we, Jimmy? The three most important things that you and your mum need to remember are to drink lots of water, eat lots of fruit and vegetables and make the time to sit on the loo regularly – even if you don't think you need to go. We'll train that body of yours to remember what it's supposed to do naturally.'

Jimmy puckered his face in disgust. 'I don't like fruit and water tastes gross. Can I have Coke?'

Julia took a deep breath. 'Water is best. Squash is fine and fruit juice is fine in moderation. All those sugary drinks will do you no good at all. They're really bad for your teeth anyway.'

Jimmy pulled his rubbery lips wide and Julia tried not to show how stunned she was at the sheer number of fillings in this child's mouth.

'But he does like his Coke, Dr Channing. Always have done, haven't you, Jimmy? He used to have it in his bottle when he was little,' Mrs Brent interrupted. 'And it hasn't done you any harm, has it, Jimmy? He's got lots of energy you know.'

Julia's grip tightened on the edge of her desk and her knuckles turned white. She just wasn't in the mood to put up with this shit today, or lack of shit as the case may be, she thought hysterically. She took a calming sip from her coffee cup, vaguely noticing the flaking nail polish on her manicured fingers. Maybe this was it? Today would be the day she started cracking up and began the inevitable slide into becoming her mother? She certainly could murder a strong G&T about now and it was barely 4 p.m. She took a deep breath and then another. If it was one thing her mother had shown her, time and time again, it was that alcohol was never the answer.

'Mrs Brent, Jimmy, you need to understand that your body is like a machine. If you put the wrong fuel in your car, it won't run properly, will it? So, if you fill your body with fizzy, sugary drinks, it will rot your teeth and you will get even more fillings. You will also find that, if you can find a way to fit more fruit and vegetables into your daily diet, you won't end up being so constipated that your bottom bleeds. None of which, I hope you understand, is good for you.'

Mrs Brent shrugged. 'Can't you just give us some more of those laxatives that Dr Bruce prescribed? They worked wonders, didn't they, Jimmy? Although we did have a few mad dashes to the loo,' she laughed.

Jimmy coloured red with embarrassment, remembering only too well how the boys at school had taunted him for weeks when he'd filled his pants at school. He shot his mother a furious look. 'I'd quite like to try something different,' he mumbled. 'And I'm fed up of my bum hurting.'

Julia looked from mother to son. As a seven-year-old boy, Jimmy could only have known what his parents had chosen to tell him and his mother clearly didn't have a clue about nutrition. Mrs Brent's skin was pocked with acne and her stomach lay like an apron in folds across her lap.

Julia felt a prickle of discomfort across her throat as she remembered how disparaging she'd been about Dan's plan to introduce nutritional counselling for their patients. His plan had been to help their younger patients, with a particular emphasis on the residents of the blighted Pickwick Estate. He'd wanted to do a few fun workshops, pop into the school and give the kids a little responsibility for their own health, rather than rely on the frankly sketchy information some of them were getting from their parents. Julia realised with a hot flush of shame that she'd shot him down, citing a waste of time and funds, to what she'd considered to be a lost cause.

She glanced down at Jimmy's food diary for the last week and sighed. It was all burgers and chips and Coke. The only vitamin that had made its way through was a glass of orange juice at a friend's house. Even at school, he'd managed to dodge the salad bar and fruit bowl.

'Okay, Jimmy, here's what we'll do for now. I'll prescribe some Mobilium that should help soften your poo and get things moving gently. And *you* will promise me to have at least four big glasses of water a day and five pieces of fruit and vegetables. Every day, Jimmy. And I want you to use this chart.'

She opened out the leaflet she'd unearthed and Jimmy giggled.

'It's called Choose Your Poo,' she explained, pointing out the illustrations that were in the chart. 'You need to write in this little table whether your poo looks like rabbit droppings, or a bunch of grapes, or chicken nuggets or here, like corn-on-the-cob.'

'Is this really necessary?' Mrs Brent interrupted looking faintly disgusted.

'Yes,' said Julia bluntly. 'Jimmy needs help and we need a better idea of how the medication is working, or not, as the case may be.' She turned her attention back to Jimmy who was happily entranced by the illustrations of all seven categories of Poo.

'The Bristol Stool Guide,' he spelled out. 'Can I colour it in?'

'If that's what you'd like. As long as you fill it in every time you go to the loo. And look, you can mark here when you've had a drink and when you've had a healthy snack.' She focused her comments on Jimmy now, because even at such a young age, he was clearly more interested in his health than his mother was. Although Julia acknowledged, it could just be that all seven-year-old boys are fascinated by poo in general.

'Any questions?' she said, trying to swallow the panic, when she saw that she was running three minutes behind schedule.

'Just one,' said Jimmy, pointing at his poo chart. 'What's corn-on-the-cob?'

The doctor's lounge was packed at 5 p.m. as Dan called the room to order. Julia tried not to stare at his tousled fringe or his un-ironed shirt. Rather than judging him for it, as she might have done only last week, his dishevelled appearance made Julia feel as though she wanted to take care of him. Noting to herself the difference between 'taking care of him' and 'controlling him', she was pleasantly surprised that this actually felt nicer.

With half an ear, she heard Dan outline the latest developments. In a nutshell, they seemed to be no further forward than they were two days ago. She saw George Kingsley looking uncomfortable and apologetic and she noted the predictable absence of Henry Bruce – lousy coward! And to think, he'd been trying to rope her in to his scheme! She couldn't pretend that the thought of an increased, steady salary wasn't attractive. She just didn't want to sell her soul to the Devil to achieve it.

She grimaced as she heard Dan's voice in her head, calling her a soulless automaton, in their last, most explosive argument before they'd broken up.

He might have had a point.

Then.

She wondered if he would even recognise her now, from the thoughts that were running through her head. Looking around the lounge, faced with the prospect of losing it altogether, she found that the people here weren't just her colleagues, to be bullied and bossed into submission.

The shocker of it all? She found that she actually liked working here. She actually liked one or two of her colleagues. Okay, so it was a long way from forming a friendship, but this nascent fondness was a dramatic about-face, from her previous position of contempt and borderline tolerance.

She watched as Holly stood up, wide-eyed and clumsy as ever, dropping all her papers in her nervousness. Again, there was a notable absence of exasperation. Instead, Julia simply leaned forward, scooped up Holly's papers and handed them back to her. 'You'll be great,' Julia whispered. 'Knock 'em dead.'

'Thank you,' mouthed Holly with a smile.

Julia caught Dan's amazed expression and blushed. How much of a bitch had she been, that picking up some fallen papers and offering support was so extraordinary?

Holly cleared her throat and began to speak. She had a dry humour and an accessible tone that made her easy to listen to. The longer she spoke, the more confident she became, until the entire room was listening to her every word. Julia blinked hard. Holly had been here all of five minutes and respect for her was written on every face in the room. Well, except Taffy Jones, who just looked like an adoring spaniel, she noticed.

'So,' continued Holly, 'rather than fighting the bureaucracy and being fobbed off at every turn, I wondered how you'd all feel about a little PR exercise. Let's make Larkford seem real to the public. Let's introduce our doctors, our nurses, our residents – if the public can identify with us, they'll be more motivated to help us.'

She carried on outlining her proposals and Julia noticed a lot of nodding heads. Holly's plan seemed to have struck a chord.

'How can they let The Practice go, once everybody knows how wonderful you all are?'

'We are,' interrupted Dan. 'You meant we, didn't you, Holly?'

Holly flushed beetroot. 'Anywaaay,' she continued. 'All of this will require time and effort and, I'm sorry to say it, a little working capital. So, I had an idea on that front too . . .'

Holly paused, clearly gauging her audience and focusing her attention on likely supporters. Julia was gratified to find that Holly was throwing her a smile too, clearly assuming she would be one of them.

'I thought we could have a concert. A town concert, to raise money. Get all of you on the stage – and any of the patients too – and have a good old-fashioned variety show, keep the costs low and charge admittance.' Holly glanced over at George. 'Perhaps we could even get Teddy to do a special thing in The Kingsley Arms afterwards for those who want to donate a little more?'

'I could do a comedy set!' called out Maggie.

'I could dance, maybe,' said Jade quietly.

'Brilliant!' said Holly. 'The more the merrier. I did just wonder though . . .'

She unrolled the large piece of paper she'd been mauling in her hands throughout the entire speech.

Take a chance with us.

Don't take a chance with your health.

Holly shrugged. 'I thought it might be a better draw, if we all did something new – something we've never had to do before. So, for example, Taffy . . .'

'He can sing like a reprobate angel,' interrupted Maggie with a grin.

'Well, quite,' said Holly, noticeably flustered. 'So maybe he should, I don't know, learn to tango, or play the guitar, or flip pancakes or something? Maybe the rugby team could sing instead?'

'Ooh, ohh,' chirped in Maggie again, her imagination clearly caught by the whole idea. 'The rugby team could do the Full Monty, like in the movie?'

Everyone laughed and Maggie blushed. Dan stepped up to join Holly. 'I think we'll probably aim for more of a family show, Mags. But do you see, guys? Look at how enthusiastic Maggie is. How great would it be, if we can get some momentum and enthusiasm going in town too? We can call in favours with most of the local publications, radio shows, do interviews. Who knows, maybe we can get Julia to do a bit on *Loose Women*?'

Taffy cat-called from the side lines. 'No pun intended.'

Julia, to everyone's amazement, just laughed, surprising even herself. 'I'd like to know how Dr Carter even knows about *Loose Women*, wouldn't you?' Glowing slightly under

Holly's laughing gaze, she shrugged as Holly sat down beside her. 'What was it you said the other day? If you can't beat them join them?'

Holly leaned in against her shoulder happily. 'Well, that went better than I was expecting.' She dropped her voice to a whisper, 'I was half expecting everyone to boo me out of the room as a Johnny Come Lately.'

'Nah,' said Julia simply. 'They all adore you.'

Holly raised an eyebrow, enjoying the new camaraderie between them. 'And how much does that piss you off?'

'Like you wouldn't believe,' said Julia. 'Sickening it is. Absolutely bloody sickening.' She spoke with just enough humour to let Holly know she was okay with it.

Holly grinned. 'It's all in the ponytail, you know!' She boggled her head around for effect.

'That and the big doe eyes under that floppy fringe . . .'

Holly sighed, suddenly wiped after all the pre-meeting nerves. 'The fringe just covers up my face. It's way better than make-up.'

Julia wondered whether her annoying perky new friend might have a point. Sitting next to Holly, who was fresh-faced and flushed, Julia felt like her own make-up had become a mask – war paint to hide her true self. Maybe a full face of make-up could be added to her *should* list – to be dropped – after all, she was a doctor, not an air stewardess.

Dan appeared to be taking a vote. Julia raised her hand in the air with pride, all those for . . .

'So,' said Dan. 'You'd all better get your thinking caps on. I gather that our wonderful Grace has already volunteered to oversee the whole fandango – so, personal profiles to her, plus ideas of anything you're prepared to do to embarrass yourself for a worthy cause.

'And if you're wondering what level to aim for, I can already tell you that myself and the lads from the Rugby Club will be putting on our very own pièce de résistance! A little something for everyone, I hope. If we big, burly rugby players putting on a show can't make the town smile, then frankly we've got bigger problems.'

Chapter 33

Holly, Julia and Taffy dutifully arrived at Elsie's house the next day. There had been no ifs or buts about the invitation for supper – they had been summoned. Word was out in the town about plans for a fund-raising concert and Elsie had been repeatedly ringing The Practice since first thing. In the end, Dan had simply suggested that they accept the inevitable, honour Elsie's position as unofficial Matriarch of Larkford and send a deputation. Originally, he had asked Taffy and Holly to go along, but Holly had found herself making excuses.

It was easy to say that she needed to be home to put the twins to bed, but Dan was already one step ahead. 'Pop home first, read them some *Meg and Mog* and hop along to Elsie's.'

How could she tell him the truth? The idea of an evening with Taffy, even with Elsie as chaperone, was simply a situation that Holly would prefer to avoid. The way her stomach flipped when she saw him at work, was early proof that moonlight and wine would not be sensible additions to the equation.

Julia, for all her aloofness at work, had stepped into the breach by insisting she be allowed to come too. Eyebrows had been raised at this, but nobody was willing to question her motivation. Julia-making-an-effort was so much nicer to work with than Julia-making-a-point.

Holly smoothed down her skirt and perched on the edge of the sofa in Elsie's drawing room. It was one of those sumptuously decadent sofas that swallowed you up in its down-filled cushions if you even dared to sit back. The soft moss green of the coverings and the light pink tones in Elsie's cushions simply made the sofa look even more like an enormous Venus flytrap.

Taffy and Elsie were in the kitchen and gales of laughter were echoing through the house. They'd only gone through for Taffy to fix a dripping tap. Now, God only knew what they were getting up to in there, but from the snippets that Holly could hear, Martinis were certainly involved.

Holly fumbled through her cavernous handbag, straightening out the crumpled plans she'd made so far for the concert. She'd meant to stop off in her favourite stationers and treat herself to a new notebook for this very purpose, but there simply weren't enough hours in the day. She'd already had an awkward, stilted argument with Milo about coming out this evening and a guilt-inducing phone call from Will, where he asked yet again for her patience and support.

Holly looked and felt exhausted. The shadows under her eyes from a late night plotting and planning were deepening as the day progressed and even slapping on another layer of Julia's Touche Éclat had made no difference. Hearing Taffy teasing Elsie in the kitchen about her sodden silk flowers barely raised a smile.

She looked up, aware that Julia was staring at her, and she self-consciously fiddled with her hair. 'What? Do I have something on my face?'

Julia shrugged. 'Just the weight of the world on your shoulders . . .' Sitting on the floor, Julia cuddled her knees to her chest and took a deep breath. 'Holly? Listen, I hope you don't mind me saying – we don't know each other that well – but when you talk about your husband, it sometimes sounds as though, well, as though you don't like him very much. Tell me to sod off, if I'm being too nosey, but why do you stay with him?'

'Crikey, you don't mess about with the small talk, do you?' Holly spluttered. Jesus, if even Julia Channing, known for her emotional reticence, was asking the question – did that mean the whole Practice was asking it too?

Holly shrugged, unsure how to answer. It would be all too easy to fob Julia off with some anodyne comment, but then, if they were really becoming friends? Might honesty be the best policy? 'My Dad died when I was young,' Holly said eventually. 'I hated growing up without a dad. So, even if we are having a rough patch – and trust me, we really are – then it's better to be together. For the boys.'

'Just the boys?' Julia asked, clearly intrigued.

'Well, obviously, once we get back on track, then it'll be better for me too . . .' Holly was very aware that her words weren't even that convincing to herself, so she blustered on, 'I just really think that boys need their fathers around, you know?'

Julia nodded. 'I can see that. Well, it just goes to show – you can get completely the wrong impression of someone. I had him pegged as all self-involved and intellectual. Is he just amazing with the boys, then?'

Holly couldn't help but let out a small nervous laugh. 'Oh Julia, you do have the ability to get straight to the heart of the issue. No. You were right first time . . . He's not really what you'd call a hands-on parent. But I have to believe, as the boys get older . . .'

'What are you two gossiping about?' interrupted Elsie, wandering through in her voluminous silk kaftan, nibbling at an olive on a cocktail stick. 'I've sent Taffy out to get ice.' She plonked herself down on the Venus Flytrap sofa and was immediately absorbed into its depths. 'We didn't really need ice,' she confided with a surprisingly girlish giggle, 'but when I heard how this conversation was going, I thought we could use a few minutes . . .'

Holly and Julia exchanged indulgent glances. Elsie's eccentricities were probably only amusing to them as relative newcomers. She must drive her family crazy, thought Holly with a smile.

'So,' prompted Elsie, 'you were saying about Milo . . .'

'It's just a rough patch,' mumbled Holly. 'It'll pass.'

Elsie patted her on the arm. 'My darling girl, these rough patches do have a habit of digging in. How long have you two been at odds?'

'Well,' said Holly, counting on her fingers, 'If we were married four years ago and the twins were born two years ago?' She grimaced, 'Shit! I'd say about two and a half years, with the odd week off for good behaviour. But that's par for the course with young kids, isn't it? No sleep, work pressures . . .'

'Affairs with their students . . .' said Elsie gently. 'I know, I know, it's none of my business either, but your boys might just prefer a happy mummy?'

Holly's face flushed as she thought of their little laughing faces at the Spring Swim with Taffy. Her flush deepened as she remembered the expression on her own face in that photo. She shrugged. 'I think we've got more pressing things to be worried about at the moment. Like The Practice closing down?' She picked up the plans and shuffled them officiously.

Elsie plucked them from her fingers and gave her a stern look. 'And we'll talk about that in a moment, but we have a small window to be frank, until our ice-bearer returns.

'Now, what are you doing to get things sorted with this husband of yours? Have you told him how you feel?' demanded Elsie.

Holly looked a little sheepish. 'Well, after the latest conversation we had, I'm not sure I'm even speaking to him any more.'

Elsie's laugh pealed out through the house. 'Oh my darling girl, you do have a lot to learn. You don't punish a man by not speaking to him; you punish him by speaking even more!' She clapped her hands delightedly. 'Oh I do so love having you girls here to chat to. It's nice to see someone using my pearls of wisdom. So, 101 Husbands and How To Choose Them.' She waved a hand at Julia to include her in the conversation. 'First, you must always play Monopoly with a man before you get married. You'll learn more about his attitude to credit than any other way. If he's mortgaged Park Lane and Mayfair before you can say "Pass Go" then you know he's a profligate spender and a risk taker and he'll do the same with your money too. Second, if the sex is no good to begin with, cut your losses: a selfish lover is a selfish man. Sex and money, you see, girls. It's always at the root of all evils. That, and greed ... wanting more sex, wanting more money, wanting more, more, more ... And never, ever, be with a man who takes longer to get ready than you do.' She gave a little shudder. 'Vain men are always egocentric bastards ...'

Holly laughed uncomfortably, Elsie's comments hitting dangerously close to the bone. 'Oh, Elsie, you do make me laugh.'

'I'm not trying to make you laugh, Holly,' replied Elsie, disgruntled at not being taken seriously. She reached out and took hold of Holly's hand. 'Your Milo has given you those wonderful twins. He's been an excellent starter husband. But now you're a grown-up and you know exactly what you do and don't want. A man should be the seasoning to your meal, to your life, enhancing the flavour of what's already there. He's not the meal itself. Seems perfectly reasonable to me, that it might be time to reassess things . . .'

Thankfully the front door slammed shut, essentially shutting down their conversation. Taffy could be heard singing, 'Ice, Ice Baby' in the hallway. 'Hellooo,' he said, poking his head around the doorway. 'Who wants Martinis?'

'We all do,' said Elsie, struggling to get out of the sofa, until Holly and Julia gave her a pull. 'Nothing wrong with going for an upgrade, Holly,' whispered Elsie under her breath, nodding meaningfully towards Taffy as they all walked through to the kitchen.

It was fair to say that Elsie's little outburst was playing on Holly's mind for most of the evening. They talked about the concert and who might take part. Taffy had some ridiculously wonderful suggestions for embarrassing skills they might learn and Julia was surprisingly relaxed and easy company.

Even when Elsie climbed onto her soapbox occasionally, they all listened indulgently. A few of her ideas were solid gold and Holly was excited about calling some of Elsie's more famous contacts to pull in a few favours. Certainly, if Elsie were to be believed, half of the BAFTA committee were in some way indebted to her.

As the Martinis flowed and the hours flew by, Holly realised how much she adored having someone older and more experienced in life to chat to. It was all very well talking to your mates, but weren't they all essentially winging it too? Elsie came with a veritable cornucopia of life skills – some of them bonkers, some of them dated, but some of them spot on the money.

Right now, Elsie was illuminating them all with theories about drinking. 'The trick,' she opined, 'is to only drink to feel even happier. Don't drink to feel happy.'

Holly rather wished that Lizzie was here to hear that one, but then quickly changed her mind, as Elsie continued.

'If you drink regularly, I mean one, maybe two little cocktails a day, it's actually healthier, isn't it? Because then you gradually pickle yourself from the inside, like a little onion, keeping your face nicely relaxed and everything else beautifully preserved – and you live longer!'

The three doctors in the room all spoke up at the same time, pointing out all the glaring errors in Elsie's reasoning. 'Science, schmience . . .' grinned Elsie. 'Now who's for another, while we plan this fabulous concert of yours?'

Elsie and Taffy disappeared again with the Martini jug and Holly and Julia flopped back into their chairs. Elsie on high-octane Martinis was a little exhausting.

Julia was still fiddling with the Lego figures and Playdoh that had fallen out of Holly's bag earlier. Her fingers worked the orange dough expertly. 'Here,' she said, passing Holly a beautiful Dali-esque teardrop, 'this is how I see you.'

Holly took the little sculpture in her hand and marvelled at the delicate curves that Julia had created.

'I sculpt things,' Julia said unnecessarily. 'Anything actually. My mind works better in 3D.'

'And this is me?' Holly said, nestling her thumb in the perfect petal-shaped dent in the teardrop.

Julia leaned forward. 'Here, in the middle is your heart – see – and this is you being stretched too thin in all these directions . . .'

'I love it,' said Holly simply, overwhelmed by the emotions that holding this little sculpture evoked. It just . . . fit somehow. 'Thank you,' she managed as she took another sip of her second Martini to steady herself. She knew she was approaching her lightweight limit, but they were just so damn tasty that she hadn't been able to refuse a refill. And now she was an emotional wreck.

'You're not so bad at this, you know,' said Holly suddenly, realising that for the first time in a long time, she was having a conversation with a female friend without bracing herself for a put-down. 'The friendship thing – I know you said you couldn't do it – but you're not so bad.'

Julia smiled weakly, still working the remains of the orange Playdoh between her perfectly manicured fingertips. 'Ah, Holly, you are sweet, but you'll see . . . I have no filter. Even now, while you're saying lovely things to me, I'm desperately resisting the urge to correct your grammar.'

Holly laughed. 'Well, me grammar never were me strong point,' she said in a silly voice, breaking the intensity that had been building in the room.

Julia couldn't resist joining in the laughter, catching Holly's glass mid-air as she sent it flying with her elbow. 'Dear God, you're clumsy! Thank God you're not a surgeon.'

Holly blinked hard, in for a penny. 'Why aren't you?' she asked bluntly. 'Only Grace mentioned . . .'

Julia flinched, caught off guard. 'Honestly? Too much guts on the patients' part, not enough on mine.'

'Oh,' said Holly quietly. 'It's just that you seem so . . .'

'Emotionally ill-equipped to be a GP?' interrupted Julia.

'I am a bit. On paper, I'm the perfect surgeon – bright, dexterous and arrogant enough to play God. But you know, real surgery is nothing like the cadavers at med school. For one thing, your patient's alive and you want to keep them that way. And that first cut,' she shuddered, 'the sensation of the scalpel, the gush, that metallic smell that just fills your nostrils and makes you want to . . .' She put a hand over her mouth, even the memory was enough to make her nauseous.

'I'm so sorry,' said Holly, entranced. 'I shouldn't have asked.'

'It's fine,' said Julia dismissively. 'I probably should talk about it more, but it's embarrassing, you know. Failed surgeon. Stand-offish GP. Rubbish friend.'

'I think you should cut yourself some slack,' Holly said. 'You're doing okay. And everyone has flaws – honestly – I know I'm way too judgemental.'

Julia raised an eyebrow in disbelief and, for some reason, Holly felt compelled to elaborate. 'Look, would it make you feel better to know that I've just essentially lost my oldest friend by being judgemental rather than supportive?'

'You mean Lizzie?'

Holly remembered suddenly that, when you live in a small town, everyone knows everyone.

Julia shrugged, looking uncomfortable. 'Would it sound a bit stalkery to say that I've seen you two together. Actually, in the spirit of honesty, I've been jealous of you two together. What happened?'

Holly sighed, in for a penny, in for a pound . . . 'She hasn't been the best friend to me lately. I won't bore you with the details, but I was furious with her. And now I'm more furious, because she won't take it seriously that I'm still really hurt. But just because I'm angry with her doesn't mean I'm not worried about her. She obviously had a reason for doing what she did . . . But at the moment, it seems she's just happier to keep on drinking her troubles away . . .'

'There doesn't need to be a reason. Alcoholics don't need a reason,' said Julia in an oddly detached tone.

'Oh, I'm not sure she'd qualify as an alcoholic, she just . . .'

'Likes to drink. A lot. All the time?' Julia said quietly.

Holly shook her head, feeling suddenly disloyal and trying to backtrack. 'Still, that's quite a label, isn't it? But then, she does like a drink these days. But then, lots of people do, don't they? It's one of the more socially acceptable addictions really.' She lifted her Martini glass, as if to emphasise the point, noticing for the first time that Julia was sipping an elderflower cordial.

'Holly,' said Julia softly, 'you need to follow your instincts on this. And please don't worry about me repeating anything you're saying. Trust me, on this topic, I'm the soul of discretion. Someone I know well, someone close . . .' Julia trailed off looking uncomfortable before taking a breath and carrying on, 'Crap this is hard, how do girls have these relationships where they tell each other everything? Alright – tell anyone this and I won't forgive you, but my mum. She drank a lot. She drinks a lot. Still. So if you want to, I don't know, talk. This one's my specialist subject, if you like. And if your friend was drinking enough to make you worried, then to be a real friend, you didn't have a choice. Trust me. Friends say something.'

There was a pause while they both regrouped and then Holly spoke up, 'Do you think we should say something to Elsie then too?'

Julia shook her head. 'Seems to me that Elsie knows exactly what she's doing.'

*

What Elsie appeared to be doing, was trying to teach Taffy the Can-Can. It was only when Taffy appeared at the doorway, begging for respite that the girls relented and followed him through.

'Now, I know we're all having a lovely time, but you've probably been wondering why I summoned you all here tonight? Well,' Elsie paused dramatically, as if waiting for a drum roll, 'I wanted to offer to compère your show. It's probably too late to teach an old dog new tricks, but I could do a little something and I like to think my name adds a certain glamour and gravitas to the proceedings. Don't you think?'

'I do actually,' said Holly, wondering why she hadn't thought of it herself. 'Are you sure it wouldn't be too much for you?'

'Pah!' dismissed Elsie. 'No problem. And then when you ring around all my friends, you can tell them I'm already in. Might sway one or two. And, if you wanted to make an old lady very happy, I could do a little scene ... maybe a duologue with Dan Carter ... maybe with a kiss?'

Taffy laughed and removed her Martini glass. 'Alright, Townsend, I'm cutting you off. I think it's a fabulous idea that you host. But I think Dan should host it with you, like at the Oscars ... What do you think?'

The imprint of Elsie's bright red lipstick on his cheek was as good as a seal of approval. Taffy smiled over at Holly and her stomach swooped once more.

'Sounds like your plan has legs now, Holls, are you ready for this?' he asked quietly. Without her asking, he poured her a glass of elderflower and passed it to her, the frisson between their fingers when they touched nearly spilling it everywhere.

'Let's hope it's enough to save The Practice,' Holly managed.

'God, I hope so,' said Taffy with feeling. 'How else would I get to see you every day?'

Holly swallowed, regretting that last Martini and wishing she'd kept her wits about her. She couldn't help the look of panic that spread across her face. She also noticed that Taffy immediately followed her lead and back-pedalled.

'Well, who else can I try my awful jokes on, eh?' he said gently, his eyes suddenly shadowed. He pulled up a stool by the worktop and sighed. 'My friend drowned in a bowl of muesli, you know. A strong currant pulled him in . . .'

Holly couldn't help it. His jokes were just so bloody awful, but they struck a note with her. She snorted with laughter and watched as Taffy's face transformed, lit up in a way that needed no translation.

Holly pressed her hand to her chest, partly to quell the nervous laughter and partly to slow her racing heart.

Elsie, quick as a dart, missed nothing. 'Don't forget what I said now, Holly,' she whispered. 'Life's too short to live in compromise and you can't fake chemistry.'

Taffy stared at Holly, Elsie's whisper being audible somewhere across the Market Place in all probability.

'Now,' said Elsie, clearly delighted to have stirred up a little trouble, 'pass me that folder, will you? I've a list of VIPs who live locally. You can have a little phone around.'

Holly reached across for a big thick folder secured with a beautiful grosgrain ribbon.

'Oh no, not that one, dear. That's my funeral file. I like to keep it up to date. Friends will insist on dying and messing up my guest list!'

Holly flinched a little, the thought of Elsie's mortality more upsetting than was logical. 'Oh, Elsie, please don't spend your time thinking about things like that . . .' she began.

'Tish tosh,' Elsie interrupted her. 'You didn't think I'd let someone else write my eulogy, did you? I've never read my own reviews; after all everyone's entitled to their opinion. And what else is a eulogy if not your Final Review? Oh no, Holly darling, that one I'm writing myself! I've drafted a lovely Obituary for *The Times* too. I like to be prepared.'

Elsie's words may have been feisty and confident, but Holly noticed a slight tremor in her hands as she spoke. She reached across and squeezed Elsie's trembling hand.

Elsie gave a gentle squeeze in return and then stood up, seemingly shaking off any concern. She clapped her hands. 'Enough of all this, Ginger darling, let's whip up a batch of Mai Tai's shall we?'

Elsie's pronouncement was like an old LP record, scratching to a halt.

There was an awkward pause. 'Do you mean Taffy?' Julia asked perplexed.

Elsie started. 'Of course, I did. Sorry, darlings, just been a long day.' Elsie looked properly rattled by her mistake though.

'Who's Ginger?' asked Holly softly, intrigued as always by every morsel of Elsie's life.

'Ginger was my eldest,' replied Elsie vaguely, choosing not to elaborate.

'Oh,' said Holly. 'I'm sorry, Elsie, I didn't even realise you had children.' There were certainly no photos of any children dotted around the house, but then maybe Elsie kept them just for herself in her opulent bedroom upstairs.

'Three actually,' said Elsie, still distractedly plucking at the bundle of fresh mint she'd been feeding into the blender. 'One dead, one drunk, one greedy. Parent of the year, I am not,' she said.

Holly caught Taffy's eye but neither of them knew what to say.

Elsie filled the yawning chasm by sighing deeply. 'Darling Ginger was the best of the bunch really, but he drove his MG into a lake on his twenty-fifth birthday. Polly lives in LA while she snorts her way through her trust fund and blames me for everything and Otto has already spent all of his. He pops round twice a year to borrow some more and drop heavy hints about avoiding inheritance tax by giving him the houses now.' She gave a small unhappy laugh. 'He's rather kidding himself if he thinks I've got another seven years left in me. He's going to be equally disappointed when he discovers I've not left him a bean.'

'Oh, Elsie,' Holly sympathised, 'I had no idea.'

'Yes, well, now you do,' said Elsie, neatly cutting off the conversation at the knees. 'And you can forget all of that until I'm dead and then you can all have a good read through my diaries and write yourselves a bestseller – how's that?' She smiled again. 'But you'll have to wait a little longer for that and you can only use the really naughty stuff once I'm six feet under.

'Anyway,' said Elsie. 'Don't mind me, I'm having a little maudlin day, that's all. All this community spirit is exhausting, don't you think? And we've had enough confidences for one evening, so I'll be off to bed now. But before I do, let's have a little toast.

'To new friends and new beginnings,' Elsie said, raising her glass pointedly at Holly. 'And to never being afraid of starting over.'

With extravagant hugs and kisses and pages of notes for the concert shuffled into her handbag, Holly leaned in to kiss Elsie goodnight at the door.

Elsie looped the treasured Missoni scarf from Holly's last visit around her neck. 'This is yours now. A little bit of Elsie to keep you on the ball.'

'Oh, Elsie, I couldn't possibly . . .'

'I shall be terribly offended if you don't wear it,' Elsie said sternly. 'I can't always be there to hold your hand and guide you in the right direction. I want you to learn to trust your instincts, Holly. Just think of this scarf as a little bit of faith to help you on your way, okay?'

'Okay,' nodded Holly, touched beyond measure.

Elsie smiled at her and patted her cheek. 'Now, listen to me, Holly Graham. You don't get married four times without learning a little something about marriage. And rather a lot about divorce too, as it happens.' She sighed deeply, her face flickering with emotions as she tried to piece together what she wanted to share. 'You know how books and movies always end when they've just got together? Well, there's a perfectly good reason for that. It's because a week later he's picking his nose in front of the TV and they're fighting over the washing up. Real life isn't like a movie, my darling girl – and I should know. But that doesn't mean you have to settle for second best. At home or at work.'

Holly kissed Elsie's powdered cheek affectionately. 'Shall I add that to my list of Life Lessons?'

'It wouldn't be the worst idea,' Elsie said, as she quietly closed the door.

Chapter 34

Dan slammed the phone down on his cousin in disgust. Okay, so Lizzie was still angry with him for taking Holly's side, but enough was enough. Why couldn't Lizzie 'fess up that she'd got this one wrong and apologise. Yeah, he thought to himself, and hell might freeze over. But, even if she couldn't bring herself to apologise, was it really too much to expect his own cousin to be a little bit helpful and supportive with the campaign to Save The Practice?

Putting aside family loyalties for a moment, as Lizzie obviously believed he'd already abandoned his – could she not see that, as a resident herself, the health of her children could be directly compromised? It was sheer, stubborn pride that was stopping Lizzie from stepping up.

He toyed with the idea of going over her head – she may be the Editor of *Larkford Life*, but he was pretty sure her publisher wouldn't be too impressed at this missed opportunity to support the community and sell some extra copies in the process.

Shit.

When did life get so complicated?

Dan rubbed his fingers methodically over the smooth pebble he used for his mindfulness exercises, trying to stay in the moment. He'd been feeling so much better, so much more like himself, since he'd been to Hereford. Chris' advice had been spot on. Dan had somehow forgotten that PTSD never really went away; one just had to manage the symptoms.

Well, he hadn't been managing himself very well, had he? Too many late nights, too much stress and no time at all for himself. More importantly, Dan had been gradually cutting back on his mindfulness programme to the point where the skills hadn't been there, at his fingertips, when he needed them.

Now, back on Chris' programme, and even with the chaos around him, the flashbacks were fewer and more fleeting and he'd actually been getting some sleep.

Obviously not last night though, since his 3 a.m. emergency call out had been a complete waste of time. He'd been met by a houseful of sheepish, slightly tipsy students. Clearly one clever dick had thought it tremendously funny to serve his housemates a high-end cat food as pâté. His idea of a practical joke had all the girls spewing copiously, but there was no evidence of food poisoning as the phone call had suggested. Dan had diagnosed psychosomatic hysterical vomiting and given them all a bit of a lecture. To be fair, the ingredients in the swanky brand he'd used, were probably better quality than the horse-burgers sold in the local discount store, but still … 3 a.m.?

Quietly driving home through the darkness of the valley, Dan had half wondered whether Taffy might fall for the same trick. He was well overdue on the retaliation front. He'd ditched the idea fairly quickly – he'd seen Taffy willingly eat far worse things than cat food over the years.

Seeing the town laid out before him and thinking about

his best friend made Dan all the more determined to step up the campaign. He'd made a mental list as he drove along of phone calls to make and favours to call in. Truth be told, he was a little aggrieved that it was Holly who had come up with the PR angle. He'd been stuck in a bureaucratic loop of red tape himself and had been close to admitting defeat.

But he hated doctors like Henry Bruce – the smarmy bastard – and his world of cronies and freebies and pharmaceutical incentive schemes. It would be a very happy by-product if he could ruin Henry Bruce into the bargain.

Now, though, he needed to focus. It hadn't occurred to him for a moment that Lizzie wouldn't leap into the fray. He'd been hoping to get her on board with a special edition of *Larkford Life* – a short notice print run to rally support. He really couldn't comprehend that, in reality, she'd just given him gip and then offered precisely nothing.

There was a knock at the door, breaking in to his reverie, and Taffy poked his head into the consulting room. 'Mate? Have you got a mo?'

'Sure,' said Dan, pushing back his chair and stretching out the stiffness in his back. Joining the Larkford Harriers had probably been a big mistake, but Chris had pushed for him to do more regular exercise and there was always the chance he'd get to bump into Lindy again and she might be persuaded to change her mind. Either way, he was stiff as a board this morning and any Taffy-style distraction was extremely welcome.

'Firstly,' said Taffy, plonking a large glass vase on Dan's desk, 'I offer you a challenge – I'm calling it First To Frog. So, here's your frog spawn, I have mine – we just need to decide on a wager.'

Dan shook his head. 'You really do have too much time on your hands, Taff.'

Taffy shrugged. 'Couldn't sleep, so I went for a jog along the river and there it was, calling to me. We can't all be Harriers, honey. Anyway, I'm in need of distraction, so what do you say? Any methods acceptable. No replacement spawn. First to a proper Kermit wins ... ?'

Dan grinned, struck by inspiration. 'If I win, you'll stop taking the piss out of Triathlons and, if you win ... That's tricky. Hmm, maybe I'll put in a good word with Holly for you. Tell her your reputation as a gigolo is only because you haven't met the right girl yet?'

Taffy coloured. 'That's too rich for my blood. I've been saving up triathlon jokes all week. Shall we go for the standard car wash and vac? Besides,' he said, not looking Dan in the eye, 'I think I'm holding my own on the Holly front. And I've made moves to improve my chances.' He rolled up his sleeve to show Dan two nicotine patches.

'I don't want her to think I'm a smoker, do I? Not with the boys about. And, I mean, it's *quite* nice not lurking outside by the bins like a social leper and there's obviously the whole cancer thing.'

Dan grinned, shocked and impressed in equal measure by his friend's cavalier attitude to his health. 'Erm, aren't those big patches the One-a-day ones, though, Taff?'

Taffy shrugged. 'Thought I'd try the low dose ones first. I just stick one on whenever I get stressed, or fancy a cigarette, but to be honest, I'm not really sure they're working properly. I just feel all dizzy and nauseous.'

'Well, did you actually read the packet? There's a maximum daily dosage of 21mg, you prat!'

Taffy looked sheepish for a moment before slowly

unbuttoning his shirt. 'Then the two on my chest were probably a bad idea too, then?'

'Jesus! What have you done to yourself?' Dan shook his head in disbelief. 'Well, I'll say this for you, Taffs, it's all or nothing with you.' Dan leaned forward and caught hold of the corner of one patch and dispatched it with a quick flick of the wrist.

Taffy's eyes watered as he took a substantial amount of chest hair away too. 'Fucking hell, Dan!'

Dan laughed like a drain, methodically stripping Taffy of every patch and handing him a large glass of water. 'Keep hydrated. One patch at a time. If you feel really unwell, you'll have to tell me. I can look it up in The Big Book of Overdoses.'

Taffy looked down at the two bald squares on his chest and the two on his arm. 'I'm not convinced that giving up smoking won't be the death of me at this rate.'

Dan was still laughing to himself. 'Well, it should certainly test your commitment to the Steal-Holly-Away-From-Her-Husband plan, shouldn't it?'

'How did she get lumbered with that prat anyway?'

'Er, because she loves him? Because they have children together?'

'Well, yeah, at the time ... But I think I'm in way over my head. Do you know I turned down a shag with Denise O'Sullivan at the weekend! I mean, where will this end? Even married to that stuffed shirt, she's probably getting more action than I am and I can't think about anyone else but her.'

'Oh,' said Dan quietly, a little blown away by his friend's confession. So much for hoping for the crush to pass then. 'You have to let this one go, mate. Focus on your frog, focus on your training, focus on the Campaign,' he suggested.

'Holly's campaign, you mean,' said Taffy darkly, looking up at Dan with tormented eyes. 'This is what happens when you let your head get involved, Carter. I've been so busy warning you off, that I just didn't see it coming myself.' He blew out his cheeks. 'Right then, I'm off to check on a dodgy prostate. Good luck with Kermit – my car is a cesspit!'

Dan sat back in his chair and yawned. 'You could try joining one of those addiction support groups? You might meet someone pretty while you're there.'

Taffy checked his watch again and leaned against the door and shrugged. 'I'm not sure that's for me, mate. Hanging around with a bunch of quitters.'

By the time his afternoon clinic started, Dan had spoken to three different newspaper journalists, sticking religiously to the script that Grace and Holly had drafted. He'd also given a radio interview that had gone reasonably well until the radio presenter had asked for his opinion of how the whole debacle had occurred. Dan wasn't entirely up to date on the slander laws in the UK, but he was now quietly hoping that Henry Bruce wasn't either. Maybe it would be a good idea to look them up, he decided. With emotions running so high, there was every chance it would happen again.

He walked through to the waiting room to collect his next patient. 'Mr Payne?' he called.

Even as the guy stood up out of his chair and walked towards him, Dan struggled to place him. The trendy media specs and scarf reminded him of someone, but he couldn't work out who.

They both sat down, door closed. 'What can I do for you, Mr Payne? I believe you're a new patient?' He flicked through the file and caught sight of the name and address,

Milo Payne. The surprise must have been evident on his face.

'So,' said Milo, 'you've worked out who I am, then.'

There was no question he was an attractive, well put-together guy. He seemed a little up himself, thought Dan, but then, he assumed that most academics worked on a different level to mere civilians. 'Great to finally meet you, Milo. I'm sure I don't need to tell you how much we love having Holly here.'

'I'm sure you don't and that's why I've come actually.' He leaned forward in his seat, looking about as threatening as it was possible for a man in Penny Loafers to look. 'I know all about you tricking her into this job with empty promises and I know all about how she's the one rallying round to save this poxy setup. But I know blokes like you, Dan Carter. You'll chew up my naïve little wife and spit her out. Be kind to her, at least. She has no idea how the real world works and I quite like her that way. So, man to man, I'm asking you – let her go now and we can move on.'

'I . . .' began Dan, finding himself speechless.

'And I know that you two have a whole flirty thing going on. Dan this, Dan that . . . It's all I get at home. So maybe, while you're letting her go, you could remember that she has a husband and two children. Not really cricket, is it, Dr Carter?'

Dan blinked hard. 'Milo, I'm not sure what Holly's told you, but I can assure you that there's absolutely nothing going on between us – flirty or otherwise. And Holly's involvement in the campaign is wonderful and entirely of her own volition. She's a valued and respected member of the team. As for who's keeping their job? Well, I'm sure you can imagine that this is a difficult time for everyone. Decisions will have to be made when the time comes.' He steepled his fingers and held Milo's gaze. 'I rather think that this is something for you to discuss with your wife.'

Milo seemed a little deflated. He'd obviously geared himself up for some verbal sparring and Dan's calm and mat-ter-of-fact response had clearly thrown him.

'Now, if there's nothing else?' Dan said, getting to his feet, furious beyond measure at the snide and disrespectful way that Milo spoke about Holly.

Milo fidgeted in his chair, small without his bluster to inflate him. 'Well, actually, Doc, since I'm here . . . I've got a really bad case of athlete's foot . . .'

Dan took a calming breath, trying to remain professional. All he really wanted to do, was to pop next door and tell Taffy it was game on. Whatever he'd previously thought about Taffy putting the moves on a married colleague? Well, that was water under the bridge now he'd met the smug, patronising git in person.

He pulled some latex gloves from the box on his desk. 'We'd better take a look. And then, maybe we should give you your Well Man check, since you're hitting middle age and we have plenty of time.'

If Milo had winced at the 'middle age' comment, it was nothing to how he reacted when Dan snapped the gloves on to his hands with a theatrical flourish.

'Now, Milo, tell me: have you ever had your prostate checked?'

Dan was feeling a little ashamed of himself by the time he met up with Taffy in the doctors' lounge at the end of the day. Taffy and Grace were munching their way through a packet of Jaffa Cakes, trying to see how many they could fit in their mouths at once.

'Look,' said Grace gleefully. 'Full moon,' she took a bite. 'Half moon,' she took another. 'Total eclipse!' she said, shoving the last of the Jaffa cake in and spraying crumbs everywhere. She swallowed hard, making her eyes water, and looked disappointed at Dan's lack of response. 'Taffy taught me,' she explained.

Dan just shook his head. 'Did you never see the ad, then, Grace?' She looked blank. 'Blimey, you'll be saying that you missed "you've been Tango-ed" next!'

Taffy obligingly stepped forward, arms outstretched to smack Dan's ears, but Dan batted him away. 'Geroff, you muppet,' he said impatiently. 'Do you want to go over this campaign stuff here or at the pub?'

'If you do it here, I could help,' volunteered Grace. 'I needed to talk to you about that anyway.'

She settled on the arm of the sofa nervously. 'I do realise it's not my department, but I wondered if you wanted me to set up a campaign website. We could include all the profiles and have a page for people to pledge their support. We could put links to it in all the press interviews too. What do you think?'

Dan wanted to do a double-take. What was it with people catching him on the hop today? Was nobody going to behave true to form? Was this really sweet, twin-set-and-pearls Grace talking? 'Do you know how to do all that?' he asked.

'I'll just use an html template and hyperlinks and we can update daily progress, take donations and sell concert tickets too. I can use SSL to ... Dan?'

Dan stopped suddenly, aware that he had been shaking his head in bemusement and seeing Grace's crestfallen expression, he quickly leapt to put her straight, 'Grace, it sounds amazing! It would be perfect actually. I'm sorry I looked so blank just then – you took me by surprise with all the techno talk.'

She blushed to the roots of her immaculate bob. 'It's no problem and I'd love to give it a go. I've been taking an online learning course,' she confided.

Dan pulled her into a hug without thinking. 'Where would we be without you, Gracie?'

She smiled, clearly delighted. 'I'll get started then.'

Dan breathed a sigh of relief, the Lizzie-shaped knot of tension in his chest slowly relaxing. 'Just as well you're a computer nerd really, Grace. Couldn't get Lizzie to do that *Larkford Life* spread we talked about.'

Grace just shrugged. 'Well, this is probably better anyway. More interactive, easier to update in real time. Print media's terribly old hat these days, you know!' She flashed him a smile and gathered up her kit. 'I'll go home and crack on.'

She bustled out of the doorway and Dan decided that he must stop making assumptions about people. Grace was a woman of many resources – but he was ashamed to admit that he tended to judge her on the fact that her husband had a fondness for the cider, her teenaged sons had a fondness for the sofa, and all three had a strong aversion to a decent day's work. But that certainly didn't mean that Grace wasn't fully motivated and up to speed. Truth be told, it probably explained why she put in longer hours at The Practice than anyone else and made the team feel like her surrogate family.

Even with so many balls in the air that evening, Dan Carter felt like a very lucky man. He looked across the lounge to see Taffy crouched beside his own goldfish bowl full of frog spawn. He was singing to it, mournfully and a little out of tune. 'It's not easy being green . . .'

'Come on, Kermit,' said Dan, flicking off the lights. 'Let's have a pint and put the world to rights.'

'Cool,' said Taffy, gathering up his fishbowl. He grinned at Dan. 'I can tell you about my *anus horribilis.*'

Dan gave him a sideways look. 'What are you, the Queen? And it's barely May. Besides, I think you'll find it's *annus horribilis*. Two n's.'

'Ah, but then you didn't have to look after Mr Proctor's prostate this afternoon, though, did you?' laughed Taffy.

Dan groaned, slow to catch the joke. 'Well no, but since we're talking about prostates, I should probably tell you about a little visit I got earlier. From the infamous Mr Holly Graham, no less.'

Chapter 35

The idea of the concert seemed to have captured the imagination of everyone at The Practice and soon other residents were offering their support. Some, like Elsie, were determined to get on stage and do their thing. Others were happier to offer printing of programmes or costumes if required.

Holly absent-mindedly clicked through Grace's amazing website, which seemed to have sprung up overnight but, thanks to Grace's well-established presence on Twitter (who knew?), it had already attracted lots of interest and nearly £300 in pledges.

Every break or lunchtime, there would be small huddles and groups, closed doors and secret rehearsals. They had all decided that a dress rehearsal, whilst prudent, might spoil the fun and spontaneity of the event. So Grace had merely put out a sign-up sheet and given each group or individual a number in the running order.

The only slight tweak to the original concept had been down to Lucy's forthright manner. 'Listen, guys, it's all very well us doing new things and putting ourselves up for a laugh, but we do run the risk of it being utterly shite. Can we maybe have a few good acts, you know, people who actually know what they're doing, just to break up amateur hour?'

She'd picked her moment well, as almost the whole team were getting their daily caffeine fix. 'It does sound like a good idea,' said Dan. 'The only hiccup being – can any of you lot actually *do* anything?'

After being bombarded by miniature packets of sugar – spirits were running a little high – they'd settled down to discuss options.

'Well, Taffy should definitely sing something,' ventured Maggie, blushing a little. 'I've heard him in church and there won't be a dry eye in the house if he does that "Raise Me Up" song.'

Grace nodded enthusiastically. 'I could put up a teaser trailer on the website if you'll record one, Taffy, looking all dishevelled and whatnot. Bring a few ladies in, won't it?'

Holly swallowed hard and fiddled with her hair clip. I really need to get a grip, she thought. I'm far too old to be having adolescent crushes. Yes, he's adorable, but he can be an adorable friend, can't he? She quite liked the idea of having Taffy as a surrogate Uncle for the boys – someone to chuck a ball around with and chat to about rugby and treehouses and stuff . . . For a moment, the idea seemed so simple, until she looked up. He was watching her, concern etched on his face.

'You okay?' he mouthed.

She nodded. Jesus, she'd have to be lying on the floor dying for Milo to take notice. A few seconds looking a bit downcast though, and Taffy was checking in.

She managed a sad smile and carried on giving herself a talking to, while Jade was offering to do a gymnastic routine that involved ribbons and what sounded like a very skimpy costume.

Milo may not be the greatest husband in history, she thought, and he certainly wasn't the most hands-on dad to Tom and Ben, but for all his faults, he was *their* dad. How could she, in all conscience, and considering herself an honourable person, do anything to jeopardise their relationship?

And Milo was finally making an effort – a slightly misguided effort – booking this night away, but nevertheless it was a step in the right direction.

Here she was, a responsible adult, on the brink of losing her job, and she was actually considering throwing away a perfectly serviceable marriage for a crush. A laugh bubbled in the back of her throat as she could hear Lizzie's voice in her head – 'He's a man for Christ's sake, not a Vauxhall Astra!'

Holly slowly counted to ten in her head to eclipse the image of Taffy as his rather shabby, slightly eccentric Land Rover Defender – certainly not in its first flush of youth, rather well worn, with a slightly torn roof, but tremendous fun. Not unlike Taffy himself.

Were cars like dogs, she wondered, sharing characteristics with their owners? Milo with his anally retentive and overly pampered Saab; Holly with her much loved, much abused Golf that could still kick in a turn of speed when required? Lizzie with her soft-top Peugeot – all style no substance? Thinking of Lizzie made Holly's stomach flip over – she missed Eric's doggy cuddles, the noise and chaos of their family home and Will's dependably dry sense of humour. She hated to admit it, but she missed Lizzie too. It had been wonderful getting to know Julia better and Elsie was like a whirlwind of positivity, but sometimes an old friend was required. Someone who didn't need any backstory – someone who had driven an acid-green VW campervan all through university – adaptable, quirky and fun – the Lizzie, in fact, that she'd been missing.

'What about you, Holls?' Dan's voice interrupted her reverie and she looked up to find all eyes on her. 'What are you going to do?'

For a moment, she froze, convinced that Dan could read her mind and wanted an answer: Taffy or Milo? Then she remembered the topic under discussion and relaxed. 'Well, for the silly, I quite fancied doing a duet – if someone wants to play the guitar? And for the other – well – I can play the cello a bit, if that helps,' said Holly quietly, almost instantly regretting the words as they left her mouth.

A few eyebrows raised and she shrugged. 'Haven't played properly for a while, though.'

Dan looked at her shrewdly. 'Now come on, Graham, is that like when Julia told us she'd once "played a bit of tennis"?'

'Oh God, do you remember?' snorted Taffy. 'And she quietly neglected to mention that she'd qualified for Junior Wimbledon! You really didn't like being my doubles partner, did you, Jules?'

Holly was amused to see Julia stiffen at being called Jules. To her credit though, she relaxed almost instantly, actually looking a little chuffed to have finally earned an endearing diminutive.

Put on the spot about her cello-playing abilities, Holly wasn't quite sure what to say. 'I'm not exactly Yo-Yo Ma but I'll be fine to play something nice.' She tugged at her earlobe nervously. 'I just don't get much time to practise really, not with everything else going on.'

She suddenly wanted to blurt out the truth though – it

wasn't that she didn't have time to practise, was it? Not really. She'd rather be playing the cello than watching TV, or cooking, or jogging. But Milo didn't like the noise. He didn't like the intense concentration that overcame Holly when she played and that made him feel left out. Although it sounded bonkers to Holly to admit it, it was almost as if he were jealous of her cello. It was the only logical reason why an otherwise sane man would be moved to banish her beloved instrument to their storage locker.

She knew that she could probably practise at a friend's house, if only she had asked. But somehow Holly couldn't bring herself to admit, even to Lizzie, that not only would her husband not allow her to have a dog, he had also banished her cello.

Which implication was worse though, she wondered, that her husband really was turning into a controlling nutter, or that she was stupid enough to put up with it? Some days, it seemed to be a miracle that he allowed her to keep the twins in the house either.

And there was that word 'allowed' again. It made Holly's heart race with the looming panic of knowing that she had to make a decision. A big decision. And soon.

Before things got any worse.

She was so distracted by her own mental melodrama that she wasn't really paying attention when Taffy asked her what piece she might like to play.

'Probably the First Bach Suite for Cello,' she answered distractedly, noting how Dan's eyes flickered to Julia every moment or two and wondering what that meant. Jesus, she had the attention span of an ADHD toddler today. 'It's my favourite.'

There was an awkward silence, before Taffy dared to say

what everyone else was thinking. 'Wouldn't you be happier choosing something simpler? Less pressure on you to find time to practise, if time's short . . .'

Holly watched as Taffy's cheeks flamed as his words petered out. She knew that the very last thing he would ever want to do was not be supportive, but he obviously couldn't bear the idea of Holly setting herself an impossible goal. He'd tried so hard to build her confidence lately, not undermine it. She felt a bit mean that she'd put him in this awkward position.

Holly blinked hard, hoist with her own petard. She'd mentioned playing the cello a bit and then blithely suggested she play one of the most challenging pieces in the cello repertoire. Alone. On stage. She wondered if now was the best time to confess that she could actually play this technically and emotionally demanding piece in her sleep? That really, at seventeen, it had been a toss-up between medicine or The Royal School of Music? But that somehow felt like bragging and Holly didn't do bragging – it made her feel uncomfortable and off kilter. She'd have been shit on *The Apprentice*. 'Maybe you're right,' she said, buying herself some thinking time, 'but it has to be Bach. He really is my favourite.'

'And the duet?' asked Grace, taking notes.

'Erm . . . I know it's a bit old school, but the Carpenters maybe? If someone could play the guitar while I strangle a cat with my singing?'

'Don't look at me,' Dan said bluntly, 'I'm all thumbs.' He paused and gave a meaningful look across the room. 'Taffy'll do it, won't you, mate?'

'No problem,' said Taffy easily.

Brilliant, thought Holly to herself. Not only did she have a raging argument running in her head, trying to be a decent person and do the right thing, but now she had to contend with Dan Carter playing Cilla bloody Black . . .

After a couple of days of practising in their lunch-break and managing to get Taffy up to speed with a few basic chords, Holly was running on caffeine, adrenalin and sheer determination. The sun was shining, the birds were singing but they were tucked away in the Phlebotomy suite amongst all the empty blood vials. Both of them tired, impatient and more than a little frustrated. Possibly for different reasons though, Holly admitted to herself.

'Listen, Holly, maybe we should pick something easier? I clearly have the manual dexterity of a wombat. In fact, I'm not entirely sure that this was your best idea, Holly. No offence,' said Taffy cautiously.

'Oh, I never said it was a good idea,' Holly replied, 'it just gained a certain credibility for being, you know, the *only* idea.' She grinned and shuffled the sheet music, quietly enjoying every moment of his nervous discomfort. 'And it is starting to sound better – well, marginally, but still better. A bit more practice on those chords and we'll be fine.'

'I'm going to look a right prat in front of the whole town, you do realise that, don't you?'

'I could be wrong, Dr Jones, but isn't that exactly what we're banking on? We put ourselves out there, take a chance, humanise The Practice . . .'

'We get laughs and support and everyone claps us on the back. Hooray, The Practice is saved and we all go home for tea and medals?' finished Taffy for her tiredly, making no effort to disguise the scepticism in his voice.

Holly flinched, as if Taffy had slapped her. 'Well, you don't have to join in, you know.' She busied herself with the music stand which seemed to have gained a life of its own and kept collapsing, until it gave one last shudder and trapped Holly's fingers in its mechanism. Tears sprang unbidden to her eyes, glad of an excuse to cry.

Glad of the opportunity to be upset for a normal, logical reason, rather than the bubble of hurt that had blocked her throat at Taffy's dismissal of her plan. Anger tussled with the upset; after all, it wasn't as though anyone else had been forthcoming with any genius suggestions, was it?

She bit down hard on her bottom lip, as she extricated her bleeding finger from the metal, furious with herself as a small sob escaped her lips.

'Here, let me see,' said Taffy quietly, reaching for her hand. He cradled her fingers in his, gently bending and flexing them. 'All in one piece. No broken bones. Let's get that cleaned up, though.' Deftly and carefully, he cleaned the broken skin and, rummaging in the freezer, turned out a bag of sorry-looking peas that had clearly served this very purpose once or twice before.

Holly hiccuped rather pathetically, pulling herself together repeatedly, only to be undermined at every turn by Taffy's attentiveness. She hated crying, but for some reason, she simply couldn't stop herself (she was not an attractive genteel crier like in the movies either; if she wasn't careful there would be full-blown snot bubbles to contend with, and that was hardly a winning proposition).

'Cheer up, chicken,' he said, after the third little sob slipped out, 'you've got a few fingers left over and it's not like you need them to play the guitar or anything, is it? You've got Muggins here for that. I'm not going anywhere, so you can relax. I'll be your Sonny, if you'll be my Cher.'

'Who?' managed Holly, bemused as ever by Taffy's

random musical references. 'Isn't that the old lady who's always wearing a leotard?'

'Sacrilege, Graham! She's won more awards than you've had hot dinners ... She's a legend in her own lunchtime! Most famous musical partnership of all time? Tch, well, as long as we don't end up like John and Yoko. Oh dear God, woman, don't look at me blankly like that ... Lennon, Yoko Ono? Split up The Beatles?'

Taffy's look of intense frustration was too much for Holly and she couldn't maintain the façade any longer. She pressed her unwounded hand to her chest to stop the giggles hurting so much. 'Your face ...' she managed, before another peal of laughter overtook her.

'You know what, Taff, sod this, it's a beautiful day: can we get out of here for a bit? Find somewhere outside to practise?'

Taffy stood up, Holly's old guitar slung across his body and his hair falling in his eyes. Holly had to resist the urge to brush it away. Credit where credit was due – you may have been able to feel the attraction between them from across the room, but Taffy had respectfully kept his distance. That first rehearsal, he'd leaned in just a little too close as Holly showed him the correct finger positions, and Holly had snapped, 'Oi, no funny business, Jones!' and he'd stuck to that arrangement. To be fair, she'd slightly regretted saying it, but it was still absolutely the right thing to do.

'Come on then, my little diva, let's go find a bench in the park and we can frighten the birds.' Holding open the door to the car park, Holly was overwhelmed by the warm sweet scent of the burgeoning wisteria that covered the front of the building. The lazy buzzing of the bees made her want to lie on a bench and switch off from it all.

As they made their way through to the Market Place and the park beyond, Holly could all too easily imagine herself and Taffy on a bench, like the end of *Notting Hill*, with the twins running around them and another one on the way . . .

She jolted suddenly. 'Get a grip,' she muttered furiously to herself.

'It's alright, I've got it,' Taffy responded, misunderstanding and tapping her guitar.

'Oh, no, I didn't mean . . .' Holly spluttered, all the while thinking, yeah, really attractive Holly. Maybe she should take a blood test, get her hormones checked? This was getting silly. She tripped over her toes a little as the ground began to slope upwards and Taffy steadied her.

'You have to be the clumsiest grown-up I have ever met,' he said with a grin.

Holly grimaced. 'It's a family trait. My dad was too and they let him carry a fire-arm!'

'To be honest, I was a little concerned when I first saw you doing stitches, but then I hadn't realised you were so good at embroidery.'

'Well, it's always the way, isn't it? You end up working harder and longer on the things you can't do.'

Taffy was suddenly silent beside her.

'Did I touch a nerve?' she asked gently.

'Well,' he hesitated, 'with me it's relationships. Some would say that I've been out with so many girls because I hadn't met the right one.'

'Some might,' Holly conceded. 'Or some might say that you're young and attractive and single and why shouldn't you?'

'Is that what you think?' Taffy asked, stopping in his tracks and fixing her in his gaze.

'I don't know what I think about anything at the moment,' Holly answered honestly. 'These last few weeks, it's as though everything I thought I knew ... well, maybe I got it wrong? And Elsie's helping me to look at things in a different way ...'

Taffy stepped forward and closed the distance between them. He looked down at her, not touching, just close enough that she could feel the warmth of his body.

'And did Elsie mention me?' he asked gently.

Holly blushed deeply. 'She might have done. She's quite the fan.' Holly lifted her hand and placed it on Taffy's chest. She'd intended it as a gesture to keep him from leaning in, but the beat of his heart under her hand was her undoing.

He leaned down slowly, giving her all the time in the world to back away, before brushing her lips fleetingly with his.

The effect was electric. Holly fought the urge to simply give in to the kiss, but she needn't have worried. Taffy stepped back, but pressing his hand over hers to keep the connection.

'I'm a mum,' Holly said, the tears rising in her throat as she looked at this man – this spaniel-eyed, floppy-haired, rogue of a man, whom she simply adored. 'I'm a mum.'

'I know you are, Holly. And I know those boys are everything to you. But I wanted you to know how I feel. It's selfish, I know. But I see you, making all these compromises, all these choices every day, with them in mind, and I wanted to say ...' he leaned down and gently kissed her injured finger, 'that you have options too.'

Holly was openly crying now and he folded her into his arms. She sobbed into his chest, past embarrassment, past caring, just loving the feel of his arms around her.

'Listen, I can't sweep you off your feet into a different life. But maybe you might let me into yours? Your boys are wonderful, Holly, because of you. Because they have such a wonderful mum, who always puts them first. Maybe just this once, with this one decision, they wouldn't mind if you put yourself first instead?'

Holly could hear his words through the pounding in her ears as she struggled to get herself under control. One decision. One simple word and their lives would be turned upside-down. The only thing Holly had to work out – was upside-down necessarily worse?

'Now then you, we have a song to practise. Apparently you get a bit down on Mondays and when it rains, so come on, let's see how it sounds.' He guided her to the same bench where she'd chatted with the Major about his wife all those weeks ago. She wondered what kind of marriage they had shared, that left him still pining after so long.

She looked over at Taffy, at his warm open expression and sighed, looking across the graveyard. She saw a bright new headstone beside the path. Brian French – Beloved Father and Husband. She gulped, as the memories swamped her. She remembered only too clearly the wrenching pain of losing her dad. Was she really so selfish and blinded by her emotions to willingly put her gorgeous boys through that?

Taffy's expression changed as he watched her and Holly knew that her thoughts must be written all over her face. He rallied a little, strumming melodramatically on the ancient guitar.

'I'm so sorry,' Holly whispered. 'I just . . .'

Taffy brushed her hair from her reddened eyes. 'Well then, maybe we can be mates? I gather it's possible for men and women to be friends?'

'So I've been told,' Holly answered sadly, feeling a small part of herself shatter.

'Well then, as mates, or indeed as the oddly incestuous Carpenters once said, we could just sing a song . . .'

'Dear God! That's awful,' managed Holly, the tension dissolving into laughter.

Taffy got to his feet and began striding around the graveyard, strumming tunelessly and singing with perfect pitch. He'd just got to the chorus of his 1970s medley, when Holly realised where he was standing.

'Taffy, get off! You're standing on somebody's grave.'

He looked down and leapt quickly to one side, crouching down to read the headstone. 'Sorry guys,' he said. 'Just got a little carried away.'

He straightened up and looked Holly in the eye, his tone light and flippant, as though he were chatting to Dan Carter in the pub, 'Did you see that, Holl? It's a family plot – three generations in one place. Jesus Christ,' he said with a waggle of his eyebrows, 'they must be stacked in like Jenga down there!'

Holly's laugh was far from respectful or ladylike, but she was simply overwhelmed with gratitude that this gorgeous, sweet man was trying his best to make this easy for her.

They walked back to work, chatting about inconsequential nonsense. Just as they neared the car park, Taffy dropped back. 'You go on,' he said, 'I just need a minute.' He rubbed a hand roughly over his face and eyes that now seemed sore and tired. 'Hayfever.'

Holly nodded. 'I'll see you later, though?'

'You can bet on it.' He paused. 'I'm always here, Holly, if you need me. I'm not going anywhere.'

And with that he turned away and Holly felt shattered all over again.

Chapter 36

Julia stood outside the window of Squire & Bates, mentally comparing each property with her own and wondering what the hell to do. Property wasn't really her area of expertise but the valuation report she'd duly received from Justin had seemed ridiculously low. Looking in the window though, at all the New Lower Price stickers, maybe Justin had a point. If she wanted to sell quickly, it had to be reflected in the asking price.

'I wondered if you'd considered my proposal,' said a deep voice at her shoulder, making her jump.

She whirled round to give Justin a piece of her mind, only to stop short when she saw Henry Bruce standing there. His suit was immaculate as always, his hair perfectly trimmed and his well-moisturised face was newly tanned. When he'd dropped off their radar, everyone had assumed he was just lying low, waiting for the storm to pass. It hadn't occurred to any of them, that he'd taken himself off on holiday!

Henry tutted as he looked over her shoulder. 'Property prices still in the gutter, I see. It's a buyers' market, Julia, not the best time to sell your lovely house. Especially when there's really no need.'

He was smooth, thought Julia, she'd give him that. He was

using his best you've-got-cancer voice, soft and supportive and incredibly confident.

'Oh, I'm not going anywhere,' Julia said determinedly. 'Why on earth would I want to leave Larkford?'

'Possibly because you're about to lose your job and you're undoubtedly in negative equity? Maybe it's time you left your pride behind and accepted my offer?'

'I wasn't aware that you'd made me one,' she parried, wondering whether this might be the perfect opportunity to turn double agent and find out what he was really up to.

Henry rested his arm across her shoulders collegially, the wafts of sandalwood from his cologne making Julia's stomach heave. Since when did men think it was appropriate or attractive to smother themselves in heavy, cloying scented products? She'd bet Henry Bruce used pomade on his hair, not to mention half a bottle of aftershave. Urgh. What was wrong with smelling fresh and showered, with a hint of masculinity – like Dan.

Julia felt instantly awkward. She'd been thinking about him more and more these last few weeks. She blamed Elsie for that. Or maybe Holly. Either way, all this chat about how to live, had forced Julia to re-examine everything she thought she knew. When it came to her job, a few small changes in attitude had allowed her to see that her colleagues could also be her friends. When it came to Dan? Well, if she were being completely honest, she could kind of understand why he'd split up with her.

She'd been broken. Broken and clinging to control like a lifejacket. She hadn't truly let him in to her life. She'd allowed him to visit. She'd set so many boundaries for herself, always thinking that if she played by her own rules, then she could avoid all the heartache.

The only problem with that scenario?

Those rules – the ones she'd constructed over the years to protect herself? Well, she was beginning to think that they might just be stupid.

She'd drunk a Martini with Elsie Townsend. Just one. It had tasted nice and given her a pleasant buzz, but she hadn't wanted to go out and drink the whole damn bottle.

She'd had an honest conversation with Holly Graham – almost as if they really were friends rather than colleagues – and the world hadn't ended. Holly hadn't betrayed all her confidences, but rather had supported and encouraged her.

Even the barmy old Major had offered her his gatehouse at a peppercorn rent, when she'd confided in him over a whisky. Bless him, he was all in favour of her selling up – true, he'd opined, she might take a financial hit, but the freedom and independence she would gain would be priceless. She had to concede that he had a point.

It was as though the focal length on the lens of Julia's entire life had shifted.

Coming at situations from a different angle had given her a different perspective and a clarity that surprised her. She didn't want to leave Larkford. Even if it meant driving into Bristol or Bath every day for work. She wanted to tell Dan she was sorry, that she knew she'd pushed him away. She wanted to sit in The Kingsley Arms, making small talk, with a packet of crisps and a white wine spritzer. Hang it all, if she was living in the crumbly old gatehouse, she might even get a dog and sod the mess.

There was one good thing in her favour with this double-agent plan, though. She'd been so aloof and standoffish over the years that nobody would question her decision to stand by Henry Bruce. They would just assume that she'd returned to her usual, cold-hearted, financially motivated ways. Besides, she didn't need everyone to believe her, she just needed Henry Bruce.

'Probably a good idea to walk and talk,' she suggested, turning away from the Market Place and striding out, Henry falling into pace beside her. 'What did you have in mind?'

Henry couldn't disguise the smile on his face. 'Well, in an ideal world, I need you and Taffy Jones. I can do without all the simpering do-gooders and admin staff are two-a-penny. I can make you both offers you can't refuse and you can still do that little TV programme you've been yapping about. Taffy can run the sports injuries side of things. And all you have to do, is help me make it happen.'

'And why would we do that? For the money?'

'Of course for the money, you daft mare. Taffy must know that all his I-need-my-freedom guff about staying a locum means he has no contract and no redundancy cheque. And, Julia, my love, we both know that you need the cash. I do my homework, you know. I'm perfectly aware that Mummy dearest is drinking her way through every rehab facility in the South-West. And go on, you can admit it to me, but wouldn't it feel good to get one over on holier than thou Dan Carter?'

Julia swallowed hard, a little frightened by how easily this could have gone differently. What a difference a day makes. If Henry had come to her only weeks ago, even being so bloody invasive and rude, she'd still have been putty in his hands, driven by money and revenge and the need for control. And now . . .

Now suddenly, none of that seemed to matter. So, she'd have a bit of a commute into work. But all the *shoulds* that she'd been shedding like old skin? It had rewired her thinking.

Turning away from the devil on her shoulder that was counting piles of filthy lucre, she pasted on a smile. All Dan's boring books about spies during the war were coming back to her.

'Well, I won't come for peanuts, Henry, you know that,' she said sniffily, trying to make it convincing. 'This offer of yours better be good.'

He didn't bat an eyelid, merely reached into his inside suit pocket and pulled out a card. Written on the back was a very large number and the magic words 'plus profit sharing'. She swallowed hard, thrown off course for a moment.

The opportunity cost of being a decent person, who considered her fellow team members, was certainly higher than she had imagined.

She shrugged. 'I'll need a car.'

Henry leaned in and kissed her cheek, his moist lips cold on her face and his sour breath wafting over her. 'No problem. You get Taffy on board and you can take your pick. I'm warning you, though, his loyalties may be a little harder to break than yours. I'm almost impressed, Julia. You handled this negotiation like a man.'

Julia breathed out slowly, resisting the urge to knee him in the nuts.

Instead she just gave him a condescending look. 'You mean because I asked for what I want and forgot to say "please sir"?'

Henry grinned. 'You've got balls, Channing. That was a pretty generous offer, you know. But asking for the car? Well, you obviously know what you're worth to me.'

'I was thinking a nice new Audi, actually. With a ragtop, of course.'

Henry's expression was calculating in the extreme. 'Well

for a ragtop, I'd probably need to see some commitment up front, you know. Taffy Jones signed up and that stupid bloody website taken down for starters. And this concert idea? Well, that needs to stop now, doesn't it, darling? All too likely to rock the boat.'

Julia was secretly delighted that the prospect of the concert had got him rattled. She had no idea how she'd go about the other things on his hazing list, but then maybe she wouldn't actually have to . . . She was just about to start milking him for information when his next words froze her to the spot.

'I'm thinking that we take your famous compère out of the equation and the whole house of cards will come tumbling down.'

'Compère?' Julia managed.

'You know, the old bird, that nosey trouble-maker . . . what's she called? Elsie something? Well, I've arranged an assessment for her.' He gave Julia a meaningful wink. 'I've called in a favour. So sad when these old biddies aren't safe to stay in their own homes, isn't it? But not to worry, she'll be safely tucked up at Willowbrook Nursing Home in no time. Such a relief for us all to know she's being taken care of. Dementia is so insidious, isn't it . . .' Henry trailed off from his little monologue looking terribly pleased with himself.

Julia had to blink hard to remind herself that she was supposed to be on his side now. She felt sick to her bones that Elsie was in such a precarious position and that Henry Bruce was so much worse than she'd ever imagined.

Was there anything more frightening than a bent doctor, she wondered. All that power, all that influence . . .

Well, it turned out that Henry Bruce knew exactly how to motivate her. And it wasn't the money.

She was going to bring him down, whatever the cost.

Even if The Practice had to close, she was damned if Henry was going to get away with this.

She smiled slowly, clasping hold of Henry's arm. 'Seems you've got that covered. How handy to have all your contacts.' She took a deep breath and took a chance. 'So tell me then, since we'll be working together soon, what exactly am I pitching to Taffy Jones?'

And so he told her. Everything.

Chapter 37

Holly lugged yet another load of washing out to the line in the garden. The twins were happily throwing sand at each other in the sand pit and laughing their heads off. The sun was shining, the birds were singing and Holly felt like they were one singing chipmunk away from a Disney movie.

It hadn't escaped her notice though, that she was the one hanging out sheets and scrubbing the floor. 'Wash the dishes, do the mopping, Cinderelly, Cinderelly . . .'

She watched the boys as they hooned around the garden, loving that they had so much space to burn off their never-ending Duracell supply of energy. They were babbling away to each other in their own little twin language again, but rather than intervene, Holly decided to leave them to it. She was actually chuffed to bits that her boys would never get lonely – they would always have a best friend to turn to, someone who knew them inside out, for better or worse.

After all, that's what friends were these days, as everyone moved away from their roots so much – friends were the new family. And old friends even more so.

Your best friend was who you turned to for life's ups and downs but without any biological compunction to meet up at Christmas and birthdays.

Maybe that's why falling out with a best friend felt just like breaking up with a boyfriend – possibly worse. You still got the heart racing, sweating palms when your paths crossed – you still carried the fear of saying something completely stupid or not looking your best. Surely looking as though you were absolutely fine, thank you very much, was *de rigueur* in either situation.

But when you broke up with your boyfriend (or your husband) – who did you turn to? Your best friend . . .

When suddenly, and for no explicable reason, that friendship died – what then?

You had to make do with bizarre role-playing conversations with yourself in the shower, saying all the things and asking all the questions you were never really brave enough to say in real life. Like, 'Why?'

Holly stabbed at the sheets with the pegs rather viciously. Lizzie may have been her oldest friend, but she hadn't been a very good friend recently, had she?

But what Holly would have given on this beautiful Disney morning, to pack up the Beast and go round to Lizzie's: to pour out her heart and soul at the kitchen table; to cook up a decent and believable excuse as to why she couldn't go away with Milo; to tell her all about Taffy Jones; to ask her advice about the concert . . . The list of things she wanted to talk to Lizzie about was growing longer by the day.

Thank God for Elsie and Julia and Dan. She'd have been lost without them.

Obviously Taffy should also have been on that list, but since he brought more to the party than simple friendship, it was probably best to leave that aside.

With the concert only days away, Holly was quietly gutted to be going away. She wanted to be here, revelling in the anticipation and preparation. She wanted to be practising with Taffy and running through her cello solo on the stage in the Little Theatre ...

And the Little Theatre was an absolute gem – the ancient tiered seating had seen better days, but the acoustics were amazing and there was plenty of space for the audience and also backstage, just as long as you didn't mind getting up close and personal.

Holly felt a thrill at the very thought.

Okay, so the only time she'd been to a performance there had been the local AmDram production of *Equus*. It was one thing seeing Daniel Radcliffe in the nude, quite another seeing the local fishmonger tackle out – and not the fly-fishing variety either. It was no coincidence that Holly had given Waves a wide berth since she'd moved here.

But Holly had a secret hope that their concert wouldn't just be good. From the little snippets she'd heard of various clandestine rehearsals, Holly was harbouring a secret hope that their concert, her concert, would be nothing short of sensational.

She followed the twins inside, as they set off on a mission to find their Bob The Builder diggers, and checked her watch. She was cutting it fine as always. Afternoon clinic, then rush back here in time to get Jean settled with the boys and away. Holly had restrained herself from commenting that Jean was always more than happy to babysit when Milo asked, but when Holly did, she was apparently taking advantage.

Either way, the time for getting out of this had passed. She'd already got through the snide comments from Milo when she'd suggested postponing until after the concert, 'Well, if you can't even tear yourself away for one night for the sake of our marriage, that tells me everything I need to know, doesn't it?'

Sadly, thought Holly, as she reluctantly pulled clothes to pack off the chair in her bedroom that was currently doubling as her wardrobe and general dumping ground, Milo's sniping was probably closer to the truth than she dared to admit.

The boys safely ensconced at Nursery and covering each other with paint, Holly somehow got to work with time to spare. She tapped on Julia's door and wandered in. Julia had another of her ghastly green smoothies on her desk and it smelled like silage. 'I don't know how you can drink that!' Holly said, wrinkling up her nose.

Julia shrugged. 'You get used to it. I keep telling myself that if it tastes that bad, it must be doing me some good.'

'Ha!' said Holly. 'When I first started here, you told me that it was all about having a refined palate and that you actually liked them.' Holly looked a bit uncomfortable and then blurted, 'I thought you were a right pretentious twat.'

'Did I say that?' said Julia, pulling a Wallace and Gromit face. 'Yeah. That actually sounds more like me. But then, in the spirit of honesty, when you first started, I couldn't stand you. So annoying! All that bounciness – all ponytail and adorable clumsiness. Argh! And then, do you remember the day we were introduced and you were all feisty and stood up to me? You know, like a little terrier that thinks it's a big dog? Well, then I thought I might have you all wrong.'

'So I'm not annoying any more?' asked Holly with a grin.

'Oh no, you're annoying as hell, I've just got used to it now.'

'Hmmm. Not entirely sure that's a compliment, but you know, the way my day's going, I'll take what I can get.'

'Rehearsals not going well?'

Holly looked at Julia, searching for some gut feeling about whether this new friend of hers was to be trusted. 'Rehearsals going very well, too well possibly.'

'Ah,' said Julia, who seemed to need no further explanation. 'And isn't tonight the Big Date Night?'

'It is.'

'Ah,' said Julia again. She wrinkled her nose. 'Maybe it's time to do some critical analysis? Pros and Cons?'

Holly waved that idea aside. 'I'm not twelve. I can't base my life decisions on a pros and cons list . . .' Holly stopped as she saw the expression on Julia's face. 'Not that there's, you know, anything wrong with people who do that . . .'

'Ah shut up, Holly, you know I love my lists. Doesn't mean you can't take a step back and see what feels right. My mum used to make me toss a coin to decide stuff. If I felt disappointed, then I knew that I needed to choose the other option. If I felt relieved, then job done. It's probably the only piece of advice she's ever given me that made sense.'

'And that actually sounds much more like me,' said Holly, wondering whether she had time for a quick 'he loves me, he loves me not' before afternoon clinic. 'Anyway, how's Operation Double Bluff going?'

Julia had spoken to all the other doctors last night, reassuring them of her support and filling them in on all the details. Holly had been quietly impressed by Julia's commitment to the cause. She knew, although Julia had never explicitly told her, that money was an issue and yet, here she was, turning down a small fortune to support her colleagues. In a world where actions spoke louder than words, it was safe to say that Julia's actions had been very well received. In fact, Holly couldn't help but notice that a certain Dan Carter had been more than a little bowled over.

Holly grinned, wondering whether, if Julia could bear to deviate from her three-year plan, that she might just get her happy ending there after all.

'To be honest,' Julia said, 'I'm hating it. I'm already living in fear that Henry will tell someone else I'm part of his dastardly plans and then I'll be back to being a social leper again.'

'Hey, you weren't a social leper,' Holly intervened. 'Just you know, private and sometimes a little outspoken ...'

'You mean rude?' Julia shook her head. 'I always told myself that I was the only one being honest – saying out loud what everyone in the room was thinking. But then Elsie gave me a talking to about filters the other day. Apparently, if I can't say anything nice, I shouldn't say anything at all. Unless it's funny ... Seems I can get special dispensation to speak my mind if it's funny.'

Holly nodded. 'Sounds about right. You can think what you like, though. No one can police what's going on in your head.'

'That's just as well at the moment. Double Agent Channing reporting for duty and all that ... But, to be fair, I think I may have missed my calling, actually,' Julia replied. 'Perhaps I should call GCHQ if I'm out of a job? Henry's just spilling the beans now, and the more aloof I am, the more he wants to impress me. He's emailing me all the financials this afternoon, so that should be eye-opening. I told him that he was all wind and piss and I needed some concrete proof that he was good for the money.' She shook her head. 'Honestly, what is it with men and this "treat them mean, keep them keen" business?'

'Don't ask me. I don't understand men at all. I don't understand why George isn't furious about all this – he's just meekly accepting the closure as a given and letting us run around like headless chickens. And I really don't understand why Henry is such a Machiavellian piece of shit. And, on a personal note, I don't understand why, after months of ignoring me, my husband is suddenly hell-bent on a romantic weekend away!'

'Don't you?' asked Julia, leaning forwards. 'You must surely see what his motivation is, even if the others elude you.'

'What?' said Holly eloquently.

'He's marking his territory, isn't he? Now you're in demand and part of the team and surrounded by fit doctors who fancy you . . .'

Holly flushed beetroot red. 'No, you don't know Milo . . . he wouldn't be that prosaic. He likes to think he's above all that.'

Julia shrugged. 'Okay then, but he was in here the other day warning Dan off . . .'

'What?' yelped Holly. 'Dan?'

Julia nodded. 'I guess he is exactly that prosaic after all. Looks like your weekend might be more interesting than you think. Maybe he's about to go all caveman to win you back?'

Holly had a sudden vision of Milo bopping her over the head with his club and dragging her off by her hair. Truth be told, albeit in rather metaphorical terms, wasn't that exactly what he was doing by guilting her into going?

'Right, enough of this chit-chat. I have a patient to assess. Reckons her friends are teasing her because she looks dyslexic. I don't even know where to start with that one!'

*

By the end of the afternoon, Holly had dished out emergency contraception, antibiotics and anti-depressants. She'd held out the box of tissues more times than she could count and she'd been presented with three different Wikipedia print-outs – it made her wonder why she'd bothered with that pesky medical degree after all, when Mr Google could apparently diagnose at the click of a mouse.

She'd had one lady refuse to take the Pill because all the hormones were going back into the water cycle and making the fish angry. She'd had another refuse to go for an MRI for a suspicious lump, because she thought the radiation might give her cancer. The wonky logic in that conversation had used up all of Holly's diplomatic reserves.

Even the news that Lance's operation had gone brilliantly, and Hattie's scan had revealed they were expecting a little boy, had thrown Holly into a spin. Her emotions were bubbling so close to the surface, she was feeling decidedly out of control.

She would definitely need to regroup before an evening with Milo.

Holly was actually quietly furious with herself about this negative state of mind she'd sunk into. Six months ago, Milo running around being all attentive would have felt like a lottery win. His 'flirtation' in Reading had knocked her self-esteem and trust far more than she cared to admit. It had taken an enormous amount of effort to move past that. But now there were three texts on her phone claiming that he 'just couldn't wait' for their time away and all Holly felt was mildly irritated.

Why couldn't they go next weekend? And what on earth had he said to Dan Carter?

Holly couldn't help thinking that she would be more

bowled over by Milo rolling up his sleeves and painting some scenery for the concert, or perhaps taking the boys to the park, or even giving her that elusive fantasy – a lie-in.

It was only in recent weeks that Holly had noticed something: she didn't need the grand gestures.

Taffy was just as likely to make her day with a well-timed Orange Club, or Elsie might make her feel loved and supported, simply by letting her feel heard or appreciated.

It was the small everyday stuff that floated her boat. Change the sheets on the bed, read the boys a story and cook me a steak: I'm yours, thought Holly, wondering when she'd become such a cheap date.

Milo was all about the grand gestures though, all flash and no substance.

Holly reached into her wallet and pulled out a coin. Heads for Milo, Tails for Taffy, she thought, wondering if she'd lost her mind.

As the coin spun through the air, Holly held her breath. In that moment, as the flash of silver rotated in front of her, Holly got her answer. 'Please be tails,' she whispered.

Holly wandered out of The Practice in her own little world.

With a toss of a coin, she had somehow found a way to connect with what was going on beneath all the logic and her need to do the right thing.

She wanted Taffy.

She needed Taffy.

Just the thought that this could happen made her feel light on her feet.

She sat on the wall that lined the car park and rehearsed what she was going to say. She tried not to think about the conversation with Milo that would inevitably ensue. Just for a while, she wanted to enjoy the momentous decision she'd made.

It was so unlike her, so selfish and pleasure-seeking. She couldn't quite believe that she was going to do this, to ignore the very rubric of her life – sod doing the right thing, sod looking at herself in the mirror every day with a clear conscience, knowing she'd been her best self ... She was about to break every rule and she couldn't remember ever feeling so happy.

She swung her bare legs against the wall, the moss tickling the back of her thighs. She wondered for a moment what Lizzie would say. Did it matter? If everyone she knew stood up and told her that this was an awful idea, would it make any difference?

Holly's pulse was racing as she checked her watch yet again and wondered where Taffy had got to. She could see Grace in the front office, shutting down computers and Dan talking to a young slim blonde girl in reception. They seemed to be having a row and Holly craned to get a closer look.

This girl was everything that annoyed Holly. She must have been in her twenties but she had the whole tiny and fragile looking, pre-pubescent thing going on, with the flicky blonde hair and wide eyes that always seemed to reduce grown men to adolescent boys. Holly knew she was too judgemental, but she just couldn't help judging the kind of guy that was attracted to that kind of girl. What did it say about them?

But then, the same could be said for the fad of huge bottoms that looked like baboons. What sort of a guy thought, hmmm, she's pretty, if only her arse was larger ... What sort of a girl filled her bottom with implants?

Holly shook her head. Although she'd said to Julia that she didn't understand men, maybe she just didn't understand people full stop.

Maybe, this time next week, people would be saying the same thing about her? Not the bottom, obviously. But her decision. Would the town of Larkford be scandalised that Holly had ripped her little family apart just so *she* could be happy?

Holly felt the first cold icicles of doubt worm their way down her back. It was all very well flipping a coin and finding relief in your subconscious reaction, but then reality had to be considered.

While all these thoughts were stampeding through Holly's mind, she'd absent-mindedly been watching the drama in reception unfold. Her attention only really snapped into gear when Taffy stepped into the room. It took all of a minute, for Taffy to take hold of this girl's arm and escort her from the premises.

His face was angry and his voice carried down the car park toward Holly. She automatically shrank back against the branches of elderflower behind her.

'Well then, tell me,' said Taffy angrily. 'What the hell are you hoping to achieve by coming here?'

The girl stood in front of him defiantly, her back to Holly and hands on her hips. 'I think I deserve some answers.'

'Oh you do, do you? Turning up here, at work, of all places. How thoughtless is that?'

The girl just shrugged. 'I've seen the website. I know what's going on. And I think it's time I laid down my marker. Nobody walks away from me.'

Taffy sighed and ran his hand through his hair. 'Look, it's not as straightforward as you think. Everything's up in the air.'

'Not my problem,' she said. The girl turned sideways and laid her hand on Taffy's arm, her head tilted coquettishly. Her pregnant belly jutted out between them, tight and high and almost comical against her tiny, girlish frame. 'I just think that a father should be involved in his child's life, don't you? Financially, at the very least.'

Holly felt the bottom drop out of her world as she watched the two of them argue. She knew Taffy well enough to read his body language. He was clearly cross with this girl for turning up at The Practice but also sympathetic to what she was saying. Their voices got lower as they appeared to find some common ground and then Taffy put his arm around her shoulders to guide her back inside.

Holly couldn't have moved if she wanted to. Other images, older images, of Milo with his arm around that student flashed into her mind. Teeny tiny blonde girls. Ruining her life.

So that was that then. A timely wake-up call that all men were basically the same. Taffy was going to be a father and she knew that he would be an amazing one – just not to her boys.

The heady smell of the elderflowers made Holly's stomach lurch unhappily.

'All plans are made to be changed,' she murmured, trying to soothe the searing pain that clawed at her chest. She looked around her, feeling disoriented and lost.

So, no Lizzie, no Taffy and, in all likelihood, no job.

But she did have her boys and, if it wasn't too late, a husband who wanted to whisk her away.

Perhaps it was always meant to be so, she wondered. Better the devil you know and all that . . .

All the justifying and reasoning kept her walking forward.

The part of her that had finally been acknowledged and heard only moments before, being soothed back to sleep with empty platitudes.

But as she turned into her road and saw Milo's car, she couldn't help but wonder – did she really need a devil at all?

Chapter 38

Holly fidgeted in the passenger seat of Milo's beloved Saab, trying to keep her feet squarely on the mat. Frankly, she'd rather be slumped in her seat with her feet on the dashboard, but if she wanted the weekend to go well, there would need to be a few compromises. Compromise number one: behave in Milo's car.

She tried not to think about the bigger compromises she was making and pushed Elsie's voice from her mind.

She felt shaken and tearful, replaying the scene with Taffy and the pregnant girl over and over again in her head. She rubbed at her temples as her headache gained momentum and she wondered what on earth she was doing.

She could acknowledge now, with the benefit of hindsight that she'd fallen deeply, irrevocably in love with Taffy Jones. A slow, affectionate burn had flared into a passionate longing and she could still feel the whisper of that fleeting kiss imprinted on her lips. Seeing him with that girl had ripped a hole in her heart that made it difficult to breathe.

He'd built her faith that things could be different and then he'd trampled it under foot.

It was time to put aside all these foolish notions that Elsie had been layering into her mind. *Should* had its place in her lexicon – as a mother and a wife and a professional, *should* was the fuel that kept her days on track.

Picking moments? Ha, well that implied a certain amount of choice, didn't it?

Picking battles? Well, who had the energy for that?

Holly ran her hand over the walnut dashboard and sighed. Her job may be in jeopardy, but she could still save her little family. So, maybe in a weird way, this mini-break had come at just the right time – to remind her of everything she did have.

For better or worse, for richer or poorer, in good times and in bad.

She tried to muster some enthusiasm; after all, Milo was making the effort. It was time she logged back in and stopped being selfish.

She watched Milo under the bonnet, tinkering away with bottles of Evian and washer fluid. She could have sworn he'd allocated more time for getting the car ready for their night away than he had for himself. It was one of the things that Holly used to find so endearing about him. She couldn't remember when that had morphed into yet another annoyance.

Milo's mother referred to him as a Gentleman Mechanic. As far as Holly could tell, that meant he never got dirty, never actually got under the car, but was permanently to be found, cashmere jumper shoved above the elbows and head under the bonnet. He claimed to know what he was doing, but since the car spent more time in the garage than on the road, Holly wasn't convinced.

One thing she did know, was that Milo adored the attention of all the passing ladies, so thrilled and impressed to see a good-looking, if slightly intellectual bloke, who still seemed to know his way around an engine. Holly was convinced that if one more female told her she was lucky, she would scream.

Truth be told, she wished he'd sell the bloody thing and buy something modern and reliable. A little something with a nod to style and nostalgia, sure, but with the added incentive that it actually worked! You know, as a means of transportation.

'Right,' Milo said, as he slipped into the driver's seat. 'I think we're good to go.' He turned the key in the ignition and the engine grumbled resentfully into life. He lightly revved the accelerator and squeezed Holly's knee without once taking his eye off the dials on the dash. 'All sorted?'

'All sorted,' Holly replied, well versed in Milo-Shorthand for 'Have you sorted out the boys? Have you filled the fridge with food? Does Mum know where to reach us? Have you packed for you? Have you packed for me? Oh, and have you brought something slinky to wear for tonight?'

Holly slid down in her seat a little and smothered a yawn. She was absolutely exhausted. Maybe Milo was right and all she needed was a night away to recharge. Even if getting ready for said night away had drained the very last of her energy, she hoped there would be time to regroup. She was longing for an undisturbed swim in a pool without floating dragons and a night in a big comfy bed with a duvet the size of Gloucestershire.

Perhaps, if she was very lucky, she'd wake up without a tiny toe stuffed up her nostril! It would probably be nice to have an evening with Milo away from his computer too, she mentally added guiltily, but if she was honest, that wasn't the main appeal.

As the Saab rumbled through the Market Place, Holly kept her eyes closed. She didn't want to tempt fate by seeing anyone who might need her.

While Milo coaxed the Saab up and down the gear box, winding their way through the hills towards Bath, Holly watched his profile. He was concentrating on the rev counter and seemed in a world of his own. His voice made her jump when he suddenly spoke.

'I'm so glad we're doing this tonight, Holly. It's what we need – a little time together to reconnect.' He changed gear again. 'I just worry, you know, that this new job of yours . . . Well, I just worry that they don't appreciate you. You work so hard and you're so good at your job, but I'm not convinced they recognise that.

'You know I appreciate you, Holly, don't you? I don't say it enough, but I do. And if you need to walk away from The Practice, I support that decision. I believe in you. I believe in us.'

Holly didn't know what to say. Milo's speech sounded rehearsed, the compliments were nice to hear, but rang utterly false. The cynical voice in Holly's mind went one step further – surely that speech was straight out of Passive Aggressive Behaviour For Beginners?

Six months ago, she knew that this conversation would have been music to her ears. Her self-esteem had been so wounded and fragile, she would have pathetically seized upon those compliments and hung on his every word. Now, though, her rose-coloured glasses well and truly smashed, she could listen with a certain detachment and scepticism.

'I just think,' Milo continued, apparently unconcerned by her lack of response, 'that people like Dan Carter are happy for everyone else to do their leg work, while they take all the glory. I'm worried that he's playing you for a fool and taking advantage of your sweet nature, Holly.'

'Dan's one of the good guys, Milo,' Holly said abruptly.

Milo looked at her sharply. 'Well, I'm just looking out for you, Holly. He's a smooth operator that one. Lucky you've got me to bring some objectivity. Seems to me that you're too close to the situation.' He sniffed. 'I rather suspect you've lost all perspective.'

'You're probably right,' she replied quietly, not bothering to point out that they were talking at crossed purposes. Perspective was yet another thing she was sorely lacking.

An hour later, as the door of their hotel room swung closed, Holly knew she was being ungracious and ungrateful, but somehow she couldn't quite contain it. She watched the red flush climb up Milo's neck, a sure enough sign of his rising temper, but somehow, she had lost the ability to edit her thoughts. She slumped into the sumptuous sofa of the hotel suite – suite! – and held her head in her hands.

'How. Dare. You?' said Milo, each word creating its own little ripple of distaste. 'I have never been so embarrassed in all my life!'

'Haven't you?' replied Holly coolly, looking up. 'Would you rather I'd waited until we were checking out, to let on that we couldn't actually afford to pay the bill?'

She swallowed hard, furious at her husband for putting her in this position and trying valiantly to be tactful. 'I understand what you were trying to do, Milo, I really do. And who wouldn't want to be whisked away to a five-star hotel for the night? Who wouldn't want to stay in the Honeymoon suite and have the Michelin-starred menu? But seriously, have you never looked at one of our bank statements? The package you booked cost more than our rent!'

Milo set his chin into that stubborn expression that made Holly want to punch him. 'So what if I want to spoil my wife? Everyone keeps telling me what a saint you are. God knows, it's hard enough to earn your attention these days. And yes, I saw that photo of you, all cozied up at the Spring Swim. I saw it, Holly. You and our boys with that arrogant Welsh git ... Wasn't flirting with Dan enough for you? You have no idea how you've made me feel. Why do you think I organised this, hmm? Obviously big, romantic gestures are wasted on you. Can't I do anything nice to please you any more, Holly?'

Holly took a deep breath and tried to order her thoughts, deliberately pushing away any stray recollections of the Spring Swim and *that* photo. She knew she should be concentrating on Milo and his heartfelt appeal. *Should.* Easier said than done. Milo's hurtful barbs barely glanced off her, compared to the pain of losing Taffy. She forced herself to focus. That was what this night away was all about wasn't it, focusing on her family and her future with Milo?

Okay, so, she floundered around, looking for the positives: Milo had been trying to do something nice for her, she thought guiltily, possibly even trying to win her back.

But he was doing it with the money she was earning, the little voice in her head whispered. The money they needed to make ends meet. And there certainly wasn't enough left over for this kind of decadence.

Would it be different if it was *his* money?

Maybe, she conceded.

But actually, they had two small children and the idea of blowing four figures – she swallowed hard as the bile rose in her throat – on ONE NIGHT AWAY??? It was insane.

'Listen,' she said tightly, refusing to be provoked about anything other than the issue at hand, 'you can be angry that I picked up the tariff sheet when we were checking in, or you can be relieved that I caught it in time. And to be fair, I think the manager was pretty calm about the whole thing, don't you? I mean, we'd already lost the deposit and he didn't have any other rooms. He could have just sent us home, you know.

'Personally, Milo, I think it's pretty cool that he let us keep this one – and for the price of the basic double. So we skip dinner and breakfast? It won't kill us – we can have a carpet picnic with this lot – look ...' Holly waved her hand at the complimentary goodie basket of fruit and wine and petit fours. 'You wanted to spend time together. Well, here we are. We can still have a swim and the massagey things are already paid for ...'

Holly petered out, exhausted, angry and feeling cheated. A night away. A night in a pub, in a little boutique hotel? Why did everything with Milo have to be such a struggle? He said he was doing it for her. But no. She couldn't believe that any more.

Milo just seemed to think that the world owed him the very best.

Even with no income to speak of, he would still wander around the deli in Larkford, spending fifteen quid on smoked cheese, while she was using up coupons to save the odd fifty pence in the supermarket. Did he think money grew on trees?

Holly was bored to tears with being the bad guy, endlessly talking about cutting their cloth according to their means. She knew that Milo struggled with the concept of sticking to a budget, but this was the clearest sign yet that he simply didn't have a clue.

She tried to tune back in as Milo ranted on about how

humiliated he felt, but half of Holly's brain had already logged out. She was using all her restraint not to bite back. How could he not see that they had actually dodged a bullet? She idly wondered just how much washing up they would make you do in a place like this if you couldn't pay your bill? Or would they have just called the police? Ice prickled her skin at the very thought.

'Milo, stop! Just stop. Stop ranting on as if this whole fiasco is my fault and take a breath.'

To his credit, Milo did just that, but his chin remained firmly jutting out. 'What do you suggest then, since you clearly know everything?'

Holly sighed, cursing Jean for suggesting the idea of a night away and cursing herself for going along with it. She looked at her watch. The boys would be in their pyjamas by now, freshly warm and scrumptious from their baths.

She shrugged. 'Well, I'm going to phone home and say goodnight to the boys. Then I'm going to have that massage, because my neck is killing me. Then I'm coming back here for a glass of wine.' She paused for a moment, collecting herself, kneading the tension along the tops of her shoulders. 'You could join in? This could still be lovely, you know. You just have to make the decision to enjoy it.'

Holly was trying very hard to take her own advice. After all, hadn't she made the decision to come, to try and recon-nect with Milo? But, try as she might, she couldn't seem to engage. She knew that she was probably over-reacting to this suite, knew that she was behaving badly. She just couldn't seem to control herself.

It seemed as though Elsie's pep talks had re-ignited the feisty, outspoken side of her brain that was now refusing to go politely back to sleep.

Okay, so the timing was lousy. Her mind was back in Larkford, thinking about the boys, thinking about rehearsals, thinking about Taffy.

But it was just one night. Milo had a point: if she couldn't even give him one night of her undivided attention . . .

Holly sighed, hating herself for being like this. Even here, in this wonderful suite, her mind was elsewhere.

Holly unearthed her phone from her handbag to call home, noticing the battery was running low and reminding herself to charge it and felt the waves of guilt wash over her.

'For what it's worth, I am truly sorry that your lovely romantic plan didn't work out and we could argue all night about why, but it won't change anything tonight. Come on, what do you think?'

He looked at her mulishly. 'Whatever. At least we're here: I was half expecting you to cancel. After all, you're the boss,' he said with feeling.

Holly looked around the stunning suite, at the heavy drapes of brocade curtains, the sumptuous quilts on the enormous bed and the huge sash windows with their price-less view over Bath. If they couldn't be happy together here, perhaps they couldn't be happy together anywhere? She reached out, on autopilot really, stroking Milo's arm. She was tired, just too damn tired, to be having this conversa-tion again.

She wanted to tell him to swallow his pride and get a job, any job really, while he was writing his book. She didn't want him to stop writing – she certainly wasn't going to be the one to crush his dream – but they needed two incomes, even supposing she could persuade him to curb his spending.

She looked at his defiant expression as he stared out at the view. So used to being the golden boy, he was rather

shattered by the notion that life didn't arrive on a silver plat-
ter, just because you felt you deserved it.

She took his hand. 'Come on, Milo,' she said gently. 'Let's
go and be pampered for a bit. What kind of massage was it
you booked?'

He finally stood up, still exuding negativity. 'It's not so
much a massage as a detox package. I thought it might do you
good. It's a wrap, I think?'

Holly's heart sank a little further into her boots. 'How
lovely,' she managed through clenched teeth, as she tugged
her swimsuit out of her overnight bag.

Two hours later and Holly lay sweating on the bed. She felt
as if every toxin she'd ingested for the last decade (and let's
face it, there had been a few) was now attempting to crawl
out of her pores. She'd been wrapped in seaweed, wrapped
in cling film, left to marinade under a heated blanket and
then pummelled with jets of icy water whilst wearing paper
pants. And, to add insult to injury, she'd actually paid someone a small fortune for the privilege! Her stomach cramped
yet again.

'Milo!' she called. 'I really do need to use the bathroom.
Will you be much longer?'

His voice echoed gruffly from the marble en-suite, 'Probably a while.'

Holly winced as her stomach spasmed yet again, triggering
a fresh deluge of sweats. 'The thing is . . . well, I *really, really*
need the bathroom. Maybe you could pop out for a mo? We
could take it in turns?'

'Daren't risk it, Holls. Having a bit of a reaction to that
detox thing. They did say I might. Probably best if I stay in
here. Just in case.'

Holly tried again. 'The thing is I had the same wrap and I really, really need five minutes in there. Then it's all yours again. Just five minutes, Milo.' Silence.

She hammered on the door, further enraged by her own supplicating tone.

More silence.

Then the sound of Holly's digestive system spasming in protest. She stood up gingerly and wrapped the belt of her huge towelling robe around her tightly. The logical part of her brain gave the headlines. Two people, one loo, first come, first served. She mentally ran through the layout of the hotel, trying to track down the nearest ladies. Surely to God the one in reception couldn't be the only one?

'Milo? Can you even hear me? Stop being so bloody selfish!'

By way of response, she heard the energetic drumming of the waterfall power shower come on and that told her everything she needed to know about the state of her marriage. This was no hairline fracture that would quietly knit back together. This was shattered bones requiring major surgery and months of rehab, with no promise of a full recovery.

She grabbed the room key from the smart Georgian credenza, doubled over once more with the sweating, agonising cramps and made a dash for the ladies' loos two floors down.

By definition, this was fast becoming the shittiest mini-break she had ever been on.

Chapter 39

Dan stepped sharply to one side, as Elsie's little Fiat zipped past him and screeched to a halt.

'Evening, Dr Carter.'

'Elsie, I was just on my way to see you. How are you?' asked Dan, leaning down to peer through the car window.

'Vibrant, Vivacious and Vaguely Vertical, as always, thank you for asking.' She smiled at him impishly. 'I've just been practising for the concert, you know. So exciting!'

'Great,' replied Dan warmly. 'Maybe you could stay in one piece until then. You could probably ease off on the speed a little, you know.'

Elsie laughed and waved a dismissive hand. 'Oh, Dr Carter, don't be silly. You know I have to drive quickly, or I forget where I'm going!' With that, she put her foot down on the accelerator and without so much as a signal, pulled out and drove away.

Dan shook his head. Elsie Townsend was proving to be a slippery customer. She wasn't quite all there and he knew it. But she wasn't doolally either. He rather wondered whether Elsie at eighty was any different to Elsie at sixty. Either way, he couldn't help but admire her.

Elsie Townsend was proving to be their secret weapon and

for all Henry's talk of immobilising her, Dan couldn't quite believe that he would go that far.

Julia, on the other hand, was convinced there was a risk and she wasn't to be persuaded otherwise. She had half the team organised to take turns popping by, on a variety of pointless errands, just to check that Elsie was okay.

Julia, in fact, was on magnificent form all round.

After spending the best part of an evening poring over Henry's financial spreadsheets together, Dan had been knocked sideways by Julia's eloquent and outspoken defence of The Practice.

How the worm had turned.

She was driven and determined, like always, but now her efforts weren't solely motivated by her own professional advancement. She was even using words like 'team' and 'together'.

Dan couldn't deny it was a winning combination for him. All the positives of this amazing woman, without all the endless bitching and one-upmanship that had led to their split.

At that thought, Dan couldn't help but smile.

They'd ended up on the treatment table in his office, snogging like randy teenagers and Dan had rarely enjoyed himself more.

All their years of history, all that water under the bridge, coupled with the growing tension about the impending showdown with the PCT, had all lent a certain frisson to their fooling around; a certain siege mentality to seize the day.

Dan ran a finger under his shirt collar as memories of the night before washed over him. He couldn't help thinking that things were looking up. He'd slept like a baby last night and felt calm and refreshed.

Okay, so George Kingsley was still being a wet blanket,

noticeably absent from most of their strategy meetings. But now, with Julia and himself finally singing from the same song-sheet? Not to mention the youth and enthusiasm of Holly and Taffy? Dan rather hoped that Henry Bruce wouldn't know what hit him.

The smile slipped from his face at the thought of his best mate. Poor Taffy.

Dan knew that Taffy had been pretty frank with Holly about his feelings. It hadn't got him anywhere though, had it? And then that pregnant girl showing up at The Practice . . . Dan breathed out sharply. It looked like Taffy had some pretty tough decisions to make and Dan didn't envy him. To choose between honour and love? There were no easy answers there.

Always supposing Holly gave him the chance, Dan thought. He changed direction and headed to The Kingsley Arms a little earlier than planned, satisfied that Elsie was safe from Henry Bruce for now, even if her own driving was probably the greater risk factor at this point.

'Really, Major?' protested Dan as he came out of the men's bathroom, with the Major hot on his heels, belt undone. 'It's the weekend. Just come into the surgery like everybody else. I'm not giving you a physical in the pub loos!'

'But you see, Dr Carter, if you could just take a quick look . . .' His elderly fingers fumbled with his belt buckle and his voice sounded a little strained. His ancient terrier sat obediently at his feet, as always, and he seemed to have shrunk at least two inches over the last few years.

'Come and have a pint with me, Major,' said Dan, 'and you can tell me what it is about our practice that stops you coming in to see me, hmm?'

Dan pulled out a bar stool for him and watched Grover, the little wiry terrier, throw himself against the legs until the Major hauled him up on to his lap. 'I'll take a Guinness then, Dr Carter, if you're buying, but you won't persuade me, you know.'

'We'll see,' said Dan easily, ordering three pints of the black stuff. 'Anything for Grover?' he joked, trying to put the old boy at ease. Everyone knew that the way to the Major's heart was through his dog. It was a wonder that the Major hadn't been into the local vet's office to get an opinion on his gammy leg.

'No, no, don't worry about Grover, Doctor. He'll share my Guinness,' the Major replied without batting an eyelid.

'So,' Dan began, trying to avoid Taffy's eye as he passed him his pint, lest he succumb to unprofessional laughter, 'how can we persuade you to come in for a check-up? Is it the other patients that bother you? The other doctors?' Dan took a sip of his Guinness and wiped away his frothy moustache with the back of his hand. He realised that, with all the drama, this was the first time all week he'd felt normal, sitting in the pub on a Friday night, with a pint in his hand and a patient cornering him for a 'quick chat'. Although, technically, he had invited the Major to join him for a drink, so maybe he was the mug. But somehow the old boy intrigued him. More than eighty years of age and never once seen in the surgery, or the local hospital. The veterinary centre he didn't know about, but Kitty and Rupert, the local vets, would be in later and he could ask them then.

The Major looked around the bar and seemed a little sheepish. Was he about to reveal his long-held terror of stethoscopes? 'You see, the thing is, Dr Carter, I don't want to lose my bet.'

'Your what now?' asked Dan, caught off-guard.

The Major gave him a slow wink. 'In 1964, my best mate Andy and I made a bet. The first one to give in and go to the doctor's would forfeit and the winner would get a bottle of his father's prized single malt. Not just any single malt, Dr Carter,' said the Major with passion, grabbing hold of Dan's sleeve, 'because Andy's dad ran a distillery on Islay. We're talking about Black Bowmore here. You could honestly buy a car for less and the taste . . . well, the taste I can only imagine.'

'Just to be clear,' said Dan, wondering how many pints of Guinness the Major and Grover had sunk before he arrived, 'you won't go to the doctor's because you might miss out on a bottle of scotch?'

The Major looked scandalised. 'Not just *any* bottle of scotch, Dr Carter. Did you not hear me say Black Bowmore!'

Taffy couldn't help but wade in. 'Seriously, Major? *The* Black Bowmore? That stuff is legendary.'

'You see!' cried the Major, waving his hands at Dan. 'Even the Welshies have heard of it. Philistine or not, Dr Carter, and I'm not doubting your medical credentials for a moment, but I cannot set foot inside your surgery before Andy McLeod starts ailing, and the bastard's as fit as a fox!'

Dan shook his head in disbelief. 'But what if you're really ill?'

'Well then, either I'll drop dead or I'll get my whisky. Shame young George is retiring,' he gave Dan a hard look. 'He always understood the stakes and never minded a quick chat off the record. And the lovely Julia often keeps me on the straight and narrow, medicinally speaking.' The Major fell silent and supped at his pint, offering it to Grover for an occasional slurp.

Taffy and Dan looked at each other over the top of the Major's greying head. Taffy gave him a grin and gestured his head towards the gents', while Dan shook his head in bemusement. 'Go on,' mouthed Taffy again, the laughter threatening and his eyes sparkling with mischief.

'You young lads never make any bets, then,' said the Major, emerging from his pint, 'nothing ever persuaded you to stick to your guns?'

Taffy shrugged. 'Our bets tend to be a bit more childish, to be honest, Major. Not the life-long variety. More the end of the week really ... which reminds me, Dr Carter,' he said, suddenly sounding very formal and with a contrived amount of pomposity, 'it is in fact the end of the week. Produce your egg!'

'Sorry, did you say egg?' interjected the Major.

Dan shook his head more and gave Taffy a look, as any remaining credibility flew out the window. 'He bet me a round that I couldn't take an egg with me everywhere I went for a whole week without breaking it.'

'And let's not forget that I had custody of an egg too,' Taffy protested. 'It's not all one-sided.'

Dan shrugged. 'Sorry, mate, it'll be my round then. I'm afraid mine was eggstremely flattened when I was doing cardiac resuscitation on old Jack Dollar.'

'Ahh, that's hardly a sporting way to win a bet, Dr Jones. The man's practically a hero. Can you not have a do-over?'

Taffy pompously pretended to consider for a moment. 'Well you see, the whole point of the bet, Major, was to prove a point to Dan. You won't know this, but our Dr Carter here, as wonderful as he may be, is in fact A Dropper.'

'I am not,' protested Dan. 'My egg was in perfectly safe hands until, well, until I dropped it. Where's yours?'

Taffy reached into the breast pocket of his jacket and unwrapped a spotty handkerchief, revealing a perfectly rounded egg. 'Ta da!'

Dan and the Major both gaped. 'You mean you've been carrying that around all week? In your pocket?' Dan clarified.

'Yup! I've been saving it for a little celebratory snack . . . First, you get another round in, then we'll have a little check of the Major's gammy leg and then, I think we need to come up with a better way of proving that you are, contrary to all logic and expectation, A Dropper.'

Dan laughed despite himself and laid a twenty on the bar.

'Same again for me, Dr Carter. Since you're buying,' chuckled the Major.

Taffy stood up and retrieved a small dish of salt from one of the tables, before neatly tapping his egg on the polished bar and beginning to peel it.

'Hang on, you cheating swine. You never said we were allowed to hard boil the bloody thing!' protested Dan as his twenty disappeared into the pub's coffers.

'Ah, but I didn't say that you couldn't,' said Taffy, taking an enormous bite of his egg and dipping it gleefully in the salt. 'The devil is in the details, Dan, you know that.'

The Major just shook his head. 'Well played, sir!' He slowly got to his feet, careful to collect his fresh pint and his inebriated terrier. 'And you boys call me mad,' he muttered under his breath, before seeking out the company of the lovely Marion for a little Guinness and sympathy.

Dan rallied almost immediately. 'Enjoy your winnings, Taffy, my car is looking forward to its full valet service. I shall have you know that my tadpole now has its back legs.'

Taffy pulled a face. 'You can enter it in the concert then,

as Kermit the frog's little nephew Robin – 'cause mine's got front legs too . . . And you should see the state of my Landy!' Taffy shook his head. 'Oh Dan, when are you going to realise that I'm in a different league, mate?'

Dan just shrugged. 'We'll see. But since you've got two left feet at the best of times, and we've got rehearsals in five minutes, maybe you should leave that twenty on the tab for later?'

Taffy grudgingly conceded. It was one thing to look like a prat on stage – it was another to let Dan Carter outshine him in a sporting event.

'Twenty quid says you can't get through the whole rehearsal without falling over,' said Taffy.

'Deal,' said Dan, shaking his hand. 'Wait, hang on, that doesn't include being pushed now, does it?'

Taffy grinned and then drained his pint. 'Oh Dan, you always have to agree terms *before* you shake. Now, will you be standing next to me in the line-up perchance? I really fancy a Chinese Takeaway!'

Chapter 40

The next morning, on the other side of town, Holly was about out of chances. She'd left Milo in Bath. Literally and metaphorically. As far as she was concerned, it was Game Over. Strike while the iron was hot and the motivation still fresh. She could be a single parent – hell, she'd basically been a single parent for the last two years, just with another body in the house.

She could do this. It was fine. Quick, like a Band Aid, that was the answer. Try not to give in to the guilt. Try not to rehearse what she'd say to the boys.

Her night away had given her perfect clarity, as the physical and mental toxins left her body: the ultimate cleanse!

She'd caught the early bus back to Larkford, reclaimed her battered old Golf and scooped up the twins. The momentum of her actions had faltered then. She'd driven aimlessly for a while. 'What's the story in Balamory?' playing mindlessly on a loop in the car.

She couldn't face going back home and she couldn't very well go to Lizzie's.

'How many bridges can I burn in one week?' she asked herself.

She pulled up outside the Spar. 'Come on, boys, let's get some breakfast.'

Being so early, there was nobody else about and Holly chatted with Marion as she ran their crusty rolls and fruit through the checkout.

'You alright there, Dr Graham?' Marion asked kindly. 'You've got a certain glow about you, but you don't look happy.'

Holly shook her head. 'Oh Marion, you are such a sweetheart. I'm fine. I am. I'll be fine.'

Marion raised an eyebrow. 'Well, you know where we are if you need us. Everybody's been talking about your concert idea – we're so touched by your support, Dr Graham. I know you haven't lived here long, but we do so appreciate all your work.'

Holly smiled. 'It's been an absolute pleasure, Marion.'

Marion nodded. 'Since it's quiet and you're not rushing, would you mind if I said something?'

Holly caught Ben's banana before it hit the floor and turned back. 'Of course, go ahead.'

Marion looked uncomfortable and intense and Holly braced herself.

'It's about your husband, actually, Dr Graham. I've been wanting to say something for a while, but there's never the opportunity, is there?'

'What's he done?' asked Holly tiredly, wondering whether he'd run up a tab, or been flirting with someone's underage daughter. After last night, she wasn't sure that anything would surprise her.

Marion took a deep breath. 'He's been buying the boys chocolate,' she burst out in the end. 'Ben too. Every week. A big bar of Dairy Milk. He says it keeps them quiet and I did try and remind him about young Ben's allergy, Dr Graham, I really did.'

Marion looked so stressed out, Holly automatically placed a soothing hand on her shoulder.

She felt like laughing – laughing in a slightly mad, hysterical, relieved kind of way obviously – but never the less laughing.

'Oh, Marion, I think I love you,' said Holly to Marion's utter bemusement.

How could Holly possibly explain the tumult of thoughts running through her head? She pulled Marion into a bear hug and scooped up the boys. Next stop Elsie's for some common sense advice about divorce.

Divorce.

No longer the judgemental knell of defeat, but the resounding toll of liberation.

As Holly buckled the boys into their seats, she ruffled their hair and planted kisses on their sticky little cheeks. 'Sorry, boys. Mummy's a bit late to the party.'

Holly wasn't sure if she wanted to laugh or to cry.

She knew now with absolute clarity that her marriage was dead. Even without the prospect of Taffy Jones waiting in the wings, she wasn't going to settle for second best. She'd rather be on her own, on her own terms.

She'd stayed with Milo because she wanted the boys to have their father around.

What a joke!

She'd fretted endlessly about Ben's hearing, health and behavioural issues – wondering how she could possibly do more. And all this time, Milo had been stuffing him full of chocolate, triggering all these little allergic reactions and bunging up his sinuses.

Jesus! What kind of father would knowingly poison his own son just to get some peace and quiet?

The answer was simple and clear – the kind of father you're better off without.

Holly slid the Golf into gear and with a sigh of relief, her conscience clear, she set off for Elsie's.

Elsie had been delighted to see them and welcomed them in with open arms. 'Boys, I have an enormous favour to ask. I seem to have made far too much popcorn. As a favour to me, do you think you could help me eat some of it?'

Within seconds the boys were in the palm of her hand. When she opened a wicker basket to reveal hundreds of tiny, polished wooden blocks, they were in seventh heaven. 'My Ginger used to play with those for hours,' Elsie told them, quickly flicking off the TV, which was paused on Mr Darcy coming out of the lake.

Holly quietly loved the fact that Elsie didn't hold with convention – so she fancied a movie at nine o'clock in the morning? Well then, make some popcorn and dig in ... They retreated to the kitchen and Holly flicked on the coffee machine, as comfortable in Elsie's home as she was in her own.

'So you've done the deed then?' Elsie said astutely.

Holly whirled around, flicking coffee grounds every-where. 'How did you ... ?'

Elsie clapped her hands in delight. 'Well I didn't know – it was a guess. You just seemed a little lighter on your toes.'

Holly laughed. 'In more ways than one.' And she told Elsie about her night away.

Elsie lived and breathed every moment of the retelling, until she slumped back in her chair. 'About time too,' she said eventually. 'It's been bothering me for a while, young Holly, how you seem to equate death and divorce as the same thing. I'm sure it was a tragedy to lose your lovely dad so young, but this is not the same scenario.'

'Nope,' agreed Holly, ladling a huge spoonful of sugar into her coffee, thrilled to finally be enjoying her favourite drink again. 'Not the same thing at all. Took me a while to get there, though.'

'And am I allowed to ask about Taffy? Did he have a role in all of this?'

'I suppose he did, in a way,' conceded Holly. 'But probably not the way you're thinking. I didn't leave Milo for Taffy. I left Milo because I needed to. For me. And possibly for the boys too, but we'll see how that pans out.'

Holly walked over and gave Elsie an enormous hug. 'I'm so grateful for all your advice, Elsie. You've really opened my eyes these last few months.'

Elsie batted away the compliment. 'Rot. I just made you stand up for yourself a little bit, made you ask for what you really wanted.' Elsie wandered over to the dresser and pulled down a small frame that was covered in dust.

The paper inside was yellowing with age, the looping handwriting flamboyant and graceful. 'I met the most inspiring lady when I was younger. Her name was Rebecca and she didn't let anything stand in her way. She used to say this all the time, so I got her to write it down for me. So I'd never forget.'

Elsie passed her the frame and Holly read the quote aloud,

'I myself have never been able to find out exactly what feminism is: I only know that people call me a feminist whenever I express sentiments that differentiate me from a doormat. Be true to yourself, Elsie. All love RW.'

'Wow!' said Holly. 'She sounds amazing.'

'A little bit terrifying, but yes – also amazing,' Elsie replied. 'So what's the plan now?'

Holly drank her coffee slowly as she thought. 'Wait and see?'

'Wait and see sounds perfect. You have to have a little faith in the Universe, I believe. You'll know what to do when the time is right. Like with Milo.'

'Hmm, I think the situation with Milo may have dragged on a little longer than necessary though, don't you?' said Holly.

'No, I don't actually,' Elsie said with feeling. 'If you'd walked away sooner, knowing you, you'd have spent your life wracked with guilt. This way, by letting everything build to a natural detonation, you can have the confidence that you made the right call – not just for you, but for the boys as well.'

Holly wondered, in that moment, whether everyone gained such clarity of vision by the time they were eighty. Did personal vision grow, she wondered, even as optical vision faded?

Holly smothered a yawn, her night in the hotel bathroom catching up with her.

'Go and close your eyes for a moment,' Elsie said. 'The boys are happy with their bricks, look. That sofa over there is the perfect length for a catnap. I may even join you.' Elsie smiled. 'If I don't get my morning nap in, I'm too tired to properly enjoy my siesta.'

Elsie was asleep in moments, the boys quietly lining up rows and rows of bricks for their toy cars to drive through.

Holly laid her head back on the sofa and watched them

contentedly. She was feeling a little fatalistic right now. The idea of putting her faith in a higher power was really quite beguiling. After the concert tonight, there would be more decisions, more choices and more confrontations.

In her heart, she knew that Taffy hadn't been the reason to walk away from Milo, but in some ways he had been the catalyst. Not as a reward, she decided, but just to remind her how it was possible to feel. And for that alone, she was grateful. So, it might be awkward being around him for a bit, but if this concert didn't do the trick tonight, then even that might not be an issue.

She closed her eyes for a moment, letting the warm waves of sleep ebb and flow. With young children in the house, Holly had perfected the knack of dozing with one ear open. The gentle babbling of the twins in their own little language was soothing as she let herself relax.

Her phone trilled beside her, announcing a new email, and Holly debated whether it was worth prising her eyes open. It was unlikely to be work or Milo, but with the concert only hours away, there was a chance it was important.

She yawned and clicked on her mail folder, the words dancing before her eyes as she struggled to make sense of them.

If she believed in signs ... Holly thought, as her mind clicked into gear.

The local representative from the Primary Care Trust was called Harry Grant. His email address was hgrant@south-westhealth – Holly's was hgraham@southwesthealth.

With one mistyped letter, the autocomplete on Henry Bruce's computer had sent Holly everything she needed to know. She clicked on the attachments and read through them at speed. These figures were very different to the ones he'd sent Julia. What a snake.

More importantly, Henry Bruce seemed to be turning down a rescue package from the PCT. 'The community of Larkford would benefit hugely from the new surgery in Framley and the medical team here are unanimous. You have our support to go ahead with the closures and, whilst we thank you for your alternative proposals, they would only have the support of a small, although vocal, minority.'

'Bastard!' hissed Holly under her breath.

Tiptoeing past the deeply engrossed building works on the carpet, Holly went into the kitchen and dialled a number on her mobile. 'Harry Grant, please,' she said. 'Yes, I can hold.'

As 'Greensleeves' strangled itself in her ear, Holly read through the attachment again. The rescue package, to her non-accountancy eye, looked very reasonable. They would need to prove local support – check. They would need to move non-urgent services to the central practice – physiotherapy and the like – no problem. They would also need to cut their GP staffing budget by . . . And this was where Holly caught her breath. Talk about a sign from the Universe!

The reduction figure was exactly the same as her own salary.

She swallowed hard as 'Greensleeves' morphed into Peer Gynt. She looked over at Elsie, fast asleep and snoring gently. She saw the boys hug each other with delight as their tower tumbled down over their feet.

She wondered if she was strong enough for yet another challenge.

A little voice in her brain was most insistent though.

There were other jobs.

And hers had never been safe.

She could live here and commute to Bath or Bristol so easily. It wouldn't be the same, but it was definitely doable.

Larkford needed The Practice, more than they needed her.

Larkford, like Taffy, had shown her what she was looking for. Elsie had helped her to realise what she wanted.

And she wanted to do this, she realised. Doing something for the greater good of the community that had brought her back to life, somehow felt right.

It felt more than right – it felt as though this was her own private mission – possibly even the reason she was here. Holly felt a quiet resolution settle in her chest. This was her decision and this time, she was going to trust her instincts.

Maybe this Harry Grant needed to come to their concert too? Perhaps he needed to see for himself, what Holly had already discovered.

Larkford was more than a community – it was a family. A very modern family, with the best of traditions at its heart.

The music clicked off in Holly's ear and a harassed voice picked up the line, 'Harry Grant speaking.'

Holly braced herself, it was now or never. 'Mr Grant, it's Dr Graham here, from the Larkford Practice. I'd like to make you a proposal.'

Chapter 41

Holly rushed around backstage, tripping over her feet, various props and a large Tupperware box full of worms. She began to wonder whether she was hallucinating, as she picked up another box and came face to face with a chirruping cricket.

She looked around for clarification. Maggie was sitting curled up on a chair, as white as a ghost. 'You know I'd do anything to support the campaign, Holly, but I'm beginning to think I may have over-reached.' She waved her hand at the stack of Tupperware boxes.

Holly crouched down beside her trembling colleague. 'What exactly were you planning to do, Mags?'

Maggie gave a slightly hysterical laugh. 'Well, you know how I can be a bit funny about things being clean, food being a certain way? Well, to challenge myself, I thought I could do a Bush Tucker Challenge – you know, like they do on the telly.'

Holly took one look at the writhing masses in the boxes. 'I think you're mad.'

'I knoooow,' howled Maggie. 'What was I thinking? I just wanted to really test myself, prove to everyone how committed I am.'

'Maggie,' said Holly calmly and sternly. 'If you put those hideous things in your mouth, knowing you as I do, I think we'll be *getting* you committed. This is supposed to be fun too, you know. We're not here to make you sick.'

Maggie's fingers gradually began to unclench in sheer relief. 'But that will leave a gap in the running order, won't it?'

Holly checked the clipboard that Grace had entrusted her with, running an eye over who else might be available. She was half tempted to volunteer Taffy to eat all those vile creepy crawlies, as some sort of karmic debt, but she figured he probably wouldn't bat an eyelid. 'Leave it with me,' she said instead. 'I'll think of something.'

Maggie went off to splash her face and offer some help in make-up, where her attention to detail would no doubt be better served.

Holly checked her watch and took a calming breath. She was wearing her favourite performing dress: a long column of charcoal jersey with a flowing skirt that perfectly accommodated her cello. Other than simple diamond studs she wore no other jewellery and her eyes were smudged with dark grey kohl, hair swirled into a casual chignon at the nape of her neck, Elsie's precious scarf looped around her.

For all the vile things that Holly had thought about her hideous detox treatment, she couldn't deny the results were phenomenal. This dress hadn't fitted properly in three years and now it lightly skimmed her curves. Her skin was bright and luminous despite running on very little sleep and industrial quantities of Diet Coke.

It was just over an hour to curtain up. Nerves were kicking in and last-minute bickers were breaking out amongst their various 'acts' as the reality of the situation finally dawned.

The Little Theatre was sold out. It was standing room only. They were about to go on stage in front of all their peers and patients and make total prats of themselves.

And, for all of that, Holly would be a lot more relaxed if only their compère had arrived. Julia had dropped by Elsie's house earlier and helped lay out her clothes, Dan had spoken to her a short while after, but still no Elsie.

Holly habitually checked her watch again, even though only thirty seconds had passed. She'd spent most of the afternoon trying to keep calm and was running out of steam.

Not only did she have to play her cello in front of an audience, despite being woefully unprepared, but she had to follow that up with a duet with Taffy Jones. How on earth was she supposed to get through that, let alone carry a tune, when even being near him was an inhuman challenge for her nerves . . .

In the way that life throws you one problem to distract you from another, she'd also had the twins to contend with. Really, they were far too little to stay up late, but where was the harm? Wouldn't it be nice for them to see their mummy up on stage, playing her cello and being a strong role model, rather than the frazzled wreck they'd been treated to lately?

Thank God for Marion Gains. She was out there now, a twin on either side and a large supply of dairy-free home-made flapjacks and smoothies to help the show along. Holly had actually been quite touched by Marion volunteering. The minute she knew there was no Milo, and by extension no Jean, on offer, Marion had been on the phone. Holly suspected that Marion rather fancied herself as a surrogate granny, since her own family were now in Australia. Credit where credit was due though, surrogate granny was doing a much better job than biological granny ever had.

Fifty-five minutes to go, and still no Elsie.

Holly looked around her, taking in the hive of activity and knowing that her preparations were all done. Cello tuned. Guitar tuned. Co-star avoided. Children taken care of. Holly slipped off her heels and pulled on her scruffy ballet slippers, making a command decision.

'Dan,' she called backstage, 'I'm going to get Elsie, okay?'

Holly ran out of the theatre, waving at the friendly faces that threatened to waylay her. Emerging from the darkness of the theatre into the early evening sun gave the Market Place an other-worldly feeling. The hubbub of noise behind her in the Theatre and the quiet stillness of the Market Place gave Holly the sensation of being caught between two worlds – which, of course, in a way she was at the moment.

She breathed deeply, the wild garlic from the woodland above wafting down on the warm breeze. This was no time to get sentimental, but Holly allowed herself a few moments to fix the image clearly in her mind.

Checking her watch again, she broke into a loping run toward Elsie's house and prayed that the sense of impending crisis that was jangling her nerves had more to do with her duet with Taffy, than any emerging sixth sense.

She arrived at Elsie's house out of breath and with tendrils of hair snaking their way out of her hairdo.

She lifted the big brass door-knocker and dropped it repeatedly against the glossy green paint.

No reply.

But Holly could see movement inside. Crouching down to squint through the letterbox, Holly could make out someone walking around in the morning room. She knocked again and they froze.

'Sod this for a game of soldiers,' muttered Holly, catching her skirts up in her arms and looking around. She vaulted clumsily up to the top of the locked side gate, hovering precariously in mid-air for a moment before landing none too elegantly and none too gently on the other side.

A sharp pain shot up into Holly's ankle, but she ignored it. The building pressure in her chest was merely adding to the sense of imminent calamity.

Hobbling along the side passage and squeezing past Elsie's recycling bins, Holly could hear a voice. An angry male voice.

Her heart leapt into her throat as she recognised the arrogant and snide tones of one Henry Bruce.

Picking up speed and wincing in pain, she headed for the back door and prayed that Elsie was in a forgetful mood. Finding the door locked, for the first time in history, Holly cursed and wondered what the hell to do. Perhaps Elsie wouldn't mind a little wanton vandalism, she thought, assessing the rocks on the rockery for throwability.

She slipped along the back of the terrace, and saw Henry Bruce striding up and down the kitchen, shouting at someone on the telephone. 'It needs to be now, Garth. They're all at the concert and I can't keep this old biddy sedated for ever.'

Holly had never been so delighted with Elsie's erratic security as she was in that moment, with her blood boiling. The French windows that led to the dining room were slightly ajar and Holly slipped inside.

Poking her head around the doorway to the morning room, she could see Elsie on the sofa and Henry Bruce now through in the hallway, fighting to open the massive front door.

'Elsie,' whispered Holly, scuttling through to her side. She pulled up short, Elsie pale face and drooping eyelids making her wonder if she'd arrived too late.

She leaned forward, watching Elsie's chest for any sign of movement.

She looked so still and so pale that it frightened the life out of Holly when Elsie suddenly said, 'You really shouldn't hover over a person like that,' and her eyes popped open.

Holly stifled a gasp – part fear, part relief – and then scooped Elsie into her arms. 'Are you okay? What on earth is going on and why did you let him in?'

Elsie's jaw set and she looked furious. 'I opened the door to go out and there he was on the doorstep, pushed his way in.'

'But are you okay?'

'I'm fine, my lovely girl, I'm fine – he tried to sedate me, though!' Elsie unfurled her palm to show two hi-strength diazepam tablets. 'I tucked them in my cheek when he forced them in my mouth – I've just been playing along to bide my time. But, Holly, he seems to think I've signed a form to go to a nursing home!' The fear was bright in Elsie's eyes for a moment, before sadness and confusion swept in. 'But I really don't think I did, Holly. You know me. I wouldn't do that!'

Holly's thoughts were running on at warp speed. Was it enough to stand up to Henry here, or did she need to take him down once and for all. 'Elsie, are you up for a starring role? I think Henry Bruce would look rather good on camera, don't you?'

Elsie's smile may have been wonky, but there was no doubting the strength of the grip with which she held Holly's hand. 'Let's take the bastard down.'

Holly tried to breathe quietly behind the curtains, her iPhone shaking in her hand as she captured Henry Bruce on film.

'Now then, Elsie, the private ambulance will be here shortly and we'll have you tucked up at Willowbrook in no time.'

Elsie's voice was trembling but distinct. 'I do not wish to go to a nursing home and I did not sign that form.'

Henry sighed. 'You mustn't work yourself up, Mrs Townsend. Do you remember, we looked at the brochures together? You said the garden looked nice?'

'I did not,' Elsie protested. 'And you sedated me!' Her vowels were beginning to slur and Holly felt a moment's panic. How quickly could they persuade Henry to incriminate himself, she wondered. Then she remembered – Elsie hadn't actually *been* sedated. She was just a brilliant actress.

She needn't have worried about Henry. His arrogance clearly knew no bounds.

'I've got all the paperwork here, Mrs Townsend. Look, how you've been permanently confused recently and cannot manage your own meds.' Henry pulled a sad face. 'Such a shame. And look, it says here you're dehydrated . . .'

'I asked you for a drink!' protested Elsie, pulling her head back upright with an effort.

'And yes, you were quite hysterical, weren't you, so I had to give you a sedative to calm you down before the transfer team got here.' Henry smiled and Holly zoomed in on his reptilian features as he loomed over Elsie threateningly. 'You'll like Willowbrook, Mrs Townsend, really you will. It's very exclusive, very expensive. Perfect for very wealthy, meddling little old ladies!'

'What's it to you how I spend my money?'

'Oh dear sweet Mrs Townsend, or Elsie. May I call you Elsie? Your money is my retirement fund. All my senior ladies are doing wonders for my pension. Such generous commission, you see, on bringing them a nice little cash cow. And it's win:win for me – because who will report on your little concert now? Without you there, it's just a roomful of tuneless wannabes. You'd have thought they'd be a little more protective of their golden goose, wouldn't you?'

'You won't get away with this. Not when I tell them what you've done!'

Henry made his little sad face again, mocking her indignation. 'Oh, Elsie, you still don't get it do you? Who do you think will ever believe you?'

'Well, I will,' said Holly forcefully, stepping out from behind the curtains, 'but then I did have the benefit of a front row seat!'

Henry's face went from puce to white to green in moments. It was a bit like watching a biological traffic light. 'As if you're the most reliable witness,' he spluttered.

Holly shrugged, waving her phone at him. 'Doesn't really matter, when I've got everything here!' Holly stepped forward and took Elsie's hand in hers. 'Are you okay?'

Elsie yawned and stretched. 'Never better, my darling. You know, once I got into the spirit of it, I really rather enjoyed that. Maybe I was a little premature in retiring. Shirley MacLaine does some excellent character roles these days . . .' Elsie flashed a wicked smile at Henry Bruce. 'And of course, I do an excellent turn as a courtroom witness.'

Henry sat down heavily onto one of the armchairs. Tall and strong, he could easily have overpowered Holly for her phone, but the element of surprise seemed to have completely thrown him.

Holly imagined that this little scenario had been played out plenty of times before – maybe Henry had become a little complacent. He certainly hadn't been expecting Candid Camera.

Holly pressed a few buttons on her phone. 'Chief Inspector Davis, I'm sorry to disturb, but could we borrow you for a moment. I'm at Elsie Townsend's house and we need your expertise.'

Holly hung up and eyeballed Henry Bruce. 'I hope you rot in jail,' she said with feeling.

'Ooh yes,' joined in Elsie. 'A pretty chap like you will never be lonely.'

Henry opened his mouth to fight back, just as his face crumpled like a sodden napkin on one side and his hand slipped off the arm of the chair. 'Iv nob goh ...' he began, the panic in his eyes betraying his fear at whatever was happening.

'Oh shit!' cried Holly, kneeling down beside him to loosen his tie and wishing she had her medical bag with her.

There was a heavy knock at the door and Holly cast a glance back at Elsie. 'Are you okay to get that?'

Elsie made her way through to the hall to answer the door.

'It looks like your private ambulance got here just in time,' said Holly, stepping back to give them access. She turned to them. 'Garth is it? Okay then, Henry here has had a stroke, so I'll let you do the honours. And when you're done,' Holly beckoned to the figure that appeared in the doorway behind them, 'I'm sure Chief Inspector Davis would love a word.'

The house was silent for a moment after Henry Bruce and his medical and police entourages had left.

Holly felt mildly deflated. All that intense panic and pressure had led to a bit of an anti-climax.

Elsie patted her face gently. 'Let's get a bit of colour back in those cheeks, shall we? And of course, we must attempt to avoid dehydration at all costs . . .' She went over to the fridge and pulled out some fresh orange juice and a bottle of vodka. She waggled it at Holly. 'Doctor's orders?'

Holly laughed, utterly in awe of the speed with which Elsie had recovered her equilibrium. 'Make mine a double,' she said. Checking her watch on autopilot, Holly gasped. 'The concert!'

Elsie passed her a drink. 'It's only five past. Relax . . . They'll wait for me. They always do.'

They clinked glasses and smiled at each other. 'I think we've all done very well,' said Elsie.

Holly took a long drink and fought the burn. 'To karma!' she said.

'I'll drink to that,' agreed Elsie. 'Although, you know, Holly, that Doctor Bruce may have had a point. About my meds. Maybe I have been muddling them up, because these ones here . . .' she jabbed her finger at a clear container holding little white oval pills. 'Well, those are supposed to help with anxiety, but I've been taking them all day and it hasn't made a jot of difference.'

'Jesus, Elsie. How many did you take?' asked Holly switching back into panic mode.

'Oh, only one or two,' said Elsie, 'and then maybe another couple . . .'

Holly reached over to take Elsie's pulse which was strong and steady. 'Do you mind if I . . .' she leaned over to get a better look at what Elsie had been taking 'all day' and then burst out laughing with relief.

Elsie gave her an arch look. 'Is my decrepitude amusing to you, young lady?'

'No,' said Holly. 'But you are. And no wonder these tablets haven't been working. They're Tic-Tacs!'

'Oh,' said Elsie, rather losing the moral high ground with that one. 'Well, at least I know I'll die with minty fresh breath.'

Chapter 42

'Did anyone order a feisty octogenarian?' asked Holly, pulling open the stage door with a grin and ushering Elsie in.

Relieved cries of '*Elsie!!!*' echoed back stage, until Grace shushed them with a wave of her clipboard.

Taffy and Julia rushed forward, relief etched onto their faces. Taffy scooped Elsie up in his arms and swung her around until she giggled like a schoolgirl. Gently placing her back onto her feet and making sure she was steady he looked her squarely in the eye. 'We were all so worried. Are you alright?'

'I am now,' said Elsie, 'thanks to this one.' Elsie pulled Holly to her side.

Holly couldn't look up. She'd hoped to insert Elsie into their midst and sneak away. Elsie's ability to recover like India rubber put her to shame. She felt shaken and nauseous and certainly not in a position to cope with Taffy.

Without waiting for an invitation, Taffy pulled Holly into a hug, dropping a lingering kiss onto her hair as Elsie breathlessly filled them in on their exploits.

Holly's mind was all for pulling away. Holly's body seemed to have other plans. She found herself relaxing into his embrace, the warmth of his arms and the comforting smell of him. It was like coming home to a crackling log fire on a snowy day. He was home. The softness of his shirt pressed against Holly's cheek and his arm tightened imperceptibly.

'I thought you weren't speaking to me,' he murmured into her hair.

In that instant, Holly was forced to remember all the reasons that she wasn't. She pulled away, just as the audience in the Little Theatre burst into a deafening round of applause.

Elsie looked dumbfounded, more shocked than she had all evening. 'You started without me?'

Grace rushed forward to explain and Holly quietly extricated herself from Taffy's arms. 'Just a little warm-up act, Elsie. We didn't know how long you'd be and the crowd were getting restless.'

'Hmm,' said Elsie suspiciously. 'Has Dan gone out to do our opening yet?'

'No, no,' soothed Grace. 'We just wanted to keep the masses happy.'

Holly tilted her head and listened. Whoever was on stage had the most amazing voice and seemed to be singing a cappella. Not only that, but they sounded awfully familiar. 'Grace? Who is that? They're doing an amazing job. You know, they almost sound as good as Barry O'Connor!'

Holly couldn't help but think how much Lizzie would have enjoyed this warm-up act. Okay, so it wasn't the real thing, but how many years had Lizzie been listening to his records on a loop?

'Well, actually, that's the thing,' Grace whispered excitedly, dabbing at her forehead and looking all overcome. 'It *is* Barry O'Connor! In the flesh!'

Holly and Elsie turned sharply, listening harder.

'Isn't it exciting?' said Grace, flushing happily. 'He even signed my clipboard!'

Elsie was softening a little, apparently happy to concede the stage to a fellow luminary but Holly was just plain confused.

'But how did he . . . ? I mean, who . . .'

Grace ferretted around on her clipboard and produced a small cream envelope. 'He arrived with this, for you.'

Holly immediately recognised the handwriting on the envelope and tore it open. What on earth had Lizzie been up to?

Holls,

Please accept this 'delivery' as a token of my wholehearted apology. Will and I have been talking and he made me see, that if ever there was a time to break my non-apology rule, it was now.

I've got my friend Dave from Breakfast News with me and he's doing a big feature on your efforts – better late than never to join the party. Don't even ask how I found Barry – I may actually have broken several laws.

I'm so sorry. Break a leg with the concert – I'm sure it will be amazing. I'll be standing at the back, wishing I hadn't been so fecking stubborn and bought myself a seat. Maybe we can catch up later? Lxx

PS Please don't tell Will that I had a sneaky cuddle with Barry – a lifetime's ambition achieved – surprisingly lecherous for an old bloke!

Holly felt the relief wash over her. Whatever had happened with Lizzie, they could sort it out. They had too much history to let their friendship ebb away. She peeked through the curtains and watched Barry doing his signature hip moves as he belted out his all-time hits.

She looked out over the crowd and spotted the twins clapping along, delighted to be hearing some songs that they recognised, thanks to Lizzie's O'Connor obsession. Marion had obviously enlisted the Major as her babysitting support, as Tom was standing on his lap, wearing half the Major's medals and looking particularly pleased with himself.

Holly spotted Lance and Hattie in the row behind. He was looking pale and a little fragile, but his arm was around Hattie's shoulders, the other hand resting gently on the bump. A little boy. And after such a successful surgery, Lance would have every chance of watching him grow up.

Holly felt quite choked.

The theatre was simply heaving, children perched on knees, seats surrendered to the elderly and Lizzie dancing at the back, a cameraman right beside her.

The atmosphere was electric.

For all her worries about their little concert, they clearly weren't short of support. Barry drew to the end of his set and the crowd roared their approval. Promising a reprise later in the proceedings, Barry left the stage, allowing Dan and Elsie to take their places.

'Thank you all so much for coming out tonight and showing your support for The Larkford Practice,' Dan began, a whoop of cheers interrupting him mid-sentence. He looked a little overwhelmed for a moment, so Elsie seamlessly took her cue.

'And may I say how heavenly it is to see you all here, old and young, on this very special evening.'

Dan cleared his throat and continued, his delivery a little stiff next to Elsie's natural charisma. Rather than looking stupid though, Holly realised he had somehow hit the perfect note. He looked young and accessible, nervous yet proud, and completely committed to their cause. 'As you are all aware, we're here, joining together, because we have a common goal,' he said. 'We share a common belief – that Larkford needs its own medical centre. That Larkford would not be the same without its own medical centre.' The cheers from the residents almost drowned him out and Elsie laid a hand on his sleeve, urging him to take a beat.

'And that the opinions that matter are not those of the number-crunching bureaucrats in London, but those of the people that live here. You, in fact. The people who rely on the team at The Practice to keep you healthy and to be there for you when you need us. And for that, I thank you.'

Dan dipped forward into a small bow, as the cheering and stomping of the audience crashed over him like a wave. He came up smiling.

Elsie, looking completely in her element, carried on. 'And rather than trotting out all our finest and best, we thought we'd throw in a few little challenges – let you enjoy seeing your medical team in a whole new light. So, to that end, we've been learning a few new skills just for you.'

There was a slight kerfuffle at the back of the hall, as the Major's terrier appeared to have broken loose and to now be challenging Eric to a duel. Eric, in response, broke into his best Clapton impression, 'Wooo-hooo.'

Everybody burst out laughing and Lizzie looked mortified.

'Ladies, gentlemen, boys, girls and assorted livestock,' said Dan, completely dead-pan. 'I give you The Pharmacy Girls!'

Half an hour into the concert and all was ticking along nicely to plan. Grace's choir had been sensational and Holly had adored seeing Julia let her hair down, donning a pair of tights as Puck from *A Midsummer Night's Dream*. The audience were in buoyant, excitable mood and met their attempts at fresh challenges with warmth and humour.

Jade's roller-skating scene from *Starlight Express* may have come to an abrupt halt, but Holly reckoned she'd probably get a few phone numbers off the back of it. Her little outfit had been decidedly skimpy for dancing, even more so for falling!

Holly waited backstage, her palms clammy and her stomach rolling. Part of her was excited that the twins would get to see their mother perform on her cello, not tucked away in the spare bedroom, but actually perform, on a stage in a spotlight, where the acoustics of the theatre would add a sensual warmth to her music. She wanted them, in a very simple way, to know that she had other talents besides an unerring knack with the Playdoh.

The other part, of course, was quietly screaming in her head, 'What on earth were you thinking? All your patients are out there. All your colleagues are back here. Don't screw this up . . .' She smoothed her palms down the long charcoal length of her dress. She just wanted to look her audience in the eye and be proud of what she could do. She was fed up of being a pale imitation of her true self.

The freedom came from knowing that, without Milo's feelings to tiptoe around, she could just relax and be whoever she wanted to be. The twins would cuddle her no matter what. Their love was unconditional – at least until they turned eight, she reckoned. Then pocket money and cake might play a bigger role.

She jumped as a warm hand settled on her waist and Taffy materialised beside her in the darkness of the wings. 'Break a leg, Holly. I'm so looking forward to hearing you play.'

He ran his other hand over the burnished wood of her cello lovingly. 'I've always loved the tones of a cello, you know? It's friendlier than a violin somehow, don't you think?'

Holly watched his hand as it stroked her beloved cello and swallowed hard. It was one thing that he was supportive of her efforts at work, praised her ideas for The Practice Campaign and played with her children like a long-lost uncle, but this complete acceptance of her cello as an integral part of who she was, made Holly feel as if she were finally at peace.

The risks, the drama and the adjustments of the move to Larkford all suddenly felt worthwhile, as she looked up into his eyes.

Everything she was feeling was reflected there and her heart tumbled slowly, as if righting itself after a long sea voyage. Accustomed to lavishing her love and attention on her boys and mad Eric, she felt completely blind-sided by this emotional, immediate response to Taffy.

Taffy Jones who'd been there every step of the way for the last few months and who now, it seemed, had the ability to tune into her own personal wavelength.

Taffy Jones, who also came with a side-order of secret, pregnant girlfriend, she reminded herself quickly.

Their timing really did suck.

She swallowed a sob and took a step back. The hurt flashed in his eyes as he followed her lead.

'Okay then,' he said quietly. 'Go and play your socks off. Then we'll show those Carpenters a thing or two.' He lingered, obviously waiting for something, waiting for Holly.

She swallowed the ball of tears in her throat, barely trusting herself to speak. This evening's emotional rollercoaster was beginning to take its toll. She nodded. 'See you in a bit then.'

He made to reach out to her, but pulled back when he saw the panic on her face. 'You've done an amazing thing here, Holly. Let's at least have a celebratory ginger ale before we go on. Keep our wits about us?'

'But you hate ginger ale,' Holly managed inanely.

'I do indeed,' he smiled, as he walked away, 'but you don't.'

Holly's fingers were sore and her cheeks were flushed, but her eyes filled with tears of happiness as she stood up to take her bow. Her performance had gone better than she had dared hope. All the emotion of that moment with Taffy had been poured into her bow work and goose-bumps had prickled her neck throughout. She'd even managed to look up during a gentle adagio to see the twins watching her open-mouthed with delight.

Half the audience knew that this was her hare-brained scheme to begin with and they rewarded her with a standing ovation. The twins broke away from Marion and ran up on to the stage, wrapping themselves around her legs. She crouched down, as Dan stepped from the wings to take her cello and she scooped their little writhing bodies into her arms.

Tom pressed a sticky kiss onto her cheek and Ben pulled back to look her squarely in the eye. 'Clever Mummy,' he said clearly and slowly. Holly thought she might die with pride.

'Ladies and Gents, I think we'll have a short interval. Teddy Kingsley has some refreshments for you all, donations only. And we'll be back shortly with a few surprises.'

*

Holly slipped down from the stage to thank Marion for all her help. Marion just smiled. 'It's actually the very least I can do, Holly. After everything you've done for me.'

Holly obviously looked as confused as she felt, so Marion simply held out her left hand, which now bore an emerald that was almost as big as the smile on her face.

The Major leaned into the conversation, gruffly adding his own thanks. 'I do hope we can persuade you to play your remarkable cello at our wedding.'

Holly kissed them both soundly, unable to find any words.

'I shall sing too,' announced Tom proudly, polishing his medals.

'Indeed you shall, young man,' said the Major with such gentleness that Holly saw him in a whole new light. The spring in his step, the softness of his gaze. 'After all, it's thanks to your mummy that I'm getting married at all!'

'But ... married ... so quickly ...' managed Holly.

The Major just shrugged. 'When you know, you know. One little fight over a sausage roll and here we are. I just needed someone to open my eyes.'

Marion and the Major looked so blissfully, besottedly happy as they took the twins off for squash and crisps that Holly felt quite adrift.

So much for life being easier for the young – it was the oldies in this town who had the right idea.

Holly turned around at the tap on her shoulder and was immediately swallowed into a tearful hug that enveloped her with Chanel No 5. 'Bloody hell, that was brilliant!' exclaimed Lizzie, having finally fought her way through the crowd to Holly's side.

Holly grinned at her exuberance and simply hugged her back.

'Can you forgive me for being such a selfish bitch?' asked Lizzie against her shoulder.

'I'm just so glad you came. I've missed you!' managed Holly. 'But you didn't have to risk arrest to bring me an apology. You can just say sorry, you know.'

Lizzie shook her head. 'I wanted my first proper apology to be a good one. And besides – I thought you wouldn't tell me to sod off, if I turned up with Barry O'Connor.'

Holly laughed and shook her head, their hug forced apart by a rather determined Labradoodle. Eric was licking Holly's hand as she spoke, lavishing her with doggy kisses. 'I've missed you too,' said Holly, 'and your mad mistress.

'There's a fair bit to catch up on,' said Holly. 'We may need to have a proper natter in the pub later.'

Lizzie shook her head. 'The deli for coffee and then you're talking.' She held out a sobriety chip from AA and looked uncomfortable.

Holly clasped Lizzie's hand and the chip tightly in her own. 'I'm very proud of you.'

Lizzie shrugged. 'Early days. But Will made me see that I couldn't keep pretending everything was okay and drowning my sorrows.'

'Sorrows?' Holly tilted her head with concern.

'Oh Holls, I've been lying to everyone, myself included. I'm so bloody miserable, juggling work and the kids – Jack of all trades and master of none – I don't know how you manage it, but I can't. I'm so sick of having to "live the dream" for the magazine. Half my work relationships are as deep as a puddle and the other half are trying to steal my job. That's why I have to be so bloody perfect all the time!

'Oh, I'm so jealous of your scruffy jeans and dated bed-linen and pitiful make-up bag. I'm fed up of living in a lifestyle spread and I just need to step off the treadmill for a bit.'

Lizzie took a deep gulping breath and continued, 'And I'm so sorry, but I did drag you here under false pretences. I wanted you here for me – because I was lonely and depressed and too bloody proud to admit it. And then you got here and you were busy, busy, busy all the time – no time for me. And all I heard from everyone was "Isn't Holly wonderful? Isn't she amazing? Such a lovely doctor ..." All your colleagues seemed to think the sun shone out of your every orifice. And, I'm so sorry, Holls, but it made everything worse and I got very, very jealous.'

Holly blinked hard, as she tried to reconcile what Lizzie was saying with the historical evidence of what she'd seen. Everything slotted together like a perfectly aligned jigsaw. All the anger and hurt seemed to release. Elsie had been right – you think you know what's going on with other people, behind closed doors, but you only *really* ever knew what they chose to show you.

Holly held Lizzie's hand even tighter. 'You muppet! Why didn't you say something? I would have understood ... And if you'd told me why you wanted me here, I would have come anyway – job or no job.'

Lizzie looked about twelve as she released her hand from Holly's and pushed her hair back behind her ear. 'What if you'd said no? What if you'd put Milo first?'

'Ah, well, we don't need to worry about that any more.'

'What?' asked Lizzie sharply.

'I decided that I'd been muddling up death and divorce for far too long. If Milo wants a relationship with the twins, he can still have one. He's still technically there for them, isn't he? I just don't have to be married to him for that to happen. I get to choose too.'

'Christ,' said Lizzie in wonder. She pulled Holly into an enormous rib-crushing hug. 'This is bloody brilliant news! If I wasn't stuck on the cranberry juice, I'd pop open the fizz to celebrate.'

Holly laughed. 'Actually, I'm getting my buzz from all of this. There's a few big changes ahead, but for the first time in a long time, I actually feel as though I know where I'm starting from. And, much as it kills me to admit it, I owe that to you and your Machiavellian, scheming ways. Moving here was the best decision I've made in a long time.'

Lizzie looked over her shoulder and her eyebrows shot into her hairline. Taffy was working his way towards them through the crowd. 'Are you and Taffy ...?' Lizzie waggled her fingers.

Holly sighed. 'Sadly no. Not for want of wishing, though.' She laughed. 'Timing never really was my thing. It seems that Taffy Jones is about to be a daddy, with a teeny tiny, pre-pubescent, blonde baby momma.'

Lizzie scowled. 'Really? Taffy? I can't say that's his usual type.' She shrugged. 'Men really do think with their dicks, don't they?'

'Seems like it.' Holly batted away the idea. 'I think it's probably best if I'm on my own for a bit, anyway. Elsie's blown open this whole can of worms – apparently we need to work out what we actually want from life. Who knew?'

Lizzie gave her arm a squeeze. 'Well, apparently neither of us, until recently.'

Taffy finally got to Holly's side and said hi to Lizzie. 'Are you ready, Holls? Dan wants us to be up next. Some shuffling

of the running order to accommodate Elsie doing a duet with
Barry O'Connor, I think.'

'And what are you two singing?' asked Lizzie, intrigued.

'Oh, I'm just playing the guitar. I'm leaving the vocals to
this little songbird,' said Taffy with a grin. 'I've a feeling she's
been hiding her light under a bushel, this one.'

Holly looked quickly at Lizzie, checking that this comment wasn't of the solar orifice variety, but Lizzie just looked
chuffed.

'Oh, Taffy,' said Lizzie, 'you haven't even scratched the
surface.'

The mood lighting on the stage meant that Holly could now
only really see the front row of the audience without being
dazzled. In fact the only place where she could safely look
was at Taffy, his fringe falling into his eyes as he scrunched
up his face in intense concentration at finding all the correct
chords.

Holly didn't need to concentrate, she just let herself go,
the melodies of the song carrying through. Even as she sang
about true love always finding a way, she felt a tingle down
her spine as Taffy looked up and caught her gaze.

Her heart flipped wildly as she fumbled slightly for
her place, the naked adoration in his eyes throwing her
completely.

What on earth had they been thinking when they chose
such a romantic song? Okay so the chords were easy, but
still . . .

Now, finally able to admit to her feelings and having shed
her husband in the process, it still seemed as though he would
never be hers.

When the song finished, Holly rushed off stage, unable

to cope with the requests for an encore, as the tears were blocking her throat.

She locked herself in the dressing room and struggled to breathe.

A gentle knocking on the door grew ever more persistent.

'Holly, it's me! Come out, please ...' Taffy's voice was magnified and echoed around the vaulted corridors. His distress was obvious even to Holly.

'I can't,' she managed. 'I need some space from all this.'

'I can give you space, if that's what you want. But, Holly, you need to tell me what's wrong. Did I do something?'

A little match flared in Holly, all of Elsie's gumption burning brightly. She yanked open the door, 'Did you *do* something?' she shouted. 'Other than coming on to me when you knew I was married? Making me fall in love with you? Having a baby with someone else?'

Taffy stepped forward, eyes bright. 'You fell in love with me?'

'That's hardly the take-away line here, though, is it? Daddy!'

Taffy shook his head. 'Holly, you're not making sense. Slow down. Please.' Concern tightened his face. 'What are you talking about?'

Holly slumped against the wall. 'You and the blonde. The pregnant blonde? I know all about it, Taffy.'

Taffy reached forward and took her hand. 'Well, then I don't understand why you're cross with me.'

'What?' snapped Holly. 'If you're going to be a father, it might have been good to have a heads-up!'

'I'm not the father, Holly,' Taffy said slowly. 'Milo is. That girl, Kimberley? She was Milo's student back in Reading and she tracked you down to The Practice after the website went

live. She wanted to confront you at work, make sure Milo
paid his dues.'

'Kimberley?' Holly clarified. 'From Reading? The student
Milo got suspended over.' She breathed out heavily. 'Well,
alrighty then.'

Taffy was looking at her as if she were a primed bundle
of semtex. 'I've been trying to work out how to tell you. I
didn't think you'd appreciate hearing it from me, in case it
sounded like I was dissing the competition.' He aimed for
a smile.

Holly looked down at her hand, at the empty space where
her wedding ring had been until yesterday.

She held up her hand. 'Not really my business any more.'

There was silence in the dressing room, only broken by
the sounds of Maggie's rendition of *My Way* on the spoons.
She left the stage to huge applause and Barry O'Connor came
back on.

'So, you and Milo?'

'Not so much,' said Holly quietly. 'And you're not having
a baby?'

'Really not.'

There were mere inches between them but neither seemed
able to make the final move.

Barry's dulcet tones could be heard to rapturous reception,
familiar opening bars of music nudging Holly's memory;
apparently love had a habit of bringing people together.

Holly looked up, the humour bubbling to the surface.
Maybe their timing wasn't so bad after all.

'I do, you know,' said Taffy, his thumb wiping away the
tears that had spilled on to Holly's cheek.

'Me too,' managed Holly, just before he kissed her.

*

The lights in the hall dimmed down low and there was a rustle of anticipation among the audience. The cast members who weren't involved were now sitting in the aisles.

The programme simply stated 'Finale', but rumours had been rife about the town since Dan Carter had walked into the sports shop and purchased eight pink leotards – all size XXL.

There was a crackle from the microphone as it was switched on and Elsie Townsend stepped into the spotlight. 'We hope you've enjoyed our evening of entertainment as much as we have enjoyed performing for you. There are so many people to thank, but special gratitude must be given to the wonderfully kind and talented Dr Holly Graham, whose brainchild this evening is. I personally owe her more than she will ever realise.'

Elsie's smile wavered then as the audience cheered and stamped their feet and she struggled to compose herself. 'But no evening of the arts would be complete without a little ballet and so, without further ado, I hope you have your cameras at the ready, I give you The Larkford Rugby Club with their own unforgettable rendition of *The Nutcracker*!'

There was a pause before the ancient sound system whirred into life and the iconic opening bars bounced through the theatre.

The spotlight shivered, before a pointed toe appeared from behind the curtain, followed by one very hairy pair of legs and then seven more. Dan, Taffy, nurse Jason and five other mates from the town rugby club tippy-toed into centre stage, tutus pert with starch.

Holly, from her spot in the aisle, a twin on each knee and Lizzie beside her, clutched hold of her stomach as the waves of laughter enveloped her. She had no idea how they'd managed to keep this a secret but it was the perfect end to a perfect evening.

The dance grew faster, moving from the sublime to the ridiculous and back again. The boys on stage had somehow managed to tick all the boxes for everyone watching. For the children, there was the fantastic sight of their normally serious doctors gadding about on stage, for the blokes there was comedy and farce and for the ladies there were tantalising flashes of toned bronzed thighs.

'Ruddy good sport,' cried the Major behind her.

Ben and Tom, and every other child in Larkford, seemed to be fidgeting around, desperate to get a better view, laughing and clapping along with everyone else.

Holly pushed back the hair from her face and leaned her head against Lizzie's shoulder.

She wanted to remember every detail of this evening. The evening she found her bliss.

She watched Taffy attempt a grand jeté, landing with a thud and a grin in her direction.

'Clever Taffy,' said Ben, again with the perfect diction.

'Very clever Taffy,' echoed Tom.

Holly couldn't help but agree.

Chapter 43

It took a while for the audience to calm down after seeing eight grown men prancing about in tutus. Everyone had taken their curtain calls and the Little Theatre was in disarray, but nobody, cast or audience, seemed in a hurry to go home. There were too many acts to gleefully discuss and one or two cast members to tease. The aisles were packed with chattering groups and laughter billowed throughout the theatre like a wave.

Somewhat disconcertingly, the rugby ballerinas seemed to be enjoying their costumes so much that they hadn't got changed, but rather were milling around on stage, surrounded by little clusters of well-wishers and with their tutus sticking out rigidly, their leotards leaving very little to the imagination.

Marion and the Major had somehow worked their magic on the twins, who were now tucked up in the Beast and fast asleep, dark lashes brushing their little pink cheeks, fringes stuck to their foreheads and thumbs duly inserted in little plump lips. Holly manoeuvred the enormous pram to one side where they wouldn't be blocking the aisle and crouched down in front of them, just watching for a moment – her little oasis of calm in a sea of chaos.

'Dr Graham?' intruded a slightly nasal voice.

Holly looked up to see a small man in a sleeveless pullover and spotty bow-tie. 'Yes?'

He held out a small, soft hand and helped her to her feet. 'We haven't met, I'm Harry Grant, from the PCT.'

'Holly,' she replied automatically. 'Did you enjoy the concert?'

'I did,' he smiled, intense blue eyes twinkling behind his heavy glasses. 'And I've also enjoyed talking to some of the residents. It has been, how shall I put this, most illuminating.'

Holly slowly let out the breath she hadn't realised she was holding, 'Not quite what you were expecting, perhaps?'

Harry nodded his head repeatedly, as he tried to formulate his response. 'Speaking off the record, of course, it seems we may have been a little remiss in how the consultation process has been handled.'

Holly swallowed hard, in for a penny, in for a pound. 'And I gather your main source of information is currently pending arrest for suspected fraud – off the record, of course.'

'Ye-es, hardly ideal. I had a very interesting conversation with DCI Davis actually. I suspect there may be further investigations required. All very embarrassing for the PCT, as you can imagine.'

'I imagine it would be,' Holly replied, rather liking this awkward chap and his genial demeanour.

'And you're quite sure about your decision, are you?' He patted the envelope that Holly had left for him at the Box Office, along with his ticket.

Holly nodded, not really trusting herself to speak. It wasn't the most considered or well-phrased resignation letter, but it would get the job done.

'If that's what it takes to keep The Practice open, then it's the right thing to do, isn't it?' Her voice cracked at those final words, her throat blocked by incipient tears.

Harry bobbed his head sympathetically. 'I can't think of anyone on my team who'd be prepared to take such a step. But if you're sure, I can get the paperwork in motion and give your colleagues some peace of mind. And, Holly, if I may say? I may not look like a man of influence, but I would be delighted to help you find a new position in the area, if that's what you'd like? I've been, ah, rather impressed by your approach. There may be something at the hospital in Bath that would suit?'

Holly managed a tentative smile. 'That sounds great, actually. Maybe we can talk next week?'

'Let the dust settle?' he suggested, his nasal voice warming with understanding.

'Something like that,' she replied.

He shook her hand vigorously, gave her his card and with a little wave, he walked away, taking her letter with him. Holly had to force herself to resist the urge to chase after him and ask for it back.

'What was all that about?' asked Lizzie, returning from the bar with two Diet Cokes and interrupting Holly's train of thought. 'I hope you don't mind soft, I had a vision of necking your wine on the way back through, so I thought I shouldn't really chance it.'

Holly sipped her drink gratefully. 'Just admin stuff,' she parried, trying to find her equilibrium – no easy feat when Eric insisted on weaving himself through her legs, desperate for her attention. 'Anyway, Stranger, how are you doing? Is that Will and the kids at the back?'

Lizzie nodded. 'They're just queuing up to get photos and autographs.'

'They don't need to queue, I can get Elsie's for them any time,' said Holly tiredly, suddenly feeling completely exhausted and a little flat. After such a whirlwind of an evening, it was no wonder that she was feeling a sense of anti-climax, but the hardest part was yet to come. She still needed to come clean about what she'd done. Looking around the Little Theatre, hearing all the buoyant voices, she wondered whether that couldn't just wait until tomorrow.

Eric, frustrated by her lack of attention, jumped up and nuzzled her face, his soulful 'wooo-ooooo' earning him a smattering of applause.

Lizzie laughed, spluttering Diet Coke down the front of her Donna Karan caramel dress. 'Shit! And this is dry clean only.' She dabbed at it ineffectually and sighed. 'I can't wait to start slumming it in jeans and t-shirt.'

Holly wisely kept quiet, knowing all too well that the jeans would be designer and so would the t-shirt.

'But look, it's not Elsie's autograph they're after, so we may be a while,' said Lizzie, pointing to the far corner of the stage, where the rugby ballerinas were lined up, feet in first position, taking turns to pose with members of the audience lying across them in their arms. For a small donation, of course.

Cassie Holland, of all people, flushed and giggling was currently taking her moment in the spotlight.

Lizzie was still dabbing at her dress and sighed. 'Well, snooty Channing was being a bitch about my dress earlier anyway. Maybe it's time to get rid of it.'

'Really?' Holly said distractedly. 'Are you sure? What did she say?'

'Oh she was all condescending and sarcastic. She said "nice dress".' Lizzie pulled a face.

Holly laughed. 'Maybe she actually meant, "That's a nice dress, Lizzie"? She's really pretty lovely when you get to know her.'

'Noooo,' said Lizzie. 'This is all my fault, I leave you alone for a few weeks and then suddenly this ... Mind you, she owes me one. The photographer who did her new headshot for the magazine fell in love with her house – made her a whopping great offer this afternoon – just out of the blue. So it turns out she's moving into the Major's gatehouse. Talk about falling on your feet – Jammy cow!'

Holly shrugged. 'I like her. She's smart and funny, not always intentionally, mind. You'd actually like her too, if you gave her a chance.'

Lizzie looked nonplussed for a moment. 'So is it lunch for three from now on then?'

'Why not? Or four even, if we invite Elsie. I'm planning on adopting her, actually.'

'Did I hear you taking my name in vain there, Holly?' interrupted Elsie, wafting over to join them, layers of chiffon and silk billowing behind her.

Holly gave her a hug, holding on for just that extra second. 'I was just singing your praises.'

'Excellent!' said Elsie gleefully. 'Don't let me stop you.'

Holly laughed. 'See Lizzie – she's trouble, this one.'

Lizzie shook her head, a little bemused. Holly could see that she was finding it hard to recalibrate: wasn't Holly the one normally in need of support and introductions at social functions? They'd only been out of each other's lives for a few short weeks, but so much had happened, so much had changed.

Mostly though, Holly had changed.

No more blushing violet, censoring her own opinions

to try and fit in. The status quo had shifted and Holly felt buoyed by the idea of a wider circle of friendship. With friends who knew her true self, insecurities, warts and all. Those weeks without Lizzie had given her a timely reminder that having all your eggs in one basket was a risky business.

Holly felt for Lizzie's hand and gave her a reassuring squeeze, knowing only too well how it felt to stand in Lizzie's shadow and how invisible it had always made her feel.

Elsie launched into a terrifically risqué story about how she and Judy Garland had always been best friends, until they'd fought over the role of Dorothy in *The Wizard of Oz*. 'I daren't tell you why I lost the part, but to be fair Judy did a fabulous job. What a waste of a wonderful friendship over something as trivial as work.' She gave Lizzie and Holly a meaningful look. 'Now, obviously, it's nice to see that you two have made up. I dare say,' she carried on casually, 'that it might be nice to include Julia in your little coven?'

Lizzie, unused to Elsie's sense of humour, looked a little offended.

Holly just laughed. 'If we have a coven then, what does that make you – High Priestess?'

'I could get used to that,' said Elsie with a cackle. 'You girls still have an awful lot to learn. To misquote the words of Glinda, the good witch from Oz – your power was always there, my darlings, you just had to find it for yourselves.'

With every passing conversation, every thank you, every hug, Holly could feel her resolve slipping. The tears that had been threatening to make an appearance were poised in the wings, just waiting for an opportunity. Nobody said this path would be easy. She slipped away, as discussions turned to the rugby boys' finale.

If only 'finale' didn't make everything sound so very final, she thought.

Watching Elsie hold court, safe and well and full of joy, Holly knew that the evening had been a resounding success on every level. She wanted to take pride in what they'd achieved. Everyone had rallied together, performed so beautifully, supported her zany scheme so generously . . . She felt a warm glow from knowing that she had made a difference, but she couldn't stay to watch their celebrations. It was just too much.

Gathering together her cello and various bits of clobber, Holly was quickly laden down with kit. She looked despairingly at the Beast and wished she'd had the foresight to bring the car. Now she was a single cello-playing parent, it might be a good idea to get over her park-o-phobia.

At that thought, her vision blurred and Holly made for the door. With single-minded determination, she knew she had to get out of there and had reached the Market Place before she was forced to stop. Pulling abruptly to a halt to avoid Prue Hartley's misjudged three-point turn, Holly just about managed to keep her cello from crashing to the ground and the sob caught in her throat.

She steered the Beast over to the War Memorial that stood sentinel at one end of the Market Place and slid her cello gently to the ground. She knelt in front of the boys, to find that they were blissfully oblivious and still sleeping soundly. It was hard not to feel a little envious.

She slid down beside them, settling on the stone steps, barely feeling their icy chill. Cars were starting up all around her, some people calling goodnight to one another, others heading happily for The Kingsley Arms. She heard her own name called once or twice, but Holly found herself unable to respond, busying herself instead with the blankets on the pram.

Lights flickered on in the windows and curtains twitched closed – everybody living their own little lives. Tears freely flowing now, she watched her warm breath balloon in front of her and shivered. So much for spring.

Looking around at this place she'd begun to call home, Holly wondered whether she'd even be here for the next Spring Swim.

The very thought made her question her decision all over again. But she knew, without even digging too deeply, that she had done the right thing. This wonderful town, this community that had welcomed her with open arms, deserved to keep The Practice. And she had made that happen. That was surely something?

So, maybe with a little luck, she might get to work nearby. It was certainly a risk. It wasn't a perfect solution, but it was better than nothing: she could still live here, live in Larkford, with her boys and her friends and a feeling that she belonged.

Blinking back a fresh wave of tears, she wished she'd listened to Lizzie about the benefits of waterproof mascara, letting out a small bubble of laughter at the very thought. A cloud flurried by and the full spring moon cast night-time shadows across the Market Place, illuminating the war memorial looming behind her and she shivered again.

There really was no point going over this – the decision was made. It was time to come to terms with saying good-bye, even if only to her working life here. She dashed at her eyes with the back of her hand and took a steadying breath, stumbling to her feet.

She looked up instinctively as a shout echoed around the

Market Place, 'Holly!' There was no doubting that it was Dan's voice, filled with urgency and anger.

She turned and her heart lurched in her chest as she saw them: three figures silhouetted against the golden light spilling from the theatre doorway.

'Were you just going to leave, then?' shouted Dan, as he strode towards her, unable to wait to express his disgust. 'All that talk – the concert – what the hell was that all about if you're just going to run away?' He skidded to a halt in front of her, waving the envelope that contained her letter to Harry Grant.

Taffy and Julia were beside him in a moment, their faces strangled by disbelief and confusion.

'Holly?' managed Taffy, his voice choked, reaching out for her. 'What were you thinking?' He stepped forward, just shy of touching her. 'I don't understand why you would do this?'

Julia interrupted him, talking over his words. 'You said we were friends.' She flapped her hands in the air. 'I don't do friends! But you persuaded me . . .' Her hand fluttered down, until it lay on the handle of the Beast, her grip tightening automatically. She looked down, almost perplexed by her own actions. 'You can't go. The boys love it here. You said you did too.' The accusation hung heavily in the air.

Holly's face collapsed and the tears flowed down her cheeks. What was the point in holding them in? This decision was breaking her heart. At the very least she'd expected these three to understand her intentions. After all, they were the future of The Practice – they got to carry on living her dream. Was it too much to ask that they'd cut her some slack while she threw herself on her sword?

'There really are no excuses for this, Graham,' Dan carried

on brusquely, as if the others hadn't spoken. 'In case you'd forgotten, we're a team.'

'Do you think I don't know that?' cried Holly desperately, her voice renting the air around them. She pressed her hand to her chest, desperate to catch her breath. 'But I saw the real figures. Surely Mr Grant told you?' She spotted him hovering behind Dan, looking apologetic.

'He did,' Dan acknowledged tightly, giving only slightly from his position of moral indignation. 'But still . . .'

Julia butted in yet again. 'That didn't mean you had to do something so . . .'

'Drastic,' breathed Taffy, his hand reaching for hers and holding on tight.

She looked at him then, just him, her eyes pleading with him to understand. 'Then you must see that I didn't really have a choice?' She pressed his knuckles against her lips and took a deep calming breath. 'I can still live here, hopefully. It doesn't have to be . . . drastic. But this way, The Practice stays.' To Holly, her logic was irrefutable and she panicked a little under their scrutiny. All her good intentions were weakening. What could she say to make them understand?

'You didn't honestly think we'd let you go?' said Dan quietly, the anger having ebbed slowly away. Now he just looked exhausted and shaken.

'You don't need me,' Holly said with a tearful shrug. Taffy's grip tightened imperceptibly on her hand.

Julia, still holding on to the Beast like a life raft, struggled to take another angle. 'But we do! We do need you. Have you met me?' she asked in frustration. 'Should I really be the only female GP at The Practice? Did you really think this through?'

There was an awkward pause as the doors of the theatre

flew open and belched another group of revellers out into the night. Hollering congratulations across to the huddle of doctors, they tumbled over to The Kingsley Arms and the night fell silent again.

Taffy pulled Holly around to face him, his hands resting lightly on her shoulders, seemingly poised to pull her into his embrace. 'Ignore everything else, just for a moment; is this really what you want?' His gaze sought the truth in her eyes and all Holly could think about was curling up against his jumper and how his arms would feel around her.

She cleared her throat, a last attempt to be eloquent and persuasive. 'I can work anywhere, Taffs, but I want to live here.' She made a sweeping gesture with her hand, encompassing all she'd come to love. 'With my boys, in a town with a heart,' she took a quick breath to strengthen her resolve, 'and The Practice is part of that. They love you guys and they need you. Please don't make this any harder.'

'And if we need you?' he managed gruffly. 'If we want you?'

Holly leaned in and kissed him slowly on the lips, not caring who saw, just wanting to reassure this gorgeous man that she wanted him too. 'I'm not going anywhere,' she said softly.

'No. You're not,' Dan interrupted abruptly, pulling Holly's arm, until she broke away from Taffy. He held up the envelope and, making sure that Holly was watching his every move, he ripped it cleanly in half. 'Julia's done the maths. If we split the budget four ways, we all get to stay.'

'It's true,' Julia butted in, nodding. 'The numbers work.' She rocked the Beast back and forth, ostensibly calming the sleeping twins, but more likely attempting to soothe her own obvious agitation.

Holly struggled to compute. 'But surely that would mean that you all have to take a pay cut? I mean, that can't be right? I can't let you . . .'

Dan laughed. 'Oh, Holly, you still don't get it.' His tone brooked no argument. 'You really don't have a choice.'

A well-timed cat call of 'Alright, Darcey Bussell?' broke the tension a little and Dan laughed. 'Look, I know I'm being a little intense, but then look what you've achieved here tonight! Hell, you've even managed the unthinkable and impressed the number-cruncher from the PCT! No offence, Mr Grant.'

'None taken,' said Harry Grant from the background, where Holly could just make out a smile.

'We need you to stay . . .' said Dan.

'We want you to stay,' said Taffy.

'And we're all prepared to make a few little sacrifices to make that happen,' said Julia firmly, her eyes fixed hopefully on Holly's expression.

Holly looked around her, choked and overwhelmed. It almost seemed too good to be true. She was touched beyond measure that anyone would do such a selfless thing to help her. The parallels to her own proposed solution had somehow passed her by.

'You guys . . .' she began before grinding to a halt. 'I don't know what to say.'

'Say yes,' said Dan easily, as if stating the blindingly obvious. He reached over and took Julia's hand. 'Live a little.'

Holly watched them share an intimate look. Their offer was ridiculously appealing.

'Taffy?' she said, with no real question in mind, just hoping he might provide all the answers.

He shook his head with a gentle smile. 'Not this time. You

have to make your own decisions now, Graham.' He stepped so close that she was forced to look up, 'Of course, I'm quite happy to try and influence those decisions in my favour.' He smiled and leaned down until their lips met in a slow and sensuous kiss.

'I can think of one or two things I could do to guide you in the right direction,' he sighed after a moment. His hand slid down to the small of her back and pulled her in closer. She felt a small release in her chest, as the knot of tension there dissolved.

'I love you,' she whispered so quietly that he might barely hear it.

He folded her into his arms and it was everything and more than she had ever hoped for.

'Is that a yes?' Julia interrupted, unable to wait for a reply any longer. 'Sorry,' she countered immediately, holding up a hand and looking embarrassed, knowing she'd overstepped. 'Lovey-dovey etcetera, etcetera ... But seriously – will you stay?'

Holly laughed, knowing now that Julia would never change. Knowing that she didn't really want her to.

Dan said nothing, quietly waiting.

Holly looked up at Taffy, her mind made up, but unable to resist one more glance at the naked hope on his face. She leaned in and kissed him again, feeling his thumb trace away the single tear that rested on her cheek.

She nodded, a smile gently relaxing her face. 'If you're sure?'

A small hand tugged at Holly's skirt and Tom stretched sleepily out of the pram. He yawned. 'Are we home yet, Mummy?' he murmured, dropping immediately back to sleep.

'Yes,' said Holly, looking around her. 'I rather think we are.'

Acknowledgements

Out of Practice would not be in your hands without the efforts of my wonderful agent, Teresa Chris, whose absolute faith in my abilities always makes me dig deeper and work harder.

Having Jo Dickinson as my editor feels a little like winning the lottery and her insightful feedback and enthusiasm for my cast of characters makes working with her tremendously rewarding and really rather fun. Thank you, Jo, for keeping the faith.

The fabulous team at Simon and Schuster have made me feel incredibly welcome from the very start and I am so looking forward to working with them. Sara-Jade Virtue over at Books and the City is intent on making this a debut to remember and I am loving every milestone we get to celebrate.

I must also thank the RNA who have quietly played a role in making my dream a reality – I am constantly amazed by how supportive and generous their members have been in welcoming a newbie to their ranks. Thank you for the wonderful friendship, cracking advice and, of course, the occasional party.

To my 'radiator' friends – you know who you are – I

thank you for your love, support and boundless positivity – not to mention your embarrassing anecdotes! (See, I told you I wouldn't mention you by name ... x)

Lastly, and most importantly, to my family – to Sam, Rosie, Bertie and Willow, who have provided laughter, hugs and unconditional love every step of the way. Oh, and the odd cup of coffee ... I am incredibly lucky to have you in my life.